MAYAN DECEMBER

D0878008

OTHER BOOKS BY BRENDA COOPER

Building Harlequin's Moon, with Larry Niven
The Silver Ship and the Sea
Reading the Wind
Wings of Creation

MAYAN DECEMBER

BRENDA COOPER

PRIME BOOKS

LAND O'LAKES BRANCH

MAYAN DECEMBER

Copyright © 2011 by Brenda Cooper.
Cover art by Scott Grimando.
Interior art by Kevin Radthorne.
Cover design copyright by Stephen H. Segal.

Prime Books
www.prime-books.com

Publisher's Note:
No portion of this book may be reproduced by any means, mechanical,
electronic, or otherwise, without first obtaining the permission of the
copyright holder.

For more information, contact Prime Books:
prime@prime-books.com

ISBN: 978-1-60701-263-4

To Russell Patrick Cooper
Good journeys, little brother

DECEMBER 14, 2012

CHAPTER 1

The hot Mexican sun created a thousand tiny diamond patterns in the sand under Nixie Cameron's feet. The stench of stale frying oil mixed with the scent of salt and seaweed in the air. The chatter and calls of hundreds of tourists and natives combined in a wild melody of mixed languages flowing up and down the beach.

Nixie absorbed it all happily, as she stopped to wait for her mom. Playa Del Carmen. Better by far than the Disneyland-like resort at Xcaret where they were staying. Her mom had supposedly picked Xcaret because it was a safe place for eleven-year-olds, but it really meant her mom could work in peace. Nearly everyone at Xcaret had children in tow, and wore fancy clothes, but here at Playa, life felt *real*.

Rich and poor, native and immigrant and tourist, Playa smelled like Mexico and magic. Nixie breathed it all in, trying to fill up her whole being with the moment. This might be her only afternoon here this trip.

Her mom, behind her, had stopped to stare at something on her phone. Huh . . . more interested in the news or her messages than the ocean right there beside them, or all the booths with jewelry and clothes and pottery and people on the other side.

Nixie frowned and walked down to watch a cruise ship plowing through the blue waves toward Cozumel. Maybe after this trip, when the end of the Mayan calendar had come and gone, she would be able to get her mom onto a ship like that. Maybe there wasn't any work on cruise ships.

The calendar was going to end, and everything was going to go on just like it was. That's what her mom said, and she should know, since she studied the old Mayans for a living. Nixie wouldn't mind if some things were different, though. Like maybe world peace and an end to climate change.

Jeez, you'd think she was a little kid, wanting impossible things like that. Easier to just hope for the cruise.

Sea foam lapped her toes; she leaned down and pulled her flip-flops off, holding onto them, remembering to notice the water and the people. A crowd of heavyset dark-skinned women and thin brown children swirled around her. Two little boys knocked her feet out from under her, and she fell down, one shoe falling in the water.

She laughed at the shocked look on their faces. They were cute.

"Nixie!" Her mom sounded like she didn't see her. Probably not, since she was now sitting on the beach on her butt, surrounded by skinny kids and their mothers' fat knees.

One of the women near Nixie let loose a string of Spanish too fast for Nixie to follow, but it made the boys who'd knocked her down cringe. Then the woman held out a meaty hand to Nixie, smiling at her.

"Nixie!" Her mom called again.

"Right here." Nixie took the brown hand. The woman was stronger than she looked, pulling Nixie up easily. One of the small boys held out her flip-flop and she took it.

"Gracias," Nixie spotted her mom further up the beach, actually past her. She slipped out from the crowd and jogged to catch up. "I'm here."

"Stay closer. I almost lost you."

"You can't lose me," Nix said. "You've got an app for me."

Her mom frowned at her, and didn't bother to acknowledge Nixie's reference to the GPS chip in her shoulder. "Did you find what you want yet?"

No. I'm trying to spend some time with you, and as soon as I find something to buy, we'll go back to the hotel and you'll work again. But she didn't say that. She wanted a perfect afternoon. "Let's go back up and look some more."

For a moment, she thought her mom was about to say they were out of time, but she smiled and took Nixie's hand, and they plunged back into the crowd.

Women and girls called out offers to plait tiny beaded braids in their hair, and children hawked jewelry. "Missy, missy, real silver." Young men in black uniforms stalked up one side of the street, pretending to watch for pickpockets.

Nixie tugged her mom into a·booth full of straw hats and embroidered shirts and handmade toys. She put a hat on her mom, and her mom put one on her, as they looked into a rectangular mirror someone had taken out of a medicine chest and mounted on the wall with nails. Twins, except for her mom being taller and her golden hair falling straight down her shoulders while Nixie's floated out in a mass of curls that made her look even skinnier than she was, and made the hat look a little like it belonged on a dwarf.

Her mom cocked her head. "Do you want that one?"

Nixie frowned. "It looks funny. Besides, it's falling apart."

An old man with wrinkles around his eyes and a potbelly looked over at them. "Ten dollars. Just ten. Authentic Mayan hat."

Good. That would do it. Sure enough, Nixie's mom—who knew what real Mayan stuff looked like—pulled the hat off her own head and walked out.

A voice called out after them. "Eight dollars."

"Come on," Nixie said. "You can't blame them for hoping we're stupid. Let's go back to town. That's less touristy, anyway." The more expensive booths were there and Nixie had forty dollars in her pocket. That should be enough for something nice, and maybe they would find a store where no one yelled prices at them.

They passed through a crowd of tourists in bathing suits with braided, beaded hair, holding signs about the impending end of the world. Nixie pushed them through as quickly as possible, hoping the signs wouldn't start her mom off on a tirade about people who didn't believe a word science said.

No such luck.

"Nothing magical is going to happen."

Nixie tried a different tactic this time. "It would be nice if it did."

Her mom stopped, mouth open and eyes widening. She let out a huff of air and pursed her lips.

"Relax, Mom," Nixie said, leaning in and giving her a hug.

The return hug started out stiff, but calmed into something warm and sweet. "I'm sorry I'm so busy."

"And stressed out," Nixie proclaimed. As they walked, she peered squinting down the sunny streets until she found one they hadn't seen before. It was part of the old town—whitewashed brick and adobe buildings with planters full of blooming birds-of-paradise and spiky aloe vera. The first shop window gleamed with polished silver jewelry full of blue and gold gemstones. The second doorway looked more promising, with painted carved wooden animals in one window and barrettes in the other. The too-sweet scent of copal incense made Nixie wrinkle her nose, but she went in anyway.

An old woman straightened up from the where she had been fixing wooden trains on a shelf near the back. Her flat face and dark eyes gave her away as more like a real Mayan than Spanish, and she was almost as short as Nixie. She looked a lot like the women at a village her mom had taken her to on their last trip down here: thin limbed, with torso and thighs covered by a shapeless off-white dress. Silver chains spilled down the front of her chest, and amber earrings made her look richer than her dress suggested. She waved Nixie and her mom in, spreading her hands to indicate they should look around.

Nixie's mom grinned widely, and said, "Hello" in English.

"Hel-lo." The Mayan took a few steps so she stood in the doorway, and watched Nixie and her mom, politely, leaving a few feet of distance between them. Well, good. Already better than the crowded beachside stores.

Nixie peered into the jumble of display cases. Barrettes, jewelry, clay plates with Mayan symbols on them, and leather bookmarks.

She could find something here. She glanced back at her mom in time to see her point at a vase, careful not to touch it. "This looks authentic."

The woman fingered the silver chains around her neck so they jingled softly against each other. She said, "I buy it yesterday from a man. He give me good price." She hesitated. "You like?"

Nixie had all of their shopping money. She put her hand into her pocket and fingered the bills, wondering how much her mom wanted the vase.

"I sell it to you for one hundred fifty dollars," the woman almost whispered.

Nixie took her hand back out of her pocket and returned to perusing the store. The nicest case of all—oak and glass with a lock—stood right up against the corner close to the door. Nearly everything inside glowed with color: beaded necklaces, a shiny brown leather purse with a tree painted on it, a coin purse shaped and colored like a turtle. And behind them all, resting across a raised wooden stand that had clearly been made for it, a thin feather took nearly the whole length of the shelf.

It was the most beautiful feather Nix had ever seen. Maybe it was the most beautiful thing in the whole world.

She knelt in front of the case and swept her gaze along the fine edge of the feather, taking in the iridescent greens, blues, reds and yellows. Perhaps a rainbow had dropped itself onto the bird. Except it really had been made of the colors of the jungle, all the colors of the jungle.

"Nix?"

Her mom's voice seemed to be coming from far away. Her mom's hand fell onto her shoulder, and Nix immediately felt herself list with the weight of it, as if she had become as light as the feather itself had to be, almost ghostly, while her mom stayed a real woman. She brushed her mom's hand off.

"What is it, Nix?"

She licked her lips and flicked her eyes to the Mayan. "May I please see the feather?"

The woman gave Nix a sharp glance and started to shake her head. Then she stopped, and looked at Nixie—really looked at her, as if she were seeing her for the first time.

Nix looked back, stilled by the woman's intense gaze. It felt like being looked into, instead of being looked at.

The old woman shivered once, and then smiled, exposing crooked yellow teeth. She made a gesture with her hands, telling Nixie to give her room.

Nixie stepped back, watching the woman use a small key tied around her wrist with yellow thread to open the case. She knelt and took the feather out carefully, using both hands. Nixie instinctively knelt at her height and held out her own hands, spread a foot apart, ready to accept the feather.

The woman laid it across Nixie's palms.

A wall of cotton fell between Nixie's ears and the honking horns and calls of people that had been coming in through the open door. But if her hearing had dulled, her vision had sharpened, so the tiny fronds that made up the feather were visible, nearly all of them elegant and perfectly formed.

She didn't know how long she held the feather, but when she looked up the Mayan woman watched her closely, a slight smile warming one side of her mouth.

"It's the . . . it's so pretty," Nixie whispered.

The woman smiled at her, and she looked a tiny bit more beautiful too. Not as pretty as the feather, but Nixie's sharper vision picked out flecks of gold and silver in her dark pupils.

They looked at each other for three breaths, neither of them moving or blinking. Nixie almost felt as if she had been given the feather, but surely, that wasn't right. "H . . . how much?" she stammered.

The woman stood and shook her head, mute. She looked as stunned as Nixie felt.

Nixie's mother's voice intruded. "It's a quetzal feather. She can't sell it. It's endangered."

The woman's gaze shifted to Nixie's mom, her eyes hardening. She bit her lower lip.

A pair of young women dressed in sarongs and bathing suit tops walked in, giggling at something one of them had just said. They smelled like salt and sweat and liquor, temporarily overwhelming the copal, then mixing badly with it. A car door slammed outside.

The woman stood and took the feather from Nixie, glancing at her mom. "It is just to look at." She replaced it swiftly—but still carefully—in the case, locked the case, and turned toward the two young women. "Greetings."

Nixie took her mom's hand and led her out of the store, not looking at her. In the door, she stopped to look back at the feather. The old Mayan was watching her, looking inexplicably sad.

Nix wished there was some way to tell the woman she understood.

Out on the street, the sounds of Playa—which had been so enchanting before—seemed to scrape at her ears and her head hurt. "Let's go home, mom."

"But I thought you wanted to find a souvenir?"

Nixie shook her head. "Not any more. I'm tired."

"Are you sure?"

If she couldn't have the feather, she didn't want anything. "It's okay Mom. If the vase was a hundred and fifty, forty wouldn't have bought the feather."

"She shouldn't have even had that feather. No quetzal birds have been seen here for decades, maybe longer. They left the lowlands a long time ago."

Nixie was sure the woman was supposed to have the feather, and even more, that Nixie was supposed to get the feather. It had been meant for her.

"You don't believe me, do you?" her mom asked.

"Yes."

"Well, it's almost time to go anyway. I'm supposed to meet that woman—Oriana—and interview her about watching you."

"Great Mom, we stay in a babysitter hotel, and then you need a babysitter on top of that."

"I love you and I want to keep you safe."

I want to have adventures. You could use some too.

CHAPTER 2

Ah Bahlam sat so still that only his heart and lungs moved. He called to his Way, his totem. *Show yourself. Feel the part of me that is you and heed my call.*

His back rested against the large buttressing root of a ceiba. The jungle crawled and skittered, and sang around him, alive to his long silence. A tapir rooted in the underbrush to his left and a green iguana moved listlessly in the winter heat. His pet quetzal, Julu, fluffed its feathers above him. Fish jumped in the sacred cenote below, flashing in the bit of light that directly reached the yellow-green waters of the underground cave.

The jaguar did not come.

He resisted the urge to shift with restlessness, knowing that any movement would return the jungle around him to silence. He needed success; tomorrow he would leave for home. If he returned to Chichén Itzá without the energy of Jaguar, he would be nothing. He would not be able to dance the dance of the Way, or play in the ball game.

Worrying would not help.

He exhaled slowly to drain all expectation from his center. He needed to become empty.

Howler monkeys chattered high in the trees as white doves called quietly back and forth to each other. The tapir grazed so close by that he could have reached out and touched its coarse fur.

He closed his eyes, feeling the growth of lianas, knowing which way the snake turned. Birds became his voice, trees his limbs, the rich soil the root of his energy.

Footsteps. Small ones, but loud in the way they silenced the world.

The jaguar? Shouldn't it be quieter?

He opened his eyes to an apparition bending down gently by the waters of the cenote. She couldn't be more than a girl, but no human looked like this. Golden hair surrounded her face and fell in light waves down her shoulders. The one eye he could see held the blue of a summer sky, and her skin was nearly the white of bones. Her legs and arms were bare, and she wore clothes that fit close to her body and were brightly colored like sacred buildings. Her clothes were so carefully made, so fine, they must have been spun by gods.

She bent down before the cenote, reaching a finger out and touching the almost still pool. Water rippled away from her finger in tiny waves, and she laughed.

What did this mean? The girl cast a reflection in the water. So she could not be a spirit or a god. Had she been sent as a sacrifice? She looked too young. Her chest was flat and her waist still slightly thick with childhood even though she had wider hips than any woman he knew.

He remained totally still, entranced. As if he had become part of the great root at his back, he could not have moved or changed the scene in front of him if he wanted to.

She slid her sandals off, put down a small bag she was carrying, and sat with her feet in the pool. The world did not shift as she did it. Rather, the sacred waters accepted her into a place no one should touch except in ceremony. She began to hum a tune he had never heard, high and light like her laughter, and then stood, stretching her arms up to the sun. She stepped into the cenote, first one step, and then another.

The water rippled away and back to her, lapping against her pale calves. Directly in front of her, the walls of the earth closed over black water.

Rumor had it that the current in this cenote flowed underground to the village just outside of Zama, a quarter turn of the sun from here by foot.

He had spent many days in ceremony here this summer, and he knew she could not go much further.

Apparently, she did not.

With a little cry, she plunged into the deep waters and they closed over her head.

CHAPTER 3

Alice sat with her fingers curled around a glass of Syrah. Late afternoon sun slanted onto the narrow strip of bar tables surrounded by running water and art deco bridges. Across from her, a small dark-haired woman sat with her hands folded under her chin.

Oriana Russo sipped her white wine. "You are? What did you say? An archastronomer?"

"Archeoastronomer," Alice corrected. "Archeoastronomy is like the anthropology of astronomy. In my case, I study how the Mayans looked at the stars."

"Which is . . . ?" Oriana asked, her bobbed hair falling forward across her face as she leaned over the table and took a small handful of over-salted peanuts.

How to explain simply? Alice knew from Oriana's resume that she had dropped out of college and spent most of her time down here diving. "The stars guided their mythology. The Mayan calendar was devised by knowing the stars and many of the ruins were built to both study and showcase celestial events."

"You sound like a textbook."

At least Oriana smiled as she said that. It stung, but she was probably right.

Oriana leaned forward. "But how did the ancient Mayans *feel* about the stars?"

"Well, they revered them. After all, the story of their gods is written in stars."

Oriana's voice dropped almost to a whisper. "I spend time in Mayan villages, and they still see gods and the future in the stars. They're afraid and excited. They can feel the great tree of life growing in the sky as we speak. They're living in the time of their myths." Oriana leaned even closer, disturbing Alice's sense of personal space. "How do *you* feel about the stars and the coming line-up?"

Alice opened her mouth, then closed it again and took a sip of wine. "I'm a scientist. I like to watch the stars on dark nights and imagine the stories they would tell me if I didn't know the science. But I do, and so I don't *feel* about them as much as *think* about them."

A soft sigh escaped Oriana's lips, almost disappointment. But she shifted the conversation. "Tell me about Nixie."

"She's eleven. She's . . . she's a good girl. Bounces between wanting to be a little girl and a teenager." Best to forestall the question about a father. "She and I live alone. Her father died when Nix was five."

"Is that hard?" Oriana asked.

She hated that question. "Not so much, not any more. She comes with me most of the time when I travel—she gets her school online. But as she's getting older, I worry more."

Oriana smiled sympathetically. "There's no place safe any more. Not even my home, Italy. Thirty people were killed by a pregnant suicide bomber in Rome yesterday. Can you imagine blowing up your own unborn baby?"

Alice scooted her chair in closer to the table to let a waiter pass, its metal feet screeching on the tile. "That's not what I mean. I do worry about her safety." Of course she did. "But she doesn't have many friends her age; we don't stay anywhere long. Maybe after this year, when the world goes on and the end of the Mayan calendar is just the beginning of a new year, I'll take a teaching job and stay in the states for a few years."

Oriana's smile was free of judgment. "None of us can read the next year yet. Shall we go and I can meet your Nixie?"

Alice had developed a skill for reading people after so many years finding guides to take her deep into dangerous jungles. Oriana seemed honest, felt honest. "Let's introduce you to Nixie."

Oriana looked pleased. "Thank you."

"Follow me." Just over the little bridge, they passed two bright red parrots chained contentedly to large perches. Faux eco-tourism—the jungle chained for visitor's eyes to feast on—no work required. But she'd chosen this place for Nixie, not herself.

They had to thread through five buildings, past a pool, and up one flight of stairs to reach Alice and Nixie's room.

Alice opened the door, holding it for Oriana, calling out, "Nixie."

No answer.

Snake, Nixie's favorite stuffed toy and traveling companion, lay across the tropical orange bedcover with its green plush head lolling sideways. No sign of Nix. Alice called again, louder. "Nixie. Nix?"

No answer.

"Maybe she went swimming." Alice led Oriana to the closest pool, and stood with her back to the falling sun, watching herds of children leap into the sparkling chlorine blue water while parents sat and sipped free drinks from the poolside bar. She squinted as each small swimming form emerged from the water.

Nixie wasn't there.

"How can I recognize her?" Oriana asked.

"A mane of blonde hair, tall for her age, thin, but strong." She glanced down at her phone and touched the tracking app to bring up Nixie's GPS signal. It didn't show. Dammit. She speed dialed Nixie's cell phone. No answer; straight to voicemail. "Come on, I can find her. She's chipped."

"Really?" Oriana blurted out. "Like a dog?"

"Like a kid who travels with me into the bush. I intend to find her if the drug cartels get her."

Back in the room, Alice tapped her feet as the laptop booted up. At home, she could always follow Nixie with her phone, but here the wireless cloud was damned unreliable. The screen brightened, throwing light across the cluttered desk. Alice tapped to get Nixie's location.

No response.

She imagined her daughter kidnapped, in a taxi or broken-down bus heading down the highway, and forced herself to picture something simpler. Nixie had just come to look for her, and something in one of the little resort shops caught her eye. Or Nixie had gotten hungry. The resort was all-inclusive. Food ran free for the taking everywhere. Maybe she went to build a sandcastle at the tiny beach.

The map began to fill in on the screen, starting with their current location and fanning out. Alice's blinking golden light took the center of the screen.

Still no blinking blue location light for Nixie.

Alice's heart sped up as the map began to redraw, searching further a field for the girl's locator. "That can't be."

The screen redrew again, its edges too far now for Nixie to have gone in anything except an airplane.

"Could her chip be broken?" Oriana asked. "Or the software?"

Alice shook her head. "We just had it checked last week when we got our shots updated at home."

"Well, it must be broken or you would see it, right? Even if—something happened to her—the chip would still work."

"Unless someone destroyed it." There hadn't been any time. She'd only been gone an hour.

Her own location light– a bright dot that looked three-dimensional - blinked insistently at her as she searched again for Nixie's beacon.

It wasn't there.

She'd let the apparent safety of the resort lull her into a sense of security.

She pushed the reboot button and glared at the screen as it crawled to sleep and then clawed back to life.

"She didn't leave a note?"

"Probably not." Alice looked around anyway, her hand shaking. Nixie almost never left, but if she did, well, she knew Alice could find her. Why leave a note when she was chipped?

The locator finished coming back up and showed exactly the same results, scanning ever wider until the whole world filled the screen and Nixie wasn't in it.

Oriana spoke into Alice's stunned silence. "What does she like to do?"

"There's ruins on the grounds. She's interested in those."

"Should we look?" Oriana prodded.

Alice bit her lip. She'd become too damned dependent on the chip. "Of course."

They sped down the steps and crossed the expanse of white concrete lining the pool, Alice still squinting at swimmers, hoping Nix would materialize.

Oriana asked, "Does she run away often?"

"No. Never." Alice shook her head. Run away? "She goes places. I mean, I work. So sometimes she goes to the community park or over to a neighbor's house. At home, she can text or call me or I can see her leave on my phone or computer, track her."

"Is it legal to chip a person?"

"Sure. It's not usual, but I have a friend in the industry. With the world the way it is and me bringing Nix here, it made sense. We've gotten used to it. It's so . . . strange not to see her beacon." Naked. It felt naked. "So she leaves, but I'm sure she didn't *run away.*"

They reached the end of the pool patio and started down a manicured path toward the closest ruin. A small temple: two stories with tall, narrow steps and a compact top just a few feet across, with a stone doorway right at the crown. Dusk bathed the gray cobblestones under their feet with orange light. It hurried Alice even more, pushing her like weight instead of light. What if Nix had fallen and it got dark and they couldn't find her?

She called, "Nixie! Ni-ixie!" She raced up the steps, looking down for a small body, fallen on the other side. Nothing. Oriana raced around the outside, bending down to look under bushes.

They shook their heads at each other, jogging side by side. The path forked and Alice pointed right, words tumbling out fast. "I'll go this way. Go left, call her name. She won't come to you; she's not supposed to go to strangers. She's got golden hair and a red top. If you think you see her, tell her that her mom needs her. Tell her to go toward the pool."

Alice's breath sped up and her blood raced through her veins, hot and worried.

CHAPTER 4

Nixie started to scream. Water closed over her head and filled her mouth. Cold. A small fish brushed its scales across her ankle. She kicked upward, seeking the surface, the cold a drag on her arms and legs. Her fingers broke into warm air and she kicked again, surging upward, gasping. She could hardly see. She couldn't have gone that far!

A thick root pierced the dark earth above her and drank the dark water. She grabbed the root, holding tight. Water streamed past her, not enough to pull her from the root, but enough to explain how she had gone all the way into the cave, and a reminder that cenotes were sinkholes formed by underground rivers. The water felt warm where it lapped her chin, but cold at her feet.

She kicked lightly to stay in place. She had swum in cenotes before, with her mom, and there hadn't been nearly so much current. She had to be close to where she fell. She turned into the water until she saw brightness in one direction. She stretched out, like in a pool, doing a swimmer's crawl toward the half-circle of brightness.

The water dragged at her, trying to force her away from the light.

She swam harder, kicked faster. When she stopped for a breath, the root appeared again.

After she calmed, she started over, not stopping, her breath hard in her throat by the time she emerged into the sunshine.

A figure stood on the bank. At first, in the quick glance between strokes, it might have been a monkey. The current let go of Nixie as she came near the edge and she stopped, treading water, just outside the light.

A boy?

No, a small man, slender, and brown like the wide tree-trunks behind him. Brown-skinned and brown-eyed, with long brown hair that curled around his heart. He reached a hand toward her, palm up.

She considered. Strangers were dangerous, particularly strange men. But her legs felt like stones trying to sink her, cold and tired. The only other place to go was back further into the dark, under the earth. She kicked forward, extending her hand so he could take it.

He was strong for his size, and pulled her up easily, his eyes rounding the moment he grasped her hand as if she'd given him an electric shock. As soon as she had her footing, he stepped back five paces, regarding her with no expression at all.

She slipped her wet feet back into her flip flops. "Thanks." Her voice sounded loud in the silent jungle. "I . . . I didn't mean to fall in."

His reply was cadenced, thick with vowels. His voice sounded like the jungle, and bits of the sounds nagged at her. She *almost* knew the language.

She was tall for eleven, but this man was only a few inches taller than she was. He wasn't old, but his eyes were like her grandfather's; too wise for a human. Like a monkey's eyes, or an old dog's eyes. He was naked, except for a rough cloth wound around his waist and hips. Another piece covered his wrist like a bandage.

Could he be part of the resort staff? Part of one of the shows they did? She and her mom had watched one just last night, homage to ancient Mayans, a swirl of color and dancing, and a scripted slow version of a ball game the Mayans used to play.

That was it. She'd heard a few words last night. *Mayan*. In fact, her mother sometimes struggled with Mayan words, sounding them out when she read other people's research. Clearly she hadn't gotten them right.

The man sat down nearly five feet from her, watching.

Two could play that game. Surely mom would be interviewing the babysitter for at least an hour. Nixie sat on a root tall enough to be a kitchen chair, and the two of them regarded each other. She pointed to herself. "Nixie."

He tried. "Ni-iki."

Close. She pointed to him.

He stayed silent.

She tried again, pointing to herself and repeating, "Nixie."

"Ni-ixi."

That was better. She pointed to him again.

He shook his head.

Maybe they didn't give out their names. She'd read about people like that in school. She picked her purse up—carefully, so she wouldn't spook him—and rummaged inside for her phone. It showed the time (5:02 PM) and her current background (a picture of a flower she had taken herself on her real camera instead of the stupid phone cam, and then added affects), but half the apps were blinking. She shook it and tried again. Must be a dead spot. She glanced at her wrist. Her new watch was supposed to show the time and the weather. No weather. She looked up. How had so much jungle gotten here anyway? The trees were taller and thicker than she remembered. She closed her eyes, listening for people. Resort carts, sandals slapping . . . anything.

All she heard was birds, and the soft sounds of fish in the cenote. A breeze smelled like dirt and salt and flowers, but nothing like people.

She hadn't gone far. Just to the closest ruin and through its small stone doorway, so small even she had to duck. She had climbed down the tall thin steps and walked down a short path, thick with big-leafed plants. The cenote had drawn all her attention, its smooth surface bright with afternoon sun. It had seemed to call her, like the feather had yesterday.

Nixie drew in a deep breath, adrift without the background noise of cars and televisions and radios and music, without the weather and news on her phone, without the scents of tanning oil and diesel and cooking food on the air.

The man unwound the cloth from around his wrist and set it across his shoulder. Leaves in a tree above them rustled, and a colorful bird fell gracefully to the man's shoulder, fluffing bright green wings as it landed. Its tail feathers nearly touched his waist.

Now she felt even more lost, dizzy. Good thing she was sitting down or she would have fallen.

A quetzal.

Was she dreaming? A hot afternoon nap dream after wanting the feather in Playa so badly?

She didn't hesitate. One foot in front of the other, slowly, she approached the man, praying the bird wouldn't get scared and fly away.

He put a hand up, like a signal to the bird. It stayed put, fluffing its feathers over and over and cocking its head at her. She looked the dream bird in the eye.

Could a dream bird talk? She extended her hand slowly and whispered, "You are beautiful. My name in Nixie. Can you talk?"

It cocked its head just a bit, and she waited, but it merely watched her. She walked around the man, looking at the bird from all angles, memorizing the color and length of its feathers.

The man watched her, as silent and curious as the quetzal.

The light had changed, falling sideways through the too-tall trees. Surely she had to wake up, or go back, or whatever she needed to do. Her mom would worry.

She backed slowly away, but the man held up his hand in the same gesture he had given the bird. He wanted her to wait.

He held his hand out, flat and close to his body, turned his palm up, and thrust it six inches higher in a quick motion. The bird launched gracefully upward. It flew in a circle around his head and then circled again just a few feet above Nixie, so near she felt the wind of its beating wings. She let out a huge "O" of surprise at the sheer beauty of it in the dusky light. It flew through a ray of direct sun, sparkling, before disappearing into thicker foliage and landing on a branch with a soft, graceful rustle of leaves.

The man made the stay gesture to her again. She stood, entranced, while he reached behind a root and took out a long strip of folded leather tied with green string. He slid the knot loose easily and opened the leather to reveal two perfect quetzal feathers as long as her arm. He picked one up, gently, and with two hands; like the woman at the booth. Nixie opened her palms to accept the feather.

It was brighter and cleaner than the one in the glass case had been, perfect. It felt right to hold it, as if the feather belonged to her, like it wanted her.

She should give him something in return. She balanced the feather carefully, fished in her shorts pocket, and handed him the wad of money.

She held her breath as he took it in his brown hand, looked curiously at it, then brought it to his face and touched it with his tongue. He nodded, and glanced at the sky, as if he, too, knew dark was coming. He didn't say her money wasn't enough, didn't take the feather back from her.

She bent down with a little flourish, a sort of a curtsy like people did in old movies. She turned to glance up the trail and then looked back at him. Was it okay for her to go? She really needed to.

He lifted his palm up to her, the way he had for the bird, his thumb holding the bills.

"Thank you."

As if her words broke a spell, he said something she didn't understand and began wrapping the bills and the remaining feather back in the leather covering.

She turned and raced back the way she'd come, holding the feather as carefully as she always held Snake.

Nothing looked familiar. She and her electronics made the only human sounds.

CHAPTER 5

Low lights illuminated the path under Alice's feet. She knew loss. Viscerally. Her stomach cramped with it. Seven years ago, after Nixie's dad died in Afghanistan, she'd cried for a year, every night after Nix went to sleep. The salt of the sea on the warm evening wind tasted like those tears.

Nixie had to be okay.

Maybe Nix was home now, worried about her. Maybe Oriana had found her. Maybe Nixie was sitting by the pool, feet in the water, waiting for Alice.

Maybe Nixie was okay.

Oriana stood waiting for Alice at the fork where they had separated, her brows creased and her slender arms crossed in front of her. She shook her head, driving Alice's nerves closer to the edges of her skin. They started back, Alice still calling out, "Nixie! Ni-xie!"

The first ruin they had searched loomed as a dark shadow to Alice's left. Oriana circled it. Alice wanted to race back to their room and see if Nix had returned on her own, but she followed Oriana anyway. Her dry throat gave her voice a plaintive edge as she called out, "Ni-ixie! Nix . . . "

"Here, Momma."

Alice stopped, disbelieving, hoping.

"Mom."

She looked up, following Nixie's voice. Her daughter sat on the top step of the small temple, dripping water onto the stones, her hair a draggled mess. She held something in her lap. Light meant to illuminate the temple doorway behind Nixie spilled up her face as she glanced down, highlighting her neck and chin, but hiding her eyes in shadow.

Alice raced up the thin, uneven steps, nearly falling, not caring. Nixie's mouth dropped open as Alice bounded toward her. She quickly set down whatever she was holding and stood.

Alice reached Nixie, folding the girl tightly against her chest, head nestled between her breasts. Nixie's damp hair soaked Alice's shirt.

Something crunched under her right foot.

"Stop mom, you'll crush it," Nixie squealed. "Pick up your foot!"

Alice took a step back.

Nixie plucked a long slender object from the stones and held it up in the light, smoothing it. A quetzal feather. The base, where it went into the bird, had been cracked and flattened under Alice's foot. "Mom!" she chided. "How could you?"

The adrenaline of her frantic search descended on Alice all at once, pouring sharpness through her teeth. "Where were you? Where did you get that?" It registered that Nixie didn't smell of either chlorine or salt water. "How did you get wet?"

Nixie sank back down on the top step, holding the feather to the light, stroking the damaged quill as if her fingers could heal it. "It'll never be the same. Never."

"I was so worried." Alice's voice sounded too clipped and firm, but she couldn't soften it. "Where did you go? I couldn't see you. Your chip didn't even register!"

Nixie leaned away as if Alice's words were slaps, her face closing.

Oriana came up the steps and gazed from mother to daughter, breaking the uncomfortable moment with a wide smile. "Hello, you must be Nixie. I'm Oriana. We've been looking for you. We were worried."

Nixie's demeanor shifted, adjusting instantly to the company of strangers. A different girl, with a polite, composed smile. She held her hand out. "Pleased to meet you." She glanced up at Alice, her eyes reproachful. "I didn't mean to scare you."

Heat rose in Alice's cheeks and she looked down at the feather. A mystery. She shivered. "I'm sorry. I thought you were . . . lost. Let's go back and you can tell me what happened."

"Wait. I want to show you a place I found." Nixie ducked under the stone lintel and stood on the far side, handling the long silky edge of the feather carefully so it missed the harsh stone. When she ducked back, her eyes were wide. "It changed."

Alice bit at her lip. "What?"

Nixie shook herself, spraying drops of water from the ends of her hair. "I . . . I don't know. There was a tall jungle and a cenote and a bird." She stopped and walked through the doorway again and then back. "It was different. Really."

Oriana bent down and poked her head through. When she stood back up she shrugged.

Nixie frowned, and climbed down without saying anything else, but she still looked puzzled. She led the other two toward the hotel.

Alice watched her back, treasuring her, searching for anything that seemed hurt or out of place or different. Except for the feather and the look of confusion, Nix seemed fine.

In the room, Nixie set her feather carefully in the center of the kitchen table. "I'm going to change," she proclaimed without being asked.

Alice glanced over at the monitor. Nixie's light burned right alongside hers, as if it had never disappeared. It was on her phone, too.

She busied herself pouring three glasses of iced lemonade, glad of something simple and comforting to do. She joined Oriana at the table. "Thank you," she whispered.

Oriana smiled. "I'm glad I could help."

"You're hired."

Oriana laughed.

Alice stared at the feather. It surely was a quetzal tail feather, but different from the one they had seen in town earlier. The edges were crisp and clean. Except for where she'd cracked the quill, the feather was perfect. She glanced at Oriana. "Do you want to stay?"

Oriana nodded. "If you don't mind. If Nixie doesn't mind. This might be a story worth hearing."

Nixie came in and sat by her glass of lemonade. "I'm sorry," she repeated.

Alice softened her voice. "I know. Tell me what happened."

Nixie glanced at Oriana, as if unsure what to say in front of a stranger. Alice spoke softly. "Oriana's going to stay with you when I have to go to meetings, starting the day after tomorrow. She's a diver, and she can teach you about the reefs here. Maybe she'll take you snorkeling off the resort beach."

Nixie's eyes lit a little, and she took a long drink of her lemonade. "When you left, I went out. I thought maybe I'd go to the pool, but I decided to walk back to the ruin, the one you found me at. It was close, and I didn't think you'd care, if I was careful."

Alice would have said no.

"I went through the doorway on the top, and down the other side. There was a path." She looked confused again. "But it's not there now. The path was in the jungle, and there were monkeys and birds."

Oriana drew in a sharp breath, but didn't say anything. Her face had tensed.

Alice shook her head to clear of it of a sudden dizzy feeling. Had Nixie fallen and knocked herself out? The feather gave lie to that. And the blank map of the world. "What was down the path?"

Nixie talked about a cenote and falling in. As Alice listened, she felt more and more uncertain. But Nixie looked completely earnest as she told them about the bird, and the man. And she'd gotten soaked to the skin somehow.

Alice interrupted, "Did the man want anything from you? Did he touch you?"

"Only to pull me out of the water."

Alice could always tell when Nixie was lying, and *she* surely believed her story. At one point, Oriana put a sun-browned hand over Alice's on the table, glancing at her with open curiosity.

How come Oriana didn't think this whole thing was crazy?

When Nixie finished her story, she blinked up at Alice, wanting something. Reassurance? Or simple acceptance? Alice wasn't sure she could give either, but she managed to nod. All she could say was, "I don't know what to think."

Nixie leaned forward. "It really happened. I know it did. Oh, and my phone didn't work, either. No bandwidth." That fit with the broken locator. Where could Nix have been? Was she confusing the ruins? Well, no, she'd found her on the top of that one. Nothing made sense.

Nixie finished her lemonade and took her glass to the sink. "Can I watch TV? I need a break."

"Sure honey, for half an hour."

Nixie's eyes brightened at the unusual permission.

Alice smiled faintly even though she still felt a little dizzy. What really happened?

Nixie settled on the big bed, picked up Snake, and turned on cartoons, as if she were a younger kid.

Oriana cocked her head toward the balcony. "Care to sit outside with me?"

"Sure." They were out of lemonade. "Would you like some tea? Or a glass of wine?"

"Wine would be great."

Alice poured two glasses of rich, dark red Syrah and the women closed the thick sliding door, muting the squealing television to background noise. It was fully dark, and the lights of the resort spread bright below them. A couple walked by one story below, hand in hand, and in the other direction, a mother chased three unruly boys ahead of her.

Oriana spoke first. "She could be telling the truth."

"How?" Alice choked out.

"Does she lie to you?"

"No." That wasn't quite right. "When she tries, the lie might as well be written on her face. She didn't look like she was lying tonight."

Oriana let the quiet hang in the hot air for a few long moments, and then spoke just above a whisper. "I have this friend, Ian. He's lived here a long time, maybe twenty years. Says he's getting ready for the world to change."

"Twenty years is more than most." So many people had come down here hoping that being in Mayan country at the end of the baktun—the great divide in the calendar that would end in eight days—would change the world into a kind of paradise. Or destroy it. "What does Ian do?"

Oriana shrugged. "Sometimes he helps with digs, sometimes he teaches scuba, sometimes he tends bar. He doesn't seem to need much." Oriana settled back in her chair, her eyes on Alice's face. "Ian says he's been to an older time. He's seen Chichén Itzá and Tulum bright with color and full of people from the past." Oriana hesitated. "But he gets there a different way." She paused again, sipped her wine, and swallowed hard. "He uses the same drugs he says the old Mayans used. Toad venom and psilocybin."

At Alice's indrawn breath she waved a hand. "Not regularly. A few times a year. In ceremony. He studies with a group of Mayan shamans. Been doing it for years."

"But Nixie couldn't have taken any of that."

"Of course not," Oriana said.

"I don't understand it."

Oriana sipped her wine, looking pensive. "But don't you think there are things we don't understand?"

Alice had spent that last decade of her life trying to understand the Mayans through the star-stories they left, and she still felt far away from really "getting" their culture. Of course she knew about the drugs. A lot of ancient cultures mixed ceremonial drugs with the sacred, it came up all the time. She'd even tried ayahuasca once, on a trip to Ecuador when she was still in college. After it made her violently sick, it gave her visions. Rivers and plants talking to her, plants singing inside her blood, reviewing her life with her, demanding she answer questions she couldn't even ask. She'd been scared, and it had seemed like a whole lifetime before she could think clearly.

She had never done it again.

Finally, she said, "There's a lot I don't understand. Including this trip of Nixie's."

"It might help you to talk to Ian," Oriana said. "I'm not sure I can find him, but if I can, is it okay for me to bring him over?"

"All right." She'd be very busy soon, but she needed to find out what had happened to her daughter. It wasn't as if she could just go ask the local police or anything. Not here. "Can you find him tomorrow?"

"I'll try."

"Thanks." Alice took the younger woman's hand. "And thanks for helping me look. Thanks for not thinking this is all crazy." Even if it was.

Oriana smiled. "I love mysteries."

DECEMBER 15, 2012

CHAPTER 6

Cauac stood with his wrinkled feet in the sea, looking out at the foamy whitecaps where shallow, bright blue waves broke over the reef. The night's strange dreams still stuck to him like honey. They danced as clearly in his head as the sea in front of him. But no meaning clarified from the images.

He needed to be alone with the sea and the creatures in it that called him family. He needed to find his Way, his spirit companion, to salve his soul and regain balance before he sent his students back to Chichén Itzá. Tomorrow, there would be no time.

Cauac took a deep breath, filling his chest, his belly. He paused. Then he let the air out slowly, blowing the sticky dreams into the world. After he was empty, he walked slowly, steadily, into the ocean, focusing on the warm water lapping his calves, on the sand under his toes.

Cauac reached water up to his chest, and turned to look back at the busy grounds of Zama. The bright red, white, and blue stone buildings and surrounding walls stood out against a soft blue sky. It sat so close to the shore that even from a few hundred feet out in the water, he could easily make out the figures of priests, serving women, and local farmers as they moved about the grounds, some certainly already busy with preparations for Ah Bahlam and the others to leave in two days.

The simplicity of Zama fit his heart, his very self. He had grown up in Chichén, been prepared to join the worshipers of K'uk'ulkan there, and perhaps to eventually wear the Feathered Serpent as his Way.

This was better.

He walked farther out, and then swam slowly, the warm water cradling him. When he had swum far enough, Cauac turned onto his back. His broad chest, his face, and the tips of his toes bobbed above the water. He closed his eyes, forgetting the upcoming journey, the dangers waiting on the road, and those in Chichén Itzá. He focused on the very center of his being, drawing all of his energy to a single point, and emptying that point into the warm waters all around him.

A simple call, energy to energy, life to life.

It flowed from him through the waters, licked the surface of the reefs, touched the sea fans and sponges, rippled through schools of bright silver fish.

He waited.

The sea filled his ears, and the sun beat on his closed eyelids. Shallow waves bobbed him up and down, and he swished a foot here, a hand there, counterbalancing the water's desire to move him toward shore.

Something bumped his right leg, just behind the knee, and he smiled up at the sky before turning and reaching for his totem animal. The great sea turtle had come alone this time, the one he called Great Old, nearly as long as he was tall. Great Old swam slow circles around him. Cauac watched, bobbing in place, admiring the fine patterns on the turtle's head and flippers, gazing into his brown eyes. As the turtle circled, Cauac smelled his salty, thick shell, heard his soft slight breath. He offered his own breath, slowly kicking circles in place, the sky wheeling above him. Turtle, sea, sky, turtle, sea, sky, and them he saw himself, turtle, sea, sky, waves, himself, turtle, sea, sky, the beach at Zama, the waves slapping the shore in play, his tiny brown body, Great Old the same size, except round. Cauac became large, larger even the turtle, than Zama, than the sea.

Large as the stars.

Great Old nudged his right hand. Cauac curled his old, leathery fingers gently around the turtle's mottled brown and sea foam carapace, carefully shifting his weight so both of his hands gripped the slippery back.

Great Old swam with him, carrying him gently, staying at the surface. Salty seawater rose up around Cauac's face, sluiced across his back, and bathed his thighs, alternating waves of sun and water. He took a deep breath, tapped his head against Great Old's house, and the turtle took him down. He opened his eyes to see the beginnings of the great reef below him. A school of groupers flashed away from them, and a bright blue parrotfish backed slowly into a crevice between two rocks. Blood-red sea fans and sun-colored tube sponges grew up from the sea floor. Cauac reveled in it all, holding his breath as long as possible, slitting his eyes for the best view. With great reluctance, he loosened his hands and floated up for air.

Great Old surfaced beside him, and Cauac smiled to feel the turtle's steady watchful energy. Two old beings, he thought, spending the afternoon together. Old friends.

He knew, without questioning how he knew, that he would never see the turtle again. Maybe it was his dreams of strange pale people or the rumors of fighting that flooded Zama. The world was on the brink of change, maybe dangerous and ill change.

Cauac slid the hard calloused ends of his fingers gently along the full length of the turtle's shell, an honoring and a farewell.

He swam slowly toward shore, washed in satisfied sadness.

Cauac climbed, dripping and nearly naked, from the water. A figure sprinted toward him along the rocky path above the white sand beach. He smiled to see his apprentice, Ah Bahlam, rushing so. Cauac let the young man come to him.

Ah Bahlam must have been watching, because the first words from his mouth were, "I wish I could call my totem so easily."

"You can," Cauac replied, "but you do not know it yet. What brings you in such a hurry?"

"I . . . I had a vision. A young girl, white as this sand, with hair like the sun and eyes like the sea."

Cauac waited for more, working not to show the tightness crawling along his shoulder muscles or the heaviness in his chest.

Confusion showed in the young man's eyes, and earnestness, as if he feared being disbelieved. "She came to the cenote, wearing strange clothing. Like the petals of bright flowers, but not. She sang to the water and then welcomed father sun, and then . . . then she fell in." Cauac wanted to ask if she had drowned, but held his tongue. Best let the story come out in its own way.

"She swam back, and I helped her to climb free. She spoke, but not in words. I gave her one of Julu's feathers from last year, and she gave me strange leaves." Ah Bahlam's smile looked uncertain. "Come, sit by me in the rocks."

Cauac followed him up the beach under the watchful eyes of a family of iguanas. They climbed up a sharp, short bluff to sit on stones at the top and look out to the sea. Ah Bahlam shrugged his bow and arrows off his shoulder, setting them carefully on rocks the wind had blown clear of sand. He unrolled the leather pouch he kept his feathers in, so it lay open on a flat stone, and reached for a set of folded green and light orange paper like the tender books kept in the sacred temples, and like the books, filled with images. They were smaller, though, leaf-sized. Ah Bahlam held one up toward the sun. "Like her speech, I cannot read her pictures."

Cauac took the paper from Ah Bahlam, running it through his fingers and staring out to sea, as if Great Old remained to give him answers. "Is the girl still at the cenote?" he asked.

Ah Bahlam shook his head. "She took the path, but when I followed, her footsteps simply stopped."

A spirit who left tracks. "Start at the beginning, and tell me everything."

While Ah Bahlam told his story, Cauac stared out to sea, listening to Ah Bahlam with one ear and to the gentle waves with the other, struggling to understand. The story made no more sense than his dreams had. He had feared the dreams concerned Ah Bahlam as well, and now he knew they must. Ah Bahlam had spent a year studying with Cauac. Other young men and women had also been sent to work with various priests, healers, and shamans like Cauac. But Ah Bahlam was special. Not because he was the eldest son of a powerful man who controlled the salt trade and sat on the high councils of Chichén Itzá. Because of—trust—a trust that Cauac had never seen in a student sent to him. A strong innocence.

Ah Bahlam would return to Chichén Itzá, where he might, or might not, be chosen to play in the winter solstice ball game that would define the new year. Afterward, unless he died on the Ball Court, he would take a place by his father's side as an advisor, and perhaps, some day, help run the city.

The whole peninsula felt the tension between Chichén Itzá and Coba, and even more, between the thirsty farms and the great city. Protection agreements fell apart as bandits roamed the Mayan roads. This was a difficult time for leadership. All his life Chichén had stood as beacon and target, and now it was more of each than ever.

Maybe he had received a sign that Ah Bahlam would truly be a warrior-priest and not just a warrior. That he would help Chichén heal its relationship to the gods. Cauac cleared his throat, signaling for Ah Bahlam to listen to him. "I have dreamed of this beach covered with white-skinned people. Of men and women wearing the fins of fish swimming in the water and speaking to each other across far distances. I dreamed of stars set back the way they started, with the black dream place overhead and the snake of time eating its tail."

Ah Bahlam shifted beside him, but held his silence. A good student.

Cauac swallowed. "I will continue to try to understand these dreams, and how they might link to your spirit girl with footprints from today." He crumpled the strange paper in his hand, then opened it again, amazed at its strength. "I fear they mean you will have a great role to play."

Ah Bahlam swallowed. "In the ball game?"

"You are a strong player." He held the paper-leaf out to Ah Bahlam. "Maybe more than that."

Ah Bahlam waved his hand at Cauac. "Keep that leaf. It is a gift. I will do my best to use all that you have taught me."

He still looked shaken and excited. Perhaps at his vision, perhaps at their impending departure. Best to focus him. "Take a few hours this afternoon and return to the jungle."

Ah Bahlam looked about to protest.

"Not so far. Just past town. Call your jaguar again, and ask it to help you understand the vision it sent you today."

Ah Bahlam nodded. "I will go prepare."

Cauac watched him walk away, wishing he had more time. Ah Bahlam had heart, and he had honed his body/self connection well enough to become a good warrior.

The gods appeared to be calling on him for much more than that, and yet Cauac couldn't read what they wanted.

How could he know if he had done enough?

CHAPTER 7

The sun had fallen halfway down the afternoon sky when Ah Bahlam finished getting ready. His slight frustration at being sent back into the jungle had been replaced with anticipation. Another chance. This time, he would find the right place to call the jaguar.

Carrying only his bow and arrows and a small water skin, he walked quickly across the grounds. As he passed the walls of Zama, he broke into a ground-eating jog, breathing easily.

He passed the village, a large cleared area where bleating goats and silent tapirs stood crowded in wooden pens outside of simple stick homes with thatched roofs. A few people waved at him, and he waved back.

Howler monkeys leapt from tree to tree above, calling to each other about him. He slowed to a walk, silencing his steps and breath. He looked for signs of water, for a good, powerful place where he could begin his call. The howler monkeys shifted their attention, going back the way they had come.

A low throaty growl stopped him in his tracks.

In the shadow just ahead, a black jaguar watched him with sun-colored eyes. The barest traces of spots, black on black, covered its slick fur.

He hadn't even called! He slowed his breathing, forcing the racing surprise in his blood to calm.

The cat took a step toward him.

Ah Bahlam kept his eyes on the animal. He had only seen a black jaguar one other time, an old one that lay on a rock in the sun looking like it waited for death. This was a young adult: strong haunches, unblemished skin, bright eyes, and a short tail that flicked back and forth as it watched him.

The cat took two more steps. It was close enough to kill him.

He didn't move.

The cat crossed one paw in front of the other, turning a bit, keeping its gaze on him. It circled him slowly.

He was being tested. He dropped slowly to a crouch, using all his inner strength to keep his muscles soft and unthreatening.

It finished its second circle and then stopped again, standing directly in the middle of the trail, regarding him. Wise. It looked wise, and very strong.

Ah Bahlam struggled for openness and silence, to become linked with the cat and the jungle. He poured gratitude from his heart into the air, and licked at a bit of sweat running down his cheek from his temple.

He fixed the image of the great head, the lithe body, and the intelligent gaze in his mind, committing details to memory so he could call the jaguar again in the future.

The cat turned and bounded away from him, sticking to the middle of the trail.

He followed, the jaguar easily pulling away from him, disappearing around a corner.

When Ah Bahlam reached the corner, the cat was gone. No leaves rustled to show its path and a ridge of stone held no tracks.

He sank down on a bare patch of ground between two knee-high roots, leaning his head against the rough bark of the tree. "Come back," he whispered, almost a moan. "Come back."

What did it mean that he had not called the cat, but it had found him? That it had run off after taking his measure? He had expected to feel full and powerful after encountering his Way, not confused and empty.

He remained between the roots, listening to the jungle shift between day and night. Snakes and hunting birds moved freely, while small game scurried under cover.

The jaguar did not return.

He waited for it until the light faded and he had to guide himself back with stars and a faint moon.

As soon as Ah Bahlam returned to Zama, he went looking for Cauac, only to be told the old man had gone to bed for the evening. He fought back disappointment, remembering that he would see his teacher with first light. He had too much energy to sleep, so he walked out toward the sea, near where he had met Cauac earlier.

The moon threw enough faint light for him to find the path. He stood a few feet from the surf, looking up at the stars.

"Ah Bahlam?" a voice whispered near him.

"Hun Kan?" he queried, although it must be her.

She stepped from the shadows into the moonlight, a slight young woman just a few years younger than Ah Bahlam. Her hair blew unbound around her face, and her eyes and lips were dark in the pale moonlight.

His breath caught in his throat at her nearness. "Little one. How are you? Are you ready to go back?"

She stepped near him, her footsteps silent in the sand. "I like it here by the ocean. The silence. It is a lesson to just be still with the ocean for a whole transit of the sun."

He kept his voice low. "We weren't born for this. It has been a gift before we start our true lives." He swallowed, feeling the dangerous journey ahead. He closed his eyes and took the last step of space between them, curling her into his arms. He should not do even this, but he could no more resist than he could stop breathing. His blood and his heart demanded more, but he made her nearness be enough.

She leaned into him, her head on his chest. "How do I know I'll be brave enough? Good enough?"

He brushed his lips across the part in her hair. "You will be." Their breathing mingled with the soft susurration of the sea. He whispered, "I saw my jaguar today. A black one."

She turned her face up toward him. "The black jaguar has the most power. Then you will have strength."

He closed his eyes, searching inside himself for the right answer. "Perhaps. It ran away from me."

"Which way did it go?" she asked.

"Toward home."

"Then perhaps we'll find it on our way."

He smiled at her optimism. If only it could be so easy. "I will pray for that."

She smelled of sea and salt and fresh air and woman, and his body yearned for her so hard he clenched his fists to keep them from trembling.

He was not free to choose his own wife.

CHAPTER 8

Noon light poured into the swimming pool, turning every metal and shiny thing into a small sun. As Alice watched Nixie and two girls from England play underwater tag, the fears that had kept her awake seemed like child's nightmares. It was hard to be scared in a place where children splashed in the pool while the adults drank free colored drinks, more juice than alcohol, and read bestsellers on e-readers.

"Alice?" Oriana's voice came from behind her and made her jump.

She turned and smiled. "Thanks again for helping me last night."

A man no taller than Alice herself stood next to Oriana. His hair cascaded down his shoulders in long sienna dreadlocks hung with homemade bone and ivory beads. The dreads didn't surprise her, but she hadn't expected anyone quite so, well, healthy. Deep tan skin spread across well-defined muscles. His teeth were as white and even as an actor's. He grinned at Alice, his smile starting at his lips and radiating all the way out to the world around him.

She stuck her hand out. "You must be Ian."

He glanced at Oriana, raising one eyebrow as he took Alice's hand. "You didn't tell me she was so pretty."

Oriana batted at him playfully. "Sure I did." She glanced at Alice. "He's impossible, and improbable, and sweet and brave." She winked. "If you're lucky he'll be more sweet than impossible."

Alice pulled her hand free, wishing she hadn't agreed to meet him.

Ian glanced down at his empty hand with a bemused expression on his face, and then looked back at Alice. "I read your papers on the equinox, and your early one on the way the Mayan astronomers used their feet as telescopes." He laughed, his voice rich and deep, but with a nearly childlike quality. "I even tried it one night, and you really can see the stars move through your crossed legs."

She glanced at Oriana. "All right, he is sweet." And apparently well educated enough to read scientific papers.

She pointed to a nearby table for four, piled high with towels and books and snorkeling gear. "We're over there."

Ian wandered over to it and picked up a mask. "You practicing?" he asked.

"It's Nixie's, and she's practicing. She's hoping Oriana will take her snorkeling. She even has a new snorkeling watch."

He sobered. "Did you ever dive here before the reef started dying?"

Alice nodded. "Maybe it was already dying, but you couldn't tell yet. The first time I came down here was 1990, and the next 1999, and then pretty close to once or twice a year after that."

"You don't look that old," Ian said.

"I'm not," Alice shot back. "I was sixteen in '90."

He pursed his lips, looking her up and down, more compliment than intrusion. He smiled. "Maybe."

He could have been flirting, if she remembered what flirting felt like. It made her squirm. "Did Oriana tell you Nixie's story?"

He nodded, looking out toward the pool. "Is she here?"

"She's—"

He cut Alice off with a gentle hand-chop in the air. "I want to see if I can pick her out after Oriana's description."

Alice watched him so she wouldn't inadvertently give away Nixie's location. He grinned and pointed. "Must be that one."

Alice turned to find Nixie a few feet away, heading straight for her. She glanced at Ian, rolling her eyes. "Very impressive."

"I aim to please." There was that grin again, the one that made it seem like everything was good and right and Ian was her best friend in all the world. Funny thing was, she could usually spot fakes. Ian didn't seem fake, even if he did have an extra helping or two of weird and one of cockiness.

She didn't want to like him, but she did. Not that she trusted him. He did drugs and studied with shamans, and most of the people like that she'd met down here were flakes. So she shouldn't like him at all.

Nixie seemed to take an instant liking to him, too. Her eyes danced welcome as she stuck her dripping-wet hand out. "Hi, I'm Nixie."

He took her hand without seeming to mind the chlorine-drenched water dripping off her, and smiled. "I'm Ian Riley. I heard . . . you took a little journey last night." Alice suppressed a gasp. He didn't beat around the bush, did he? She hadn't even brought up the subject today.

Nixie smiled, seeming relieved. "I did. I met a Mayan man, and he gave me a feather. I gave him twenty dollars for it."

Ian nodded gravely. "Had he ever seen money before?"

Nixie shook her head. "I don't think so. He tasted it."

Ian laughed. "Did he like it?"

She laughed back, a bright girlish laugh. "He didn't say anything." She frowned. "I couldn't talk to him. He spoke Mayan, and I don't."

"How did you know it was Mayan?" Ian asked.

"We heard it at the Xcaret show the other night." She grabbed a blue hotel towel and wrapped it around her waist, grinning at Alice. "And sometimes you try to say some Mayan words."

Ian raised an eyebrow at Alice before asking Nixie, "Can I see the feather?"

Nixie glanced at Alice, who nodded, then Nix raced off toward their hotel room, the towel flapping against her legs.

Alice turned her attention back to Ian. She chose her words carefully. "Oriana tells me you believe you've gone back in time? Like maybe . . . *maybe* my daughter has?"

He shook his head. "Not like her story, not if I heard it right. I've only seen the old world, but she touched it. I couldn't have brought a feather back. I'm in awe."

"I'm worried sick."

"Worried about?" Oriana asked quietly. She hadn't spoken in so long that Alice had nearly forgotten she was there.

"If she's lying, or been deceived, then what really happened? Was she stalked?" Alice hesitated, her stomach rebelling at the idea of even saying the next words. "If she's telling the truth, then what if it happens again and she can't get back?"

Oriana chewed her lower lip, and Ian watched her quietly. Finally Oriana asked, "But don't you worry that it's happening at all? What if it's happening all over?"

"The old world washing over the new one?" Ian mused.

"I'm trying to ignore that," Alice snapped, the words out before she thought about them. She laughed softly. "I'm sorry. But I worry about my daughter first. The world is too big to worry about." She'd lost Nixie's dad trying to keep the world safe. She couldn't keep the world safe. Maybe she could keep Nix safe.

Oriana leaned back, giving Alice an appraising look. "I thought it was all dreams and visions for Ian," she glanced over at him, "but then when I heard Nixie's story last night, well, I didn't sleep too well. Could it happen to any of us?"

Alice took a long sip of her drink, which had once been a piña colada, but now tasted like warm, sour pineapple. "I don't know." She glanced at Ian. "What do you think?"

He spread his hands out wide and gave an exaggerated shrug. "Perhaps there's something special about Nixie. Or maybe about her age. Through the eyes of a child, and all that."

He didn't seem overly concerned. Like strange things happened to him every day. She shivered and wished he wasn't there all over again. But he was, and something *had* happened and there were too many witnesses for her to deny it. "I hope it's not something special about her," Alice whispered, thinking of the shopkeeper back in Playa kneeling before Nixie for that long moment. She glanced toward their room. "Here she comes."

Nixie carried the feather across a towel, balancing it as if she were a ring bearer at a wedding, the look in her face solemn and intent, imbued with the same eerie grace Alice had noticed yesterday afternoon with the first feather.

Alice listened for the silence that had fallen over the store, but the kids splashing in the pool and the babble of conversation about them remained the same.

Nixie presented the folded towel and feather to Ian, who set it carefully on the table and looked at it without touching. He pointed at the crushed quill. "What happened?"

Nixie glanced at Alice, who said, "I stepped on it. An accident."

His eyes flashed surprise and regret at Alice before he turned back to Nixie. "Well," he said, "It's still the prettiest one I've ever seen. What will you do with it?"

Nixie's cheeks reddened and she took a half step back. "Look at it."

"Okay," Ian said. He fished in his pocket and brought out a carved stone bead on a leather string.

Nixie gaped at it. "I don't want to trade."

Ian smiled at her. "Of course you don't. I'd like you to have this. If you find the cenote again, or you go anywhere else that's like that," he ran the bead through his thumb and forefinger, "I want you to have this to trade in case anyone else gives you anything. I made it, so I'll know it if I ever see it again, but I don't want you to put anything from today, like money, into that time."

Alice reached a hand out and put it on Nixie's arm. "But I don't want you to go anywhere like that again." She waited until Nixie looked directly at her. "Promise me?"

Nixie shook her head. "I just walked there, Mom. I didn't try to go there."

"I know, honey. But try not to, okay? I was really scared." Talking about it made it real all over again, and sent flutters of heat up her spine. She wiped an arm across her face, looking down as it came away damp with unshed tears.

She stood up and turned toward the pool, watching a big boy try to dunk a smaller one. The younger boy dove down of his own accord and swam along the bottom of the pool, surfacing a few feet away and turning to laugh at his would-be tormentor.

Alice felt small arms slide around her from behind, and the comfortable weight of Nixie's head just below the wings of her back. "I'm sorry I scared you."

She turned around and held her daughter. "You didn't scare me, honey. But I was scared for you."

Nixie looked up at her. "Can I have the bead?"

What harm could it do? "Sure." She glanced at the table. "I can watch your feather if you want to swim."

Nixie shook her head. "No, I'll put it away." She took the leather loop and bead from Ian's outstretched hand, placed it carefully beside the feather, and walked off toward the building their room was in.

Alice collapsed back into her chair. "Oriana, Ian, I'm sorry. I didn't sleep much last night. It's all so overwhelming."

"Of course it is," Oriana whispered.

"I've worked all my life to be here now. But ten years ago, I didn't expect the world to be so hard, or that so much attention would be on this place in this time." She swept her hand toward the busy pool. "I bet every one of these people knows this is the end of the Mayan calendar. They don't understand it, they just read the cheap novels and the flashy books from the last few years, and watched the silly movies and TV shows. They're here to escape riots and car bombings, flash crowds, and maybe even floods or the drought at their own homes. They're hoping for something that can't happen . . ."

Ian whispered, "Why not? Why can't something happen? Something good?"

"And then, to almost lose my daughter . . . " She shook herself, feeling rude and self-absorbed. "Maybe something good *will* happen. But I'm still scared."

"Maybe we all need to be a little more open to magic right now," Ian said simply.

This was what she'd sworn not to get sucked into. Crazy beliefs. False hopes. Dammit, she was a scientist. A mom. She'd earned respect. Been published. She wanted to say all that, to talk about science and reason, but what came out was, "I don't believe in magic."

DECEMBER 16, 2012

CHAPTER 9

"Mom?" Nixie stood in the kitchen, clutching a towel. "Oriana doesn't get here for an hour. Can I go down to the beach?"

Her mom wore work clothes; khaki pants and a neatly ironed white shirt, her hair pulled back into a high ponytail. Her face had pinched up tight. "I'm sorry, honey. I don't have time to go with you today."

It wasn't fair. She needed air and sunshine. "You let me go the day before yesterday. I came back in an hour like you wanted me to, and I didn't go in the water, except up to my ankles, just like you said." She tried to sound innocent. "There aren't any waves at that beach, and there's a lifeguard. I'll come back in half an hour this time."

Her mom looked away, out of the window, and for a minute Nixie thought she saw a tear sliding down her cheek. It took two sips of coffee and a cough before her mom turned back to her. "I have some free time tomorrow. I'll take you then. Why don't you draw a picture of your feather, or watch TV or something?"

"You never want me to watch TV." Nixie picked up Snake and her book, a paperback about flying horses, and went out onto the porch, not quite slamming the door behind her. She curled Snake into a soft green pillow for her head and crossed her bare feet in front of her on the railing. She opened her book, but instead of turning the pages she fingered the bead Ian had given her, and looked out over the low broken jungle canopy between their room and the water.

How had she gotten to that old time? Her mom must think it had been real, or it would be okay to go to the beach.

She tried to read her book, but the words kept fading to hash marks. She fetched her journal and colored pencils, and drew the walkway below her, and the tops of the jungle trees, and the bright blue sea meeting the paler blue sky. The ruin she'd walked through yesterday stuck up just above the trees, and from here, it was clear there was no tall-tree jungle and no cenote. Just resort.

She added color and a quetzal bird flying up toward the sun, then sat and stared at her drawing. It hadn't seemed scary to be there, or maybe she should think, *then*. But what if there hadn't been a path home?

After a long while, her mom came out and stood beside her on the balcony. "Nix, do you want ten dollars to go shopping with Oriana today?"

"Where?"

"I'm going to ask Oriana to take you on one of those tours to Tulum. You haven't been this trip, and you liked it before."

Nixie blinked at the new plans. "But . . . but I thought Oriana was going to take me snorkeling."

When her mom didn't answer right away, Nixie said, "You don't want me near the little ruin. Tulum's just a big ruin."

"But there'll be a lot of people there."

Like strangers would keep her safe? "Mom—I promise I'll be careful."

Her mom's arm snuck across her shoulders and she found herself looking into her mom's blue eyes, at least two shades paler than her own. Summer sky washed by the sun. She looked really, really worried. Maybe even a little scared. "Please Nix? For me? Unless you'd rather stay in the pool." Her jaw quivered, and she looked away, out toward the cluster of ruins. "You'll have fun."

At least there was a beach at Tulum. She didn't remember if it was okay to swim there, but all of Tulum looked down on the ocean. It was the prettiest ruin in Mexico; a neat, whitewashed set of Lego-like buildings perched by the open sea and surrounded by a low stone wall. She brightened at a stray thought. "Will Ian come with us?"

Her mom shook her head. "Just Oriana." She held out a ten dollar bill. "American money will be fine anywhere on the resort, and you should be able to use it in the little shopping village outside Tulum, too. I'll give Oriana a little more for snacks, but this way you won't be broke."

"Thanks." Nixie shoved the bill into her pocket. "Will you be home in time for dinner?"

"No. I have to go to a party."

Nixie brightened. "A party?"

"Boring. Archeologists and scientists."

Oh. "I like scientists." Fat chance of her going.

"You can take Oriana to one of the restaurants. We get two adult passes with the room anyway, so Oriana can use our extra one. She can get towels, too." She bent down over Nixie's drawing. "That's very good." Her voice quivered as she asked, "But why did you color the ruin blue?"

Nixie bit her lip. That was the color the ruin had been yesterday, from the magical old side. She remembered that now, the steps red, and the lintel the bright blue of the sea more than the blue of the sky, maybe even brighter. Like the blue in the quetzal feather down by the spine, a shining blue. "The colors are pretty."

Her mom was silent for a few moments. "I must have told you that in the old days, the Mayans used bright colors on their houses and temples. They're only gray today because the color has all worn off."

Nixie didn't remember that, not exactly. She just remembered what she saw.

A knock sounded on the door. While her mom let Oriana in, Nixie picked up her drawing materials. Before she went inside, she stood at the edge of the balcony, looking at the sea.

Nixie laughed as Oriana zipped the car into a tiny parking spot at the edge of the gravel-strewn parking lot under a small copse of trees. She climbed out, swinging her backpack over her shoulder and clutching her camera. The dark oily smoke belching from the tourist buses running between them and the entrance to Tulum stank, huge things with high dark windows and sun-cracked paint. The sides were pasted with big, bright signs saying things like, "*Riviera Maya 2012! The dream of a people,*" and "*Best sacred places tours. See Tulum and Xel-Ha!*" Painted snorkelers the size of whales swam along the sides of some of the buses, peering at painted fish the size of Oriana's little purple Volkswagen beetle.

Nix stopped to snap pictures.

Oriana grinned. "The morning crowd will be gone soon. That's why we drove—they come here in two big clumps for the morning and the afternoon tours, as if two hours were enough to see this place." She held her hand out, and Nixie took it, liking the dry, rough scratch of Oriana's palm against hers.

They threaded through a pile of busy open-walled shops just outside the ruins. Nixie stopped to take a photo of brightly dressed young men hanging by one foot from a pole high in the air. The pole began to spin, and the five men descended slowly, upside down, each tied by a single rope wrapped from thigh to ankle and held at their waists. The pole turned faster. The men swung in fast, wide circles high above the heads of the crowd, eliciting entranced sighs from the audience.

"Do you want to stay and watch?" Oriana asked.

Nixie shook her head. She'd seen the same dance at Xcaret, only with the men in bright red-and-green macaw feather headdresses and white loincloths. "Let's go in."

"All right," Oriana said. "Can I be your guide?"

"You bet! The last time our guide was a fat guy who kept making bad jokes."

Oriana clapped her hands together and started toward the entrance. "How old were you last time you were here?"

"We came two years ago, so I was nine."

"Do you remember much?"

"It was a place for priests."

Oriana nodded. "It used to be called Zama, which they think was a word for "sun." It was a sacred place, and also a trading port. See how small it is compared to Chichén Itzá? The archeologists think the priests and warriors lived inside the walls, and that they held ceremonies here. But most of the people lived in villages outside, or came here by traveling. This was a key defensive spot, the way it's on the ocean here."

"Can we go to the beach?" Nixie asked.

"Sure. But we have to get in first." They fetched up against a line of tourists shifting impatiently, waiting to gain entry. A pair of gray-green iguanas watched the people, cocking their heads from time to time, as if having a silent conversation. Nixie used the 3D setting on her camera and got two good pictures before a little boy in bright yellow shorts came too close. The reptiles skittered under rocks.

Ten minutes later, she and Oriana were inside, going upstream against tourists beginning to drift back toward the shopping area and the parking lot. "Can I walk you around once before we go to the water?" Oriana asked. "It's emptying out some, and this would be a good time to go see the temples."

Nixie looked up at her. "Can we go to the beach, first? Please?"

Oriana cocked her head at Nixie, as if deciding whether to assert her adultness. Then she smiled. "Okay." She led them down a wide dirt path flanked with brown grass and short palm trees. They picked their way around a corner, and the path gave way to fine white sand that clung to their tennis shoes. In front of them, the sea stretched light blue in the midday sun. Small waves licked at the beach. Oriana pointed. "See how there is a huge break in the reef here? That's part of why they built Zama here. They could get boats in and out."

Nixie frowned. "I wish I'd brought my fins and mask."

Oriana shaded her eyes and looked out. "There are better reefs just off the resort." She pointed at an old Japanese couple walking slowly through water over their knees. "Sometimes they don't let anyone in the water, but it looks like it's okay today."

Nixie grinned. "Good." She took off her shoes and raced down the beach, the hot sand stinging so much she cried out before plunging into the sea. She went as far out as the old couple, water lapping her thighs. She turned to look back at the beach. Oriana clutched Nixie's pack in her right hand. She walked quickly across the sand, set their gear near Nixie's abandoned shoes, and waded in, her face tight and her brows drawn together.

Oriana slid easily toward Nixie, as if she and the water were the best of friends. Her brown eyes snapped with the reflection of the sun on the sea as she said, "Don't do that. Please. I only want you to go in the water when I'm with you."

Nixie glanced at the couple, now wading shoreward, hand in hand, heads bent close in conversation. "It's safe here."

"But if I'm going to teach you to snorkel, I need to know you're going to do what I tell you around and in the water."

Nixie stiffened. But Oriana had brought her down here and, in truth, she sounded more worried than mad. "Sorry." She turned, looking away from the gray stone bones of Tulum toward the vast Caribbean. Something flashed in the warm water at her feet. She bent down. A school of tiny fish. She pointed. "Look."

Oriana peered at the seafloor. "Baitfish." She glanced over her shoulder at the ruins, and then said, "Let's go out a little further. Maybe we can find something more interesting."

"Does it get deep?"

"Not for a while." Oriana waved a hand out towards the open sea. "It changes color when it gets deeper. Stay on this side, where the water is lighter. And stay close to me."

"It's so clear." Small stones and bits of shell speckled the white sand, disappearing as Nixie's steps sent clouds of fine white powder up into the water, a trail of fairy dust following her.

"Be careful," Oriana said. "Watch out for sea urchins or stingray tails— they look like barbed brown sticks poking out of the water. Shuffle your feet so you won't step on one."

"Wow." As Nixie obeyed, the cloud of fairy dust thickened.

"When we snorkel, we'll see parrotfish and angels and big groupers. We might see baby turtles. Last summer's first crop should be big enough to swim to the reefs. I saw one yesterday morning, off of Akumal."

Good. All she'd seen so far was more of the little silver fish. She headed further out, the sand sloping ever so slightly under her feet. She stubbed her toe on a rock and hopped up and down on one foot, losing her balance and falling sideways in the water. She same up spluttering, but laughing. "Sorry."

Oriana was laughing, too.

Her mom wouldn't have laughed, at least not this year.

Nixie stood dripping in the water, still laughing, stopping when Oriana's eyes widened at something over Nixie's shoulder. "Ssshhh," she said. "Look."

Nixie turned. Just a few feet behind her, a turtle poked its yellow-green head out of the water and regarded the two women. It was gray and green, with pinkish spots, and ridges that went from the front to back of its shell. "That's no baby," Nixie said.

It was almost longer than Nixie was tall. "An old leatherback," Oriana whispered. "That shouldn't be in here. Not this close to the beach."

Nixie took a step toward it, holding out her hand.

CHAPTER 10

Alice sat in the back of a small hot bus, surrounded by locals going to work at Chichén. She'd left her car in a lot in Cancun. Gas was so dear, even in Mexico, that she'd started taking local buses on long trips.

Today, she drew attention from the brown faces around her as she glanced repeatedly at her phone. She'd turned the tracking on even though she knew the webs were lousy on the roads. It worked, though. Her light blinked in the center, Nixie's at the edge. As she watched, the background re-drew, showing Alice's movement away from Nixie, toward Chichén Itzá. She licked her lips, wishing Nixie were beside her.

The bus dropped Alice off near the gate. The lot looked more crowded than she'd ever seen it. To get in, she dodged buses, rental cars, and gaggles of brightly dressed tourists gathering around guides with megaphones. She headed directly toward the gate, where she flashed a pass to get in.

Just beyond, two men and a woman sat on a gray stone bench, watching for her. Her friend, Don Carlo Agapito, and two people from IndiStudy, a private foundation he funded.

The woman, Julia Highland, spotted her first. Julia was dressed almost identically to Alice, in khakis and a light shirt with wearing a dull green canvas expedition hat to shade her fair skin. Even dressed alike, they didn't look alike. Julia might have stepped out of a magazine cover, complete with makeup and blonde hair that looked bouncy even in the humid air.

Alice shook her hand quickly. "Hello, Julia. You look wonderful."

A nod. "Ready?"

Alice met Don Carlo's sparkling brown eyes. She genuinely liked him. Two summers ago, they had traveled together with some graduate students on a trip to decipher the paintings on a new mural unearthed north of Merida. He had been respectful and curious, if sometimes slightly drunk and talkative after dinner. Although he had the dark skin, delicate features, and wide brown eyes of a Yucatecan Maya, Don Carlo had been raised in the United States. He'd invested the millions he made in technology to study his heritage, anonymously funding Mayan research and schools. He smiled down at her. "Hello, Alice. You're as beautiful as ever."

She blushed a little at his comment, even while knowing it for his usual manner with all women.

Michael Lingen looked like the perfect tourist, all tan and lean muscle, almost six feet tall, blond and confident. He wore jeans and a T-shirt. The hand he clasped Alice's hand with was cool and soft. "Pleased to see you."

"Likewise." Michael was better looking than Don Carlo, except his flirting wasn't as harmless. But he could give her more work. She was traveling on the last of the money IndiStudy had paid her, and she needed a way to feed Nix next year. A tough line to dance on. She smiled along that line, stepping back a bit from him. "What can I show you?"

"Can we start at K'uk'ulkan?"

The temple of the snake god. At least he didn't call it "the castle" like so many tourists did. She glanced over at Julia and Don Carlo. "Is that all right with you two?"

Julia said, "Sure," and Don Carlo grinned, his smile lightening her mood. He felt like an almost-authentic version of Ian. Funny, since Don Carlo was native and Ian imported. She shook her head to clear the thought and led the trio toward the large stepped pyramid, falling a little behind to glance down at her phone.

No Nixie. Damn. She pushed the message button and whispered an instant voicemail to Oriana. "Is everything okay?"

Michael waited for her. She must be showing her worry because he echoed, "Is everything okay?"

She nodded quickly, an instinctive reaction in front of a client, and then shook her head. "I think so. My daughter is at Tulum, with a friend. I was just checking on her."

He looked as if she'd just brought a monkey into a crystal showroom. "Trixie? Isn't she young?"

"Nixie. She's eleven. I brought her down to see this." She struggled to keep her voice light and even. "Something she'll remember her whole life." She smiled at him, hoping to disarm.

His smile didn't reach his cool, blue eyes. "Tulum's got enough military presence to keep it safe."

"I'm sure you're right." But she couldn't help glancing down at her phone. There was no reply, and Nixie's light was still missing.

As they dodged a woman pushing a baby stroller awkwardly on the cobbled walkway, he changed the subject. "We appreciate your work. I'm looking forward to being here when the stars line up like the legends."

"Not legends," she said. "Science. The Mayans were excellent astronomers."

"So have you noticed anything different here?"

What was he looking for? She chose her words carefully. "Chichén has become a popular destination. Mayans are coming, too. In droves."

"Will there be trouble?" he asked, echoing the tabloid headlines.

She held her hands out, shrugging as if to say she didn't know. "We saw some protests yesterday in Playa."

Michael sounded worried as he said, "Miss Marie's having an international environmental conference starting in Cancun in a few days. Conferences seem to need demonstrators and terrorists."

One more way the world was going crazy all at once, trying to hold to a world view that was slowly killing them all. Then the name he said sunk in. Marie Healey.

Marie Healey, the President of the United States' Science Advisor and Director of the Office of Science and Technology Policy. The woman who ran his international program of shared responsibility for climate change. A mixed success, but more than anyone else had managed.

"I went to school with her," Alice said.

"Really?" He sounded intrigued. "What was she like?"

"Smart." Alice could see her, a year older, laughing as she came to Alice for last minute tutoring, or chided her for studying too hard. Marie the lucky, the one who always knew the moment to strike, the act to take, the person to meet. Marie who might be saving the world. No other woman at Stanford had burned as bright as Marie. "She's brave. We used to get in trouble together."

"So are you brave?"

Alice shook her head. "Marie used to make me brave. Besides, courage is for the young."

He arched an eyebrow at her. "Really? You're brave enough to come down here on your own."

They were near the bottom of the pyramid, and Alice stopped so Julia and Don Carlo could catch them. Maybe she could start them all up the steps and then call Oriana again. "Ready to see if you're in shape?"

Julia's eyes flashed at the challenge. Don Carlo showed his white teeth in a faint grin, and Michael simply started up. His long legs made the tall steps easy, while Julia climbed slowly, placing both feet on each step before taking the next one. Although she stayed close to the metal chain running up the center of the steps, she didn't actually grab for it. Don Carlo went up at Julia's pace, at her side, but one step at a time. He looked like a Mayan priest might have, taking the steps reverently, his back straight and his head high.

Alice glanced back at her phone. Nothing new. She sent another message and forced her legs up instead of letting them run back to the parking lot and hail a cab to Tulum. Midday sun whitewashed the sky to barely-blue and heated the steps so they produced faint shimmers of heat.

Seven steps from the top, her phone vibrated. Alice hesitated, suddenly scared to listen. She pulled ahead of the other two, rushing her breath, and sat down on the top, her toes barely reaching the step below her. She tapped her wrist. "Oriana?"

An unfamiliar voice said, "Call for Ms. Alice Cameron."

Her hands shook so hard she almost dropped the phone. "I'm here."

The voice on the other end of the line was very formal. "Please hold for Director Healey."

Surely it was coincidence she'd just been talking about Marie. Although maybe it made perfect sense they'd both be here at this time.

Marie was calling her?

"Alice?"

She recognized the voice. Marie *was* calling her. "Yes? Hi. How are you?" She sounded like a tweener talking to a kid-band lead singer.

"I'm fine. A little busy lately." Marie's warm tones calmed Alice's racing blood. "Are you sitting down?"

"Yes."

"I want you to show me around Chichén Itzá."

Alice's mouth dropped open. "I'm . . . sure! I'm there right now. When?" What a dumb question. Surely for the summit.

"Me and a few of my best friends. On the twentieth. Yes I know the site is closed. But not to us."

Wow. The V.I.P. showing. Oriana could watch Nixie. If Nixie was now . . . Damn. Alice licked her lips. "All right."

Marie's voice warmed even more. "Look, I saw your name on a list of people who could do this. So I picked you. I'd like to see you again. There's a dinner afterwards, too. For even more of my best friends. Can you come to that, too? The president will be there.

"I . . . I'd love to." Her knees felt watery. Not a good thing on top of a pyramid. At least she was sitting down. Marie Healey. And the President of the United States, and other leaders of the free world. Or the not-so-free if you counted China, where they kept up an invisible electronic wall that almost worked around the whole country. "I . . . yes. I'll be happy to do it. Of course I'd like to see you again."

Silence fell for a beat. When Marie continued, her voice was serious. "I wanted—*needed*—someone I can count on. Someone who won't play politics."

Michael's impatient voice called to her. "Alice!"

She shook her head at him. He glared at her with an *I'm more important than you and you work for me* look. Don Carlo showed up beside him and said something Alice couldn't hear and the two men stepped away. Alice refocused in time to hear Marie ask, "Are you busy?"

"Not too busy to talk to you." Unless my daughter calls. But she didn't say that. "I'm honored. Should I meet you here, and when?"

"It's not that simple. There will be background checks. I need you to meet with my security people. The first session will be tomorrow morning."

"Tomorrow." She'd planned the morning off, promised Nix she'd take her to the beach. "Hold on."

She flipped to her calendar, noting along the way that Nix still didn't appear to be in the real world if you counted on GPS. You could build great applications, but a bad network could take them all down. Or magic. Not. Surely not.

Her schedule popped up on the screen. Maybe she could rearrange her noon meeting, keep her date with Nix. It mattered. "I can be free at noon."

Marie responded. "Staff has time at nine in the morning. At the Cancun Marriott. I'm sorry, I can't change it. If you want to do this, you'll have to be flexible. I'll make sure to fix anything it does to your schedule. You'll be paid, of course. For all of the time."

She'd have to leave before breakfast. It was just wrong to leave Nix in the lurch, but December, 2012 would never come again, and she needed the money. And Marie Healey! "Of course I'll do it."

"But do you want to?"

Alice swore she heard something almost pleading in Marie's voice. "Of course I do."

"Okay. Be at the Marriott at nine. There'll be follow-ups, too, I'm afraid."

Alice let out a long breath. "I'll do it."

"Thanks."

Alice was wondering what to say next when it came to her. Don Carlo. "May I bring someone who can help?"

Marie sounded startled. "Who?"

"Don Carlo Agapito. He's American. Used to own a tech company he sold, uses that money to help Mayans down here. He'll be good for PR."

She could almost hear laughter in Marie's voice as she asked, "Is he your sweetie?"

Alice did laugh. "No, I don't have one of those. But he's helped me get work down here, and I can use someone I trust to help me if the group gets too big. He can answer any question about the Mayans themselves. And they should be represented."

"Hold on." The phone went silent, and Alice heart her heart beating too fast for a long time before Marie came back on the phone. "He's already on the possible list. We'll move him up a notch. My folk will contact him."

"Thanks," Alice said again, a little surprised at her audacity, at how easy and hard it was to talk to Marie, all at once. Just like it used to be. "I'm looking forward to seeing you."

"Okay. I'll have the security squad contact you. You can give them your friend's particulars."

"All right."

"Look, I've got to go keep working to save the world. But I'll see you in a few days. I'm glad we found you and you're down there. Bye."

"Bye." But Marie had cut the connection before she even said that. Alice sat up straight and looked out across the jungle. Wow.

"Are you ready yet?" Michael called.

She stood up quickly. "Yes, sorry."

"Was that Nixie?" he asked.

"Just . . . " What to say? "An old friend. Someone I wouldn't have been able to call back if I hadn't taken the call."

He frowned, but led her around the top of the pyramid toward the others as if he were the guide.

She frowned, but followed him. He paid her, after all.

They came upon the others looking down at a whitewashed four-step pyramid.

Alice shook herself. Nixie . . . well, what could she do? Nixie had to be all right. She needed to focus, to do her job. Speaking of the job, she pointed. "That's the Temple of the Warriors below you." Tall stone columns holding up nothing but air and imagination surrounded a building as steep as the one they stood on, but squatter and shorter. "No one knows exactly what the columns held up. It'll be decorated as a market for the equinox. Those are the tallest freestanding columns found so far in Mayan architecture, even though they look small from up here."

Julia spoke softly, "It's like looking down on the bones of a world. With all we understand, we don't know what it looked like when the culture was alive. Maybe we never will." She turned to Alice, sounding morose. "What if we had to look at our own bones some day?"

Don Carlos said, "Our bones keep being rebuilt and restored. Perhaps they'll never be as bare and unclothed as these. Or as strong." He looked down on the Temple, musing. "Imagine hundreds of my people, thousands, walking on the paths, going about their business. Artisans carrying pots and mosaics, warriors practicing, women with water and weaving."

Alice liked his word pictures. "Scientists and mathematicians—all priests, but they had people who did my job." Like ancestors, in a way. A heritage she could almost feel when she came here. "They're going to try to decorate some of this the way most archeologists think it would have been. You should have heard the arguments! We won't get it right, but you'll see your color."

Don Carlo smiled yet again. "And there will be real Mayans acting as the artisans and warriors."

She couldn't bring herself to tell him that only a quarter of the actors would be Mayans. Many had been hired for their looks: tall, tanned people more like the American and European ideal of Native Americans than the small, wiry Mayans.

They came upon Michael staring fixedly toward the Ball Court. He turned as they approached, laughing, "What took you so long?"

Showoff.

"We stopped to admire the view," Julia said sweetly.

Michael grunted.

Her phone vibrated again and Alice turned her back on Michael, no longer caring what he thought. She sat down.

"Everything's okay. We were in the water, so didn't have our phones." Oriana sounded excited. "We swam with a turtle. It was the most amazing thing. A big old leatherback. They never come in there, not that big, not at Tulum."

Alice let her breath out, yet she still felt full of air, almost like she could spread her arms and fly from the pyramid. Nix was okay! She glanced down, looking for Nixie's light. It wasn't there. So Tulum was just a dead space in the wireless network. Alice smiled as Oriana continued. "We're going to dry off and wander through the ruins. We'll call you later. Don't worry."

"Okay." She dropped her hand to her side.

Julia sat on her right and Don Carlo stood beside them, calm and serene. Alice looked below them, the pyramid steps almost as steep as a ladder from this height. Chichén Itzá spread out below her, and for the first time that day, the magic and mystery, the sheer timelessness of the stone world filled her again. Years of her life had been arrowed toward this week. She needed to lighten up and let that in, enjoy it. Quit worrying.

Michael cleared his throat. "Was *that* Nixie?"

"Yes." She smiled and made a little ceremony of shoving her phone into her pocket. "Let's go. What are you waiting for?"

CHAPTER 11

Heat dried the saltwater from Nixie's back before they even made it off the beach. Nothing, ever, had been so cool as the big turtle. Not even the Mayan man with the quetzal bird. Why was she so lucky?

"That was . . . wow." Oriana said. "You are magic. I've seen a few leatherbacks before, but never so close in or so . . . so . . . it came to see you!"

Nixie smiled. "I've never seen one before. I wish we'd gotten a picture."

"Come on, let me show you the ruins."

Nixie blinked at her. Might as well. Nothing could be as great as the turtle, though. Its eyes had been so old, so like her grandfather's eyes. They gave her that same feeling like she was just perfect exactly like she was, like she would always be perfect. She looked out at the clear, calm water. "No wonder you love to dive."

Oriana put a hand on Nixie's shoulder, and Nixie had to strain to hear her soft voice. "I've been diving down here for years, and I've never seen a leatherback act that way. It might have been a pet."

Nixie screwed her eyes tight against the glare. "It didn't want to be my pet. It wanted to tell me something, I just know it."

"But you don't know what?"

"No." She shrugged Oriana's hand off and started up the beach. "But let's go. I want to draw a picture. Maybe we can find a good place to sit so I can draw the ruins. Mom would like that." She pointed up at the rocky bluffs just above the beach. "Maybe there."

"You don't want to walk around?"

"Not yet. I want to think about the turtle."

As they crossed from sand to grass, they passed five young Federales dressed in black, aliens among the multinational tourists in Bermuda shorts and Hawaiian shirts.

Nixie and Oriana settled together on a wide rock with a view of both the ocean and the ruins. Both pulled on shorts from their packs to protect their swim suits from snags. A tourist path ran between them and the ruins. "Our view's going to be interrupted," Oriana said.

"I don't care. I want to see the ocean."

"Are you waiting for the turtle to come back?'

Nixie shook her head. "I don't think it will. Not today. It would have just stayed. But we live in Arizona, and there's no ocean there." She dug through her pack and pulled out her journal and her drawing box. "You can use my pencils. If you want, I can tear out a piece of paper for you."

Oriana smiled. "I brought my own journal. It's no good for drawing, but I have a pen. I'm quite content to just sit here and pretend I'm an iguana basking in the sun."

Nixie laughed. Good enough. She'd had to sit still for years, following her mom to archeological sites and lectures and stupid adult parties full of teachers. She'd learned to like it. Sitting still, that is. She pulled out a black pencil to sketch in the outline of the Temple of the Descending God, easily visible from here. Maybe she could do something as neat and orderly as her mom's scientific drawings. It would be easier without her mom looking over her shoulder.

She waited for the path to clear of people, steadied her camera against a rock, and took a picture of the ruin from exactly where she sat in case she didn't have time to finish. The outline was pretty easy, just a square on a square, and the rough outline of the rocks between her and the ruin. The gentle scratching of Oriana's pen soothed her, and she'd gotten all the way to trying to shade the darker gray of the stone lintels before she looked up.

Oriana whispered to her, as if hoping not to disturb her. "I'm going for some cold water. Would you like a bottle?"

"Sure."

"Do you want to come with me?" Oriana asked.

Nixie shook her head, glancing over at a family with two young boys that had settled near them and were pulling out a picnic lunch. "I don't want to lose our place. But I'm hungry, too."

"All right. I won't be long." Oriana pointed at a silver cart with pictures of bottled water and ice cream sandwiches on it. "I'll get a snack, and we can have a real meal back at the hotel."

She thrust her journal into her pack, shouldered the pack, and headed off. What did Oriana write in there? Had she written anything about Nixie and the quetzal feather? Nixie sighed and shifted her position to keep her right foot from falling into pins and needles.

A soft sob rose from her left.

There was no one there when she glanced over. Must be someone on the beach.

But it hadn't sounded like a kid, more like an adult, and adults didn't cry in places like this. She bent her head back to her drawing, listening carefully. There it was again, so quiet she was sure whoever cried didn't want to be discovered. The deep sadness of the cry sank into her bones, making her feel light and cold.

She set her journal down carefully and crawled the three yards over to the edge of the rock on her knees, leaned over, and looked down.

Below her, three rough canoes were pulled up on the beach, and a young woman with black hair sat between the canoes and the rock, her face buried in her hands.

There was a way down, if Nixie was careful. A thin scrabbly path she hadn't seen from the beach.

She glanced back toward her stuff.

It wasn't there.

It was happening again.

She drew in a deep breath and looked around. Two men with towels or something wrapped around their waists walked away from her, toward the temple. She gaped at the bright blues and reds, skewered in place by the liveliness of temples that had been dead to her eyes five minutes ago. The sky seemed deeper blue and the air clearer, as if everything in this time breathed sunshine.

She shouldn't be here. She hadn't known before, but this time her blood raced.

A muffled noise below her reminded her why she'd come to the edge of the rock. Carefully, she let herself down, toes scrabbling for purchase. She risked a look down. Not far, but steep. The young woman's head jerked up as Nixie's feet scraped a trickle of small stones down the rock. She had dark hair, swept back from her face and held with bone clips, and a round face with dark eyes rimmed in red. With her big eyes and thin frame, she almost looked like a Mexican anime character.

She stood, scrambling back, watching Nixie carefully. She wore a rich red, green, and brown woven smock, and a string of bright green and brown beads hung to her waist. Her fright was so palpable Nixie could feel it. More than anything in the world, Nixie didn't want to scare her away, not when she'd been crying so. She froze on the rock, looking down. How old was the girl? Maybe fifteen, maybe less. It was hard to say.

It seemed like a long time before either of them moved. The Mayan girl said something softly. It sounded like "ba-ox," or "hello" in Mayan, a word Nixie had learned. But the accent was so far off it took her a breath to figure out.

Nixie licked her lips and dug her toes in further. He hands hurt where she gripped the rock. She said, "Hello," and then, "I won't hurt you."

The girl looked puzzled, but ventured another step closer.

Nixie took two steps down, and stopped. When the girl didn't move again, Nixie finished her trip down to the warm white sand. "Are you okay?" she asked, sure the girl wouldn't understand her. She extended a hand, slowly, remembering a school lesson on the Lewis and Clark expedition where the teacher said an open hand was a universal sign for coming in peace.

The girl slowly closed the distance between them, reaching out to touch Nixie's hand. She drew her hand right back in surprise, then touched Nixie again, then again, feeling her hand and her arm and then touching her hair.

Maybe these people had never seen a blonde. She recalled the man who gave her the feather looking surprised when he clasped his hand over hers to drag her from the cenote. She probably did look different from them, but that didn't stop it from feeling weird to be stroked all over.

To make it even, Nixie reached out and fingered the long necklace. The girl gasped and brought a hand to the stones, then stood still, shaking. Nixie dropped the necklace. Maybe now they could stop touching each other. She looked the girl in the eye and pointed to herself. "Nixie."

The girl was quicker than the man she'd met, because she pointed right at herself and said, "Hun Kan."

Nixie repeated it, and shortly they had each other's names. The tears in the girl's eyes had dried.

There was no way to tell how long she'd have here. The beach was empty, but the idea of seeing a lot more people made Nixie nervous. Surely Oriana was worried by now. Maybe her mom, too, if she noticed Nixie wasn't in her world. Nixie still had her camera in her pocket. She slid it out slowly and pointed it at Hun Kan. She held her breath as she pressed the button to take a picture, smiling when the camera gave a satisfying little click. She took two more pictures in quick succession, then circled the girl and took another one from a different angle, hoping it wouldn't scare or offend. After all, the girl couldn't know what a camera was anyway.

Hun Kan smiled at her, and sat on her knees on the sand, patting a spot beside her. Nixie took the hint and sat down with her legs crossed.

Hun Kan took off her necklace and handed it carefully to Nixie. Nixie took it, and ran it through her hands, feeling the smoothness of the green beads. When she handed it back to the Mayan girl, Hun Kan draped it over Nixie's head in two big loops that tinkled against each other. The weight of it felt solid and comforting, making the girl and the beach and the strange time seem more real.

Could she take it? She remembered the bead Ian had given her, and fished it off her neck. It was only a simple bead on a leather string, nothing like the finely worked necklace she now wore. But Hun Kan's eyes glittered approval as Nixie dropped it into her hand.

She seemed more enamored of the string than the bead. It was a rounded leather string, probably made with machines of some kind. Maybe Ian hadn't thought of that.

Ian hadn't said anything about bringing things back, but the necklace was far more beautiful than the bead.

Hun Kan reached for Nixie's arm and fingered her watch. She couldn't give it to her, not according to Ian, but it was just a little thing. Not as big a deal as money. She could buy another one with the cash her mom had given her this morning. The weather feature didn't work in this time, but Hun Kan wouldn't know what she didn't have. Nixie took it off and held it out. Her unease almost evaporated as Hun Kan held her wrist out delicately, like a small bird, her face glowing with pleasure.

The neon blue band showed bright against Hun Kan's tanned skin. Nixie struggled to fasten the tricky hidden clasp around the girl's slender wrist so the watch was a cool, unbroken circle of color. Hun Kan stood up and twirled slowly in the sun, watching her wrist the whole time.

Noisy calls came from the path down to the beach. Boys. They sounded like boys from 2012, laughing and jeering. She couldn't see them yet, but surely they were coming this way.

Hun Kan's eyes widened.

Nixie stroked the back of a hand gently across Hun Kan's cheek, looking deep into her new friend's eyes.

Hun Kan took Nixie's hand in hers and smiled. Surely now they were friends. Nixie squeezed Hun Kan's dark hand in her light one and vaulted up the path, hoping it would lead her home.

CHAPTER 12

Cauac twisted and turned, his face bathed in the sweat of an old man's dreams. He sensed more than heard someone call his name, and sat up on his sleeping bench, hot even under the palm thatch roof.

"Cauac!"

He opened his eyes. It was Ah Bahlam, crossing the central space of the compound that Cauac shared with seven other teachers. The girl, Hun Kan, was with him. It jolted him into a memory of them together in his dreams, walking a dark path, their feet bathed in strange lights. "I'm here," he called out.

Hun Kan stopped to pour Cauac a dipper of water from the clay vessel outside in the common area. She'd given thought to his needs even though something had agitated her so much that her hand trembled as she handed him the ladle. A ring of too-bright blue glowed on her arm. Brighter than a feather, brighter than the sky, or the sea.

He drank slowly, giving her a few moments to calm down, then handed her back the oiled wood dipper. "Thank you." He inclined his head and waited for Ah Bahlam to start.

After he and Hun Kan sat, Ah Bahlam said, "She saw the same vision. The golden-haired girl. Here. On the beach."

Cauac took three breaths to think. "How do you know it is the same one?"

"Can there be two?" Ah Bahlam asked.

There were many in his dreams. There could be as many as there were Maya. "Please, each of you describe this girl."

He listened carefully and asked for another dipper of water. After he drank, he sighed heavily. "I believe it is the same girl. After all, Ah Bahlam, you saw her wearing the bright blue thing she gave Hun Kan on her own arm."

Hun Kan fingered the odd bracelet and then took a single bead on a string from her neck and held it out to him.

Once it was in his hand, he knew that it too was from the same spirit world as the green leaves and the blue bracelet. But only because the stone and the leather cord both felt too smooth. He bit into the leather near the back, away from where the stone bead hung. His teeth left marks. All of this was real, if unknowable.

"But why did she come to me?" Hun Kan asked.

She was so earnest and so innocent. So young. And truly beautiful. He glanced from her to Ah Bahlam. "The gods often choose hard roads for those they love the best. This year has been one of preparation. Perhaps she is a sign of favor for your journey."

"She is not a god!" Hun Kan exclaimed. "I touched her, and she touched me."

"Do you not think the gods can touch us?"

Hun Kan fell silent at this, but doubt rimmed her eyes. He had his own doubts, tied with his dreams, but what else could she be? The smooth leather in his hand and the way the green papers felt had convinced him the golden girl was not Toltec. Maybe albino, like the animals sometimes born as if the gods had forgotten their color brushes? But such animals were weak and sickly, and this girl wasn't described that way.

"I gave her an offering," Hun Kan said. "She . . . she found me crying and came to offer comfort." The girl's dark eyes bored into his, wanting answers. "We touched each other."

"Why were you crying?" Cauac asked softly.

Hun Kan averted her eyes. "I don't want to go back. There is so much trouble in the outside now, and Chichén has so much death." She glanced at Ah Bahlam. "I have been very happy here this year."

Cauac let her fall silent. He had chosen to turn his back on his own duties to Chichén many years ago. It had taken a long time for the world to find peace with him over it. "So she has come to each of you in times of great emotion." He glanced at Ah Bahlam. "When you could not call your Way," and back to Hun Kan, "and when you could not see your direction."

Ah Bahlam asked, "What should we do?"

"Let us gather the god's favor for your journey." He stood, reaching for a puma-skin bag he kept high on the shelf. "Bring fire," he said to Ah Bahlam, "and water," to Hun Kan. He started toward the temple. He did not look back until he had climbed the steep steps and ducked under the figure of the Descending God. Inside, sun splattered the brightly colored walls through the single window that faced the sea. Cauac sat on one wide stone bench, waiting for the other two to join him with fire and water.

Earth would be the ground they sat on, and the sky was above them.

Silently, Hun Kan and Ah Bahlam entered and sat across from him.

"We will give blood?" Ah Bahlam asked.

Hun Kan looked pleased as he nodded in reply. Good. Both of them were brave. And each might be called for far greater sacrifice at the end of the journey home.

Perhaps if he set up the journey well, Ah Bahlam would begin to find his Way, so that he would run with the jaguar instead of watching it run away. It was a good sign that it had come to him, and progress. If Ah Bahlam found the heart of his Way, he would be truly formidable.

Cauac set shells out in the four corners of the stone room and sprinkled dried leaves in the pearled bottoms, then bits of whitish copal highlighted with amber-yellow. He spoke quietly to the two young people. "Enter this ceremony as you enter your Way. Bring all of yourselves to this time, this place, this moment. Be your breath and be the temple and be the sacred place dedicated to the Descending God."

He stood, breathing in the place, the time, the world, breathing out everything that separated him from these things. Even though this temple was young, its power drew from a place that must have had a natural sacredness. It thrust through him with a shock of recognition, and at the same time, slew him so that he stood as someone that Cauac watched, more than someone that he was.

He reached for the wooden bowl that Ah Bahlam held out for him, and carefully slid the loose stones that sheltered the coals aside. Using two long leg bones from a puma, Cauac picked up one small coal for the south shell. "Bless this corner of the world. Let the centering world tree that holds up the sky hear our prayers and let them waft up to the gods." Slowly, slowly, the southern gods and stars enveloped him, a silence and a weight that strengthened his blood as the gods of the stars joined him, filling his heart.

He repeated the ritual words again in the north, and then in the west and east.

When he finished, he stood in the center, full of stars and gods.

He slid a worn gray stone bowl from his pouch, setting it on the floor in the middle of the four shells, in the place of the tree-that-holds-the-world, and next to the still red-bright coals. He freed his ritual knife from the pouch, the obsidian glittering in the window light as he plunged it into the coals, heating and cleaning it. His hands rose high over his head, reaching toward the low top of the temple, and he pulled the Descending God down into the stone knife so it quivered and bucked in his hand, and then rested, hot and full.

He gestured for Hun Kan to pour a small amount of water into the bowl, and then he held his arm out above it. Using the knife, he made a sharp, sure cut near his wrist, but not all the way across the life-veins. A thin trickle of blood turned the water rose-colored. Cauac held his arm bleeding over the bowl until the water was dark with it.

Ah Bahlam then took the blade, purified it in the coals, and drew his own blood. His face remained stoic and his body only tensed once, at the moment of incision. Good.

Hun Kan bit her lip to keep from crying out, but her hand was steady.

Their blood mingled in the water.

Together, the three said, "We call the Descending God and his family with this blood."

Cauac spoke next. "Guide Ah Bahlam and Hun Kan on this journey. Grant them signs and portents. Let them stay true in their hearts and perform the duties of the gods of the Itzá. We will live or die in peace and power."

If only he, Cauac, could be sure the power in Chichén was clearly dedicated to the gods.

Silence descended on them all, and Cauac offered up his heart prayer to the silence. *Help me understand the dreams you send me. Help me harness your strength and glory for the good and beauty of all my people.* The chaos of the new non-Mayan people, the brown-haired ones from the north, and the decline in food and trade all seemed worth praying about, but something held his tongue, and instead he added, *Keep the golden-haired and the dark-haired ones to their path. Keep the Way in front of them, the Earth below them, and the sun and the sacred tree above them. Keep them within the four corners of the world.*

In ceremony, what his heart chose to speak, especially into the silence, often surprised him.

He let the silence remain, the copal smoke teasing his nose.

Ah Bahlam shifted. Hun Kan's left eye blinked, then closed tightly again. Cauac smiled, but let the silence stay longer. He was still not entirely shrunk to the being that was Cauac, and there was no reason to hurry the gods. After they had all been still ten more breaths, he nodded and said, "It is so."

He poured the bloody water onto the stone, adding the power of their life to the power of the stone. He emptied the shells, leaving the copal to continue burning on the bare floor.

Stepping outside, the force of the naked sun fell on Cauac as a man reborn with new skin, bathing him in heat and light.

CHAPTER 13

Alice breathed a sigh of relief as she watched her employers drive away in a green Land Rover, the sun glinting off of a metal rack on top. She dug into her pocket and dialed Nix, and her daughter's hello on the other end sounded like heaven.

"How was your day?"

Nixie sounded tired. "You were right, Mom, Tulum was fun."

Alice started toward the queue for the buses. "I heard about the turtle."

"It was big, and it seemed like it wanted to swim with me. It let me touch it, and ride on its back. I'll tell you about the ruins when you get home."

"You were there the whole time?"

"Sure."

"I couldn't see you half the day. I hate the tracking chips."

"Does that mean I can take mine out?" Nixie asked.

"No." She'd probably get home after Nixie went to sleep. Better to tell her now. "Honey? I have to work tomorrow morning. Something came up that I need to do." Alice winced at the word "need" as she took her place in line, the soft voices of the Mexican women waiting with her making it harder to hear.

"Then can Oriana take me swimming?"

Nixie didn't even sound upset. Must have been some turtle. "We'll talk about it in the morning. I've got to get on the bus. Don't forget I'm going to the party."

Nix's reply came too fast. "That's fine Mom. Oriana's going to let me watch television tonight."

Something didn't seem quite right, but perhaps it was just the weird day, and hearing from Marie after all these years. Or that Nixie seemed happier with Oriana than with her. "Okay, honey. I'm going to try to be home by your bedtime."

"We're going to go swimming and then eat."

A little part of her wished Nixie did mind her being gone. "Have fun. Call me if . . . if anything goes wrong. Tell Oriana, too."

"You're the one who's traveling around," Nixie replied in a dry voice.

Alice shook her head. Damned kid was so smart. "I'll be careful if you will. I love you."

"Love you, too." Nixie ended the call before Alice could add anything more. At least Nix wasn't crabby any more. People who told her being a mother was the hardest thing in the world were right.

She turned to take a long look back at the ruins bulking into the sky. The Mayans had built—and thought—big. The next time she saw the temples and observatories, they would be decorated for the turn of the baktun, and today's crowds would be nothing. The heavy stone buildings looked almost new, if bleached gray and white. What if Nixie really had stepped back over a thousand years? For all that Ian and Oriana and Nixie herself had said, it was still tough to believe.

During her first visit to Chichén, the ruin had taken her breath away, the way a beautiful wild waterfall or the twisted peaks of the Grand Tetons did, and the first time she climbed K'uk'ulkan and saw the vast jungles from above, she had knelt on the hard stone and let the feel of the world wash over her. She had felt part of a mystery. Part of all the grandeur of life and the cosmos, small and large all at once. She knew that she had felt that, remembered it, but she couldn't recall what the actual feeling was, like a name lost on the tip of her tongue.

But that had been before—before school, and astronomy and archeology classes, before getting married and having a kid. Before a roadside bomb in Afghanistan changed how she and Nix would live forever. She was over it, and she wasn't mad at anyone anymore. There never had been anyone to be mad at.

She fought a sudden urge to go back in, to climb K'uk'ulkan herself and stand there with no distractions. Maybe all the wonder and awe of that first time would come back.

The bus door opened in front of her and she stepped inside.

The University of Arizona had rented most of one of the smaller hotels just outside the tourist district proper in Cancun. When Alice arrived, the party was already in full swing. Every Mesoamerica researcher with any funding at all had figured out how to get down here.

Some faces were familiar. Old graduate students with work of their own now, past teachers, people she had toured with or met at conferences. Here and there, Mayans and other Mexicans mingled with the otherwise mostly American crowd.

Alice waved at Steven Blake, an older man with white hair who'd been her cultural anthropology professor back in graduate school, and a mentor through her first few big projects. A slight stoop in his shoulders reminded her it had been over five years since she last saw him. He smiled, and waved her over. "How are you?" He asked. "I thought you'd be here. I saw your paper in last week's *Mayan Journal*. The one on Venus. It was quite good."

The praise pleased her. "Thank you."

"I'm here," he said, pointing at the hotel floor. "Where are you staying?" he asked.

"At the resort outside Xcaret. I've got my daughter with me."

He plucked a glass of wine from a tray bobbing past them on the arm of a dark-haired teenager dressed in white. He handed it to Alice. "Turning her into a Mayan expert?"

"She went to Tulum today. She always travels with me." Alice took a sip of her wine. "When did you get in?"

"Yesterday. Did you hear about the storms in the Midwest? And at the same time there's idiots at the capital demanding lower gas prices."

She held up a hand to forestall him. "Some days I can't stand to listen to the news. She remembered the conference. "Anything new between China and India?"

"Not this week. The UN declared North Korea a disaster zone today and sent in troops to guard a food caravan." He took a sip of his own wine. "So what do you think will happen?"

He didn't have to say "when." At the end of the calendar. Now. Soon. She shook her head. "A big ceremony, a few demonstrations, people who claim some kind of religious experience, and then the next day will dawn."

"And the world will keep sliding downhill," he said softly, his eyes full of sadness. "I would hope for something better, but like you, I don't see what it could be."

His cynicism grated. She sipped at her wine, looking around for food. A tall man wearing a waiter's white uniform passed her with an empty tray. She turned back to Steven. "Maybe everyone will wake up and love their brothers and sisters, or all the hungry will be fed." Something *was* happening, and it had caught her daughter up in it. She wanted tell him, needed to. But Steven would laugh at her, like she would laugh at anyone who told her a girl had traveled back in time. Or would have, two days ago. She needed a safer subject. "How's the food?"

"Great. I'm going after some more. Want to join me at the appetizer buffet?"

Steven's specialty had always been finding food. He did a nice job of weaving through the crowd, and by the time they reached the table, he'd picked up three other people she knew in passing. The whole line of Steven followers were chattering about the weather and the jungle, and who might still be funding archeological research next year. As she listened for clues to possible future employers, she ate salty chips and ceviche, and pork marinated in lime juice and wrapped in small flour tortillas.

The talk turned to current events—flooding and drought, methane out-gassing in the arctic. Things she couldn't control.

Alice drifted away and wandered through the crowd, wrapped inside herself. Why was she here anyway? Just because everybody else was? It was the cool party? She should go home to Nix.

A hand descended on her shoulder. "Alice!"

She looked up to find Ian smiling at her.

"What are you doing here?" Her cheeks flushed red. "I mean . . . I didn't expect to see you." She didn't want to see him here, except his smile had made her smile.

He lifted his hand from her shoulder and turned toward a young dark-haired man. "Peter Wood. This beautiful lady is Dr. Alice Cameron."

Peter was scrawny, but his handshake was firm. "Hi. I'm with the University of Texas."

"Impressive." They had a good Mayan studies program, including the Linda Schele Library.

"I'm a grad student in their Information Studies Program."

Her face must have shown her confusion, because Ian said, "Come on. Let's sit in the bar. I think you'll be interested in why Peter's here." He didn't wait for assent, but took her by the hand and led her through the crowd. Ian's hand folded around hers. He smelled like sweet jungle flowers and beer.

As they worked their way through the crowd, at least three people greeted him by name. He responded warmly to everyone, but kept his grip on her. As if by magic, he found a tall round table just being abandoned in a corner. A garish red and gold hanging lamp bathed the yellow table in light. Ian hopped up on one of the tall stools. "This is great. I'm glad we ran into you."

She wasn't sure she was glad.

Ian's brown dreads had been pulled back into a thick ponytail and tied with a white ribbon. He looked both older and more serious than he had by the pool. He turned to Peter, who was setting up a bright red ultra light computer he'd pulled out of a battered green backpack. "Can you get us a few plates of food and some wine?"

Peter nodded and plunged back into the crowd. Ian grinned his wide bright grin and she found herself caught up in it against her will, as if she were a girl on a date. "Is he a friend?" she asked.

"I've known Peter for years. We've been following each other on social networks for years. He has ideas you might be interested in. He thinks we're near singularity and that the end of the Mayan calendar might mean the birth of a new species of human."

She still held a glass of Syrah in one hand. She took a careful sip, trying not to choke. "Surely you're kidding."

He laughed. "It's not as bad as it sounds. And you can't exactly discount that something is happening. After all, you know time is flexing, right? Nixie experienced it. I have." He stopped for a second, looking at her quizzically. "Have you?"

"I don't seem to attract magic."

"You attract me," he replied, so offhand it startled her. "I mean, you're interesting. Why did you start studying Mayan stars?"

She twirled her now-empty glass in her hand. "Because I fell in love with this place the first time I saw it. And I read science fiction when I was a kid, so I guess the two things went together in my brain." She wanted to tell him about Marie's call, but it might be breaking security.

Peter emerged from between two old men arguing and a pair of female grad students in skimpy white shorts. He balanced three glasses and a plate piled high with appetizers. Alice took the plate from him and he set the three glasses down with a flourish. She should be leaving instead of listening to Peter as he asked, "So what stories has Ian been telling on me?"

"He said I might be interested in why you're here."

"Okay," he said. "Let's figure out what you know. You're an astronomer?"

She nodded. "Archeoastronomer. That means I'm as much a historian as an astronomer."

"Okay. But you've had math?"

That made her want to scream. Plus, he could stop saying "okay" any time. "Why don't you just try me out? I'll stop you if I don't understand anything."

"Well, you know how pyramids all over the world have been built with more geometry than the ancients could have had?"

She stiffened. "That's a common misperception. It sells pre-technology cultures short." She pointed at his nearly translucent screen. "You don't need computers to have math. You need things to count, like stones, or stars. Ancient populations had plenty of hours to study the sky."

He didn't seem to notice her tone. "Well, okay. Sorry. But you have to admit that all the way back to Sumer there's stuff that's hard to explain?"

She nodded, as much to humor him as anything.

"Well, okay. This great tree in the sky, it only happens once every turn of the Mayan calendar, right? And the last time was the beginning of this calendar round, right? I think that means we'll go through some kind of information field. Information is creative. You know how they're finding that robots with more access to raw information and more possible processing algorithms are able to pass first grade tests now?"

She hadn't. "Like Turing tests?"

"Not that. But they can deal with less certain information, answer multiple choice questions instead of just true/false ones, even on topics they have to research. Fuzzy logic. And quantum computing is going to make something too smart to pass the Turing test. You know how the test is about whether a human can tell if it's talking to a human or a computer?" His voice had gotten higher and sped up. "It used to be because the computer was too dumb, but soon it's going to be too smart." He shook his head. "Okay, I'm way off base. I'm just trying to say that information is creative, or can be. That raw data can have a creative force."

She licked her lips, and glanced over at Ian, who had just stuffed a bit of fried banana in his mouth. Some help he was. Did *he* believe any of this? She turned back to Peter. "So if I buy that, then how do you think this information is getting here?"

"Well, through space, obviously. Maybe we're just about to be at the right place in the universe to access some new information. Like a radio signal only with more data. Well, more like a laser beam. Or an artificial intelligence." He was practically bouncing in his seat. He was actually cute, in an uber-geeky way. "A friend of mine was postulating that AIs could use any stratum at all to hold together. Air. Space. They would just be bigger or smaller, denser or more diffuse . . . they could compute with whatever molecules are there, as long as there are basic building blocks, because with nanotech, an AI could change one thing into another. As needed. The only thing it couldn't do is live in a pure vacuum."

She cleared her throat and sipped her wine. If that was the case, why didn't a single AI take over the whole universe? She didn't ask.

"Sorry. I just get so excited about this stuff. We live in the best time ever. I just know something good is going to happen."

Well, at least he wasn't as despondent as Steven. Hope was good. Of course, Peter clearly lived in his head. Maybe that explained the run-on sentences. He continued, "Or metaverses. You understand those? Multiple universes?"

She nodded, listening to the high-pitched screeches of a band tuning up not far from them. In a few minutes, they probably wouldn't be able to talk here.

"Okay. Maybe we come closer to the boundaries of another universe. Then all kinds of things would happen, could happen—we might stretch and change, gather raw information from some other place or some other time. Did Ian—?" he glanced at his friend, who nodded. "Well, he told you he might have seen old Maya? Maybe that was in a parallel universe. Not this one at all. One where the Maya stayed ascendant."

Right. "Cultures don't stay static for hundreds of years. Even in alternate universes." She gave Ian a wry look.

He grinned. "I told you you'd be interested."

"So you believe this?" she asked.

"I'm not even sure I do," Peter answered before Ian could. "But isn't it interesting to think about?"

The band started, a combination of pan-style flutes, lap-based string instruments, and hand drums; not as loud as she'd feared. Ian pushed himself up from his chair. "Want to dance?"

She did. She bit her lip and turned away. "I have to get home to Nix."

She stood up, grabbed her purse, and started across the wood dance floor. He stopped her with a gentle call of her name. He stood close to her, put a finger on her cheek, and lifted her face so he could look into her eyes. "Don't let all these ideas, mine or Peter's, or even yours, scare you. Something is happening, and none of us knows what it is yet."

She swallowed, feeling his physical presence so strong that she took a step back. "He doesn't have a theory. He just has hope and a bunch of pop science."

Ian grinned at that. "I know. But he's kind of refreshing. And smart."

"Okay." She laughed, but Ian didn't seem to get the pun on Peter's language. Maybe that was a good thing. The kid was likeable, if strange and intense.

Ian cocked an eyebrow at her. "Sure you don't want to dance?"

Some inner person she hardly recognized wanted to dance so much that Alice barely choked out, "I haven't danced in years, and I have to go. I have an appointment in the morning."

He looked genuinely disappointed.

How long had it been since a man attracted her? And what was she thinking? Ian was at least a little bit crazy, as far as she could tell. She bit her lip and looked him in the eyes, trying to look resolute. "Maybe another time."

He pursed his lips and his eyes clouded over. He seemed to be thinking hard, nervous, even though she'd have sworn it wasn't an emotion he was very familiar with. But when he met her eyes, he flashed his bright, full smile. "Maybe I should follow you home."

"No." She didn't let men follow her home.

He stopped, close to her. "I'd like to hear Nixie's story."

She rolled her eyes. "You already did."

"No. From today."

"Huh?"

"Nixie did it again," he said.

She drew in a deep breath and held it while found her phone and checked. Nixie was at the hotel. "How do you know?" she challenged him, suddenly angry that he had information she didn't. About *her* daughter.

"Shhhh," he cautioned. "I talked to Oriana."

"Well, so did I!" But she hadn't. She'd called Nixie directly. "When?"

"At Tulum. Oriana went to get them water. She turned around as soon as she got into line, and Nixie wasn't there. She ran back out of line and looked but Nixie wasn't anywhere, and Oriana lost her tracking, too. You know that shouldn't happen with the local net between two linked devices."

She already knew Nixie was safe. But that didn't keep her from shaking. They should have told her! The sudden anger bracing her spine made her blurt out, "You knew I didn't know about it! Or you would have talked about it. How could you hide that from me?" She balled her fists and stuck her chin out. She struggled for something to say, and ended up snapping at him, "How dare you!"

He blinked at her, looking barely disturbed, and certainly not looking guilty.

Anger choked her chest and her eyes were hot and wet with tears. She had to get away from him. She dived into the crowd, looking for the women's bathroom.

There was a line. Used to be science was so much a man's game it was never a problem. She went for the closest exit, keeping her head down. Outside, tears stormed down her cheeks. She headed for the parking lot.

Ian called her name from behind her.

She ignored him, almost running to her car. It was tough to spot in the dimly lit and crowded lot, especially since she'd gone out a different door than she came in. She wiped at her face, struggling to clear her vision after she tried two rows with no luck. Ian didn't call for her again, but she swore he was nearby. She could feel him.

She finally found her car by pressing "lock" on her key fob to make the horn sound and the lights flash. Alice unlocked the car, opened the door, and got in. When she went to close the door she felt resistance and looked up to see him holding the door open. "Look, let me talk about—"

"You should have told me!" She was almost shouting. She never shouted. "You should have told me as soon as you saw me. Not . . . not wasted my time with Peter's crazy ideas."

"I thought you'd need some ways to think about this." His tone was so reasonable it made her angrier.

"This is my daughter. You can't possibly have any kids! Never, ever—"

A pair of dark-clothed figures stepped up to them, stopping her diatribe in mid-sentence. The closest streetlight was dim, but enough to see both the typical Federale rifles, and that the two had concerned looks on their faces. "Haga usted tiene que ayudar a la señora?"

"No. I don't need help." She slid into the car. With the Federales there, Ian let her close the door. She rolled down her window and said, "Gracias," to the soldiers. Ignoring Ian, she pulled away slowly, noticing that the Federales had engaged Ian in conversation.

Good.

Once she reached the main highway, she sped up.

CHAPTER 14

The bright lights of resort entrances streamed by Alice: gold exclamation points tourism had dumped onto this once-pristine coast. She cursed as she had to stop for a military convoy of dented trucks and unimogs painted with the color of jungle camouflage.

What had happened to Nix? Why had she gotten so mad at Ian that she hadn't asked him for more information? But he should have come clean. And was he really there innocently? She shook her head and got going again as the road cleared. Ian had to have been in the same place on accident. He had known people at the party.

She pulled in, stopped the car, and sat in the sudden silence, breathing hard. She had to be calm. For Nixie. She placed a hand on her stomach, and felt her breath lift it up and down like she used to when she was pregnant.

The lights of another car reflected in her rearview mirror made her blink and put her head down. She sighed and got out, immediately hearing her name. "Alice, I'm sorry."

Ian.

Damn him. She didn't turn to look at him, just stared at the hotel lights shining on stylized paintings on the stucco walls. Two glasses of wine weren't enough to impair her driving, but it had apparently impaired her emotions. She wanted him to leave in the worst way. But then who would she talk to about her daughter traveling into the past?

Damn. Her voice came out stiff. "Come on. You drove all the way here."

At least he was smart enough to follow her up in silence.

When she led Ian into the house, she found Nixie still dressed, sitting at the table with Oriana, playing a game of gin rummy. When Nixie looked up at her, she had a guilty look in her eyes. "Mom, it was my fault. I told them not to worry you. I made Oriana swear."

Oriana watched Alice silently, her face a mask. Neither of them seemed surprised to see Ian. He'd probably called them from his car. She hadn't, afraid she'd say the wrong thing.

The energy in the room felt fragile, as if a single wrong word could shatter a truce.

She pulled a coffee cup from the tiny cupboard and filled it with water, put it in the microwave and punched the button to boil it. "Does anyone else want mint tea?"

She ended up making four cups. Done, she settled slowly into the one remaining chair, between Nixie and Ian. She leaned over and gave Nixie a hug, savoring the salty smell of her hair, the fact that she was actually there. "Tell me what happened."

"It was after we went swimming with the turtle. Oriana went to stand in line and get us water." She must have felt Alice stiffen because she hurried to say, "I could see her, and she could see me. I stayed because I didn't want to lose our place on the rock and so I could watch for the turtle. Then I heard a girl crying, or someone crying. I didn't know it was a girl yet . . . but I climbed down the rock to the beach and she was just a little older than me, and she was crying hard. But she stopped after a while. Her name was Hun Kan."

Why didn't Nixie sound scared instead of excited?

Ian leaned in. "Say that again."

"Hun Kan."

"One Sky," he said. "That's a powerful name."

Alice flinched. She should have been able to translate that. Would have. She just wasn't thinking about anything except Nixie. She took another sip of tea, trying to clear her head.

Nixie continued. "That's about all. We learned each others names, and then a bunch of boys were coming toward us from the beach and I came back."

"Just like that? You decided to come back and you did?" Ian asked.

"Well, I took the trail up that I'd taken down. And at the top, there was my stuff, and the tourists, and Oriana looking mad at me."

Oriana laughed. "More like worried."

Something felt wrong. Nixie didn't lie, but she omitted. "What else happened?"

Nixie swallowed, and her hand went to her wrist, turning her watch around and around. Alice could have sworn Nix's watch was blue, but this one was her new favorite color, yellow.

"Why do you have a new watch?"

Nixie glanced at Ian rather than at Alice. "I gave Hun Kan the stone, like you said. But I also gave her my watch." She clamped her mouth down tight, but didn't take her gaze from Ian.

"And what did she give you?" Ian asked, not a shred of doubt in his face or posture.

Nixie reached for her neck and pulled out a long chain of jade and amber stones on a knotted string. It had been hidden under her shirt. She set it on the table, the amber glowing in the warm interior lighting. Alice blinked at it. The stones were smooth, but not perfectly round. They each had holes in them, nearly all the same size, but clearly hand-done. A strip of thin, flat brown leather held the beads together, and the clasp was a round jade stone that the end of the leather looped over.

It was stunning. It belonged in a museum, or an art gallery. Not on her table. Not on her eleven-year-old. "It looks . . . beautiful."

Alice had gone past angry to cold and shivery. Frightened. She looked over at Ian for the first time since the parking lot in Cancun. "What do you think?"

He picked it up, holding it so the light interacted with the amber. "Fit for a princess."

"Why would the girl give that away?" Oriana asked, her voice awed.

"She touched my hair. The first time she touched me, she looked afraid." She glanced at Oriana. "I'm sorry I hid the necklace from you, too."

"So that explains why you wouldn't climb into your pajamas, huh?" Oriana said, her voice disapproving.

Nixie ignored the comment. "But I . . . I don't think I traded her enough. It was a cheap watch. Maybe I'll see her again."

Ian looked serious. He set the necklace on the table. "If you do, no more watches. No electronics. *Nothing* from this time. That's why I gave you the bead."

"I'm sorry, but the necklace was so pretty and the single bead was so small." Nixie brightened. "Although she loved the string it was on."

Ian sighed. "I should have thought about that. At least it's leather and it'll rot." He glanced at Nixie. "No more plastic." He grinned. "What will the archeologists think?"

She giggled. "I don't know. I took pictures."

Oh. Oh! "Did they come out?"

"Of course. Why wouldn't they?" The look Nixie turned on Alice made her wince. Nix was right. Cameras didn't need networks until you wanted to do something with the pictures. But what was she supposed to say? *Gee, I'm sorry honey, I'm still a little shocked?* All she could get out was, "Did you print them?"

Nixie gave her the 'duh' look and went over to the desk, putting three pictures on the table. In all of them, a Mayan girl with mussed dark hair stared back at her. The camera had captured fear in her eyes, and maybe something else. Awe? The girl wore the necklace that now graced the table. Hun Kan's clothes looked hand-woven and hand-dyed, and her forehead sloped back, a sign she was aristocracy, had endured a board tied to her head to impart the look of the rich and powerful.

Behind her, three canoes graced the beach. Alice yearned for a look at the handwork on the canoes. The digital pictures themselves should be much clearer if she zoomed in. "Did you save them in our shared file?"

Nixie grinned, wearing her I'm-proud-of-myself-and-I-gotcha look. "I saved the best for last." She dropped one more picture on the table between Alice and Ian.

Alice gasped as Ian picked it up, his hands trembling. Behind Hun Kan, in a corner of the picture, the Temple of the Descending God was bright blue and red.

Through everything else—the feather, the necklace, even the pictures of the girl, some part of her had not believed Nixie's "time travel" was real. That part of her just shut up and stared at the picture. She knew that ruin—no, she corrected herself, that temple. She knew it. And neither Nixie nor an army could have restored it. Or faked it.

Ian broke the fragile energy. "Guess you better carry your camera everywhere you go, huh?"

Nixie nodded, looking pleased. "Or my phone. But the camera's better. My dad gave me my first one."

Ian nodded, and had the brains to hold his tongue.

Nixie turned to Alice. "I wasn't gone very long. I really wasn't. And I didn't try to make it happen. It just happened."

Alice let out a long breath and gestured for Nixie to come over to her. Only when she held her daughter, solid and firm with wild blonde hair that tickled her nose, only then could she speak. "I know, honey. I know. Whatever this is, it isn't your fault."

"What are we going to do?" Nixie asked.

"You're going to go to bed." She swallowed hard. What was she going to do?

Nixie leaned in and gave her a hug, then started toward the bathroom. "Shower, first," Alice called out automatically. "You were in the ocean today. Get the salt off your body."

She waited for the ritual argument, but Nixie didn't make it. A few moments later, the sharp rattle of water hitting the glass reassured her.

Best worry about tomorrow before the next day. Oh god, tomorrow. The Secret Service. "Oriana, can you be here earlier than I asked? I have an unexpected meeting in the morning, in Cancun. I'll take you two with me and you can go to the beach by the hotel." Nix would be close to her.

Oriana nodded. "I'll come at seven. Is that okay?"

Alice nodded. "How about the twentieth? I got some new work. Can you watch her then?

Oriana grinned. "Sure. I kinda like the kid, and who'd miss this mystery?" In spite of her grin and ready agreement, she sounded a little apprehensive.

Oriana had kept Nix's adventure from her. Surely they were planning to tell when Alice got home. The circle of people she could talk to was tiny—

Oriana, Ian, Nix herself. Maybe Peter. Maybe she'd try Steven after all, before she went stark raving mad. "I appreciate the help," she told Oriana.

Oriana hesitated. "I'm sorry I didn't tell you right away. Nixie said your meetings were important and she was safe anyway, and, I mean, why make you worry?"

Alice nodded. Anger at Oriana flickered, but only for a moment. "She gets me that way sometimes, too. But I want—I need you to promise that you'll call me if she ever goes missing again, even for just five minutes? And that you'll keep her away from ruins? I don't want her near any more ruins unless she's holding my hand."

"I understand," Oriana said. "Sorry." Then she grinned. "But you should've seen the turtle."

"I would have liked that," Alice said, suddenly exhausted. "Can you two go now? I want to be alone."

Ian leaned over and pulled her close in a friendly hug. "This is amazing, you know. Really amazing."

She shook her head. "You're as crazy as your friend Peter." She sighed. "I'm still mad at you. You should go."

He nodded. "I will if you want. But think about it as good. She always gets back, and I think she always will. Maybe Nixie's just innocent enough to see things we can't."

She blinked up at him. "Is this happening to anyone else? Do you know?"

He shook his head. "I'll ask around."

"How do I reach you?"

He sent his contact information to her phone, and then he and Oriana left.

The room felt horribly sterile and silent.

Alice took the necklace into the kitchen and looked at in the brightest light she could find. The amber alone was worth hundreds, maybe thousands of dollars, the beads clear gold and red with hints of green. The jade beads? She had no idea. But she knew who might. She emailed Steven to see if he could meet her for lunch, and then carefully set the necklace back on the table.

She sat in the chair closest to the bathroom door, listening to Nixie sing in the shower. The whole time, she stared at the picture with the bright-colored corner of the temple.

DECEMBER 17, 2012

CHAPTER 15

Stars faded into the brightening sky as Ah Bahlam and fifteen others gathered at the gates of Zama. He shifted his stance to balance the weight of the wooden shield on his arm with the spear and bow and arrows he carried. His glance slid to a young man standing beside him, Ah K'in'ca. His friend stared down the road they would run along soon, apprehension momentarily showing on his face. "It will be a good journey," Ah Bahlam said, as much for him as for his friend. "We will be safe."

Ah K'in'ca raised his shield. He spoke loud enough to cover the uncertainty in his eyes. "We will travel well."

They would. Their clothing, spears, shields, and helmets shone from the long peaceful season at Zama, which had been full of warm evenings with time to talk while their hands polished and mended their tools and dress. They would be an imposing sight.

Three women stood in a bunch: Hun Kan, Nimah, and Kisa. All were from ruling families, all maidens, all sent here to prepare for noble sacrifice, or to become wives of important men; women with roles to play in the squabbling elite. But for now, they all looked beautiful and solemn as they stood watching the travel preparations.

Five older men ranged back and forth along the slowly forming line, joking about returning to their families. Guards for families of the Lord of Itzá, they had accompanied the students from Chichén and would return with them.

Ah Bahlam looked back at the temples of Zama, catching the exact moment the sun rose over the gray water and brought them to life for the new day. He would miss this moment, this crack between night and day that was far more beautiful here on the coast than inland. He offered a silent prayer to K'inich Ahaw . . . *God of the sun . . . protect this place even while I and my spear leave it.*

Ah Bahlam understood Hun Kan's tears about leaving Zama, but he would look ahead now, look toward seeing his father and toward the ceremonies of equinox. The ball game. He had dreamed all his life of this return to Chichén, to becoming part of the blood and heart of the powerful city.

Cauac and the other teachers would surely appear soon and start the rites.

He went and stood a small distance from Hun Kan, watching her. She wore a loose dress designed to allow free movement and, if she was needed, hand to hand fighting. Her dark hair had been caught up in a knot on top of her head. Wooden sticks with round jade beads held her hair in place. A wide strip of beaded leather wrapped around her wrist, covering the bright blue ornament she had received from the golden-haired girl, Ni-ixie. The single bead hung around her neck.

She smiled at him, silent, ready, all traces of sadness gone or buried. Seeing her reminded him of the scent of their mingled blood, and copal, and the strength of the ceremony. He wanted to touch her. He returned her smile and went on, walking past her so her beauty wouldn't distract him from being ready.

The beginning of a journey mattered.

The stars had all disappeared by the time the teachers lined up in front of the travelers. An apprentice, barely five summers old, carried a shell full of embers, herbs, and copal, fanning the smoke onto each of them with a serious and intent look. Cauac, Ah K'an, and K'ahtum followed the boy, blessing each warrior. When it was Ah Bahlam's turn to stand in front of Cauac, he stood as straight as he could, held as much control as possible. He might never see the old man again. He looked into Cauac's eyes and flinched at the unexpected worry he saw there. Had he dreamed more disturbing dreams? There was no time to ask.

The other four teachers waited for the full shamans at the head of the line, until the seven made a long barrier in front of the travelers, forming the top of the World Tree.

Dressed in bright red, green, and blue finery, all of them except for Cauac wore masks made of feathers, bone, shells, and wood. Their chests were adorned with necklaces to match, including jaguar teeth, puma and tapir teeth and bones, and even the small sharp teeth of vipers bleached harmless by three seasons of sun on top of the walls.

The procession began to move, led by two of the seasoned warriors.

As he passed Cauac for the last time, Ah Bahlam kept his face forward and looked to the path in front of him. It was time to know all that he learned in Zama and bend that knowledge to a safe journey, to watching for signs of bandits and people-of-unrest along the roadside, to keep his feet sure on the path and his spirit balanced with the jungle.

With any luck, stories would return to Cauac to make him proud of his student.

CHAPTER 16

Nixie felt a hand on her shoulder, shaking her awake. She'd fallen asleep in the car. The car door was open, and her mom's voice called her name from far away. She couldn't tell what her mom's face looked like since it had grown dark, and the only light came from above and behind her mom's head. "Are we home?" Nix asked.

"Yes. At the hotel. Come on, wake up and eat something. You need dinner."

"I'm not hungry." She and Oriana had eaten empanadas and fried tortillas with sugar, and drank sweet orange sodas in little round glass bottles. She struggled out of the car, dragging her backpack after her.

Her mom led the way up the steps, calling back, "I'm sorry you had to stay in town all day."

"I still want to go snorkeling. Surely the beach is safe enough."

"When I can go with you."

Nixie winced at the sharp tone in her mom's voice. "Look, mom, I don't know why it happens, or what places make it happen, but I don't want to spend my whole time here wandering around hotel lobbies and stupid tourist shops. Cancun is like when you took me to Vegas last winter. Same stuff."

Her mom held the door open, frowning down at her. "I'm sorry. I know this is hard for you. But if I lost you . . . " She smothered Nixie in her arms, making it hard to breathe. "Maybe you and Oriana can go to Isla Mujeres tomorrow and look in the shops there."

Nixie pulled away. "Look, nothing bad happened." She remembered Hun Kan's face shining up at her, dark eyes alight with curiosity. "I want to see Hun Kan. I want it to happen again. Maybe we should go to Tulum and you can try and go with me."

The look on her mom's face said she'd just pushed it too far, so she changed subjects. Sort of. "Do you have the necklace, Mom?"

Her mom dug the towel-wrapped necklace out of the bottom of her purse and started to set it on the counter. Nixie reached a hand out. "Can I have it?"

Her mom hesitated.

It was hers. Hun Kan had given it to her. Nixie stared at her mom, willing her to do the right thing.

It took a long time, but finally her mom set the whole bundle in her outstretched hand. "Take care of it."

"What did the man say about it?"

"The materials are worth a lot of money."

She didn't care about that. It was her link to Hun Kan. "Did he say it's old?"

Her mom shook her head. "He says it was made like the old ones, but the materials are new."

Nixie clutched it to her. "I'm tired, Mom. I'm going to bed." She walked to the fake mantle over the fake fireplace and picked up her quetzal feather, then headed for her room.

Nixie felt a hand on her shoulder and then her Mom's voice, too cheerful, saying, "Let's get in our pj's and read in bed. I'll sit with you in your bed until you go to sleep."

Great. A moment. But then again, she was tired. "All right, but first I want to put the necklace away."

"Put it someplace where it can't fall."

Right. Like she didn't know that. She carried it carefully to her bedside table, nestled the towel into the drawer beside a Gideon Bible that no one had apparently opened in years, and laid the necklace out carefully. She could wait until her mom went to bed and take it out and look at it. She set the feather on top of the dresser since it was too long to fit in the drawer.

She managed to put her pajamas on and get into bed before her mom got there, adjusted the light so it was just perfect, tucked the covers around her bare legs, and opened the book in her lap. She was interested in the story by the time her mom climbed under the covers, but having her mom there made it hard to concentrate. She stared at the words, frowning, and turning a page every once in a while.

Her mom wasn't reading her book either, and Nixie wondered which one of them would say something first, and then decided it wouldn't be her. She was too tired to talk about something she didn't have any answers for, and nothing interesting had happened today, except she and Oriana snuck into one of the hotel pools and dangled their feet in the water; the sneaking in had been exciting.

Her mom would never sneak in anywhere.

As she expected, her mom broke the silence first. "Do you want to talk?"

Nixie set her book down. "I wasn't really reading anyway. I was just pretending, like you."

"Were you scared when . . . when you got the feather and when you met Hun Kan?"

Nixie shook her head so hard her hair flew across her cheeks, but she smoothed it away before her mom could do it. "No Mom. I wasn't scared. I think it's exciting. I want it to happen again."

"I don't want it to happen again." Her mom breathed the words out slowly, and Nixie tried not to be sucked into feeling sorry for her. She picked up the feather and ran her hands along its broken spine. Maybe her mom was jealous? She studied the old times, but Nixie had gotten to see them firsthand. "Even if it happened to you? Would you mind then?

"Especially then. Who would take care of you?"

Nixie turned her face up to look at Alice, and said something that surprised her. "Why is it happening to me?"

"I don't know."

Some help adults were. She set the feather down carefully and rolled over on her side, pretending to sleep so her mom would leave her alone.

CHAPTER 17

Alice listened closely as Nixie's breath slowed into the neat rhythm of sleep. Her features relaxed, releasing the face of a younger Nixie, a true child. Alice timed her breath to Nixie's, comforted by the feeling of connection brought by such a simple thing.

She should get up and go to her own bed in the living room. Her limbs felt like lead weight, and her eyes couldn't quite stay focused on the yellow-orange wall in front of her.

It just felt so warm, so perfect, to lay still and breathe with her daughter.

Macaws called above Alice's head, and she pushed aside the leaves of a strangler fig and peered through the opening she created. The sharp edge of a dry leaf brushed the back of her hand. She jerked at the sensation and opened her eyes to the dimly-lit hotel room, then slammed them shut again, immediately finding herself standing where she had been, fully aware this time that she dreamed.

Vividly.

Winter orchids blooming somewhere nearby released a sweet, almost sickly scent. A road of white stones with white mortar ran in front of her, raised, clearly built by hand, and largely smooth. Here and there, small jungle plants poked up through the stones, particularly at the edges, but no more than a few.

A sacbe. A Mayan road. Sacred.

She had seen the remnants of sacbeob, unearthed from dense covering foliage, or sometimes even still largely holding their own against the hungry jungle for yards at a time.

This road stretched far on either side, a tree-lined oasis in the midst of dense jungle.

Alice stepped toward it, moving slowly, leaves rustling against her calves. She shuffled her feet to avoid tripping on uneven roots, to feel the ground hold her weight even in the dream, finally reaching the edge of the road. She hesitated, her stomach light yet full of a sense of impending change. Stepping up onto the road would change her. There was a stretch of restored sacbe on the grounds of Chichén Itzá. But not like this, whole and long, and surely recently dedicated with blood and ritual.

She lifted her foot, stopped in mid-stride, took a breath, and set it down, stepping on fully, lifting the other foot, walking. She couldn't quite feel the road, but it held her up—like walking as an avatar in a full-sized virtual world. Except that the trees and the stones, and even the smells were better than any virtual rendering she'd ever seen.

"Mom!"

She halted. Nixie. Here, in her dreams. She looked back to where she had stepped out of jungle. Not there.

"Mom! Here."

Nixie was ten feet in front of her, standing easily on the roadbed that had been empty and clear before, her head cocked. "Mom, come on. Someone's coming." Nixie reached her hand out, and Alice took the steps needed to grab it, surprised to find Nixie's hand warm and a touch sweaty, as if they were in the middle of a normal day.

They walked up the road quietly, holding hands.

Nixie stopped, then pulled Alice to the side, scrambling up a pile of rocks Alice hadn't even noticed. It wasn't a natural pile, nor was it a building. A place where the Mayans quarried?

"Mom!"

Her attention had wandered. She would have to watch her dream self. "Who's coming?" she whispered.

"Get down behind here," Nixie said, crouching so that only the top of her head, from her eyes up, showed above the rocks. Alice scrambled around to crouch next to her, a sharp corner digging into her knee until she shifted. So she could feel here, but the pain felt odd—not as sharp or intense as in the waking world.

Since when did dreams hurt at all?

Nixie pointed back the way they had come.

A group of people walked toward them at an easy, ground-eating pace. Maybe fifteen or twenty of them. It was hard to count, to focus. Every new thing caught her attention, a feast of information and glory.

A lifetime of study, given flesh.

Sunlight glinted off beads, shells and metal worked into breastplates, helmets, and around calves. The men carried shields and spears, and in two cases, arrows. Trained Mayan warriors, at least in the front. Real ones, not made up for tourist shows. They were both shorter than she expected, and fiercer. Their foreheads slanted back. Their bare sun-touched thighs and calves showed deeply defined musculature, and thick belts clung to their waists over skirts made of leaves.

They continued toward Alice and Nixie's hiding place on silent footsteps, watchful, alert. They seemed to belong on the sacbe, in the jungle; they moved like big cats; easy and powerful, almost as if they were dancing instead of walking.

The first two rows of three warriors carried only shields and spears. The next row carried bulging sacks across their back, but the weight hardly seemed to affect the carriers at all. Behind the burdened men, three women walked apace, heads forward and up, warriors flanking. They too wore artifacts of the natural world, including bright macaw feathers that hung from their necks on strings over simple woven dresses. Behind the women, two more warriors walked nearly sideways, able to see behind the group.

Nixie whispered. "See her?"

Alice squinted. The woman to the left could be the one from the picture. It was hard to tell with her hair pulled up and away from her face, but she seemed to have the same eyes that had looked so intent in Nixie's pictures. She wore a single bead on a string around her neck. Ian's bead. "Hun Kan?" she asked, verifying,

Nixie nodded. "Shhhh . . . "

The jungle around them had quieted, as if honoring the presence of the travelers.

Nixie's hand squeezed hers so hard pain shot up Alice's arm. What is it?" she mouthed.

"Him." Nixie's whisper sounded so soft Alice could barely hear it. "The man who gave me the feather. He has his bird with him."

The man closest to Hun Kan in fact did have a bird on his shoulder. Alice had missed it in all his feathered finery. A quetzal, perched easily on a wide strip of leather that ran from the man's neck to his left shoulder.

Could the Mayans see them? She had to resist the temptation to stand up and find out. Surely she and Nixie dreamed, but these people walked the sacbe in the real world.

The group came close enough to hear the muted jangle of shells and beads. Alice held her breath. Did Nixie have her camera? No, this was a dream. Nixie was dressed in jeans and a favorite T-shirt, but had no purse or electronics with her.

Along with the beauty, danger and the ability to deal death surrounded the Mayans, sending a cool heat up Alice's body, as if her dream-self carried more nerves than her real one, every one alight with what must be the wariness of prey.

The first warriors were almost directly across from them now.

Sound slammed into her. The high scream of macaw fear, the roar of a jungle cat, the chattering of monkeys. All talking to each other.

Wrong.

It sounded wrong, felt wrong, *sang* wrongly in her body.

The warriors stopped, eyes scanning the jungle, dark bodies crouching lower.

She gathered Nixie close to her, curling her slender form inside the cage of her arms and legs, feeling Nixie tremble.

Arrows and spears flew through the air toward the travelers.

A warrior in the second row crumpled, a spear protruding from his neck. Blood stained the white road.

Nixie screamed. Alice clapped a hand over her mouth. Nixie's teeth closed on the flesh of her palm.

Alice tried to wake up in the hotel room. Her eyes were already open here and opening them wider didn't help. Blinking failed. Her heart pounded with fear, worse than in real life, worse than in the real world. A dream become nightmare.

Men boiled around them, nearly naked, carrying spears and shields but simply dressed. Nixie turned a terrified face toward a pair that leaped over the top of the stones two feet from her, but the men seemed to look right through them. Still, Alice kept her hand clamped over Nixie's mouth. Men kept streaming from behind the rock, behind trees, from the ground behind thick vegetation. Twenty, thirty of them. More from the other side. The original warriors on the sacbe surrounded the women, facing out, lifting their spears and shields.

The attackers closed.

An obsidian blade glinted in Hun Kan's hand. The women stood back to back to make a triangle, hand-to-hand combat now swirling about them, too fast for Alice to follow.

The quetzal bird flushed up in a bright-colored startle and landed in a tree above Alice and Nixie, chirping loudly, almost a bird-scream.

Attackers fell. Warriors, too, but three or four of the others to each of the original warriors.

Ambushers swarmed over the fallen, ripping the spears and even the clothing from the bodies. A warrior stood over a man struggling to strap on a stolen shield, yanked up his head, and slit his throat, roaring like a bear or a cat, triumphant, turning on the ball of his foot, kicking at another man before four of the attackers brought him down.

The warriors were better, but there were too many of the others.

Openings appeared where the attackers could get near the Mayan women. Two men grabbed the smallest one—not Hun Kan—and covered her face with a cloth, taking her away, kicking, melting into the jungle. Others advanced on Hun Kan and the remaining woman, now standing back to back, their faces as fierce as the warriors'.

Nixie ripped Alice's hand from her mouth and stood, yelling, "Hun Kan! Hun Kan!"

Alice grabbed her around the waist. "No!"

"Hun Kan," Nixie hissed, twisting in Alice's grasp.

An attacker grabbed at Hun Kan, ripping at her necklace. The bird man broke his spear over the man's back and grabbed Hun Kan's hand, looking around frantically.

A jungle cat's roar drove a physical shiver through Alice's bones. The sound filled the air and bounced from the jungle, the stones, a sound so great and so long and so demanding that nearby leaves quivered.

The fighting below paused as attacker and attacked all stopped, eyes drawn to the top of the stones where a jaguar stood just above Alice and Nixie. Alice sat down, hard, pulling Nixie onto her lap.

The cat stank of power and blood and sweat and glory.

Nixie stilled, her eyes fastened on the strong jaw and the gleaming white teeth. Close to them, so close. Alice could have touched it.

The black jaguar roared again.

The black on black of its coat rippled, great uneven squares of darkness on an ebony background. It stood looking down at the carnage, completely focused, its golden eyes bright and intense. The tip of its tail moved, slowly.

It turned its head, and its gaze rested on Nixie. Mesmerizing. Dangerous. Alice herself had gone beyond fear into silence. Into acceptance. The jaguar had all the power of the world inside its eyes, all the speed and danger and savageness of the jungle, but it had not come for them.

Movement resumed below them, and the jaguar's gaze returned to the road.

The bird man and Hun Kan broke free and raced *toward* the cat, toward them all. A man started to follow. One of the three remaining warriors grabbed him by the neck and twisted, throwing the limp form down in the ground and turning to face another attacker.

Hun Kan and her companion stepped close to Alice, between her and the jaguar. A gash on the man's leg dripped blood. Hun Kan's hair had come down, falling in a dark wave around her small shocked face.

The cat leaped down the stones, flowing more than running. The bird man and Hun Kan followed, fast, scrambling on all fours, coming so close Alice or Nixie could have reached out and touched them, but neither stopped in their rush toward safety. The cat paused in a small cleared spot just beyond the rocks, waiting. As the Mayans reached the bottom of the rock pile, it turned and all three disappeared into the jungle.

Alice blinked at the place they had gone, mesmerized by the swaying leaves until they stopped and there was no sign of their passage except their footprints.

"Look," Nixie whispered. She reached a hand out and picked up the necklace. It must have fallen from Hun Kan's throat in the mad dash up and over the pile of stones. Broken leather protruded from Nixie's fist.

Alice glanced back at the melee. One Mayan warrior from the original group raced away, in the direction they had first been going. Someone to report the deaths of all the others?

He wasn't followed.

The attackers had already stripped the bodies of clothing, weapons, and finery. They melted into the forest, all of them leaving from the far side, taking the other girl as well. At least they weren't following Hun Kan and the bird man.

The white road in front of them was littered with bodies, the two groups different even in death; the Mayan warriors all well-formed and well-fed, healthy. The attackers looked thinner with rougher hair and clothing and scarred bodies. They shared the same features, though. Not Toltecs then, but Mayans. An underclass. Maybe farmers? Evidence in front of her that civil unrest had helped bring down the Itzá.

Alice swallowed hard, wanting to hide Nixie's eyes, knowing it was too late. But Nixie wasn't watching the road or the bodies; her attention was on the necklace. She held it out toward Alice, her eyes wide and shocky. Alice reached out for it, but her hand passed through the cord as if it were not there. She shook her head. "I can't . . . "

Nixie looked away from her, back the way they had come. "We have to go."

Alice felt it too, a pulling, as if her dream body wanted to lose its form.

Nixie stood, disentangling herself from Alice. "I have to leave this here."

The jungle and the road fuzzed in her vision, but she wasn't touching Nix, couldn't—wouldn't—return without her. She forced her energy into feeling the stone, her body to movement. "Why?"

Nixie shook her head. "It belongs here."

Alice swallowed, suddenly in awe of her own daughter. "Set it on the stone." Nixie jumped down a level in the stone pile. "I need to hide it." She climbed all the way down, carefully not looking at the bodies and the road.

Birds chattered again, and the incessant drone of insects filled the white space between their conversations. Wind sang in the trees above her. Alice looked up for the quetzal, but it was gone. She climbed down beside Nixie, staying close enough to reach for her. The chalky, iron scent of blood wafted toward them on a soft breeze.

She forced her focus back to Nixie, who had picked up a stick and broken it so the ends were sharp. Nixie dug a hole in the ground underneath an egg-shaped rock, poked the bead and cord into the hole, and covered it up.

When she stood up, sweat shone on her forehead, and one cheek was streaked with dirt. "We have to go," she whispered.

Macaws called, and monkeys. Real ones, not the calls the attackers had thrown into the sky before their ambush.

Nixie took her hand and led her back to the sacbe. While Alice gave a last glance at the plundered bodies, Nixie did not. She screwed her face up in concentration and kept Alice's hand in a tight grip, and ten steps later the orange walls of the hotel greeted Alice's eyes. She gasped, feeling for the soft covers on the bed, gripping them in her free hand like an anchor.

Beside her, Nixie trembled and blinked, disoriented. She gulped in the dry conditioned air like a drowning person. Alice's stomach flamed and she bent double, then raced for the bathroom, retching and retching, Nixie's hand on her back.

When she could finally push herself up to crawl to the door and collapse against the wall, Nixie sat beside her, clutching her hand. Alice took Nixie's face in her hands. The smear of dream-dirt crunched beneath her fingertips. "Tell me what you saw."

"The . . . the jaguar roared and they got away. I buried the stone."

Alice sank to the floor, pulling Nixie down next to her and stroking her hair.

Nixie's face was buried in Alice's side, but Alice heard her whisper, "At least they got away."

CHAPTER 18

The jaguar led Ah Bahlam and Hun Kan along nearly invisible paths, and they often had to duck to keep from being trapped by thickly entangled lianas. The cat ran easily, outpacing Ah Bahlam's breath so every step knifed through his lungs. His calves stung, particularly the right one that had been spear-struck. It still bled slowly, a thick trickle of blood oozing down his leg when he extended it to leap over roots or downed trees. All he could do was keep his focus on the black cat, call on the cat inside himself that answered to his totem, and move without stopping.

Turning, they climbed shallow hills and descended again, twisting in so many directions through the jungle that he'd have to wait for the stars to brighten the night sky to fully orient himself.

His training would let him run for days, but this was a sprint. His lungs screamed at him. The cat in front of them didn't slow. A dark shadow spinning its shadow under the shadows of trees, hard to follow. He often reached back for Hun Kan's hand to help her negotiate roots and short, steep drops. She began to wheeze and make small moaning sounds. He looked over his shoulder to see her miss her footing and fall to her knees.

Almost despairing, he reached for the jaguar in his mind as he stopped. *We're stopping. Stop. Stop!* He knelt beside Hun Kan, unable to tell if the cat responded. His body demanded attention. They needed water. To drink, to clean up with. They'd escaped with nothing but what they carried, and here he did not know where to find a cenote. Water ran everywhere under the jungle floor, but only breathed air periodically.

As her breath slowed to a rasp she could talk through, Hun Kan looked up at him. The anger in her eyes barely touched her voice as she simply said, "Thank you," and then, "Do you know where your Way is leading us?"

He shook his head, admiring her pluck and control. "We must keep going. If the jaguar waits for us, it will not wait forever."

"It waits."

He licked the stinging salt of his sweat from his dry, cracking lips, and looked down the path. Sure enough, he spotted the jaguar, a black shadow sitting in shadow, with only the slight movement of its breathing giving away its presence.

Cauac would be proud.

Ah Bahlam looked up at the sky, verifying west by the now-steep slant of the sun angling down through the canopy and making small spots of brightness in the dark jungle.

He took Hun Kan's extended hand and helped her stand up, balancing her while she tested her limbs. She didn't limp from her fall, but she refused to run, shaking her head and walking close behind him, quickly, but walking nonetheless. The jaguar again led them, slower, its pace fallen to match Hun Kan's walk. A hundred steps past where it had lain in the shadow, the jaguar turned down an even slimmer path, perhaps the way peccaries and tapirs took, and stopped in front of a pool of shaded water.

A small cenote.

Two gray-green iguanas sunning on rock in the only shaft of direct light in the small clearing eyed them and then wandered off into the jungle as if they had simply been out for a walk. The jaguar drank, then faded into the trees and stretched out on the ground, its great head resting on its forepaws, clearly signaling a stop.

He helped Hun Kan lever herself down to sit on a moss-covered rock, making sure she was comfortable before he gazed at the cat. *Thank you. We will rest here awhile. Stay, or hunt and return. But continue to lead us.*

The cat licked its jaws. It did not appear even a little tired. For a moment, its eyes met his, and he imagined it saying, "If you just ask for what you want, I can give it to you."

Ah Bahlam smelled the water, suddenly beyond thirsty. *K'uk'ulkan, gods of the jungle, thank you. May our presence bless this water, may this water bless us.* He had seen Cauac honor strange cenotes in this way, using his blessing and respect to appease or temporarily drive away any spirits that inhabited the area.

He found a large leaf and bent it to carry water, bringing Hun Kan a sip.

She leaned toward him and held out her small, pink tongue against the bright green leaf, sipping like a baby bird. "You saved me," she said.

"The jaguar saved us both." She was alive. Nimah and Kisa might be dead by now, or saved for ransom. He suspected not. Their captors had looked too desperate for patience. *I will protect you!* he thought.

The people-of-unrest lived in many small villages in the jungle, often moving every year or two, building no permanent structures. When the time came for their young men to serve at Chichén, they hid. According to rumors brought by the traders who put in at Zama, this defiance grew across the peninsula. For three years, the summer rains had come thin and seldom; the maize crops had yielded less harvest than the people needed.

People blamed the Itzá for their empty bellies.

If their rulers communed well with the gods, no such damage would befall their people and the rainfall and crops would be good. Chichén had fallen ill.

The Itzá had to change, and Ah Bahlam and his friends meant to help, to communicate clearly with the gods so they'd bring water and plentiful food again. They would build strong armies in case the Toltecs came in greater numbers. And to lead, they must be strong and sure of themselves. He must be. "The jaguar is helping us return to Chichén in time for the ceremonies."

"Good." Hun Kan stood and went to the pool, dipping the leaf he had used into the water and bringing a small flood of cool sacred liquid to his lips. After she brought him three leaves of water, she returned to filling herself, dipping the leaf over and over again in the cenote, drinking some, pouring some over her body. She dipped it in the water one more time and stood. "Come here," she said softly, and when he stepped near enough to smell her, she washed his cut, scrubbing so hard he nearly cried out. After she finished, she looked up at the fading light in the sky. "I'll find dinner."

"Stay close to the pool." He glanced at the jaguar, which still watched them. "Maybe it will hunt with me." He had lost his spear and spent two of his arrows, but he still had two.

"We could fish."

He eyed the cenote. No ceremonial marking showed, only the worn thin paths of animals. "Very well," he replied, watching her gather her hair back and begin to search the area for edible plants.

Tired and footsore as he was, this moment of building a meal and a place to sleep together tugged at him. He turned away from her to hide the yearning in his heart. If they chose on their own, they would not be welcome at home. The High Priest of K'uk'ulkan had to bless noble marriages. To live like the men who attacked them would give them both sickness and anger.

As Hun Kan became totally immersed in her task, he watched the jaguar. It was entirely still, except for the tip of its great tail. Ah Bahlam crouched on a rock, hoping to get his Way to meet his gaze. It had stopped for them, but that did not mean it would do his bidding for small things.

As if it heard his thoughts, the jaguar stood and stretched as he approached. It walked off sedately into the jungle, ignoring him completely.

He watched it go, suddenly ashamed of himself for thinking it might feed them. It had brought them to water and food. Should it feed them, too?

He tried five times before he finally scooped four small wiggling fish from the cenote, and started a fire in a rock ring using the flints he carried in a pouch on his waistband. As he cleaned the fish he remembered to be grateful that at least he had not lost his small knife.

Hun Kan returned with an armload of roots and herbs, and a flattish stone that would be adequate for cooking on. She, too, had kept her knife and used it to cut the plants. "Where is the jaguar?" she asked.

"Hunting," he said.

By the time they were done eating, drinking, and gathering enough wood to keep the fire going, it was full dark. Hun Kan had curled up under some branches, and lay sleeping, her open mouth and small snores telling him she dreamt. Stars shone through the thin jungle canopy, but the fire kept Ah Bahlam's eyes from seeing as clearly as he wished. He turned his back to it and stared out at the jungle, watching for predators and all the while praying the cat would come back to them. With no other warriors to help protect them, they couldn't return to the sacbe. He could get them to Chichén but it would be far easier if the cat led them.

The wheel of the sky had turned more than halfway before he woke her to watch.

She came straight up to a sitting position when he touched her shoulder, looking around for danger.

"All is well," he said. "Just time for me to sleep."

She smiled at him and touched his cheek briefly, then went to care for her body before coming back to sit a bit away from him. "So sleep," she said.

He lay down. He drifted, deep tiredness making sleep hide. His cut throbbed in spite of the herb salve Hun Kan had made for it, and every nerve seemed to feel the jungle and to listen for the cat all at once.

Maybe Ni-ixie would return. Maybe if the cat did not return, she would. Was she Hun Kan's Way like the jaguar was his?

Hun Kan began to hum, drumming her fingers softly on her knees, and the sweet sound carried him into the dreaming world.

DECEMBER 18, 2012

CHAPTER 19

Alice sat on the edge of Nixie's bed, rubbing soft circles on her back, as much to calm her own shaking hands as to comfort her daughter. Nix was so small, so precious. Her eyes were closed now, her breath rising and falling in the even rhythm of sleep, Snake clutched close to her chest.

Alice pushed herself up and wiped a shaking hand across her dry, nasty mouth. She changed into the oldest shorts she had with her, a yellow T-shirt, and bright blue socks. She brushed her teeth and hair, wishing for a way to brush the circles from under her eyes. She went to the kitchen and poured a small glass of white wine, staring out the window into darkness. The wine hit her stomach like ice, and she poured it out and made hot tea, letting it sit untouched to cool.

She paced back and forth—only three steps in the tiny kitchen—then started circling the floor.

Her battered olive suitcase and Nixie's newer rose-colored one were stacked in the hall closet. She lifted them out, scraping their wheels against the door jamb. Starting with the living room, which served as her own bedroom, she pulled open the drawers of the chest that doubled as a TV stand and began removing clothing. She layered her shoes, underwear and socks carefully in the bottom of the case, adding neatly folded shirts and her one light sweater. She pulled her now-dry bathing suit from the bathroom.

She closed her case and opened Nixie's, tiptoeing in and emptying Nixie's dresser as silently as possible. She packed Nixie's flip-flops, her bathing suit, and her book, which had fallen to the floor.

She slid the drawer by the bed open, holding it up a little so it wouldn't creak, and peered at the necklace. Her hand reached for it, hesitating. Nixie should pack it. She hated it when Alice touched her things. Besides, Nix had bundled it in so carefully with the towel, doing exactly what she'd been asked to. An unexpected tear splashed onto Alice's hand and a sob rose in her throat.

She closed the drawer as carefully as she'd opened it, walking fast from the room, her hands on her face. She stood staring down at the suitcases, tears spilling from her eyes and blurring her vision. She sank down to the floor, her back leaning against the bed, the ceiling fan blowing loose ends of her hair softly against her cheek until they got wet and stuck.

It was two AM and she was crying in a hotel room. She should get up and pack their shampoo and jewelry from the bathroom, but her legs seemed glued to the floor.

Moments passed. Long, silent moments, filled with the sound of the fan and her uneven, shaky breath.

Was she planning to run out on Marie, who might still be her friend? Who might give her more work, pay for more of her research, and provide a living for Nixie and her? Was Nixie safer anyplace else?

How could she leave here now? December, 2012?

She went and stared at Nix's sleeping face, listened to her soft breath.

She found a handful of kid's cereal at the bottom of a box on a kitchen shelf, and ate it slowly, one piece at a time. It calmed her stomach.

Her voice shook as she told her phone to call Ian.

She had a pot of coffee brewed and was nursing her second cup by the time he knocked at the door. The suitcases were still full, but shoved behind the bed on the far side so she didn't have to look at them. She poured him a cup of coffee as he sank into a chair in the tiny seating area by the front door. "Where's Nixie?" he asked. "Is she okay?"

"She's asleep." Alice sat on the narrow couch and tucked her feet up under her. "I don't think I'm ever going back to sleep."

He raised an eyebrow. "What happened?"

She started at the very beginning, skimming through her interviews, her lunch, her meetings after lunch, but withholding Marie's call. She slowed down as she described their homecoming, telling him everything she could remember about the dream. When she was done, he sat quietly for a moment, and she swore she could hear him thinking.

"So you couldn't touch the necklace, but Nixie could?"

She nodded.

"But you could feel the rocks and the leaves?"

She nodded again. "Not . . . quite right. I mean, it wasn't the real world. Almost. I could smell the jungle." She shivered. "And the cat and the blood."

"That's really weird." He drummed his fingers on his knee. "But the Mayans didn't see either of you?"

"No." She sipped at the cold dregs of her third cup of coffee, no longer sure if her hands trembled from the dream, from telling the dream, or from too much caffeine. "But I swear the jaguar saw her. It looked right at us."

"Did it see you, too?" Ian probed.

"I don't know. She was in my lap, but it really looked like it was watching her. The other weird thing was Nixie's always gone at the same time of day. I mean sunset here and sunset there, or afternoon here and afternoon there." The words almost stuck in her mouth. "Just in a different year. But this time, it was night for us—we were fast asleep—but day where we went. And it wasn't even the same place, like Tulum."

"But you don't know where you were." A statement more than a question. "A lot of the old sacbeob have been mapped. The abandoned chicle industry railroad runs along one for a while and bisects it later."

All the energy had left her when she called Ian. Her nerves, her nausea, her fear. She was wiped clean and too tired to know what to do next. And she had to go see the damned Secret Service again in just a few hours.

She brushed the hair back from her face and sat up straight, struggling for some clarity. Did she really have to go? Nixie mattered more than a tour. Maybe finding out if the dream was real mattered more, too. "Do you think we can find the place we were? Only now?"

He grinned at her and leaned a little forward, smelling of coffee. "We can try."

She needed to do this. But why? "What will it tell us? What do you think is happening?"

His knee almost touched hers. He spoke carefully, a serious Ian instead of the funny or the beaming Ian. "I can only guess. I first saw the old world in June, and that was on a guided shamanic journey. That means I was in a trance, and I saw the ruins of Tulum when they weren't—when they were new, when men were even still building them, so many Mayans . . . ." His voice trailed off. "I didn't know what to make of it, but my guide, Don Thomas Arulo, said it happened to him at Palenque, almost a year ago. He was just sitting in the jungle, minding his own business behind the Temple of Inscriptions, and it all came alive in front of him. People and colors and the jungle taller and thicker. He had done a journey that week, but not that day. So it happened with no sacred plants in his system at all. Don Thomas attributed it to leftovers, though. He told me it happened two other times, with toad venom. Strong stuff." He grinned. "Even Don Thomas admitted he couldn't tell how real *that* was."

She remembered her one ayahuasca trip again. A mild hallucinogen compared to what she'd heard of toad venom, which glyphs suggested had been used in Mayan rituals all over the Yucatan to commune with the gods. Some of the young cultural anthropologists had even suggested that toad venom had let Mayans spirit-travel to other stars. "So a Mayan shaman and you have seen the other world. And now me, in a dream, and Nixie, who's been there. What about other people?"

"I tried to find Don Thomas yesterday to see if he knew anything else, but he wasn't in his village." He shrugged. "That's usual. He shows up when I need him, not when I want him."

"You still haven't told me what you think is happening."

He stood up and stretched, the tips of his fingers nearly brushing the ceiling. "I think time is more unreal than we think. I guess I've always thought that, but I never had proof before." He looked down at her. "And now that I'm getting proof, I'm nervous. Whatever separates us from the past seems to be getting thinner, more permeable. Maybe because we're near the end of a baktun."

Alice felt unstuck from the world. They were talking of clouds and religion and not of science. "So, if we find the place, and we recognize it, we'll know the dream was true? I mean, we didn't bring anything back."

"But Nixie buried the bead."

Right. That would be looking for a needle in a haystack. But she couldn't just sit here and let things happen to Nix. She needed to understand. Or she had to leave, and she just couldn't. Not in December, 2012. "Can we go look tomorrow?"

"Tomorrow or today?" he asked.

She yawned, blinking at the window. The first light of day was slipping light gray over the black sky. She glanced at her watch. It was almost five-thirty, and sunrise proper would be a little after six. "Today."

"Then you best sleep," he said, pointing to the bed.

"I don't think I can. I'm going to check on Nixie."

Wisely, he was quiet as Alice walked into her daughter's room. She found Nix completely still except for soft breathing, one leg kicked out of the covers.

When she got back to the main room, her body headed for the bed even though she meant to return to the couch. "Okay, I'll lie down. But I don't think I'll sleep."

She stretched across the bed, fully clothed in the shorts and T-shirt she'd pulled on after she called Ian. He lifted the far edge of the light bedspread up and covered her shoulders with it, and she closed her eyes, which stung from tears at his simple act of tenderness. Nobody had tucked her in for years.

"I'll wake you in a few hours," he said. "We should go by eight or nine since it's a full day trip."

She'd have to cancel so much. She'd have to unpack. A short laugh tried to escape, but since she lay prone it came out more like a choking sob. But it felt right. Laughing at the suitcases. Staying. Going for the bead. She closed her eyes so she would at least look like she slept.

CHAPTER 20

Hot sun beat down on Ah Bahlam's eyelids. He opened one of them. K'inich Ahaw had been shining for almost a quarter of the day. Memory rushed back, and he lifted himself to look around, his arms and legs stiff. The jaguar wasn't where it had been, but Julu fluffed his feathers in a branch just above him, staring as if to scold him for sleeping so long. Hun Kan sat on a rock by the cenote, rubbing mud in the cracks of a hand-woven basket.

"Have you seen the jaguar?" he asked.

"Good morning." She laughed, her voice playfully mocking. "It is a beautiful day and my hands and eyes have been too busy to watch for your Way."

Ah Bahlam suppressed a good-natured growl, sure his body would have slept a whole day if it had known itself somewhere safe. His limbs all worked, even if they were stiff, and the edges of his cut had started to knit. Hun Kan had been a good healer for him, and now she was almost done making a way for them to carry water. And no hurry; the new baskets would need time to dry.

He stretched his muscles out, first one leg then the other, then one arm, then the other, the various combinations, following a sequence that Cauac had taught him. It took a long time before he could move so freely that yesterday's run was only a memory to his body.

The jaguar was nowhere to be seen.

He found a path upwind of Hun Kan and crouched on a high root, becoming his own jaguar, waiting. He didn't return until he had scattered a herd of peccary and picked one off for breakfast with a heavy rock.

As he held the meat over the fire on two sticks, Hun Kan held her two small-mouthed baskets near the flames, upside down, letting smoke and heat permeate the mud. By the time they were done eating they had two oily, slightly smelly baskets that would hold water reasonably well. Twigs and leaves gave them shape. Hun Kan had coated the interiors with mud and pressed leaves into it, making a barrier between the mud and the water inside.

They were not works of art, but they would get them through a day. Or, he looked up at the sun nearly high overhead, more like half a day.

Hun Kan set the baskets aside, and stripped the leather from the blue wrist-bracelet that Ni-ixie had given her. "The symbols change." She held her arm up for him to see. "They seem to mark time." She pointed at the first symbol, a straight up and down stick. The one next to it was a circle, and beside it there were two others that changed as he looked at them. "The stick showed itself at about this time yesterday morning."

"How did you see it while we traveled?"

She grinned. "I wrapped the leather so that I could peek at it."

He shook his head again, bemused. "We can look again tomorrow and see if the stick is there at this time." He drew his brows together, thinking about Hun Kan's idea. If it was true, it meant that Ni-ixie had powers like the astronomers who kept the records of time at Chichén. More. He held his hand out. "May I see your gift?" he asked.

He expected her to hand it to him, but instead she held out her wrist. "I cannot take it off." She smiled shyly, her cheeks suddenly red. "And I don't really want to. What if I can't put it back?"

The bracelet was loose enough to spin on Hun Kan's wrist, although not easily. It could not be pulled off over her hand. It wasn't tied on, or buckled, but seemed to be a whole, as if it had always been there. As he watched, the circle became a stick, so the symbols that didn't change as often were two sticks. He felt as if it told him to hurry up, to keep going.

The jaguar had not returned, although Ah Bahlam thought perhaps it was close by. Its tracks went north and a little west, and Ah Bahlam started out following them. He lost the tracks in a rocky patch, and stuck to the animal trail, which was wide enough for them to follow, at least for the moment. Still, he stopped to look around regularly, and to call to the jaguar. In his heart, he knew it was close, and also that he must not depend on it; a warrior found and used his Way but depended on himself and his connection to his gods. He watched carefully for any sign of the people-of-unrest, as well as for vipers and other dangers.

CHAPTER 21

Morning light poured through the hotel window. Nixie lay in bed, watching the brightness, her eyes wide open and her body still. The whole real-dream tumbled in on her. It wasn't a television show or a video game; she had seen living people die. Even at home, where people died of weather or riots, and where pictures of dead bodies from the famines and wars in Africa showed up daily on the news nets, she had never seen real death, except for animals. The dream had been exciting, fast and confusing, with Hun Kan and the bead and the jaguar to focus on. She didn't like it, people dying. At least . . . Hun Kan! And the bird-man. Were they safe?

Nixie padded into the living room. Her mom slept sideways on her bed, snoring lightly. Ian sprawled across the couch, face up, with his mouth open and his long hair falling down his chest, not snoring.

Ian! She'd wanted to see him again. Except not right in the middle of her morning at home. He shouldn't be here. This was her quiet time with her mom, whether they cuddled or talked or fought or what.

But it was Ian. She poked his foot with her finger.

His eyes didn't open, but he smiled. "Good morning, Nixie."

"G . . . good morning," she stammered back, then retreated to her room to change out of her pajamas.

Her drawers were empty. "Mom!"

"We're having an adventure," Ian called. "Come wake up your mom."

They loaded backpacks, walking shoes and a huge pile of snacks into their daypacks. Nix could barely eat the mango, papaya or cereal at the resort's main buffet, but at least she could watch the waiters and keep her mind off the dream and the death, and her mom packing them up. That had been close! They couldn't leave now; she had to find out if Hun Kan and the bird-man were safe. Besides, her mom would never forgive herself if she didn't see the end of the calendar, whatever it turned out to be. Especially if it really was anything.

Ian had to boost Nix into his camouflage-colored jeep. It was extra-wide and had an open back with three brown seats in it, and big wheels. They picked up Oriana at her house. She wedged herself into the second backseat beside Nixie, who was in the middle. Nixie told Oriana about the dream while they drove out of town. She nearly had to scream the story to keep the wind from stealing her voice. When she finished, Oriana leaned down and gave her a big hug, the wind blowing wisps of her black hair like tiny sharp knives against Nixie's cheeks.

She settled back against Oriana and drowsed until they stopped in front of an older hotel about halfway to Cancun. A thin dark-haired man wearing all tan clothes and tan sandals with purple socks, and carrying a briefcase, jogged over to them. Ian turned around to face her. "Nixie, this is Peter. He's my friend, and he wants to go with us today."

She already knew they were going to try to find the bead, but why were there new people going? Someone she didn't even know? Nixie had to work to get out a smile and shake the man's hand. She scooted as close to Oriana as her seatbelt would let her go.

As soon as they started off again, Peter started pointing at the cars they passed and making up stories. "See that little purple beetle? It has the last surviving singer of a famous band in it."

Nix smiled in spite of herself when they passed the car and a young Mexican woman sat behind the wheel. She pointed to a battered green truck with a faded picture of a grocery store on its sides and spoke solemnly, "That's the Ambassador of Peaches. He's come to meet the aliens that are landing on the twenty-first."

Oriana joined in, so it seemed like only a few minutes passed before Ian stopped the jeep by a thin dirt road that led into the jungle. After a long ride over washboard roads, they came upon a big sign on a flat board propped up against two trees with "cenote" painted on it in red and "Real Mayan Village" painted in black under it. She tapped her mom on the shoulder. "Can we eat soon?"

"Yes." Her mom turned around and laughed, reaching down to pour water onto a little scrap of towel and hand it to Nixie. "Wash your face. You're all dust."

The water on her skin made her feel a little better. After about fifteen minutes of slow, bumpy riding, Ian pulled into a dirt parking lot and two men came over to him jabbering in a mix of Spanish and Mayan. He answered them the same way, the words coming easy to him. He spoke almost as fast as the men. After he climbed out of the jeep, he clapped the men on the back, all three of them smiling. Nixie picked out a few of their words: road, sacbe, water, food, cenote.

They climbed out and followed the men past a ground-level cenote, the place where the water faded back into its underground river a dark hole covered over with green bushes. About a dozen sun-faded wetsuits lay piled on a wooden picnic table next to three neat huts with dirt floors and thatched palm leaf roofs. Inside the biggest hut, which had wooden walls, they found four more people, all sitting where they could see the door. When they sat down, too, they made a whole circle. Oriana, Ian, Nixie and her mom made up one half of it, and the two men and two women made up the other half. The women were both older than her grandmother, with wrinkly sun-browned skin and friendly eyes. One of them only had half her teeth. The men were younger, with strong backs and dark hair that brushed their shoulders.

Oriana introduced all four of them, but Nixie could only remember one of the names, Marco, which didn't sound Mayan or Mexican. Food appeared on white paper plates: crackers and fruit they'd brought from the hotel room, and limes and corn chips provided by the Mayans. After everyone had eaten at least a little, Oriana asked, "Is Don Thomas Arulo here?"

Marco answered. "Is the wind here?" He shrugged and picked up a cracker. "He has not been with us for two days."

Ian frowned. "He was not at his house yesterday, either." He fell silent for a moment, then said, "We're looking for a place that was very near the Coast to the Chichén sacbe, a place where the old Mayans quarried rocks, probably to use for building."

Marco brightened. "We can walk there. I will show you the way to go."

"Will you lead us?" Ian asked.

"I have work this evening. It will take an hour to show you where it is and get back."

Nixie glanced at her mom, but she was watching Ian, who asked, "Can you show us a place where the Mayan's quarried?"

Marco shrugged. "I can show you the sacbe, and the way to go toward Chichén. There are rocks beside it in many places." He glanced down at Nixie. "You must bring water. The jungle has taken most of it back." He stuffed another handful of crackers and cheese in his mouth, still sitting.

He was like the waiters who always took forever to bring the check. Mayans and Mexicans did things on their own time. Her mom was always cautioning her not to be a rude American, but at this rate it was going to take until tomorrow to find the bead. It was hot and dusty, and a load of real tourists could come by any time and distract everyone. She didn't want to complain, so she stood up and brushed the chalky limestone dust from her pants.

Surprisingly, her mom got up, too, standing over the four Mayans and Ian. "Can we go now?"

A half an hour later, they stood by the metal bones of a now-rusted railroad line. It didn't look anything like her dream. The stones under the rails were gray and tangled with roots. Marco pointed northwest. "You can mostly follow it for a few kilometers here, until you get to the end of the rail line. After that, it's pretty overgrown." He glanced at the women, focusing for a second on Nixie. "Be careful. Bandits and Federales and drug runners use the old road to avoid each other."

"Is there a difference?" her mom asked.

Nixie had seen her face Federales down when they stopped them on the road and wanted to search their car. Now, her mom's eyes had that hard look she got when she was working, the one that drove her to write late into the night sometimes or to stay out at a site until dark, drawing perfect pictures of weathered images carved in stone. Maybe packing and then not leaving after all had made her stronger.

Good. Nixie didn't want to give up.

Ian turned to Marco, holding out two twenty-dollar bills. "Thank you. Please watch our car."

Marco frowned down at the money, as if he was trying to decide whether to take it.

"Go on," Ian said, "Give it to the women if you don't want it. Take them out to dinner."

Marco took the bills.

Ian smiled. "If you see Don Thomas, tell him we are here, and I am looking for him."

Marco nodded and turned back, a small dark man with a bright blue plastic water bottle clipped to his belt, swinging gently against his right hip.

Ian turned back to them all. "Mark this place carefully. See how it looks so we'll recognize it again."

Nixie pulled a bright yellow hair-band out of her pants pocket and wrapped it around a tree branch.

Ian laughed. "Good idea."

As they followed the metal railroad ties, Nixie wondered how they would ever find the bead. There were big stones everywhere, not so neat as the stones in her memory, but would it be a neat pile anymore? What if the Mayans used the stones they'd stood on last night to build temples or the Mexicans to build railroad houses? What if they used them hundreds of years ago?

For the first hour, Peter carried the car game forward. "See that tree? A famous painter once painted the fork in it and sold the painting for six dollars. It sold at Sotheby's for two million last year." And, "See that part of the railroad? A car got stuck there. It had so much chicle in it that the sun melted it to the tracks." It wasn't as enchanting out here where there was no little Mexican woman driving the beetle to give lies to his tall tales, and Nixie stopped before he did.

She stuck as close to the right edge of the tracks as she could, moving so slowly her mom or Oriana called her to hurry more than once. She kept looking for the egg-shaped rock, even where there weren't very many big rocks. She surprised a small snake once. Later, three wild pigs rooted through the group, separating her from the others for a few moments, and making her and Peter and Ian laugh.

They were never going to find the bead this way. It was going to take more than just walking down a dead railroad. The sacbe—she was sure they were on the sacbe—had become so jumbled it had no edges anymore. Trees grew up from it, roots snaking over the metal, usually in ones and twos, but sometimes in clumps they had to work their way around or through. They were just going and going without a plan, walking till they ran out of time. "Can we rest?" she called forward to her mom.

"Of course." They waited for her.

Peter looked around, finding a jumble of rain-worn rocks and sitting down on the edge of one. "I'm ready to bird-watch for a few minutes."

Nixie sat on a rounded rock and took a long drink, water dribbling down and splashing on her neck, cooling her.

After they all drank and sat for a few minutes, Peter stretched his long skinny legs out in front of him, his socks the only purple in view. "Let me get this straight. We're out here looking for a single bead that got buried in this jungle roughly a thousand years ago?"

Ian laughed. "Think of it as an act of faith."

"Because it sure isn't an act of archeology," Nixie's mom said.

Oriana laughed. "At least it's pretty."

The trees around them had clearly been cut when the railroad was made. They'd grown back of course, but the taller canopy started a good hundred feet or so from the road. Lianas, bromeliads and mosses decorated the trees. A burst of orange and yellow flowers hung almost twenty feet above them.

Nixie's mom glanced at her watch. "We'll have to start back in an hour. Maybe we should move faster."

Not faster, better. This would be her only chance; they wouldn't get back out here. Nixie closed her eyes and imagined her dreamscape, the white road glistening in the green jungle, the monkeys in the trees, and the flash of bright bird wings. The smooth slap of feet on the road.

Her mom's voice, quiet, near her. "Are you okay, Nix?"

"Yes." She opened her eyes, keeping them soft, trying to keep the glowing dream in front of them and still see the tumbled rough road of today. She shuffled forward slowly so she wouldn't stumble, trying not to look at the tracks. Sweat salted her forehead and she tugged scraps of flyaway hair back into her clip.

She wanted a breeze.

Her mom said something to Ian, too soft for her to hear, but she heard his answer. "Leave her. Watch."

So she ignored them, made them not there in her mind.

A breeze did come up, from behind her. She stood in it, smelling the jungle dust and flowers. She found a good flat place for her feet and closed her eyes again, listening. Leaves rattled softly against each other. Small birds chattered in the trees by the road, and somewhere further off, a pair of macaws scolded each other.

Oriana started to say something and Nixie held up a hand, her eyes still closed.

The breeze was almost wind higher up in the canopy, a warm breath. She imagined Hun Kan and the bird man. The black jaguar with the golden-yellow eyes. The jaguar's coat clarified in her imagination. As the black on black of his coat began to shimmer, she knew how far they had to go. She licked her lips and turned back to the others. "We aren't there yet. We're not very close. But I know where it is, so we can hurry."

Peter looked puzzled, but Oriana winked at her. As they neared her, Nixie spied a flash of fear coming through the determination in her mom's eyes and reached out for her hand, holding it in hers. "It's okay, Mom."

"I know."

Nixie kept going, moving faster. The others followed her, sticking close. When Peter started talking to Oriana, Nixie shushed him. She needed to hear the jungle and the wind, needed to smell her way, feel her way. She needed as little of today as possible inside her senses.

Her mom stayed really close to her, so Nixie could reach back and touch her if she wanted to. A guardian. Someone to keep her in this time while she was half in that time.

She didn't want to see the dead warriors again.

The wind freshened more and the blue sky faded to soft gray that darkened to deeper gray, and then to charcoal. The air felt full of water and electricity.

"Nix?"

Nixie turned to find her mom handing her one of the cheap clear plastic rain ponchos that she always bunched in the bottom of her pack. Nix stopped and gave her mom a hug. The hour had surely almost passed, and they still had a ways to go. She couldn't let them stop and think, let them get all adult and turn around. "We have to hurry."

"But we *can* all stay dry," her mom noted, using her mom-voice.

For answer, Nixie pulled the poncho over her head and turned back. Her legs were tired, but she made them move a little faster.

The air stayed hot and damp and the clouds above Nix felt like anvils that could fall and crush her.

The poncho made her feel like a sandwich in a plastic bag in the sun. She bunched it up over her shoulders, walking so fast she was nearly running, pushing her way through the small trees that poked up in the middle of the path.

The trees thickened, becoming a wall decorated with strangler figs and flowers. The tall buttressing roots of kapoks grew across the remains of the sacbe, becoming barriers up to a few feet tall in some places.

What remained of the road was a white stone here, clutched in a twisting root, and another one there, half-buried under dirt and rotting leaves.

The clouds emptied on them, a waterfall of rain. They huddled under the tree canopy while the rain sheeted the more open sacbe behind them as if glass covered it.

"It's the end of the railroad," Ian said.

"Why would they stop a railroad in the middle of the jungle?" Peter asked.

Her mom answered. "Because they ran out of chicle contracts." Nixie's mom looked at her sadly. "We'll have to turn back."

"Not," Oriana interrupted, "until this stops."

They couldn't turn back. They were too close. The rain wouldn't last long. Fifteen minutes or so. The Yucatan's daily splash bath. In an hour, the jungle would look as dry as when they started. Nixie struggled up onto a kapok root, balancing on one foot, trying to look through the dense jungle. This hadn't been cut in years, maybe hundreds of years. She couldn't see a path.

She closed her eyes.

CHAPTER 22

Late afternoon sun slanted through the trees. Hun Kan's mud baskets were nearly empty, and Ah Bahlam still hadn't seen the jaguar again. Julu flew above them, always staying nearby.

They had found one pool so far today, a small rushing sliver of water beside a thickening in the animal trail they followed, the lips of an underground river kissing the sky.

"We'll be late," Hun Kan said.

Yes. They should be arriving tonight, and have two full days of preparation before the equinox. "If we get there at all."

A human call floated through the jungle. He stopped, feeling Hun Kan stop beside him. Bandits? Or the people-of-unrest? Monkeys chattered above him and Julu fluffed his feathers, muttering softly in the language of birds.

Hun Kan took his arm, and he looked into her eyes, finding a trace of fear, but more of determination. He smiled to see it, happy she was the one who had been spared to accompany him. A fierce companion.

It was hard to tell the direction the single voice had come from. They could stop, but waiting might not avoid any enemies. What would Cauac do? Or his father, for that matter? He was stuck between Zama and Chichén, and needed to choose between a sorcerer's way and a warrior's.

Perhaps, in this, the two ways were not far apart.

He closed his eyes, feeling Hun Kan's hand still resting on his arm. He drew a picture of the jaguar in his head, letting it fill him, black spots on a black coat, until he could see the eyes. The yellow-gold orbs in his mind stared at him, unblinking, full of power and purpose. He would be like the cat, whether it came to him in the flesh or not.

Ah Bahlam started forward again, slowly, being careful to keep his steps uneven and not to snap twigs. He ghosted forward, following the thin tracks of a pig family he had been hoping would lead to more water and perhaps a meal.

It did not take long to come to a dusty fork where animal tracks mixed with humans. Bare feet, and so people of the jungle, whatever kind.

Should he follow the pigs or the people?

He stood in the fork listening to his breathing, to Hun Kan's, watching for a sign.

None came, except a deep conviction that this was *his* choice. In fact, Julu, too, had disappeared, a further sign that he must decide. He wanted to keep Hun Kan safe, but safety might not lie in either direction.

He followed the people.

He was destined to be a Lord of Itzá, and anyone this close should pay tribute to Chichén. Perhaps he would learn something that his father needed to know, bring information back to Chichén. If not, well, they could have died yesterday and instead they had been saved. That was something to trust in.

The human tracks were fresh. The path was wider, allowing for slightly faster travel.

Dusk had made the forest-of-shadows taller than the living trees, when he smelled burning wood and heard the deep, measured rhythm of many drums. They slowed, keeping even their breath low. The sky was nearly dark when he detected the murmur of humans and the crackle of bonfires.

He led Hun Kan in a circle around the people, carefully, staying unseen. The flat ground kept them from being able to see anything, and the thick undergrowth made walking silently hard and slow. They were close enough to hear men calling back and forth to each other and the thunk of new wood being thrown on the fires.

He looked up, searching for a thick trunk with good handholds and strong upper branches. The last of the light let them shinny up a kapok tree, using the twisted vines of a strangler fig for handholds. They surprised three green tree-frogs with bright red feet. A good sign, the frogs.

He clambered out on a sturdy branch, followed by Hun Kan, seeking a clear view through the thick forest. Her breath blew warm on his thighs, then his shoulder, as she inched carefully up beside him.

Flames flickered and lit the rising smoke from below, turning it blood-red. Copal had been thrown on the fires, and the scent of it drew him into the memory of other ceremonies, small ones for blessing the morning hearth and large ones for blessing the year's crops. Dizzy, he squinted, trying for details.

He looked over the roofs of rough palm-thatched huts and storage buildings that edged a large manmade clearing. On the far side of the clearing, the dark hole of a deep cenote was edged in golden light. From here, he could not see the water, but such hard cliff edges nearly always led to deep pools.

Warriors danced circles around the fires. Ragged warriors. Tens, many tens of tens, a full hundred or more, bodies glistening in the last of the day. And around them, more men, older and younger and all ragged. People-of-unrest.

The number of them took his breath away and he gripped the branch tighter. He listened, trying to make out what was happening, but the voices were a jumble. Power filled the clearing. Many kinds: The raw power of shamans—an angry power calling out to the gods, the complex power of the cenote and the jungle, and the simple power of so many men. They were not gathered here for nothing. All this power and anger was directed at Chichén, at his home, his family.

This was more news than he had expected to gather.

Hun Kan gripped his hand, then pointed. Her eyes were wide and dark, her jaw clenched. He looked in the direction she looked, following her brown and shaking finger.

Nimah. She had been painted blue, dressed in white robes, decked in yellow and white winter-blossoming orchids, and stripped of all other ornamentation.

He saw no sign of Kisa.

Between Nimah and the cenote, a small wooden platform had been built.

She had been prepared for sacrifice.

Ah Bahlam swallowed, nodding at Hun Kan to tell he had seen. Smoke blew the scent of the fires to them.

Nimah's blood would strengthen these people greatly, add to the threat they presented for Chichén. It made him dizzy to think of it, and to think of the danger to Hun Kan. To him.

Hun Kan's gaze slid back to Nimah. She was completely still. He had seen Hun Kan and Nimah together at Zama, sometimes swimming and other times gathering flowers or roots or sitting in the sun weaving baskets. They had laughed like two young girls laugh, and sometimes wore each other's clothes.

Hun Kan would know there was nothing they could do, not two people against a small army. This must be Nimah's fate. Her Way.

When he had imagined what might happen to the two women who had been captured, a full sacred sacrifice for the good of an enemy had not crossed his mind.

They should leave now, and use the last scrap of light to see by. He could protect Hun Kan from Nimah's sure fate and Chichén from the damage that could be done by losing Hun Kan, too.

He swallowed hard and gestured to Hun Kan to back down the trunk. She looked blankly at him for a moment, her face pale. Then she shook her head and mouthed, "No. I need to see."

He understood. Without them to witness, Nimah would go to her death with no friendly spirits to mark her passage. He licked his dry lips and resettled on the wide branch, watching.

It would not take long. The cracks between day and night held the most potential for communion with the gods. Hun Kan drew in a sharp breath as two men came forward, taking Nimah's hands. They led her to the front of the platform and laid her down, and two other men came to take her feet, so that she was well pinioned.

She did not scream and the platform was too far away for him to see if she cried or moved her lips in prayer or trembled.

A man dressed in a quetzal feather headdress, a polished bronze chestplate that might have come from any of the warriors they'd traveled with before the ambush, and a simple leather skirt with matching leggings walked out of the smoke from the nearest fire and stood beside Nimah. A priest. Or a man who styled himself as one.

The false priest should be killed. But he couldn't do it from here. Not with Hun Kan to protect.

The priest stood beside Nimah until the entire clearing stilled, all eyes watching him, waiting.

Drums began a heartbeat rhythm, soft and sure, a promise to the gods. The Priest began to chant and the crowd returned his words, as proper as if the ceremony happened at the grand Chac-Mool in Chichén. The sound made Ah Bahlam shiver and sweat.

He wanted to reassure Hun Kan but couldn't take his gaze from the scene below them. His stomach lurched and he felt dizzy. He smelled the tree they clung to, the moss above his head, the sweat and fear and hope of the men and women below them, the acrid fires. He clutched the tree harder, digging his toes in to keep from sliding free of the branch. He blinked and his vision sharpened and grayed all at once. The lights of the fires fuzzed to indistinct brightness. Light appeared also over the people, and a brightness enveloped Nimah.

The jaguar's vision.

This could be his fate, or Hun Kan's. Here, or at Chichén. They could be called to do what Nimah did, to give up their lives with honor. *If that is ever me, let my death serve my own people.*

Ah Bahlam pulled his own small knife out and held it poised over the place he had cut in the ceremony with Cauac.

The priest's arm came up and his obsidian blade caught the last flash of the sun god's rays. As it fell, quickly, to pierce Nimah's pale chest, Ah Bahlam brought his own blade down on his arm, whispering, *Gods of Chichén, take this sacrifice to the glory of Chichén, twist it away from any use meant to harm us.*

The priest held Nimah's heart up triumphantly, cupping it with two hands. At that same moment she cried out, the last cry she would ever make, the cry coming moments *after* the priest raised his hands full of her severed heart.

The four men holding her took her four limbs and tossed her body into the cenote at the same time that the priest cast her heart onto the nearest fire.

Noise rose, the crying and calling of many voices reaching for their gods, so Ah Bahlam did not hear Nimah's body hit the water.

When Ah Bahlam looked back at her, Hun Kan's cheeks were damp and her eyes burned with fierce anger and loss. But she, too, had not cried out. He reached a hand back and wiped the water from her cheeks. In that moment, a terrible purpose seemed to flow between them, a bond deeper than any he'd ever felt with anyone. Her eyes told him she felt it, too. "We will bring this news," she hissed quietly.

"Yes."

A few moments later, they dropped to the forest floor, and began edging slowly away from the clearing.

Someone nearby called out, "Stop!"

He took off, racing, checking to make sure Hun Kan followed. Their baskets fell to the side of the path, crunching together. Starlight threw faint shadows, helping them step around twisted roots and depressions in the jungle floor.

Their pursuer called out sharply, clearly trying to bring others to help him. Ah Bahlam caught sight of him once, a big man with long hair, a spear in one hand.

The trees and underbrush seemed to rise up against them, threatening to trip them or tangle them in roots.

Ah Bahlam called on his inner jaguar yet again, trying to see like the cat did, to have the dark be as much a friend as the light.

Other voices cried out, more pursuers. But only the one was still close.

The great cat roared. Behind them. Between them and the others.

Ah Bahlam didn't hesitate, or turn. He raced as fast and hard as he could. Julu appeared in front him, Julu who did not normally fly at night.

He followed the bird and trusted the cat to keep their back path free. He breathed the jungle, felt it, heard and felt its creatures. He knew where each root was, each bush, each down tree, each hole in the limestone floor. He was Hun Kan and the jungle and the bird and the cat. One being, with one purpose. To get two humans home to Chichén Itzá.

CHAPTER 23

Alice watched rain obscure the path they'd just rushed down and hide the top of the trees so only the five of them seemed bright colored and alive. Water stuck like jewels to Nixie's hair and Oriana's, dripped from Ian's dreads and Peter's hat. It fell so fast it pooled in the hollows of the porous limestone under their feet.

She'd been so sure they'd find Ian's bead.

But the dream was years from this broken road, and Peter's words kept sticking in her head. A single stone bead in a jungle was worse than a needle in a haystack.

At least a needle would be shiny.

Nixie had been so sure of herself, and dammit, Alice had *trusted* that sureness. She blinked again, feeling the close-in walls of the torrent holding them here at the end of hope.

Maybe they could come back tomorrow and find a way to start from here. Except there wasn't time. When she'd called to put the Secret Service people on hold for a day, the woman she'd talked to had been incredulous, and had barely promised to let Alice come in the next morning, early.

Alice put a hand on her daughter's shoulder, squeezing softly through the clear plastic of her poncho. Surely Nix was disappointed, crushed.

Nixie didn't turn around.

Alice let her hand fall, willing to wait Nix out at least until the downpour stopped. As she turned back to watch the rain, Ian came up beside her, circling her loosely with his right arm. She stiffened, then let out a deep breath as Ian reached for Oriana with the other arm. Safety in numbers.

Peter hooked himself to Oriana, and the four adults stood together looking down the road they'd come up, everyone in a different colored plastic poncho, no more than bags with hoods, and holes for their arms. If there was someone down the road to see, they'd look like jelly beans.

The constant backdrop of cicada song had stilled. Water splashed on the plastic, on their heads, dripped from the roof of the trees. Ian pulled her in closer, smelling like jungle and salty sweat and the freshness of water. She closed her eyes, accepting the pressure of his arms in the group embrace. Conscious that her own arms and torso were still stiff, she took a deep breath and relaxed. She heard water and his breath and her breath; all of the other jungle sounds in abeyance, waiting.

The water stopped.

Cicadas and birds sang.

She opened her eyes to a clear blue sky, dizzying blue, and pearl white stones in neat rows under her feet. Nixie, behind her, gasped. "Let's go!"

The four adults let loose of each other in a tangle of arms, turning. The wall of trees might have never been. In front of them, the sacbe stretched clear, clean and fresh, the jungle to either side tamed, but taller and closer in.

Nixie was already loping down the white road.

Peter yelped. Oriana gasped. Ian touched Alice's arm, propelling her the only way a mother could go.

After her daughter.

Oh my god. She bit back a screech and grabbed for Ian, who clutched her as he whispered, "We did it. She did it."

The road under Alice's feet was solid, more solid even than the dream, as solid as reality. She dropped down and touched a stone, feeling its rough edges. "Wait, Nix!" she called.

Nixie stopped and turned, her face glowing with excitement. "We don't have much time!"

You'd think she was at Disneyland instead of back in a hostile past. "Wait," Alice said, and lifted her still-soaked rain gear over her head. One by one, the others also stripped off their bright plastic ponchos.

"Come on," Nixie encouraged.

Alice glanced up at Ian, who was looking all around him. "It's magic." He must have felt her gaze. He looked down at her. "We're here for a reason. Let's do it, since I'd bet we can't get back until we do."

She shut her mouth on an argument about that idea. She didn't buy it, but the look on Nixie's face demanded a mother's strength. She took a step, and then another one, and didn't fall down. This time was real like her own except it smelled better. Another step. And then Nixie was smiling at her and she caught up to her daughter and stood beside her, looking up the white road.

They followed Nixie in a line: Alice, Oriana, Peter, and in back, watching behind as well as in front, Ian. Their warrior. His presence gave comfort even though she had no illusions of safety. They could never outfight either band of Mayans, formal warriors or ambushers.

The jungle around them was taller, but drier, showing signs of stress: brown branches, fewer new shoots. Certainly it had not rained here today, maybe not for days. But life still teemed. Monkeys tracked them from the treetops. Bright red and green birds—parrots and macaws—startled Alice repeatedly, flashing across the sacbe in jewel-colored streaks. More, many more, than in 2012.

It had been time to turn around, in that other time, the one where their phones collected worldwide news from the air and they had a car tucked safely by an *Authentic Mayans Here* sign. In this time, they kept going, the following of Nixie inevitable.

Peter's eyes were too wide for Alice to imagine he could find his tongue anyway, and Ian and Oriana had gone into deep states of alertness.

Alice focused on Nixie, on a bob of her hair that had escaped her ridiculous big clip, on the rise and fall of her hips, on the bright blue of her shirt, her feet handling the smoother by far, but still uneven road. Step, step, skip, step, step, long step, step-step, step.

Stop.

Alice nearly ran into Nix. Oriana and Peter fetched up at her back and Ian stopped beside her. Peter gasped out, "What? Is this—?"

Nixie held up a hand to silence him and focused on Alice, her eyes the blue of the sky here in the past. She whispered, "Recognize it?"

Alice blinked. She walked a few feet up the road and then turned back. "It's where we came in. From the dream."

"Okay," Peter said. "Okay, how do you know what time you're in? We're in?"

Alice was far more curious about whether or not there would be a pile of dead Mayan warriors around the bend. The questions related, though, at least a little. "We don't," she said. She suddenly wanted to finish this, get the bead and get back. Except if they got the bead from this now, then what? If the dream was a promise, then what did it mean to find the bead? "Nix?" she said. "Are you scared? Do you think we should go home?"

Nixie swallowed and chewed on her lip. Finally, she said, "I feel heavy here."

Alice knew exactly what she meant. Stuck. She nodded and took Nixie's hand, the memory of the dream-carnage thick in her throat. This was no dream.

They walked around the bend.

There were no bodies. Red ants coated the white rocks, carrying blood-stained twigs and leaves and other small things. Each ant was half the size of Alice's little finger, and the river of them all was as wide as she was tall. Alice swallowed and held Nix close to her. "They're cleaning up."

Ian dragged a downed tree and threw it over the ants. "Hurry," he said, demonstrating, walking along the wood above the insects.

Nixie and Alice followed. By the time Peter stepped from the wood onto the white road, thin pulsing veins of ants swarmed over the tree. Ian dragged it back, off the road, and Alice smiled in silent approval.

Just past the ants, past the scene of the fight, the pile of quarry rocks stood just as it had in their dream. Alice reached a hand out and put it on Ian's arm. "That's it. That's where we dreamed we were."

He grinned at her, looking pleased, then stopped in the middle of the road and looked around, as if absorbing the location.

Her good expedition camera was deep in the bottom of her pack. "Nix? Do you have your camera?"

"Of course." Nixie sounded more excited than awed now, as if passing the ants had freed her of some dread. She snapped pictures of the scene with and without people, directing, sure of herself.

Peter and Oriana took phone pictures.

Alice tensed when Nixie ran back to kneel near the ants, capturing them carrying bloody leaves. When she came back, her eyes shining, she looked up at Alice. "Ready?"

Peter had only lost a little of his shell-shocked look. "Maybe I better find it. I wasn't in the dream and I haven't been in the past."

Alice glanced at Ian. He nodded softly and climbed up near the top of the rock pile, choosing a vantage point much like theirs had been in the dream.

"I want to find the bead," Nixie protested.

"You can take pictures," Alice replied, using her best dig-boss voice, the one she'd developed last summer keeping piles of barely post-grad students in line.

Nixie settled on a flat spot on a stone just a little above the egg-shaped rock so she could get a nice, easy picture of Peter. She spotted the disturbed place where she'd dug the hole and pointed to it.

It only took a few moments to find the bead. Peter held it up, his gaze into the camera deadly serious, his face white. Late afternoon sun coated even the dull stone of the carved bead in soft gold. He whispered, "It was just where she said. Okay. So this has to be the past. Okay." He looked at Alice. "You were right. No alternate universe could be so like our past today. Okay?"

He was clearly scared, but heck, so was she. It didn't help anything. "Yes, Peter, we're time-traveling."

Her immediate concern was getting the hell back. She still felt—how had Nix put it? *Heavy in this world.* The warm, too-dry air stuck to her skin, the chalky limestone dust made her want to sneeze, and all of the sounds were wild.

It was late . . . everyone sun-painted like the bead in pre-dusk pale gold. Oriana had gone over to Peter and taken the bead in her hand, and Nix was snapping a picture. "We should go," Alice said, looking up at Ian. "We got what we came for." Maybe not enough proof for anyone else, but enough for her.

"We can't get back to the car without walking the jungle at night," he said. "The old sacbe and the rusted tracks would be tough in the dark."

"We're time-traveling. How do we know we won't get back in the morning there?"

"Want to try it?" he asked mildly.

She shivered. She didn't really want to stay here. The fight had been here, and she didn't want to run into the ambushers—or the jaguar—any more than she wanted to trip on old metal right now. It would be really dark soon.

Primitive dark.

Starlight! My god, she could see the ancient stars. She didn't want to go back, after all. Not yet. "No," she said. "No, I don't." She climbed up the stones easily, her feet remembering where they had gone the night before. She found a flat rock to lean against, a foot or so from Ian, close but not touching. "I suppose the people here won't have night vision glasses and semi-automatic weapons," she said, making sure she was speaking too softly for Nixie to hear. "But I saw them kill each other."

Ian stared silently out over the jungle. Even though his features softened in the fading light, there was unmistakable readiness in him. "My journeys before were preparation. The bead was just proof. I made it then, and we found it now. But why you and Nixie? She's a kid and you don't believe in magic."

"Tough to deny it right now."

"But you'll try to deny it when you get back."

She winced. "I hope not." She watched Nix and Oriana trying to catch more pictures before the day faded entirely. Nix's blonde head and Oriana's dark one made a pretty contrast from above like this. Peter seemed to have become a little more like himself; he had his little computer out and was furiously taking notes. "But what is there to learn here? These people were as bloody as we are. And based on what we know so far, they weren't noble savages. The Lords of Itzá chased power as surely as any of our worst leaders. So what's the message?"

"Maybe that's why you. You're enough of a cynic to report accurately. And you're an expert." Laughter floated up toward them from below. "And maybe Nix is just innocent."

She bristled a little as his use of her pet name for Nix. She scooted a little bit away from him, and immediately felt better. He noticed, and gave her a long, silent look, but didn't say anything.

Another reason she was here had clicked in her head. "I'm touring Marie Healy around Chichén day after tomorrow."

He stilled, then grinned broadly. "The climate change conference."

"Right. I think I'm touring them all."

"Why didn't you tell me?" he asked. "It's the chance of a lifetime. How many people get to talk to the leaders of the whole damned world?"

She should be as awed by it as he was, as delighted. It was downright strange that she wasn't. "It's just . . . it's not as important as figuring this out, and keeping Nixie safe. Besides, if I don't get back tomorrow for more meetings with the Secret Service, I won't be touring anyone."

"Mom!" Nixie called up, delighted.

Just at Alice's eye level, a quetzal bird perched on a branch still quivering with the weight of its landing. Alice blinked at the bird. "Hello," she said, feeling a bit silly.

The bird preened, and looked from her and Ian down to Nixie, calling *keow-kowee-keow*. Its voice had more strength than beauty, a contrast to the bird itself, which seemed to be perched precariously. The combination made her laugh. "Too bad I can't take you back with me."

"It's the bird-man's bird," Nixie called up. "So I know they're safe. It would be sad if they weren't."

Alice bit her tongue. Birds with feelings (real or imagined) were no stranger than anything else that had happened in the last day. She stood up. "Are we all agreed to spend the night here and walk back with first light?"

Peter was rolling up his computer keyboard. "Can we get back?"

"I'm sure we can," Ian said, standing next to Alice and surveying the area. "But I don't want to pop back into the jungle on our side at night. Do any of the rest of you?"

Alice didn't think they even could go now. She still felt solidly here. But something in the back of her head, her heart, didn't mind. What a gift to be here, in this time. "I want to see the stars. This may be my only chance to ever see them the way the old Mayans did."

Nixie was climbing up near them. "Me, too."

"Can we build a fire?" Peter asked.

"No," Alice immediately answered. "To truly see the stars you need the blackest sky possible."

"And we don't want to attract attention," Ian added.

Alice shivered.

They made a simple meal of the leftover snacks: potato chips, apples and Gatorade.

By the time they finished eating, there was barely enough light to see to put the bags and trash back in the backpack, and hang it from a tree in hopes it wouldn't attract ants. They gathered close together, Alice and Nixie on one rock, Peter and Oriana each close by, and Ian above them. Ian looked up at the velvet-black sky shot through with stars. "So, you're the archeoastronomer."

He pronounced it right. She smiled. "I am."

"What would the old Mayans have seen in this sky?"

"They knew most of our constellations, but had different words for them. What we call Monoceros and Canis Major, for example, are—roughly—the paddler gods, Stingray and Jaguar, in a celestial canoe. They tracked Venus very carefully, and knew its orbit more precisely than we did until the 1970s. Hold on . . . I think I can find it." She should be able to do this easily, but the banquet of stars made it tougher. "There." It hung low on the horizon, brighter than any stars around it. "Do you see it?"

She heard a soft laugh from Ian. "I think so," and an "of course," from Nixie, who had sat out with her at many observatories while she was working on the paper she'd just published.

"But what's most important is they saw the stars as gods, as teachers, as guides. They understood complex astronomical terms that we didn't document until much later."

"So no one had to teach them the Earth isn't the center of Universe?" Peter asked sleepily.

She laughed. "No, I don't think so." She licked her lips. It was a good question. "I don't know. They did see the stars as influencing them and their world. Maybe I'd say they saw the Earth as *a* center, but not *the* center."

Oriana asked, "What about in our time? I keep hearing about something special in the stars, some way they line up that's very rare. Ian tried to explain it to me once, but I don't think I fully understood it."

In the moment Alice gave Ian to respond, Nixie said, "The equinox sun lines up with both the dark hole in the Milky Way and the center of the galaxy."

Oriana giggled. "Okay. Pretty easy. Alice, how rare is that?"

"Oh," she said, feeling a little giddy, "That happens about once every thirteen baktun's. That means once every fifty-one centuries. It's supposed to be a time when there are a lot of solar flares, too."

"Ah," Oriana said. "Rare."

Peter spoke up. "There have been more flares lately."

They all watched the stars in silence for a long time. Peter said, "We'll need to set watches. Do you want me with Oriana or with you?"

So she and Ian had become joint leaders of the expedition? She swallowed. Ian was the strongest, and Peter the weakest, perhaps even weaker than Nixie. "I'll take Oriana," she replied, and Ian looked over at her, the starlight illuminating a conspiratorial wink that tickled her below the belly, making her warm and uneasy.

She and Oriana drew the first part of the dark of night. Good. She'd have stayed up anyway.

Ian and Peter lay out their ponchos on large flat rocks and stretched out on them. Alice couldn't imagine how they'd actually sleep, but at least Ian hadn't pulled the man card on her.

As Alice and Oriana climbed up to find good watch-spots, Nixie called up, "Mom, I can't sleep. Can I sit with you?"

Alice reached a hand out to help Nixie up. "Sure."

Nixie tucked herself next to Alice, head on Alice's shoulder, and mother and daughter looked up together at the bright blaze of stars.

The dark rift in the Milky Way hung black as an iris above her, surrounded by the light of billions of stars and galaxies. If she closed her eyes halfway, softening her focus, it was easy to imagine being an astronomer in this ancient world. Half her time would have been spent in the glory of nights like this one, which progress had stolen from the world.

The river of stars sent enough light for Alice to make out the dark lines of Nixie's eyelashes. The brilliance of each individual star shone clearer than she had ever seen from ground-based expeditions or photos. And unlike satellite shots, written over with numbers and dates and captured on square screens or scraps of paper, this sky had fullness. Dimension.

"It's magic," Nixie whispered.

That would have to do. Even if she didn't believe in magic. The thought was wry now, and she smiled as the magic of the stars above penetrated all the way to her bones.

DECEMBER 19, 2012

CHAPTER 24

Birds sang the dawn home in time for Alice to open her eyes and see the ancient stars fade into a softening sky. She lay rooted to the stone, amazed at the variety of bird calls, the soft touch of the cool breeze, the rustle of animals in the dry trees and bushes. The weight of Nixie's head no longer pinned her shoulder to the hard rock beneath her. She jerked up to a full sitting position, her eyes tracking to whispers across the white road.

Nixie and Oriana stood on the far said of the sacbe, using the first blush of dawn-light to take pictures of each other, of Ian sitting silhouetted against the red-orange sunrise, of Peter sleeping with a skinny arm over his long face, and of Alice herself stretching out the pain of sleeping on rocks.

Daylight made them visible. They couldn't be caught here, not by old Mayans. The Secret Service! Adrenaline juiced her into sitting up, then standing and stretching. "Come on, we should get breakfast and go."

Ian stood, stretching, a dark silhouette against the dawn, a wild man who could belong in this time. Then he turned and the light fell on his face and he looked like himself again, grinning at her.

She made a hurry-up motion with her hands, but couldn't help smiling back.

By the time the sun painted brighter greens into the canopy, they were walking down the white road. The ants were gone, the road so clear that except for a few dark stains, the fight might never have occurred. Efficient little beasts.

Alice took the lead, making sure Nixie was close to her, driving the group quickly.

The sun and walk warmed Alice during the hour it took to reach the point where they had switched time, where the railroad ended. It did not appear under their feet and trip them. The road remained clear and open, new, the stones in neat rows, the spaces between filled with plaster made of white limestone dust and water.

Alice licked her lips, but stopped herself from stopping, made her feet go one in front of the other.

Ian must have sensed her unease; he came up beside Alice and said, "It will be okay."

Absurdly, she wanted to call her Secret Service contact and warn her she might be a few minutes late. But of course, her phone would not work here. She looked up at Ian. "If you see a water source, stop."

"Sure." He skipped a few steps on the path, looking happy. He didn't seem manic, or even silly, but just at peace with the situation. Kind of like a little boy.

But maybe cheerfulness was how he reassured himself. In spite of his clowning, he remained watchful and alert.

He took a few more dance-like steps and reached for her hand, encouraging her to join him.

She swallowed hard and took his hand, which was almost big enough to fold hers entirely inside it. She managed a few dance steps for Nixie, and then a few for herself.

It was okay.

Alice danced another few hundred feet, feeling silly and mystical all at once, before she blushed and fell back, letting Ian take the lead. She walked in the middle beside Nixie and listened to Peter and Oriana chatter about artificial intelligences and alternate universes and communication between stars.

Ian kept dancing.

She watched the side of the road, hoping to see something familiar even though it was surely madness or blind faith to even look, what with the clean, white stones underfoot. Still, they must be getting near the path back to their car. What if they passed it?

A dark-skinned man dropped down from a tree onto the road, directly in front of Ian.

Oriana screamed. Alice tensed, ready to run. Nixie gripped her arm. "He's us," she hissed with all the righteous indignation of an eleven-year-old who knew something her mom didn't.

Alice blinked. The man could have been Mayan. Probably was Mayan. Now Mayan. He wore Nike sandals and a Hawaiian shirt over cut-off blue jeans, his dark, bare legs thin under a broad torso. The man reached for Ian and clucked him under the chin. "I thought I'd find you out here."

Ian laughed, and hugged the man. He turned toward the others. "This is my Mayan benefactor, my teacher, my friend, Don Thomas Arulo." Ian was grinning ear to ear, as happy as if he'd just won some great award. Ian introduced everyone around, leaving time for each of them to say something personal and welcoming to Don Thomas.

He saved her and Nixie for last. Don Thomas bent down to meet Nixie, taking a few extra minutes to gaze at her. "You," he said, his English slow, "You did this." His hand swept across the group of them. "Brought these people."

Nixie was solemn as she gazed back at him, then she winked. "I brought Ian, too."

Ian spluttered but didn't deny it, laughing.

Don Thomas reached a hand out to Nixie. "Congratulations."

She blushed, but shook his hand before turning to Alice. "This is my mom, Alice Cameron."

Don Thomas' dark eyes reminded her of an older version of Don Carlo, sure and regal but yet still full of warmth and humor. Maybe it was an indigenous Mayan trait that Ian had picked up, too. Alice saw the sea and the sky in Don Thomas' eyes, even though they were brown rather than blue. It made her dizzy to be near him, and she breathed easier when he gave her a curt nod and turned his attention back to Ian.

The old shaman took Ian aside and spoke to him in low tones. Alice watched closely, interested, but still tapping her foot as time passed. Ever since he'd dropped down and startled them, she'd felt lighter, more split. As if his very presence made them no longer *heavy in this world*.

When Ian and Don Thomas stepped back toward the group, Ian looked at Alice. "I'm going to Tulum with him. He says time is so thin we can see it like it was."

Of course they could. Nixie had done it just yesterday. Alice frowned, suddenly feeling alone. "We need to get back."

Nixie bit her lip. "I can do it. I can get us back. You go on."

Ian laughed. "We will go back together. Don Thomas and I will drive to Tulum. After all, it's a full day's walk from here."

Alice blinked. "So you're going back to the cars with us?"

Don Thomas shook his head but said, "Yes."

She felt tension leak from tight muscles in her back and shoulders as he took off for the side of the road, the sun finally hot enough to make heat-shimmers on the road behind him. He turned around. "Come on."

Not heat-shimmers. The branch with Nixie's yellow hair-band wrapped around the end nearly brushed Don Thomas' head. Alice walked, certain this time that it was Don Thomas she followed through time rather than her daughter. The thought didn't bring as much comfort as she might have expected. Now that the adventure—this part of the adventure—was over, the strangeness of the whole thing hit her and she clutched Nixie's hand as they walked, her senses searching for any shift as they moved from now to now.

She turned around after they went through, looking back for Peter and Oriana. They seemed caught in a tunnel, the white road behind them, first clear, then fuzzy. As they passed the hair-band, the jungle was simply there, the broken stones and rusted railroad testament to when they all were.

In spite of her need to hurry, Alice called, "Wait!" and raced back by the yellow marker, passing it, moving fast. She only stopped when she nearly tripped on the old broken road. She looked up and down. Everything here was from now. She wanted to scream for joy, but settled for doing a few more dance steps like the ones she and Ian had done on the old sacbe.

Nixie retrieved her hair band and shoved it in her pocket.

It seemed to take only moments to get back to the tourist village and Ian's jeep. A beat-up rusty brown VW bug with Mexican plates was tucked beside the jeep.

No one came to greet them. Maybe they still slept, or were out. Alice glanced down at her phone, now ringed with icons for news and weather and GPS satellites.

It was 7:00 am or AM. She had promised to be in Cancun at 8:30, which meant she'd be late. Her brain was filling itself with the comforting logistics of clear tasks. Shower. Get her car. A meeting with the Secret Service goons to prepare for Marie and a talk at another conference. She had been nervous about it, and now it seemed normal, small, and comforting. She laughed.

Ian stepped over near her, really quite close. "Take the jeep. You can leave it in the lot at your complex. Oriana can stay there with Nixie."

She didn't want him to leave; maybe she'd worry. But there was no place for him in her day, either. "You're really going back?"

He nodded. "How could I not? We need to figure out what's happening, right?"

She nodded. It wasn't as if it were her choice.

He leaned down so close she felt the soft brush of his hair against her ear. "You'll be all right?"

"How do I know? Is anything going to be all right? Are you going to be all right?" She glanced over at Don Thomas. "Can he get you there and back? And when will I see you again?"

Ian grinned and leaned even closer, pulling her into him, covering her lips with his. She stiffened, and then his hands caressed her back and she gave in, too off balance to resist. His lips were warm and she was suddenly hungry for him, returning the kiss. It felt like fire and heat and food, like losing herself. She hadn't kissed, not like this, not in years.

When he pushed gently away a few moments later, her eyes felt damp and her center warm. As he gazed at her, she laughed at the sparkle of mischief in his eyes. "Take care of yourself."

He turned away from her, toward Don Thomas.

She glanced over to find Nix had her camera up to her face, laughing and blushing. She looked pleased. Alice frowned, her cheeks suddenly hot.

Behind her, Ian said, "Peter? You coming with me?"

And then Don Thomas, Peter and Ian were folding themselves into the tiny old beetle, Ian in the driver's seat, Don Thomas beside him, and Peter in the back with his head bowed a little so he would fit. The car started up with a chugging rattle.

Ian held a hand out the window, signaling, "After you," and she scrambled into the jeep, noting that Oriana and Nixie were both in the back seats, seatbelts on, ready.

She pulled out and preceded Don Thomas down the bumpy road toward the *Real Mayans Here* sign. She felt like singing.

CHAPTER 25

Ah K'in'ca spilled color slowly into the jungle. Ah Bahlam's legs burned, his lungs burned. The cut on his calf had split open again partway through the run. Not as badly as the first night, but warm runnels of blood dripped down his ankle. They had sprinted all night, the jaguar's footsteps soft behind them, pacing them. He felt its great energy, its body, its potency, and the power of its yellow eyes, all lending him strength and surefootedness.

Hun Kan ran ahead of him, shifting from dark ghost to girl in the growing light. They followed the bare footsteps of herders and herds down a well-used trail. From time to time, a breeze blew in the fire-scent of town and the faint, welcome aroma of goats.

The jaguar's steps faded from his hearing and then the morning sky was split by a single, chilling, full-throated roar. Ah Bahlam caught Hun Kan and whispered with broken breath. "It is no longer needed. We are nearly home."

She smiled, but did not reply.

"It will guard our path." His legs faltered, and he began to lurch as much as run.

Hun Kan pulled ahead again, called to him. "Follow me!"

They ran up over a low rise. Animal pens and fields stretched out in a large cleared area. One of the roving villages that ringed Chichén, people who cut swathes through the jungle, farmed a spot for two years, and moved on, but stayed close. The people he saw now all lived inside the circle of safety promised by the Lords of Itzá.

Home.

He had not been so close since the day after the last winter solstice. He hadn't missed it, but now he ached to see his parents, his brother and sisters, his teachers, even the family servants.

A small boy out with five goats turned toward them and held up his short spear as they approached. Ah Bahlam laughed. They must be a strange sight. Hun Kan's hair was loose and awry, her ceremonial travel dress rumpled, stained, and ripped. He was dressed like a warrior who had been fighting, and bloody to boot. They both breathed hard from their long run.

He patted his shoulder and Julu flew down, landing with a thunk. He reached a hand up and the bird gently took his fingers in his beak, giving him a greeting.

The boy stared at them, assessing.

Ah Bahlam thought he might run, but instead he handed his water-skin over to them solemnly, as if this were the most serious moment of his short life. Good for the boy. He recognized them as belonging here, seeing through the outside disorder to the cut of their clothes and the slope of their foreheads. Julu, of course, might also have impressed the boy. Quetzals came from higher and wetter jungles far away from Chichén, and only families with power and wealth could trade for them.

Hun Kan took the water skin from the boy's outstretched and shaking hand, and drank. He noted the way her jaw moved, the aristocratic tilt of her slender neck. He and his Way had helped bring her home, helped keep her safe. *Thank you, Feathered Serpent and Jaguar God for bringing her home safely.*

She noticed his gaze and passed him the skin. He drank deeply, handing it back to the boy with a sip of water left in it. "Thank you," he said as the boy's small hand closed around the mouth of the vessel.

The boy nodded. "Is there going to be a war?"

Ah Bahlam thought about the hundreds of men he had seen in the jungle. Not enough to take Chichén, not even close. But they must have some kind of plan, and he had not learned anything about what it was. "Perhaps. Run and tell your village to post watches, and to keep their spears near them."

The boy started to turn, but Hun Kan placed a hand on his shoulder. "First, which is the fastest way to Chichén?"

He pointed at an angle from the path they were on. "That way. Go up here and turn onto the wide path and then don't leave it until you cross the sacbe."

Hun Kan smiled at him. "Go."

He went, opposite the way he had sent them.

Refreshed by the water, Ah Bahlam and Hun Kan ran on. They came upon three small huts that looked deserted for the day, but generally lived in.

Hun Kan made use of their well, drinking, cleaning her face and hands and then washing Ah Bahlam's leg and opened cut. She tore a strip from her dress to bind it with. "Will you tell them about Ni-ixie?"

Of course he would. "Why do you ask?"

She pressed leaves against his cut. "They will barely believe we saw so many people-of-unrest in one place. Who will believe in a girl with skin the color of sand and hair the color of the sun? One who is and is not a goddess?"

"Perhaps that part is a story for the priests. They'll know if she is a goddess or not." He raked his hand gently through her tangled hair. "I don't understand how Ni-ixie fits in with the bandits and the people we saw, but there were enough warriors to hurt Chichén. They are the most important story we bring. That part must be told first."

"We should hurry. The ball game is the day after tomorrow. And we are a day late."

The festival would already be starting. The huts around them were probably empty for that very reason. During festivals, people took their harvests and tribute in, trading goods for goods, playing music, praying. Dancing. Only the elite would actually see the game itself, but Chichén would overflow with people for the next four days. "We must get there soon so they can increase the guards before they all start drinking too much balché."

She laughed softly. "They will protect us even if they do drink balche."

As soon as they reached even the outskirts, he might be separated from Hun Kan. They came from different families, and would have duties. Perhaps they could stay together long enough to report on what they had seen, but no matter what happened, this might be his last quiet moment with her.

She finished tying the binding around his leg and, still kneeling, looked up at him. Her eyes were warm and brown, tender. "Thank you," she said simply.

He reached down and touched her face again, like when he had brushed away her tears after Nimah's sacrifice. She leaned in, her warm cheek pressed against his palm. He inclined his head and swallowed hard, wanting long moments with her. "We came home together," he said. "You helped me."

"And you me." Julu chattered at him from above. A rabbit stirred the underbrush. Hun Kan's hand was warm and small in his.

Their duty mattered.

He pulled his hand away gently and offered it to her, helping her stand. "We must go."

She nodded. He sensed she wanted to delay their homecoming as much as he, to stop and freeze time and be together. But that was a path with no honor, and they had not lost that in the year they studied at Zama. So they continued toward Chichén, finding the sacbe only a few hundred steps past the huts. They bowed their heads as they came onto the sacred white road again, and reached for each other's hands, squeezing them together.

He spoke in the voice he reserved for addressing the gods. "Thank you for keeping us safe. May we speak with your voices to the people of Chichén so that we may join with you and bring good luck."

Hun Kan squeezed his hand one more time, hard, and released it, separating a little from him. They broke into the ground-eating jog of warriors. They ran easily on the even road, passing the scattered homes of healers, artists, pottery-makers, and then small animal farmers, serving both the wandering villages and the city. And finally, they neared the city itself: the minor lords, the leaders of warriors, the builders, the merchants who traded for feathers and jade and amber and fine art from afar, and the weavers of fine clothes.

They began to see other people from time to time on the white road, but the urge to get home drove them past.

At the point where the great walls and the tops of the temples rose from the jungle, bright and full of power, Ah Bahlam stopped. He had been glad to leave. The simplicity of the months in Zama, the simple hard study, the nights talking with Cauac or the other teachers, or sitting with his now-dead friends were behind him. The power and complexity of the city called to him. All that mattered in the world was decided here.

Hun Kan stood beside him, also looking. She had cried at the idea of coming home, but had run beside him all the way. Sweat glistened on her forehead and shoulders, the back of her hands. They both breathed hard, the scent of exhaustion seeping from them. As one, they started running again.

Because of their news, they passed their homes and went on to the gates of the city, clogged by a crowd making their way in for the second festival day. People gave them room, perhaps seeing their disheveled state and reading the determination in their eyes.

Inside the gate, they pushed through merchants setting up stalls under a high thatched roof held up by great stone columns more than twice Ah Bahlam's height. Colorful banners hung from the wooden roof supports. Artisans laid out pottery vessels made locally and carved jade brought in from far away by the salt trade. Some of the best booths held intricate mosaics, while others displayed simple clay figurines of various Ways: rabbit, peccary, macaw, jaguar, and deer. He and Hun Kan returned the greetings of merchants they had acquired goods from in years past.

Finally, they stood in front of the Temple of Warriors. The imposing roof held carved statues along the top and reliefs of K'uk'ulkan. He gave silent homage, his head raised. The power of the god stole the breath from his stomach. He waited, gazing fixedly and quietly, Hun Kan beside him, until he felt full of the god. With a strong shrug of his shoulder, he sent his bird off and used hand signs to tell it to wait.

His body wanted to collapse. But first, they must tell their stories.

Hun Kan turned to look up at him, apprehension showing in her eyes. This was not a place women normally entered, but she was part of the story they had to tell.

Inside, light poured through small windows and illuminated the center of the room. Murals of old battles looked down on four men who sat on small stone benches in the shadows.

The Chief of War, a small but very fast man who had proven himself in battle at the age of ten. Ah Beh, the man responsible for organizing all festivals. Beside him, the High Priest of the Feathered Serpent: the spiritual heart of the community.

It took a moment to decipher the familiar features of the fourth man, who sat mostly in shadow. His uncle, Hunapa.

The men were so wrapped in quiet conversation that they didn't notice Hun Kan or Ah Bahlam for a few breaths. Hunapa looked up first, and cried out, racing to Ah Bahlam's side and grabbing his arm, giving it a hard squeeze. He stalked around him, looking carefully, as if he hadn't seen him just last spring. "You live!"

Ah Bahlam grinned, suddenly understanding. "Yes, uncle. We two live."

"Ah K'in'ca said that all of you died, and your family mourns you." He glanced at Hun Kan. "You, also."

Ah Bahlam understood. Ah K'in'ca must have escaped also, and run back along the road. "We got away near the end of a battle. Many people-of-unrest attacked us. Four or five twenties at least. More than we could hold off. I saw most of us die, and then later, later we witnessed the heart of Nimah bless their cause."

His uncle put a hand up. "Let me send a messenger to tell your father he is lucky." He went to the door and called a small boy who had been squatting outside, giving him instructions. Then he stood, ushering Ah Bahlam and Hun Kan onto a spot on the benches and handing them his water skin. Grateful, they drank. Hunapa's voice and facial expression were formal and serious, as if simply being in this place was a serious matter. Perhaps it was. Ah Bahlam had been here twice with his father as part of his education, but never during a meeting. Hunapa said, "I am pleased you live. Sit. We must hear your story, but quickly. There is more news than yours surrounding this day."

Ah Bahlam licked his lips and looked around the small space. The War Priest was painted and masked, which should not happen until the ball game the day after tomorrow. The stiff air inside the room felt serious and heavy. He told of their journey, and of seeing the great crowd of warriors less than a day's run from Chichén. Here, the War Priest stopped him and questioned both him and Hun Kan. His mask hid his eyes, but Ah Bahlam watched his mouth grow thinner and angrier, and the lines of concern around his cheeks grow deeper. All of them winced and moaned at the loss of Nimah, and the evil power that her death may have given to Chichén's enemies.

When they finished, Ah Bahlam asked, "What other news?"

Hunapa answered him. "Three outlying towns refused to pay tribute in builders or goods, and three more have been attacked. We believe the towns that refused to pay tribute helped the people-of-unrest attack the three towns that stayed loyal."

Ah Bahlam swallowed, but remained silent. This was outright revolt. The power of the Itzá was waning, more than his worst fears. "Perhaps this year's celebration will bring rainfall, and a year of good crops," he said, keeping his voice neutral.

The War Priest nodded. "You need rest."

A dismissal. He glanced at Hun Kan, sure she read the question on his eyes. Her small face was resolute, as always. Fearless. She nodded, telling him yes, they should mention Ni-ixie, and then before he could speak, she did, her voice clear. "There is more to tell you. Before we left, at Zama, we were visited by . . . ." she hesitated, "by a spirit. I do not know if she was a goddess." She glanced over at Ah Bahlam. "Cauac thinks so, but I do not."

The War Priest glared at her as if she should not have any thoughts different than Cauac's.

Hun Kan ignored him and continued. "She appeared as a young girl, with hair as yellow as K'inich A'haw's, and skin as pale as the mist in the morning or as sand."

The War Priest stood straighter. He glanced back at the High Priest of K'uk'ulkan, who nodded. "Tell us. Quickly."

First Ah Bahlam and then Hun Kan told their stories of meeting Ni-ixie, and Hun Kan shared how she learned the girl's name, and what Cauac had said. She recounted the bloodletting to nods of approval.

The High Priest of K'uk'ulkan moved in closer as they spoke. He also wore a mask, but his dark eyes were visible though the blue and green feathers that surrounded them. They grew hard and cold, and while Ah Bahlam did know the man well enough to read him well, he sensed distrust.

Hun Kan must have felt the same. She shrank a bit into the wall, as if needing some space between her energy and his.

As soon as Hun Kan finished, The High Priest stood up, intimidating in his finery, his legs and back straight. He smiled, the jade inlays in his teeth showing beneath his mask. His arms were folded across his chest. "This is a very difficult story to believe. If . . . if this person you saw is a goddess, why show herself to you and not to Cauac, Ah K'an, K'ahtum, or the other Priests or wise women of Zama? Why to some child?"

Hun Kan's voice trembled but her chin and gaze remained firm. "We do not know. Nor do we know why we were saved and brought home and the others were not."

Hunapa smiled. "Perhaps my nephew is a good warrior and a good man."

Ah Bahlam warmed; he had received more admonishments than praise from his uncle as he was growing up. He spoke up. "Hun Kan was also brave and good in the jungle. We both contributed to the success of our journey." They hadn't mentioned the jaguar, since he knew his uncle had trouble calling his own Way, the peccary.

The High Priest glared at Ah Bahlam. "Can you produce this woman? Perhaps your Ni-ixie is simply one of those people born with no color, or came down from the north. I have heard rumors that some people in the north have light brown hair."

Hun Kan's hands moved in her lap, twisting at the leather on her wrist. Ah Bahlam understood, and fished for the pouch that held the strange leaves Ni-ixie had given him the day she blessed the cenote. Hun Kan beat him to it, and stood, holding her hand over her head so her wrist met a beam of light coming in one of the square windows. The band around it glowed a brilliant blue, drawing the eyes of everyone in the room.

The High Priest walked around her, stalking her wrist like a cat. He held a hand out and touched the band. A finger traced the strange round button with symbols on it. His face held puzzlement, and a little bit of anger, perhaps at proof positive that Ni-ixie must be something outside of the normal, that in fact, she had visited these two and not him. Ah Bahlam struggled not to see the look as petty. This man spoke to the gods better than he did.

Perhaps.

The last few years had not been good for Chichén. Ah Bahlam filed the thought away, shocked at any idea that the High Priest might not be capable. It was death to say such a thing, and perhaps death to think it.

The High Priest held out his hand. "Let me hold the gift."

Hun Kan shook her head. "I cannot remove it. I have tried." She laid her wrist in his hand, shaking, her eyes wide.

He licked his lips and shifted his weight, watching the priest turn the band in circles around her wrist. The priest looked puzzled, but curious. He tried pulling the band over the heel of Hun Kan's palm. It did not go. It didn't even stretch. Puzzlement gave way to frustration. He spoke words over the band. It didn't budge. He hissed, "What did this Ni-ixie mean to say to us through this?" He glanced at the other men in the room, receiving a blank stare from Hunapa, and a hurry-up look from the War Priest. Ah Beh watched the High Priest and Hun Kan with a focused, curious gaze.

The priest's lips were drawn tight with determination. He rubbed oil on Hun Kan's wrist and tried once more to pull the band from her. He twisted each small section as if checking to see if the material would rip.

Hun Kan sat still and stoic, except for a slight extra rounding of her eyes and a tremble in her chin.

Ah Beh cleared his throat. "Perhaps it was truly given to *her*," he said dryly, his tone so disparaging that Ah Bahlam jumped. The High Priest of K'uk'ulkan snarled under his breath, but stepped back.

He called out, and the two men guarding the doorway came in.

"Take her to my temple," he said.

Hun Kan threw her hand over her mouth, covering up her instinctive call of "no," so it sounded like a muffled cough. In the temple, she would be at the mercy of the High Priest, with no one watching over her.

Ah Bahlam glanced at his uncle for help. Hunapa's eyes met his, containing understanding, but Hunapa shook his head in warning.

The men closed on Hun Kan, taking her arms gently.

She hung her head but didn't fight. Before they turned her to take her out of the door, she raised her head and her eyes bored into Ah Bahlam, pleading.

He should obey Hunapa. But he could not. He stood up, looking the High Priest of K'uk'ulkan in the eyes, defying him. "Leave her free. She has fought hard and run hard to come home. Let her see her family."

Behind him, his uncle gasped.

The priest snarled at him, and Ah Bahlam stepped back. He kept his gaze on the High Priest, feeling for his Way. The jaguar answered him, filling him until Ah Bahlam could feel it inside the room, a presence. He was sure the jaguar's wildness shone from his eyes.

The High Priest took a step closer to him.

No words came. It was unthinkable to challenge the High Priest even though he wanted that more than breath. Without the ability to challenge, there were no words.

Deep inside the priest's eyes a brightness glowed, gods or madness or both. Ah Bahlam trembled, fought for breath.

The priest moved toward him again.

Ah Bahlam dropped his gaze.

When he looked up, he saw the back of Hun Kan as she was led away, her head bowed. It took every bit of self-control he had not to scream.

CHAPTER 26

Nixie and Oriana had no specific instructions. Her mom had rushed off in a worried flurry, brushing her wet hair and throwing a quick, "I'll call you," over her shoulder as she flew out the door.

Bright sun shone on the paths outside their window, and even though it was still breakfast time, the cheerful sounds of children in the pool already wafted in the open window. Nixie grinned. "Let's go eat by the beach. They have the best breakfast there, and then we can make sand castles and maybe swim."

Oriana yawned. "Aren't you tired?"

"Aren't you hungry?" Nixie replied. She rushed to put on her bathing suit, pulling a gold sundress over the suit and sliding white sandals onto her feet. She returned to the main room and sat on her mom's bed, holding Snake.

Oriana blinked at her, then went to the sink and splashed water on her face. "All right."

Twenty minutes later, they stood in line by the thatch-covered buffet restaurant, waiting to be seated. Nixie asked the small dark-haired waitress for a table over the water, which earned them an additional wait, but as they sat down Oriana looked happier than she had so far this morning. The clear bay that served as a swimming beach washed gently against the pilings just below them. The deck chairs and umbrellas were already half full of visitors sitting in wooden Adirondack chairs and reading, or laying face down on chaise lounges, showing already-red skin to the sun. Unlike in the States, even the morning sun burned here, and Nixie felt in her pocket for her sunscreen.

Children played on the white sand or waded in the clear Caribbean-blue water.

They filled their plates with fruit and small Mexican cakes, and Oriana got herself two cups of coffee at once. Nixie laughed at her, and got two glasses of juice.

When they got to the table, Oriana took a big gulp of coffee and leaned in close to Nixie. "Are you okay?"

Nixie nodded. "Of course. This doesn't scare me much." Oriana had laughed with her before they went to sleep, giggling at the memory of Peter and his computer. She wrinkled her eyebrows. "You were having fun, weren't you?"

Oriana gave a little half-smile that only partly touched her eyes. "I was. It just seems weird now. Like being here is suddenly—not certain."

"I've felt the same way ever since the second time."

"Not the first time?"

"Well, I didn't know what was happening. But what about you? You look . . . tired."

Oriana looked out over the water. "I didn't sleep much. I kept thinking about how I love the sea and the wild and the jungle. How I love diving in the caves. Being out there. I've always thought I was a nature girl, you know?" She shook her head. "Maybe not. I've never been someplace I couldn't see or hear anything that wasn't modern before. I thought I had, but I've learned differently."

"Yeah, I get that." Nixie looked out over the sun-sparkled water. "But what about seeing the old places new? I mean, I guess you didn't really, except the road. But you should have seen Tulum all painted and pretty. Like a new house, or something. Like it breathed then, but it doesn't now. Or now it just breathes out old dreams."

"Anybody ever tell you you're really smart for a kid?"

Nixie laughed. "Sometimes." She picked up one of her glasses of orange juice. "I'm hungry like one, too." As she dug into her breakfast, she thought about the things that weren't in the past. Hun Kan never got to eat at a restaurant or stay in a resort, or fly on an airplane. How weird was that?

The clear voice of a young girl called from the beach. "Look Mom! A turtle!"

Nixie craned her neck. A small girl, maybe five, and her slightly older brother stood knee-deep, looking down at the water where a smallish turtle swam toward them. Because they were above it, Nixie could see the turtle's four legs and long-stretched-out neck. A woman who must be their mom came down to see, and held her hand over her mouth.

Cries of "Turtle!" and "Another one!" and "There!" began to rise up from all along the little cove. Nixie stood and leaned over the balcony. She could see at least seven of them, none much bigger than her foot.

"Wow." Oriana shaded her eyes with her hand and stared at the turtles. "Green turtles. They're not hatchlings, they're too big. That's really weird."

Nixie leaned further out.

"Careful," Oriana cautioned. "Don't fall in."

"You're right!" Nixie abandoned the rest of her breakfast and headed for the walkway to the beach, almost knocking the tray out of a thin blonde woman's hand.

"Wait!" Oriana called.

Nixie didn't stop. When she looked back, Oriana followed, a cup of coffee in one hand and a pastry in the other. They weren't supposed to take food out of the restaurant, but Oriana was an adult. Besides, no one would notice. People who had been in line for tables were breaking away and walking down to the sand, craning their necks. Nixie slid quickly through the crowd. She kicked off her sandals and threw them on an empty wooden chair.

The warm water welcomed her. She stopped with both her feet in, surrounded by the cries of children and the savory scent of warm salt water. She settled into it all, absorbing it. Although she was clearly here, now, the air tasted like the past, clean and healthy.

Nixie lifted her chin and walked out past the littlest children. She stopped for the first turtle she saw, stroking its back with her forefinger. It was softer than the big one she'd swum with in Tulum, the way the top of a baby's head is soft. She smiled at it. "Hello, little one," she murmured.

She went on, walking out on the soft sand, small turtles swimming up to her, kissing her calves. The turtles bunched around her legs until the water was brown and green with them. She looked toward where the sea ran into the protected cove, hoping to find her bigger turtle, but it wasn't there. Only small ones, maybe hundreds of small ones.

She didn't look back until she got far enough out for the water to stick the tips of her hair together and weigh down her unruly curls. She still wore her dress, soaked past the waist now. She turned and floated, surrounded by turtles.

The lifeguard was calling to people, "Protect the turtles. You can see them from the beach. Come on out."

Nixie ignored him. Turtles surrounded her, a song of beings. There were so many she couldn't turn. She floated on turtles. It felt . . . peaceful. Easy.

The lifeguard pointed at Nixie. "You, in the dress!"

A male voice called out, "No! Let me get a picture!" She looked up to see a well-dressed man with sandy hair leaning over the balcony almost right where she and Oriana had been eating. He noticed her glance and called back, "Don't look at me. Look at the sky, or the turtles, anything."

She turned surprised eyes on him.

"No!" he said to her, mouthing the word as much as saying it. "Forget I'm here. Please?"

Well, she was a photographer. She usually wasn't the subject, but she understood what he wanted. She gave it to him, falling into the moment and forgetting him so she'd be the perfect subject, unaware entirely of the camera like her mom when she took the picture of her and Ian kissing. The thought made her giggle and she stifled it, clamping her mouth shut to keep from inhaling water.

She relaxed, feeling the sea, the warm sunshine on her face, her dress floating around her, her legs and arms mixed in with turtles, fingers caressing them while they kissed her. They tickled, making her laugh. Some were no bigger than her palm, and the biggest only the size of her head.

They had come for her. "Why?" she asked them silently, knowing they didn't need words. She'd seen reliefs of turtles carved into stones, gods climbing from their backs. But she was a little girl and these turtles were too small to hold gods. "Why?" she repeated.

The turtles bumped her gently, and for a moment it felt as if she floated on them instead of in the sea, that she could rise up on the backs of tiny turtles as if she were a cloud.

The turtles didn't answer her except by staying with her, and she took deep slow breaths, letting herself go, feeling them bump gently against her sides, their feet stroking her as they swam, as if she were one of them and caused them no fear at all. It felt as if she and the turtles, and the warm sea and the sunshine on all of them was the whole world.

Oriana's voice distinguished itself from the background noise. "Leave her be. She's okay." Nixie heard the calls of people on the beach, some afraid for her, some in awe. The children were merely curious and hopeful.

The next time Oriana's voice was closer. "Nixie. Come in. Before you turn to a prune or get us kicked out."

Nixie carefully asked her legs to sink, slowly, so she wouldn't step on any turtles. Oriana waded slowly close to Nixie. She held a hand out and Nixie took it. "Are they all here?" Nixie asked. "All around me?"

Oriana laughed. She seemed translucent in the bright light, like an angel. "Almost. Some are just swimming around."

"Are they visiting the other kids?"

Oriana pursed her lips, holding back another laugh, maybe trying to hold onto being the adult guardian. "If you come in, they might."

"Just a minute." Nixie sighed. "Here, Oriana. Help me figure out what they're saying."

Oriana spluttered, finally letting the laugh out. "They're saying you cost me a cup of coffee."

"No really. Just stop."

Oriana did, and Nixie stood completely still and let the turtles surround her. They seemed to be saying *Look at me. I'm alive. I'm greeting you. I'm here for you. You. You. Pay attention to us, to the world, to the magic. You pay attention. You.*

Nixie grinned. She didn't understand in any way she could say, but a gift had been passed to her. She ducked her head underwater and whispered, "Thank you," her words bubbles that broke into the sunshine and clear air above. She looked at Oriana. "Pull me?"

Oriana obliged, pulling her toward the shore carefully, the turtles a river behind her, following.

Sure enough, when Nixie and Oriana stood back on the shore, the turtles began to swim in ones and twos, greeting the little children.

Nixie stood on the beach, watching, for almost half an hour. Soon there were fewer turtles, then fewer again, then the cove was empty of them and the lifeguard called, "All in who want to go. Be careful."

CHAPTER 27

Alice stood on the sidewalk outside of the Cancun Marriott with Don Carlo. The endless sounds of engines and machinery and people in a modern city felt jarring after her long quiet night. The Secret Service interview hadn't helped, either. What the heck did her second-grade teacher have to do with anything? "Wow," she said. "That was tough."

Don Carlo nodded, but said, "It wasn't too bad." He'd been through it the previous day, when Alice canceled, and somehow she suspected the security goons had been even harder on him. Damn good thing he was an American citizen, or he might not have been approved at all.

It had vaguely surprised her that no one had asked about the day before. Maybe she should be glad they were busy interrogating Don Carlos then. Direct access to the Director of the Office of Science and Technology Policy, and maybe even the president, not to mention other world leaders, came at a high price. She knew way too much protocol now. Don't touch. Don't speak unless spoken to, or as part of her tour guide job. Don't bring up her own views unless asked. Don't talk to reporters before or after the visit. Show up a half-hour early so you can be frisked completely. She'd bet dinner that diplomats didn't have to go through that, although surely they were more actual threat than simple scientists like her and rich do-gooders like Don Carlo.

Rich do-gooder or not, she was glad to see him. "Coffee?"

His voice was soft. "I'd like that."

"Let's get over to the Gran Caribe," Alice said. "I won't have to worry about being late." As it was, she wouldn't have time to go over her notes.

"Of course."

It took twenty minutes to get there and park, so they bought lattes from the lobby bar and sat in big, soft tan couches under bright skylights. As soon as they were settled, Don Carlo cocked his head at her, curiosity shining through his placid gaze. "What happened yesterday?"

"Something came up that I had to do. A . . . friend needed help."

He seemed willing to accept her lack of information. "Thanks for getting me included."

Actually, if the world were fair, the Mayans would be inviting her. She swallowed. "I'm a little nervous. It seems like such a responsibility."

"You'll do fine. You really are good with people."

Well, she'd learned to get along with the native Mexicans, to be polite and dress modestly, and ask instead of demand. But that was completely different. "What if I say something stupid? Or don't say something I should say?"

"You'll do fine," he repeated.

Or I miss the whole thing because Nixie or I or both of us decide to go time traveling? "Don Carlo?"

He waited.

"Do you . . . what do the Mayans think about time?"

He blinked at her and licked his lips. He was never quick to respond to questions, but he hesitated more than usual. Or was she making that up? Eventually, he said, "They studied time. You know that. They thought this time, our time, is important. You know that, too."

She felt a hand on her shoulder from behind and looked up to find Steven standing there. "Hello."

"Look, a miracle has occurred. They're running a few minutes early. You should go now to get set up for your talk."

Frustrated, she spread her hands apologetically toward Don Carlo. "This is Dr. Steven Blake, one of my old teachers." After Don Carlo nodded a hello, she asked him, "Will you come hear my talk?" After all, he'd helped her get the funding for it.

But he shook his head. "I have a class to teach." He smiled at her. "Good luck."

She followed Steven to the Baile Plaza Room where the lectures were being held. She'd clipped a printed picture of Nixie's shot of Tulum in color into her papers. Maybe Steven was the right person to give her perspective. "Can you meet me after the talk? Just for a few minutes?"

He slowed down and turned around, a big grin on his face. "Sure. If you tell me what you know about the turtles. That was Nixie, wasn't it?"

"What turtles?"

"Really? You didn't see the picture? She's all over the Internet. Search for 'Turtle Girl.'"

Alice fumbled with her phone. Steven must have seen her frustrated look because he said, "We'll pull it up on the presentation screen."

Well, that would be private. Not.

The conference was on a break. Nearly half the crowd stood by the wall-sized screens, pointing. As soon as she saw the two huge twin images, Alice drew in a sharp breath. Nixie. Twenty-feet tall in the projections, laughing, floating in the water in her good gold dress, surrounded by thousands of turtles. A professional quality picture, every golden hair on Nixie's head visible, the turtles so clear their claws and tiny tails could be seen, the wet dress clinging to Nixie's hips so she looked like a sixteen-year-old-goddess instead of an eleven-year-old girl.

Damn.

Alice was going to kill her for going in the water in that dress. No, she wasn't. At least it was in this time. Damn it. She tried to keep Nixie out of pictures and off the nets. Safer that way. Damn.

"You're gaping," Steven said.

She breathed out slowly, unable to tear her eyes away from Nixie's bigger-than-life features, the pure joy the photographer had captured on her face. A spiritual joy, as if Nix were a water nymph instead of a girl. My god, her baby. On display for the whole world. "You're right. It's Nixie."

"You didn't know about it?" Steven prodded. "It's an AP photograph—all over the world in thirty seconds."

She bet the photographer uploaded it right from the spot. Didn't they need permission for that? Her voice shook. "Is there more?"

"There's a story with it. And some tourist's grainy YouTube video from a bad angle. But you'd better get your presentation loaded up."

She turned the external display off before shoving the USB drive into a free port and starting the copy. While she waited, her fingers flew across the keyboard bringing up major news sites. Nixie was on all of them, one of those weird stories that gets the world's attention for thirty seconds. In this case, because of the picture, and the heading "Turtle Girl." The story itself was simple:

This morning, a flood of turtles approached a hotel beach near Xcaret on the Mayan Riviera coast. They seem to have come to see young Nixie Cameron, and gathered around her for a half hour. Soon after Nixie left the water, the turtles disappeared. Local naturalists have no explanation. Some people are tying the strange visitation to the impending end of the Mayan calendar.

Below the article, streams of comments had already shown up. There was no time to read them—the conference moderator was already calling people back to their seats. But she could imagine what they said: a sign of the times, a portent. How pretty Nixie looked, how nearly magical. People were probably seeing the Virgin Mary in her daughter.

To hell with the crowd. Alice turned around, put her back to the room full of people, and called Oriana. "Is everything okay?"

Oriana answered almost immediately, her words coming fast and furious. "I'm sorry. I don't know how that happened. The man asked someone, it wasn't even me, for permission, and the story was on the television before we got back to the room."

"All right. Stay inside. Download Nixie's pictures from last night or something."

Oriana hesitated. "We can't stay. We're packing. There's reporters banging on the door. The hotel is sending someone to pick us up in a cart and take us someplace they can secure."

Damn. They should have just stayed packed. She couldn't deal with it now. "Just keep her safe," Alice hissed as the moderator started to introduce her.

Turning to look at the crowd she froze. She wasn't ready. She'd prepared, but the last week felt like a year.

She took two deep breaths, letting a long silence fall before starting. Three or four sentences into her talk, she hit her stride, focusing on Mayans and Venus, Venus' position in the sky now and when the Long Count calendar was created. A half-hour of excruciating detail, smiling at people when she really wanted to bolt away from the wooden podium and run home.

She took three questions, giving short answers but at least making the crowd laugh once. There were still hands up in the audience, but she'd done enough. She could walk away and feel like she'd delivered.

The moderator held up a hand. "Just a few more questions?"

Alice nodded and took a sip of water to gain a moment of peace. A tall thin woman in a conservative blue dress in the back looked like the kind of questioner most people ignored.

Alice called on her.

"I saw the picture of your daughter with the turtles."

Alice stiffened.

"Three people swore they saw a family of quetzals at Xamen Ha yesterday and there's been reports of lights on top of the Temple of the Inscriptions at Palenque. Is all of this tied to the coming solstice, to the end of the calendar? Will it be the ending of this world or the beginning of a new one or both?"

The question skewered Alice in place. She stood there for so long the audience shifted uneasily. Whispers floated up from the seated crowd.

A week ago she would have said something like, "People see what they expect. And if they expect strange things, that's what they see. But that's not science. For science, we have to wait, and watch, and measure." She'd have had to bite her tongue to keep from saying it was all delusions. Now all she could croak out was "I don't know."

More hands went up. She shook her head. "I'm sorry, but we should leave time for the next speaker."

At least no one had the guts to mention there were fifteen more minutes scheduled for her presentation. As she walked away from the podium, she felt as if a tsunami were tumbling her carefully preserved academic life, pouring magic and fear onto the foundation of her very soul.

Steven trotted up to her and put a hand in the small of her back, guiding her through a door into an empty hallway. She was clutching her papers, and the Tulum picture, to her chest. "Wait," she said. "Just a minute?"

"Sure."

She stepped away, staying where she could see Steven, and called Oriana again. "Okay. I'm done with the talk. But how are things?"

Oriana laughed. "Fine. They took us to Xcaret and gave us a guard and tickets to swim with the dolphins. There's only so many people allowed in at a time, and we can't get mobbed. We put Nixie's hair in pigtails and changed her clothes, and the worst thing that's happened is a little kid came up and asked her if she was the turtle girl."

"What did she do?"

"She just looked at him and asked if he liked dolphins. When he said yes, she asked him to stay close to her when they swam."

The very Nixie reaction made Alice smile. It was an hour's drive back to the resort, but her hands shook with the need for food. "Are you okay for a few hours? I want to eat before I come back."

"We're fine. I've done this before. It's safe."

So had Alice. But not Nix. She'd love it. "I wish I were there. I'll be home in time for dinner. Thanks." She hesitated. "Did you hear from Ian?"

"No."

"All right, call me if you do." She closed the connection.

Steven's hand on her arm pulled her focus back to the Gran Caribe. "Is there someplace quiet we can go? Someplace to eat?"

Bless his soul, Steven led her out a back door and through the parking lot and into a smallish restaurant one block off the beaten path. "This place has the best empanadas in Cancun, and," he swept his arm around at mostly local patrons, "it's where the locals go."

Trust Steven to know about food. She never could figure out why he wasn't so fat you had to roll him down the street. But he wasn't. Except for a little belly that was as much from being old as eating, he looked good. He immediately ordered chips and bottled water, and virgin margaritas for them both, and had the common sense to wait until she ate enough to feel like she was back in her body. The way he watched her, she could tell he was waiting for her to start a conversation. "I didn't know about the turtles. But Nixie swam with one in Tulum a few days ago—said it was huge, though, as big as her."

He raised an eyebrow. "Big turtles are rare."

She licked at the salt on her glass. "So are hundreds of little ones in one place. But . . . hold on." She fished through her papers and found the picture Nixie had taken of Hun Kan, with her flat forehead, the beaded necklace, and the restored—no original—Temple of the Descending God. She pushed the picture across the table at Steven and waited, almost wishing that there was tequila in her margarita.

Steven looked at the picture for a long time, silent. When he looked up, he was very confused. "Where did you get this?"

"Nixie took it."

"When?"

The same day she swam with the big turtle at Tulum." She had to think about it. "Three days ago."

"That's the necklace you brought me day before yesterday. But who modeled it? Shaping the forehead like that is illegal now. I've never actually seen it."

Alice needed him to come to his own conclusion. She waited.

"You know it wasn't taken at Tulum. It couldn't have been." He raised his eyebrows. "Unless it was altered?" He sat back for a moment, holding the picture up to the light as if trying to see through it. "What about this lady who's watching Nixie? She was there this morning, too. She could be staging these things. This morning could have been staged, too."

Right. As if Oriana owned a turtle farm. She licked her lips and forced her hands to stop toying with her glass. "I don't think it was doctored," she said. "We don't have the software to do it at my hotel, not that well, and Oriana and Nixie didn't go anywhere." Why couldn't she just tell him what she'd experienced? *I dreamed about a battle in the time the sacbeobwere new and freshly-made, used as roads by wild Mayans. I traveled back in time. I found ants finishing off the bloody remains the next day. And I saw the stars the way the old Mayans saw them, a wheel of brightness the likes of which can't even exist in modern times.*

If their positions were reversed, she wouldn't believe herself. "A lot of strange things are happening. And a lot of them are happening to me."

He knew her fairly well, even after all these years. "But you believe this picture is real? That it's what, from some other place or some other time?"

She managed a small nod, but couldn't meet his eyes.

He sighed. When he spoke his voice was his old teacher's voice rather then her friend's, cool and professional. "Go home. You need to get some sleep. The next two days will be busy."

She needed him to believe. But his chin was set tight and his eyes cool and distant.

She understood.

He couldn't follow her down this path or he might become as crazy as she felt. Or as alone.

CHAPTER 28

Ah Bahlam woke to the scent of corn cakes. His belly swore it was the best smell in the world, better even than a woman or the sweat of mock battle. The thought brought back the stench of true blood and fear mixed with courage, the smell of real battle, the eyes of the High Priest and Hun Kan's pleading look. These things would have driven the hunger from him if his body didn't need food so badly.

He pushed himself up from the thin mat on the stone bench, swinging his legs onto the floor. He found his mother and two sisters just outside the door, watching over two kitchen slaves doing the hot work of baking corn cakes over fire-heated stones.

His mother smiled at him, her eyes warm and pleased. When he saw her earlier they had been red from tears of mourning, but she had not cried at his return, only held him.

She had held him a long time.

When she stepped back, his two younger sisters and one younger brother had leapt on him, clambering for news of his journey, of the fight. His mother had watched while he answered their hundreds of bird-like questions, and finally taken him and made him lie down, shooing his siblings off into the market, saying, "Go get something to sacrifice for the coming war and make us strong."

Now, he came up to her and kissed her. "Thank you for the rest."

"In a moment, you may have the first corn cake."

"Father is not home yet?" He had not been here when Ah Bahlam arrived, either.

"He's in the city."

It would be time to light the torches and small marking fires shortly. "I am pleased to be home." She was smaller than he was, smaller even than Hun Kan. It was something he had barely noticed before, and it saddened him a bit. Surely she was not yet old enough to shrink and so he must have grown. He touched her cheek gently, noticing even in the fading light that more gray showed now. "Has it been a hard year?"

"It is a good year that has brought you home alive." She gestured to the older of the two slaves. "Bring my son the first corn cake and pour him some bal balché che."

Ah Bahlam had eaten three corn cakes with avocado and fish by the time his father returned. When his father came in, he too, appeared smaller than

Ah Bahlam remembered. Still, he had to look up a bit to meet his eyes. "It's good to see you."

His father nodded, giving away his pleasure with his gaze. "I have been in the city meeting with Ah Beh and the War Chief."

"Will they increase the guard outside the city?"

His father smiled broadly, clapping him on the back and sitting down beside him. His mother brought him a plate herself, and then went back for one of her own. "The news is that my oldest son is home, and that he brought both news and mysteries. Yes, they'll increase the guard, and no, you don't have to go tonight. Tell me what has happened to you. I wish to hear it from your mouth."

Stars filled the sky by the time Ah Bahlam finished. His father had asked many questions, and his mother cried out when he spoke of Nimah's death. When he finished, his father swallowed and said, "You did well. Truly the gods brought you home to us."

Ah Bahlam inclined his head in respect, and the three of them watched the fire in silence for a long time. "The extra guards, will they be enough?"

His father shrugged. "The priests prepare additional sacrifices. Our warriors are stronger and better fed than theirs. If I knew how many, if any, will be brave enough to attack us, I could tell you how many of our men may die. But we will be enough."

Ah Bahlam sat back, watching the small fire in front of them. Because it had been so dry for so long, firewood was plentiful, and the flame burned brightly. "We will not be enough forever, Father. There are many people who depend on us, and yet we have not given them the water they need. We must do better this year."

"The gods give them what they need," his father said. "Or not. It is not us. That is a belief for little boys."

Ah Bahlam cringed, but continued. "And a belief the priests have spread widely. We had best hope that we can influence Chaac to send rain."

His father sighed. "We have all prayed to Chaac for three years. He appears to have turned his back on us. There are rumors that we need a king, and rumors that all of the priests should themselves be sacrificed, and rumors that Chichén will fall. It will not fall this year, and kings do more harm than good."

"But what about the priests, Father? I did not like what I saw in the high priest's eyes today when he looked at the gift from Ni-ixie. He looked like he felt Hun Kan is a threat to him."

"You'd best hope he does not think that. He is looking for sacrifices."

"I want to marry Hun Kan."

His father frowned and when he answered his eyes looked sad. "You may not get what you want."

"I can imagine a life with her, but I cannot imagine one with anyone else." Ah Bahlam looked into the fire. "For the first time today, I'm not sure that I should trust a priest."

His father put a hand on his shoulder. "Never speak such a thing where they can hear."

DECEMBER 20, 2012

CHAPTER 29

At 4:00 am, Alice was already sipping her second cup of coffee, staring out over the balcony of the new—and bigger—room the hotel had assigned her and Nixie as refuge for the turtle girl. Elite and private, it was near enough to the sea to hear waves washing on shore. Darkness still wrapped the world loosely; faint stars dusted the sky.

She scratched notes on a single sheet of hotel paper. A dream. Not a dream like the one that eventually led to the bead, but a normal dream. A dream with Ian in it, with his neat dreads and wild smile. Not a proper academic boyfriend. Not safe. A wild man, a force, a worry. In her dream, she had nestled beside him on the steps of an old temple, a gray and lifeless one from today, so generic it could have been a partly-restored-at-best small building at any of the sacred sites along the coast. Xel Ha, or even one of the ruins here at the resort, like the one Nixie walked through when the bird-man gave her the feather.

The stars in her dream had been now-stars, dull and lonely compared to the rich starlight of the old times. Would stars always look dull, now? Or would she forget?

She jotted a few words, "Ian," and "Alice," and "Nixie." Like a school girl. She glanced at the picture Nixie had snapped of her and Ian kissing. She'd found it propped up by the coffee pot, waiting to greet her when she turned it on. Nixie had framed the shot well. Both in near-profile, their lips locked. Ian's hand rested on her shoulder. She hadn't seen the picture until this morning, which was probably exactly what Nixie had meant to happen. A sticky note on it said, "Good luck." Maybe a wish for luck with Ian, maybe a wish for Ian, gone still, or a wish for Alice's day with Marie. Impossible to tell; Nix and Oriana were still fast asleep.

She forced herself back to the fading wisps of dream. She and Ian had talked the way conversations run in dreams, spinning from the feel of silk to the taste of green tea in Japan. A normal dream and a dream-normal conversation as much with herself as with Ian. Except she had smelled him, the sweaty, wild, jungle smell of him: limestone chalk and palm leaves and orchids and salt. Even now, she sniffed the air for some trace of him, as if he had truly been in her bedroom. But she only smelled the ocean.

It made her breath shallow and fast even to think about him.

If she could walk out in the wild now, walk the beach barefoot and watch the dawn, she would. Maybe it would center her, make it easier to think about Ian, or to see Marie, or to ponder the trip down the white road.

But what if she ended up in the wrong time and didn't make it to Chichén Itzá this morning? She wouldn't have Nixie or Don Thomas Arulo to help her. Best to stay someplace that couldn't be in both times, because it was only in this now. Like this room, on the second floor of a resort, filled with computers and televisions and machine-made clothes.

She wrote words on the paper in front of her. A quote she'd heard more than once, used a few times, but hadn't thought of directly before the words came out in blue ink all over the bottom of her paper under her scrawls about Ian. "Advanced technology is indistinguishable from magic."

She didn't believe in magic. In hope, yes. Like Ian believed in hope, like Nixie swimming with the turtles looked like hope. But hope wasn't magic, and whatever was happening wasn't either.

She wouldn't be herself any more if it was magic.

Would she?

By the time she finished her coffee, the stars had dulled in the firmament above her, and it was late enough to turn on the shower and think about getting ready, about starting early to make sure she was on time.

Alice drove all the way to Chichén Itzá, without even checking Nixie's GPS signal once. Whatever mystery engulfed them, Nixie rolled with it. She was scary-competent there. Something inside Alice had clicked over enough to trust Nix—oh, not to trust the world, not to trust what was happening, but to trust Nix. Still, she left the sound on her phone so she'd know if Nix called.

Or if Ian called.

At the gate, guards checked a list and her picture, radioed someone she couldn't quite hear, and then bowed and let her in.

She climbed the temple of K'uk'ulkan and sat at the top, feet barely touching the next stair. Below her, the decorated Temple of Warriors glowed with promise even though the morning was sultry and had grown overcast, the air thick with rain. Beginning tomorrow at dawn, there would be a market set up down there. A real one, where tourists rich enough or lucky enough to get in could spend money on a vague hope or a thing they didn't need.

For now, it was empty. Strings of Federales and American soldiers wandered in and out of the open places. Some of the Americans led dogs. She was too high up to tell the breeds, but as they stood their backs were near their handler's waists. Big dogs. Alice laughed, the sound slightly bitter. A conference about saving the world that needed bomb-sniffing dogs.

"Alice?" A soft voice, almost tentative.

She turned her head to see a tall slender woman with shoulder-length hair stride toward her. "Marie?"

"May I sit?"

Wow. "Are you here with no handlers?"

Marie shook her head. "They're nearby." She smiled wryly. "Sometimes they give me fifty feet of rope."

Good enough. Alice patted the hard stone next to her. She'd seen pictures and news articles and speeches, of course, but she remembered the college girl, a bit older than she was, a tad more beautiful. In those days they were both beautiful. It wasn't something they thought about. In Marie, beauty had been replaced by dignity and worry-lines. She now looked a decade older than Alice, older even than Alice of death and single parenthood and money-worries. Marie's hair was shoulder-length, and no longer the original color. Something redder and full of fake sun stripes: hair colored for the camera.

As Marie settled next to Alice, she gazed out of the same shockingly blue eyes Alice remembered from college coffee-houses, except now they were surrounded by thin wrinkles. Alice swallowed. "Thank you for asking me."

"I wanted to see you. After I got scheduled into the conference, I asked my advisers for a list of women scientists who studied the Mayan people. I saw your name." Marie hesitated. "I know I didn't bother to keep in touch, but I'm busy. You were always honest with me, and I don't know if anyone is anymore. So I asked for you."

Alice liked being remembered as honest. She was, she always had been, but since she didn't speak up that often, how would most people know?

Marie pushed the hair from her forehead. "Remember when we flummoxed Dr. Liebert? When we emailed his whole class bad instructions about the lab?" Alice laughed in spite of herself. The air in the lab had been so dense with smelly fog that everyone's clothes were soaked. "Remember his face?"

Marie giggled, and Alice joined her, reveling in an image of the laughter of the obscure scientist and the most politically important scientist in the world mingling and flowing down the steps of K'uk'ulkan. It carried so far on the wind that one of the soldiers below looked up and shook his or her closest neighbor, who did the same. Soon the whole line waved assault rifles in one hand. Their faces were brown and white flowers looking up.

Marie waved back. She picked up Alice's hand, asking her to wave, too. Alice grinned wryly, caught in a moment that wasn't hers. "They aren't waving to me."

"But you can still wave to them." Marie lifted Alice's arm above her head. "You can still appreciate them. Thank them for keeping you safe."

Alice waved. She blushed. And not because the Secret Service had told her to do what the director wanted, but because Marie had always been able to get her to do silly things.

Like Ian, who had gotten her to dance on the sacbe.

Did she always need someone else to get her to laugh? When was the last time she'd just laughed on her own?

Marie grinned and shook Alice's shoulder lightly. "Hey, I heard about your turtle kid. Did Nixie like it? What did she think?"

"How did you know?"

Marie was still grinning, but a touch of uncertainty had crept into her eyes and voice. "You've been watched ever since I asked for you. Surely that's not surprising?"

"Of course not." They hadn't watched too closely. No one had followed her into the past.

Marie might have been reading her thoughts. "They lost you yesterday. They don't lose people. They were following you through the jungle, and lost you. So they watched your friend's jeep, and you just—oh, I dunno. They said you just showed up." She laughed softly. "You should have seen their faces trying to explain it to me. And then the picture with the turtles and Nixie. They wanted to revoke your visit, but I overrode them. Losing followers you don't know you have is no crime, nor is nearly drowning in turtles." She searched Alice's face. "That's why I came early. Fabulous things are happening to you. I want you to show me."

Show her? Take the Science Advisor to the President of the United States of America back to a world where they threw captive women into wells as offerings to gods? She shook her head. "I don't even know what's happening." She didn't say: *It might be dangerous so I wouldn't show you anyway. How could I risk you? You are a hope of the world.* She looked up at the clouds. "Besides, it's about to rain. Feel it?"

Marie fixed her blue eyes on Alice, her gaze one that demanded, expected, cooperation. The gaze of a power rather than a student. "So tell me. Tell me everything you know. We can work this out together."

An echo. Marie had been a year ahead, and she'd helped Alice pass her first calculus class, and Alice had helped Marie with basic astronomy. That was how freshmen and sophomores got through the tough early curriculum at Stanford. They'd lost touch in the later years, the ones full of even harder classes that told the real secrets of their disciplines. Alice shook her head. She was in awe of her old friend. "I wasn't even there when Nixie swam with the turtles. I was getting cleared to meet you. I saw the picture on the news before I saw Nixie."

Marie put a hand on her arm. "What did she say when you saw her?"

Alice laughed. "She said she loved the dolphins. To get her away from reporters, the hotel gave her a free pass to swim with dolphins at Xcaret. She was so full of the dolphins I didn't ask her about the turtles. I just . . . went home and slept. When I woke up, Nixie was getting ready for bed, and she told me about the feel of dolphin's skin, and how they swam right up to her."

"Like the turtles?" Marie asked.

"I think the dolphins at Xcaret are trained to swim up to everyone."

Marie let out a long, low whistle. "So there has been so much happening in your life the turtles were not a big deal?"

Alice stared, flummoxed. Marie had always been smart, but wrapped in herself. Alice hadn't expected her to have become this intuitive. She'd thought they'd smile at each other across a distance and remember they knew each other, but not that Marie Healey would ask about her life. "I don't know how I could explain it all. But Nixie swam with turtles another day, not so many, and she has a quetzal feather she loves, and . . . " Her voice trailed off. She'd love to talk about it. She needed to talk about it. But it was too crazy. "She's had weird dreams, and I had a weird dream, too. And we both remembered the same thing when we woke up."

Marie's voice was so soft Alice strained to hear her. "I dreamed of a tree growing in a sky so bright with stars it almost blinded me, and there was a snake, but it wasn't the biblical snake or the biblical tree. They were Mayan. Stylized like the trees and snakes you see here."

"I can help you with that during the tour. It's powerful Mayan symbolism." Alice shivered in the heat. "Did you meet anyone in your dream?"

"No. Did you?"

"Not meet," Alice said. "But we saw old Mayans. I mean young ones living a long time ago, like the stars you dreamed of were from a long time ago. "

"Were they? The stars?"

"Sure. No light pollution." It was like teaching her astronomy again. Maybe Marie remembered that, too.

"They were magnificent." Marie pursed her lips, determined. "Where did you go yesterday?"

Alice looked away, hating herself for shaking at the idea of telling Marie the truth. "I had to help a friend find something. I'm sure your people just missed us taking a turn or something. They must have been good. I never saw them." Did they see her kiss Ian? It made her cringe at first, then she grinned. Heck, Nixie had gotten a picture. Maybe Marie's goons had, too.

Since Marie held her silence, Alice kept talking. "In my dream, the old Mayans were walking down a white road, like the sacbe here, and they were fierce and beautiful. Both like I thought they would look and not. Healthier and more powerful, and as wild as I expected. Then they were killed in a fight with the poor."

"Like we might be?" Marie rubbed her hands together. "People need so much. Cities are dying, the middle class is half-gone and the only sectors with more jobs and people are tech and medicine—both of which pull from an international labor pool. We're lucky so far—but there's still riots all over the world. The climate makes that worse." She stopped and shook her head. "You'd think I was talking to the press instead of an old friend. Sorry."

"You're right," Alice whispered. "Some days it already feels too late—the whole thing's a scaling problem. We're doing so much, but it's too slow. I saw a great TED main conference video the other day on how worldwide demand is outpacing the increase in clean energy."

"There's still too much oil. It's too damned cheap." Marie was silent for a few moments. "If we fix the climate—stabilize it, move faster . . . well, then maybe we can get to a little more peace. The president feels like he has to do better on the environment."

"I agree." Like in spades, but Alice didn't say that.

"I'm grateful for the press that'll bring. But it means we all have extra security, and the president can hardly sneeze without three Secret Service officers offering him a handkerchief." She glanced around as if checking on her guards. "I hope they didn't bother you too much."

"I didn't even see them. But will they follow me after today, or will everything be normal again?"

"After tomorrow, they'll stop. Unless you see me again."

Alice heard the yearning in her voice, and wondered that it seemed real. "I'd like to see you again," she said, glancing at her watch, "but now I need to get searched, or I won't be able to see you today."

"And I have to go get formal. That's why I came up here." She looked around. "To see you before I put on my power."

"You have it on now, whether you know it or not."

"Not all the trappings. I also came to see Chichén Itzá like this, empty, with no one to watch me be amazed."

"Except a few hundred soldiers and two or three Secret Service people."

"That's as good as it ever gets," Marie said. "This is as good as it's been for months, anyway."

She couldn't imagine what Marie's life must be like. Yet she always looked confident and smiling in the news, or at least confident. "Will any good come of the conference?"

Marie wiped at a strand of her too-red hair. "It's important for us all to be in the same place, look into each other's eyes. China's a problem. They think being extraordinarily good in some areas, like their new eco-cities and green buildings, makes up for being the worst coal polluters left in the world. India and the EU are both moving forward. Too slowly. I can only push so hard." Marie sighed.

Alice wasn't going to pretend she knew the right thing to do. She settled for draping her arm loosely around Marie, the way they had once expressed friendship at school. She whispered, "Good luck. I hope it goes well."

Marie pulled Alice in close to her. "Me, too. This is supposed to be a time when the world changes." As she looked out over the gray ruins under the gray clouds, she looked worried. "I want it to be for the good. I have the most power of any scientist in the world to make it be for good. *And I don't know what to do.*"

"I'm sorry." Alice sighed. "And I don't understand what's happening. I'm losing control. The turtles . . . "

Marie made a soft sound of agreement. Pensive.

"And our dreams. Is the whole world dreaming strange dreams?"

"I don't know. Maybe . . . " Marie's words trailed off.

Alice blinked in sudden sunshine. Unfamiliar noises—flutes and chatter in alien languages and the bleating of animals tickled her ears. She swayed, disoriented, her stomach sinking as she realized what had to be happening. Her hold on the real world felt like gossamer. She glanced down and pointed, watching Marie's eyes for some sign Marie saw what she did.

Marie gasped, and a sound was starting to come out of her throat when Alice clamped a hand across it. "You don't know who is nearby," she whispered. "Maybe nobody. Maybe not your security guards."

Marie turned wide, but not frightened, eyes on Alice. She nodded and Alice removed her hand.

Below them, the covers over the market stalls set between the columns of the Temple of the Warriors were no longer new canvas but old palm-thatch turned straw-colored by years of sun. A turtle had been painted across the top, clearly meant to be seen from where they stood. A long line of festival dancers snaked through the open space between the bottom of the pyramid stairs and the beginning of the market. People gave them room, small dark people dressed in cotton and bright woven clothes, busy, chattering with each other.

Alice licked her lips, looking down. Slanted heads. Masks. Feathers. Finery. Faces, some pealing into laughter but many walking in sullen silence. The grass was sere and brown, sere-brown instead of the green she had walked across an hour ago. The stones at ground level were bright red and smooth, like the sacbe except for the color.

It looked so intense . . . as if a bit of desperation touched the whole scene. A monkey rode on a woman's shoulder. A little girl threaded through the crowd leading a goat. Here and there, people carried trays full of pottery or carved bones or jewelry, stopping to trade with small crowds that gathered for them.

Marie tugged at Alice's hand, pulling her up. Where they stood, the steps were old and gray, and below them, near the bottom, everything was bright and sharp, the edges of the steps less worn by time.

Marie took a step down the face of K'uk'ulkan, toward the differences.

Alice pulled back, resisting. She couldn't go back, not today, not with Marie. Not without Nixie.

Marie took one more step, her arm holding Alice's hand fully extended now. Alice shook her head, frantic. She raised her eyes, looking behind her. A plane flew in the clear blue sky. Marie's gaze followed hers.

When Alice looked back, the roof of the market was again new, and boringly uniform with no bright symbols painted on it. The market stood empty. Marie looked at her accusingly, almost angry. "You saw that? You've seen that before?"

Alice nodded, for a moment unable to speak. She licked her lips and said, "Only once. The day before yesterday. Not here. But we walked in the old world. We could tell because the road was perfect and new, a Mayan road." She just couldn't quite go into the relationship to the dream or the bead.

Marie took the steps back up, stopping one step below Alice, looking up. She'd lost the anger, replaced it with intensity. "What does it mean?"

"I don't know."

Footsteps scraped the stone behind her, and Alice turned to find a man and a woman in black, standing close. She hadn't even heard them approach. What had they seen? Their faces gave away nothing. She gave Marie a hand back up the last step. "I guess we better go."

Marie nodded, her voice louder and more formal. "I need to get rigged up. I'll see you when the tour starts." She followed the two guards, clearly heading for the chain that made it safer to walk down the steps.

Should she have let Marie plunge them down into the past? In that moment of Marie tugging her downward, she had been sure it would kill them to go back.

But now, with the world solidly normal, she wondered if she should have gone, like some old fairy tale of King Arthur visiting Camelot. Except the Mayan world believed in blood and science while tales of King Arthur were chivalry and religion.

She should have had the presence of mind to take picture. She was a scientist, dammit. She could have at least used her phone.

She needed Nix.

Alice let them get halfway down before starting herself, watching Marie's back as she walked easily down the narrow, uneven stairs, ignoring the safety chain and her watchers. And Alice.

Marie didn't look back even once.

CHAPTER 30

The mid-afternoon heat sent runnels of sweat down Ah Bahlam's back, and he was merely standing still. His mother leaned in from behind him, carefully knotting the black sinew ties that held the jaguar pelt to him. She stepped back, admiring her handiwork, and then moved close again, straightening the pads on the shoulder where Julu landed. "That bird," she muttered. "Birds do not land on jaguars."

He leaned in and gave her an awkward hug, hampered by the thick costume. "This one does. Besides, if you had not sewn these on, he would land on you."

His mother screeched exaggeratedly, mocking him, laughing. "No, he would not. I am too bony." She smiled and stepped back. "You look strong." The pelt, which hung down his belly and back, *was* beautiful even thought it wasn't black. Perhaps his jaguar would not care. The costume had belonged to his grandfather, the last person in his family to have been chosen by Jaguar. The base color of the pelt was a soft wet-shell white, its spots a light brown ringed with darker brown. Its teeth hung around his neck, and his mother's hand held the mask he would don before the dance started. She had worked on the costume, fixing frayed edges and restringing the teeth while he was gone, preparing for her son's return to take his place as a warrior-priest of the Itzá.

Perhaps her prayers had helped him come home.

His father waited, already dressed in puma skins and holding his own mask in his hand. Ah Bahlam leaned down and kissed his mother on the forehead. "We go."

His father looked into his eyes, his gaze full of all the things he had shared with his son about the power of the dance of the Way. *Release. Let go. Believe. Let your Way become you and you become your Way.* But he added nothing now. He just nodded solemnly at Ah Bahlam, then winked. A final exhortation to remember that the dance could be done with humor regardless of how deep its meaning and how much the people needed their lords to succeed.

A path had been cleared for them. They walked, slowly and smoothly, as close to gliding as possible, until they had joined twenty other dancers milling at the bottom of the stairs up the Temple of K'uk'ulkan. Two others were cats: an ocelot and his father's puma. His uncle wore the brown skins of a peccary and his heavy mask was made from an actual peccary head, split open and widened to fit over his uncle's large skull, giving the pig's face a puffed-up look. A wooden stake ran from the base of the mask to his waist to take some of the weight. He would have to dance with a straight back.

Ah Bahlam should have been surrounded by young men his age, but there was only Ah K'in'ca. He wore a wealth of macaw feathers in glittering green, and ruffed about the head and neck in scarlet. His mask left his eyes and mouth visible, although a great wooden beak hung out, the long pointed top jutting from his forehead and the small bottom beak cupping his chin. When he looked straight on at his friend, Ah Bahlam made out Ah K'in'ca's smile and clasped his friend's hand. "Good dance," he said.

"And you," Ah K'in'ca replied. "Dance your path."

"Have you heard anything about Hun Kan?" Ah Bahlam asked.

Ah K'in'ca shook his feathered head. "Rumors only. Her sisters banged on the door of the high priest today but were sent away."

"If you—"

"If I hear anything, I'll tell you." He paused, watching the men sort themselves into order for the dance. They would be last. "Now is not the time. Focus on your Way."

Ah Bahlam swallowed. The jaguar had brought them both home. Had it brought Hun Kan back to serve the high priest's desires? And if so, what were those? The world was duller for not knowing if she was safe. But he still had his duty. He nodded at his friend, repeating, "Good dance."

Ah K'in'ca turned away and followed the men up, his wide red wings tucked in close behind him as he negotiated the stair carefully. Ah K'in'ca had never walked easily up or down the thin steep temple steps, even though, on the flat, he ran as if the wind pushed him.

Ah Bahlam took the last position, the dried seed-pods fastened around his ankles chuttering softly as he ascended. He fit the heavy jaguar mask over his head as he neared the half-way point. It smelled of oil and old fur, and he breathed hard into it, struggling to make its scent part of him, to give it his. He nearly gagged before he could breathe clearly.

He stopped on the top step, sweating, so close to Ah K'in'ca that a feather tickled his face, even through the mask. In front of Ah K'in'ca, the next youngest, and then the men ranked by deed and position. The pride and hope of Chichén, regal, raw, and beautiful.

His father and uncle were lost to his sight, near the front. Ahead of them, standing at the edge of the steps down, would be those with most powerful Ways: the White-bone Snake, the Vision Frog, and the Maize God.

These were the Lords of Itzá and their adult male children.

The most elite warriors of Feathered Serpent were already there too, waiting on the sides of the great platform, ready to escort the dancers. Were there fewer, leaving some of the best to handle the unrest outside the city?

The mask hid enough of his vision it was hard to tell. It only mattered a little. The linking of the gods to the Itzá here during ceremonies meant as much to Itzá's safety as her warriors. For the first time, his responsibility to the people felt like it was here, now. The dances and games of these days would feed and water the people for the next year.

Or not.

The lilting drums and flutes that accompanied the maidens rose and fell, and wove through the last steps of a dance to the sun god, K'inich A'haw. The beat made his sandaled feet want to shuffle, and he remembered how lithe the young women looked twirling slowly side by side. But then the sun god had seemed well pleased for years. It was Chaac, the rain god, who hid from them.

The maidens' music rose and then stopped, and the watching crowd called out to them, clapping and making the sounds of jungle animals, a great chorus that seemed to raise the very sky.

Even though he couldn't see the front of the line, or down below to the people waiting for the dance, Ah Bahlam's memories of these moments were so vivid he could see the next few moves in the familiar rite. The High Priest of K'uk'ulkan must already be standing at the top of the steps, sunlight glinting on the shells and beads woven into his net skirt. Red feathers adorned his powerful calves and arms. His mask hid most of his face and his ceremonial headdress, nearly as tall as he was, bobbed with every move. Ah Bahlam knew the moment the priest raised his arms by the silence that settled slowly over the crowd until even the children no longer called out to each other.

Drums boomed in the heartbeat of the waiting warriors, of the gods, and of the lords who would dance to become them.

He felt the high priest begin his stately walk down, flanked by seven warriors. He counted time in his head. When the high priest was halfway down, the Lords of Itzá would follow him.

And they did.

The crowd of costumed lords thinned out.

Before he was ready, the steps were in front of him. Below him, the crowd looked up almost as one being, flowing about the great flat space, a field of color. They thronged around the street vendors, to and from the Wall of Skulls, touching it for luck in battle, and came as close as the guarding warriors would let them get to the Venus platform and the path the dancers would follow to surround it. Ah Bahlam closed his eyes, calling to the jaguar, conjuring up once again the golden eyes and the black face, the lithe form.

The jaguar hovered in front of him, inside him, and then spilled away.

He was out of time, and took the first step down alone, clothed not in the jaguar but only in the costume. The last dancer, although one of the warriors walked beside him. Ah Bahlam focused on the immediate. Head up. In front of him, now, so high, only the blue, blue rainless sky. Another step. Another. Careful. The drums told the timing. Two full heartbeats for each step.

Should he call to his Way again, now, on the steps, or just get down?

The crowd below had become a heavy weight. He could not see them, but he knew they were there. They clapped softly, in rhythm with his steps, all the other steps.

The high priest would be near the bottom, preparing to mount the Venus platform in the middle of the square. There, he would start the dance alone on the raised surface, visible to all, the many Ways of the dancers below him.

Ah Bahlam took a deep, steadying breath and called the jaguar's visage from the blue sky in front of him.

His right foot missed a step, slid, the seedpods scraping and crackling against the stone. His knee buckled. Before he could lose his balance entirely, he put his hands out, feeling for the steps.

Scattered gasps rose from the crowd below.

A strong hand caught his arm, pushed him back against the steps, giving him a moment to find stone under his foot. "Stand," the warrior's voice hissed, insistent.

He stood, shaking.

"Move," the voice continued. "It happens."

Ah Bahlam did not remember any Lord of Itzá falling down the stairs. But he had only missed one, and scraped himself a little. His knees shook. He managed the next step, and the next, and before they came close enough for the crowd to hear, he whispered back to the warrior. "Thank you."

Silence.

How much damage had he done? And he had been worried about Ah K'in'ca. He let the heartbeat of the drum pick him back up, fold him in its rhythm, and by the time he came to the last step he moved easily again.

Now he could see the crowd clapping and singing and the sway of the dancers in front of him, feel the slow, even steps as they began to surround the stone platform. It had looked easy when he watched the dance, yearned to become part of it. Now, he fought just to stay with the others, to keep his steps in line.

Incense burners surrounded the Venus platform, sending the smoke of sacred plants and mixed venom from vision toads into the air the dancers breathed. It made his eyes water, but changed nothing about who he was.

He could not imagine the jaguar coming to him here in this crowd, in this moment when all of his attention was required to keep his balance, ignore the smell of his costume and know the position of all the others around him.

CHAPTER 31

Nixie stood on a dark rock by the lagoon in Akumal, enjoying the early afternoon warmth in spite of the clouds bunching above her like gray beach balls. She glanced up at Oriana, wrinkling her nose. "For someplace called "place of turtles," you have to admit that it's a bit of a disappointment."

Oriana put her hands on her hips and leaned down, so serious she was funny. "Did you expect lightening to strike twice? We've already seen three turtles. Nesting season was over in October. Three is good." She frowned, suddenly serious. "Especially now." She waved her hand at the sea floor. Earlier,

she had pointed out invasive corals and algae that loved the warmer waters but strangled native species, and shown Nixie bleached coral bones that used to be vivid red or yellow.

Nixie looked down, frustrated. Why did she have to be born just when the world was dying? She liked Mexico because the green, watery jungle felt so much more alive than most places in Arizona. The turtles had made her feel magical yesterday, as if she mattered. She'd watched for them all day today. The big turtle hadn't come to her, and neither had the swarms of adolescents. None of the turtles they did see had treated her as anything special at all. In fact, she couldn't see any right now.

A blue tang swam by just below her, a bit of sky against the white sand bottom. A bright spot surrounded her for a moment and moved on, a beam of light pouring through the clouds, one of many making parts of the lagoon so blue that others looked deeper and grayer. She wanted to draw. But she was afraid to get her pens out with the air so thick and heavy with impending rain.

It was the first time she'd been to Akumal, which Oriana called snorkelers paradise. They had seen parrotfish and tangs and angels, and had swum over nearby wavy corals on the beach, then had come here to snorkel the lagoon. It was pretty, but somehow the very ordinariness of the day seemed like a letdown. "Oriana?"

"Yes."

"Did going back in time and finding the bead make you want to go again the next day? Or today? Do you miss it?"

Oriana waded into the shallow water, her orange water socks looking like goldfish on her feet. "Yes. But it scared me a little, too. What if we had been there at the wrong time and gotten in the middle of the fight you dreamed about?" She shrugged. "I don't think that time is done with us yet anyway."

Nixie was sure of it. She *knew* she'd see Hun Kan again. Unless she stopped it. But she wouldn't. "But why us? Why me? I mean, I love it there, but I'm just a kid."

A soft wind made Oriana brush the dark wisps of hair that had escaped her ponytail from her eyes. "Maybe that's exactly why. You are a kid. I mean, you haven't been scared yet."

Not really. Especially not at first. But it was getting more confusing and more people were tangled up in it, and Ian was gone and hadn't come back. "Well, the closer we get to tomorrow, the more I think maybe I should be scared."

"Do you think being scared will help?" Oriana asked.

"No." A school of tiny fish flitted through a water-filtered sunbeam below Nixie. "But I wish I knew what was going to happen. Maybe then I wouldn't be scared at all." She skipped a stone across the water. "The turtles were trying to tell me something, but I still don't know what."

Oriana leaned down and picked up a shell, held it out toward Nixie. "Take this. Look at the inside."

Nixie sat down and turned the shell over and over in her hand. It was the kind that curled inside itself, tapering from a rough pointy top to a thin, almost elegant bottom. "I can't see the inside. It's a pearly white going toward it, but the center is hidden."

"So you'd have to break the shell to see it?"

Nixie nodded. "It's too perfect. I don't want to."

Oriana took the shell from her and put it back where she found it. "Every day has its own center that you have to imagine, but you can't know about in advance. The turtles were like that yesterday. Would it have been as magical to swim with them if you woke up knowing you'd see so many?"

Nixie shook her head. "It'd be like today, when I thought I'd see more."

Oriana smiled, her eyes suddenly unfocused, like she was looking at something inside herself. "My mother taught me to like every day. She's dead now, but I know she had a great life. Because every day was the center of a shell for her."

Like the turtles yesterday, a surprise . . . she wanted to see more turtles today, or even the same ones again. Except . . . "I guess I wouldn't want to swim with so many turtles every day, anyway. It was hard to move my legs."

Laughter brought focus back to Oriana's eyes, and she splashed over to sit beside Nixie.

Oriana wasn't that old. Younger than Mom, anyway. What must it be like to be without a mom? Sure, Nix fought with her mom, but she couldn't imagine life without her. Nixie patted Oriana's knee. "I'm sorry your mom died."

Oriana shook her head. "Thanks, but I'm not. I mean, I miss her. Like I said, I know she isn't sorry. She accepted everything." Oriana raised her eyes and looked out over the lagoon, and it felt like Oriana had gone somewhere else, gotten light, like maybe the real Oriana was in the sea. "I think we need to appreciate every day. That's what our time teaches us. You know the world is changing fast. It's hard to know how long we'll live."

"Because the climate's changing and the animals are dying?"

"And the wars. The poverty. You don't see it here," she swept a hand around at the beach full of tourists, "even though the rich people are nervous, too. But before I agreed to watch you, I sometimes helped out at a free medical clinic. More people are getting diseases, but more people are getting cured, too. There's hope." She let her voice trail off, and her eyes had gone all unfocused again.

Nixie had questions about Ian and the medical clinic and Oriana's life. Too many to know which to ask. She dangled one foot in the water and sat quietly.

Oriana continued. "So we just have to enjoy every day's magic."

Maybe Oriana was talking to herself instead of to Nixie. A light breeze ruffled Oriana's hair and fat raindrops landed on Nixie's hand and her head. "Should we go sit in the car?" she asked.

Oriana smiled, although her mouth was a little drawn down. "No." She walked out into the lagoon, rain plopping all around her, the drops so big and hard they splashed Oriana when they hit the nearby water.

A fish jumped.

Oriana kept walking.

Nixie swallowed, remembering Ian and her mom dancing on the sacbe the day before. She slipped her own yellow water socks on and stepped slowly into the lagoon, following Oriana. The uneven footing went from rock to sand to rock and she had to focus on each step.

The rain fell harder.

The lagoon wasn't really deep anywhere, but Oriana found a place where it came up past her waist, then settled down into the water so only her head showed. Nixie stood beside her, her head just a little taller than Oriana's. Oriana took Nixie's face in her two hands and smiled. Her eyes shone. "See. We're already wet. I don't know what's happening to us, to the world. To Ian. But we're already wet now, and we just have to decide to like the rain, and to be curious. It's a good, warm rain today."

Nixie nodded, sure she understood in her gut even if her head didn't really get it. But it was nice to sit with Oriana, in the warm lagoon in the warm rain, with the warm wind on her face and fish swimming by to tickle her feet.

She felt like a turtle.

CHAPTER 32

Ah Bahlam swayed unsteadily. The red-painted stones underfoot, the brush of other dancers around him, the calls of the crowd and even the drums were barriers between him and his Way. He rained drops of sweat onto the ground. He breathed in sickly-sweet smoke, the thickness of it slowing him, making every moment of failure available for him to examine. His first chance to dance his Way, to do the real work he'd been born and bred for, and his head felt thick with clouds while his feet seemed to wear rocks.

He circled the Venus platform once, twice, three times, and then lost track of how many times. Each step took long moments, each trip around seemed like a day.

Other dancers began to call and mimic their Ways. Macaw and monkey, hissing snake, even the grunts of the peccary. Perhaps he now danced alone, the only pure human left in the gathering.

Keeping his head high and his back straight became a struggle. The costume, light when he donned it, had turned to a heavy weight smashing him toward the floor. It kept his feet from moving easily and trapped his spirit in a heavy, human body.

He was going to shame his father, his people. Cauac. Hun Kan. Their faces danced in his imagination, frowning at him. Hun Kan's eyes inside his mind became large and watchful. Cauac stood back at the edges of his consciousness, frowning.

Wings fluttered near his face, a streak of green and blue across the small bit of sky available to him from inside the mask.

Julu landed on his right shoulder with a thump, as if to say, *I am here, where is your jaguar?*

If Julu could find him, why not his Way? He reached a hand up and offered his bird greeting. *Thank you.*

His vision began to feel, well, *wrong*, the colors to fuzz out and soften. The sky expanded and grew higher above him, the smells carried on the wind grew stronger: sweaty dancers, and beyond them, birds and orchids, peccaries and mice. The thirsty abundance of the jungle surrounding Chichén became an extension of his own soul, as if his bird brought the wild to him.

He had been looking outside himself, like when the jaguar led them home. The jaguar of the dance struggled to come to him from inside his belly, to infuse him from the center of being out. Strength seeped into his legs. Lightness and the wind filled him. He fell to all fours, his paws slick on the smooth surface of the ceremonial ground. His slow steps, so carefully matched to the heartbeat drum, fell into a rhythm of their own, almost gliding. Sound flooded his ears: the Ways all about him (footsteps of puma and peccary, light hopping of birds, slither of serpents), voices lifted and separated, becoming clear even from the far back in the crowd. A child's voice, "See the jaguar," and a man whispering, "I do, son."

Air filled his stomach, his chest, bubbled through his lips in a soft growl and then ripped through his throat. The deep growl of the jungle cat.

He slid around each of the other Ways, around the great red floor, his head full of the scents of other animals and of the humans. He walked differently, still upright, but with the grace of the cat full inside of him. He felt lighter and stronger, his jaw heavy, and his vision shifted, nearly making him dizzy.

He danced into new muscles until a barrier stopped him.

The feathered serpent stood in his way. He had a sense it had faced others. A small part of him deep inside identified the high priest. That part lay quiet and watched as his jaguar crouched, its head low, shoulders hunched, feline eyes meeting the dark orbs of the winged snake writhing on the ground in front of it.

The jaguar should drop its head, pay respect.

It stayed completely still, the two great beasts watching each other in silence.

Drop, Ah Bahlam encouraged himself, his jaguar. The two were now so one that he addressed them both at once.

Except it was stronger. It held its pose.

He struggled to make his silent inner voice as strong as possible. *Drop.*

The two beasts began to circle each other slowly.

You are my Way, you must obey me.

This man smells wrong.

Never had his Way spoken to him clearly. *He is K'ul'ukan* he reminded the jaguar in him. *K'ul'ukan.*

His days are numbered and mine are not. Humans will always need jaguars to live, but they will be done with Feathered Serpent soon.

Ah Bahlam nearly gibbered. The Way was the path, the destiny. His destiny. He and this wild thing inside him did need to do something, help change something. But this was not the moment. He knew it. He wasn't ready. He was too young. Why did the being that held him insist? Why did his own path show disrespect?

Control. Cauac had driven control into him. And the power of sacrifice.

He breathed in, feeling *his* energy fill the beast's lungs.

Good. He could become a little more himself, a little less jaguar. Was it the dance and the smoke that made the jaguar far too strong in him today?

You are my Way and I am your Way. I doubt him, too. An image flashed in his mind: Hun Kan being taken away. *But this moment he has the power. He has all the power of Chichén. We will have our day, but this day is his. For the sake of my people.*

His legs straightened, his stance shifted. His Way was no longer bigger than he was, no longer stronger. Still, it fought him, slowing his movements. It did not agree.

The tail behind him flicked and twitched, an unfamiliar extension of his haunches.

In front of him, Feathered Serpent swayed, seeming to grow bigger.

The high priest's eyes met his, commanding. The older man and his Way were clearly one, undoubtable. Strong. The feathered serpent in truth.

A god.

His head, the head of the jaguar, bowed as one, man and reluctant beast accepting the power of a greater being.

When he looked up, the high priest glared at him from inside the feathered serpent that rode him. *I'm not done with you.*

Nothing in the jaguar was afraid, and it gave no answer. Ah Bahlam quivered. He felt small compared to the two Ways.

K'uk'ulkan slithered around the jaguar. Ah Bahlam rose to two paws, still paws, his tail a balance, and danced.

The jaguar no longer fought him. He sensed it had gotten enough of what it wanted. For now.

The jaguar inside and outside of him, the jaguar that was him, flowed: paws barely touching the ground, back even, great head watching to both side of him, tail twitching. Its essence flooded him with joy in spite of his fears, joy so great it swept away all other emotion, taught him to glide and sway and roar.

The puma that shared the body of his father momentarily walked beside him, step for step, and a great growl of joy burst from his throat into the air. His father fell back and he circled a last time, walking now to the heartbeat drums, a man carrying the warm vestige of a beast inside him.

He stepped aside to the cleared place designated for the dancers to finish and fell to all fours and then to his stomach, prone between his uncle and Ah K'in'ca, gasping for breath.

CHAPTER 33

A woman in a black uniform gave Alice a flat emotionless stare over a cool smile. "You're cleared. Five minutes."

Don Carlo had been here when she arrived, in quiet conversation with one of the female agents. Alice had been interrupted by the woman in black before she could greet him, and now he still looked busy.

Her confusion at the brief glimpse of old Chichén she'd shared with Marie had turned to anger. What if time wouldn't damn well stand still? Why hadn't Ian called? Come back? She stared out the window, trying to ignore the hum of conversation behind her.

Don Carlo appeared at her side with a cup of coffee. She took it, nodding her thanks, curling her hands around the cup. Her stomach wanted food. She spied a long table full of sweet sugar buns, mangos, and grapes. She popped a grape into her mouth and took a bun in her free hand, savoring the very idea of thick, heavy bread to sop up the bitter morning coffee.

Before she could finish even half the bread, the biggest black suit stood in the doorway. Cross-chatter stopped and the twenty or so folk in the room started heading toward him, forming a pre-arranged line.

She glanced at the half a roll in her hand and shrugged, stuffing it into a napkin and shoving it in her pocket. Don Carlo saw her and winked. Alice walked over to stand next to him in line, her coffee cup still in her hand.

A young man dressed in black plucked the cup from her and placed it on a nearby table

Alice barely suppressed a nervous giggle. Best not to walk out and meet the important people holding a disrespectful—perhaps dangerous—cup of coffee.

As she passed through the door, the sun was so bright it almost made her duck. Clouds hugged the southern horizon, but the rain had apparently bypassed Chichén this morning. They rounded a corner, a neat line, everyone moving to their pre-assigned places.

Alice's place was a few feet away from Marie, who had in truth transformed to a power in look as well as feel. She wore sensible but elegant slacks and a short-sleeved beige explorer's shirt without a single speck of dirt on it. A Mayan-styled pin that represented two butterflies caught her hair up elegantly. Her cheeks had a slight glow to them and her lips were redder, brighter, and fuller.

She glanced at Alice, her blue eyes cool and appraising.

So serious. Should she should be worried? Had she said the wrong thing? And then Alice caught her breath as the President of the United States came up alongside Marie, speaking in a low, familiar voice. He wore khaki slacks and a white polo, and might have been any young professional by his dress and stance.

He walked near Alice as he greeted the President of Mexico, a tall man with raven-black hair and eyes, and wearing a three piece raven-black suit, apparently unfazed by the hot sun beating down on his dark clothes. A smaller man in a rumpled brown suit stood beside him, looking more at ease than his boss.

Huo Jiang, the Minister of Environmental Protection of the People's Republic of China, came next. His formal suit matched the President of Mexico's. As the two men shook hands, they looked like penguins ready for a formal ice ball in the middle of the tropics.

Huo Jiang was accompanied by three equally formally dressed men, and a young woman with black hair pulled into a severe bun.

Even before the formalized greetings between Huo Jiang and the presidents finished, the Indian prime minister, Aditi Roy, drove up in a new Toyota hybrid car. When she climbed out, only two people accompanied her, one woman and one man, each in light flowing clothes that looked perfect for the heat. Because of her briefings, Alice identified them as a prominent climate change scientist and a bodyguard. Alice liked seeing the prime minister here, like the presidents.

Following on their heels, Emelio Pella, the European Union's Commissioner for the Environment, emerged from a big blue bus in the parking lot, followed by seven others, the largest contingent of all.

Alice watched the dance of official greeting solemnly, reviewing the right honorifics for everyone in her head.

Did they have dreams of old Maya?

What if she led these people to the old world?

Maybe if she just thought about modern things like cars and climate change and the European Union. While touring an ancient ruin. Right. Alice shifted on her feet. Sweat poured down her temples. There was nothing for it, not now, but to be her best.

Marie finally brought the heads of state over to meet her and Don Carlo, allowing each of the dignitaries to introduce their entourages.

It took a wry look from Marie to shock Alice into acting. "Please follow me." She led the group toward the Caracol.

The first part of the tour was normal, unless you counted the extra company of security-types with the tense demeanor of herding dogs.

Between locations, whispers spun behind her back. When she started talking tour-talk, the conversations stopped. Her audience asked informed we've-just-been-briefed questions, but with the exception of Aditi Roy, they were far more interested in each other than in Alice's presentation. Prime Minster Roy walked next to Alice, smiling, her bright blue and yellow sari adding cheer to the late morning. She felt like good company, almost like a generic version of an old friend or a grandmother. Madam Roy was rumored to have diplomatic teeth. If so, she didn't show them now.

Don Carlo's official job was to tour the hangers-on and aides, ostensibly so that each group was small enough, although Alice suspected it was to allow the whispers she heard behind her to go on unencumbered by minions. Her friend seemed to be doing well. Bursts of laughter floated over to her group.

The tour was paced by a tall black man in a white shirt and loose white karate-style pants who had appeared as soon as they started to move, and who gestured Alice onward from time to time. The man in white, the more congenial counterpart of the woman in black from this morning.

And of course, guards waited, watching. Not following—simply standing. Some with dogs. Close enough together that Alice never really felt like she could breath easily.

They started down the white road toward the cenote of sacrifice.

The old sacbe had nearly glowed with perfection. The surface of this re-creation was rougher, as if the archeologists couldn't quite imagine the Mayans had done a true, finely finished job.

She gave them time to gather at the edge of the viewing platform for the cenote. It rested on top of a cliff, and the deep well of water glittered nearly twenty feet below, a perfect circle of azure surrounded by pale green and white limestone, and a multitude of healthy jungle greens. The scent of hot water and rotting vegetation rose faintly under the sweeter smells of flowers that lined the cliff. Alice said, "This is why they built Chichén Itzá here. Places had power to the Mayans, and by their actions they could augment the power of places. Water *always* had power.

"There is another cenote on the grounds which was used for daily access to water. This one served as a sacred place of power. People traveled here from far away, a little like pilgrimages to Mecca today. Rulers controlled important trade routes and resources, and water was the most precious of all."

Commissioner Pella, the Italian, stared down into the water as if it both fascinated and horrified him. "Didn't they perform sacrifices here?"

Alice frowned at his condescending tone. "There were skeletons found when this cenote was dredged, but many more other artifacts. Blood sacrifice was for wars, for major ceremonies, and for hard times. Daily wishes were simpler and less costly."

Marie stared down at the pool. "Still, imagine being thrown into such deep water, trussed up so that you couldn't move. Imagine drowning in such a pretty place."

Emilio Pella laughed, condescending. "Your heart would have been cut from you first."

Marie glanced over at Alice. "Would that have been true?"

Alice nodded. "There are many legends and some glyphs that suggest that people chose to sacrifice themselves for the sake of their people. Kings are depicted decapitating themselves in some Mayan centers."

Marie looked away for a moment, then back. "Dying for your country is not new. Kamikazes. Suicide bombers."

"No," Pella said, "But surely most sacrifices didn't choose to die; they were simply murdered." He glared at Alice, a subtle dare in his eyes. "This culture was no better than yours, or mine. History was bloody. We must rise above it."

"History has lessons for us," she said, trying to keep her patience. "But you're right, perhaps many sacrifices were just brutal killings by our standards." She paused. "We're still learning about the culture that lived here."

Emilio seemed to lose interest, shifting and looking at his watch.

Alice turned to Marie and then Madam Roy. "There is a legend that the offering of a prayer at the sacred cenote of Chichén Itzá has special power. In light of your work to broker understanding between nations—peace and a healthy climate—we obtained permission for each of you to toss in a coin from your own country." She dug into her pocket and pulled out a dollar, a yuan, a euro, and a rupee. They glittered in the sunshine.

Huo Jiang came forward and took the yuan, tossing into the cenote with an air of disdain. He said nothing.

Alice bit her lip. This had been her suggestion.

Aditi Roy glared at Huo Jiang and took the Indian coin. She held the rupee to her heart and murmured silently, then tossed it in a graceful arc into the still water.

The President of the United States took the dollar coin from Alice's outstretched hand, and spoke out loud. "I wish for a better world and a healthy land, for all of our children." He tossed the silver dollar, which turned over and over in the air before falling into the deep pool. When he rose, he smiled.

Pella licked his lips and looked at Alice and the last coin she held in her hand as if he were watching a snake. He glanced at Huo Jiang and back at Alice. Then he laughed. "A good tourist trick. I will play." He took the euro and tossed it high into the air almost immediately, watching it fall. When it splashed into the water he spoke a single word. "Peace."

Next, they climbed K'uk'ulkan, the long line of dignitaries trying to keep their dignity while coping with the steep, narrow steps. At the top, photographers lay in wait, vultures snapping picture after picture. The tour group was clearly used to this; they posed for a few minutes and then ignored the journalists. They answered no questions.

Alice got included in a few shots before she was politely elbowed out of the way. She took the opportunity to look down from near where she and Marie had stood this morning, her heart catching for a moment at the dark faces and hair below her. But it was only local people bustling about with decorations and testing thoroughly modern sound systems.

After the photographers finally backed off, the whole group rested at the top for a few long and surprisingly easy minutes, the view across the multi-greened wave of jungle canopy enough to shock almost all of them to silence.

For the first time since early this morning, Marie stood close enough to Alice for a private conversation. She leaned down, pointing at something imaginary off in the distance. "This morning. How many other people is this happening to?" she whispered.

Alice answered as softly. "Everyone that was with me the day before yesterday, and yes, we were in the past, then." She grimaced. "In a place I dreamed of before I went there. But I don't know of anyone else. Until you. Can you investigate?"

Marie raised an eyebrow. "Can't you see the headlines now? PRESIDENTIAL SCIENCE ADVISOR INVESTIGATES MAGIC?" She laughed. "I can't do this. Can you?"

"I've been trying." There wasn't much time. "If I learn anything, how do I reach you?"

Marie handed her a piece of paper. "This phone number is direct. It's good all week."

Alice slid the paper into her pocket.

Marie's smile was tinged with mischief. "I'll try to catch up with you during dinner."

Alice felt immediately forgiven and trusted. Before she had a chance to reply, Marie turned back to Huo Jiang, her formal face forward.

Alice swallowed and signaled to the guy in white pants that it was time to gather the group for the climb down. It always took longer to go down than people expected.

She had told them the Caracol was built to align with the solstice axis, to allow the Pleiades to be viewed from a high window, and to let astronomers inside see the extremes of the rise and set of Venus. They had already known about the fabulous snake of light and shadow that cavorted along the steps of the temple of K'uk'ulkan every equinox.

She'd kept the Ball Court for last.

When Alice and her string of important ducklings arrived, the huge space was already being prepared. Barriers had been erected so that only those with special tickets or dispensation could get in. Bleachers stained the space at either end—an evil sacrifice for the god money, even though she and Nix had seats there for tomorrow. A small army of volunteers carefully hung colorful banners along the walls.

She raised her voice over the background of workers. "Gather in please. I'd like everyone to hear this." Alice centered the group in the middle of the Ball Court. She stood just behind a stone disk with a relief carving of the sun passing through a circle on it. They obediently gathered around her, Marie standing closest to Alice, then Emilio, Huo Jiang, and tiny Aditi Roy, with all of their hangers-on behind, but near.

Don Carlo stood beside Alice. The sun struck her almost full-face, summoning beads of sweat onto her forehead.

She pointed down at the stone. "This replica was made by a contemporary Mayan shaman, to replace one that is now in a museum. This marker identifies the center of the sacred space that the Ball Court represents. The symbol here represents the ball passing through the ring," she pointed at a great stone ring suspended from the Ball Court wall, "which in turn represents the sun passing through a number of centers. The rebirth of the sun, if you will."

She took a sip of water and cleared her throat. "I've told you how remarkable the Mayan astronomers were, and how much they meant to their society. We, for example, seldom plan a building based on its alignment to the stars. In most of our cities, we cannot even see them." She paused, giving a beat of silence to her words. "Have any of you been anywhere so remote that no night lights chased the stars away? Not a ski resort in the mountains or even the America desert—total darkness no longer exists in either place. Perhaps the Arctic? Or the ocean, in a boat darkened for the sake of seeing stars?"

A few of the hangers-on, and Aditi Roy, nodded, and all of the rest were quiet. Alice turned to the Prime Minister. "How did the darkest night sky seem different to you?"

Madam Roy smiled. "I have been to the South Pole. It was like seeing the faces of the Hindu pantheon dancing on velvet."

Very nice. "When there is no surface light to fight it, the sky is very bright. In almost any small space, small enough to circle with your forefinger and thumb, there are too many stars to count. The universe appears to go on forever, to be as deep as infinity. The brightest stars cast light and sometimes even shadows, the way that the full moon can cast your shadow faintly upon the ground."

She stopped to wet her lips again, to check. They still paid attention. "The

Milky Way is truly a river on a velvet night," she nodded at the prime minister, "and in that river, there is a black hole, a dark space in which few stars shine. And tomorrow night, that black hole will be directly above you." She paused, letting them all look up, checking to be sure that they did. She continued in a slightly softer voice. "Now, you know how when they teach you about the orbits of the planets in astronomy class, there's almost always a mobile with the sun in the middle and the planets circling it in ever-bigger circles?"

Even though they all spoke English, a few translators had to work on that one. When the babble stopped, Alice continued. "The mobiles are true representations. If you turned the solar system on its side, the sun would be in the middle and all of the planets would spin around in front of each other, as if they got built in a nice neat line. In other words, they spin around the sun almost as if they had been placed on a flat plate and pushed like marbles. That plate is the ecliptic plane." She waited again until it looked like everyone got it.

"So, back to the starless spot—the dark rift—in the Milky Way, which will be right above where we are standing. There will be a cross in the sky, centered on the dark rift. The arms of the cross are made by the Milky Way itself, and the ecliptic plane. This is a very rare alignment that only happens about every five thousand years.

"The Mayans thought of tomorrow as the ending of a great age and the beginning of a new one, a time of death and recreation. The Mayans saw this cross in the sky, this rare alignment, as the tree of life."

Madam Roy whispered. "It is similar to the Hindu turns of the ages."

The prime minister had spoken so softly that her words seemed to be meant for her own ears, so Alice simply nodded. "Much of this has been written about in popular New Age literature for some time. So has my next point, although less so. Right there, through the middle of the dark rift, we on Earth will be looking directly at the center of the galaxy. This is a rare and awe-inspiring astronomical event, and we will all be able to see it."

She let silence fall, looking up at the blue sky. This was the last message she wanted to leave with them.

Marie's voice was the next one she heard. "Thank you, Alice."

There were things she could say—please help us save the world, please find solutions to the morass we have made—but she settled for "Good luck."

Marie nodded.

People clapped.

The man in the white pants herded the group toward their next event.

Don Carlo nodded at her, a compliment.

Now that the dignitaries had left, more workers poured onto the floor of the Ball Court, carrying bunting and chairs and banners and sound equipment. "Look, we're in these people's way. I'm going to find something cold to drink."

Don Carlo shook his head. Reluctantly, she thought. "I'll see you tomorrow."

"Please stay a moment. I want to ask about time."

"What about time?"

Surely he remembered her asking at the Grand Caribe. "What did the old Mayans think about time? Or the people from today, for that matter? Do they think about it like we do?"

He looked at her for a long time, an American Mayan man standing on an ancient Mayan site in thoroughly modern clothes. "Time is . . . " He sighed, and closed his eyes for a moment. When he opened them, he said, "I was talking to an old man who is one of my language research subjects. He told me that the breath of the galaxy is usually even, but at times it is less fixed. That was the word he used. Breath. He said that with enough innocence, or need, or ceremony, time bends. I don't know what he meant, but the other Mayans in the room seemed to believe him."

"Did he say anything else?"

"No."

"Thank you."

He nodded. "I don't think I believed him." He leaned in and kissed Alice on the cheek. "But you never know." His gaze was soft. "I have to go."

"Bye." Maybe there was never going to be a clear answer to a breathing galaxy that bent time. She sighed, watching him leave, sensing he might be as confused as she was.

She called Nix, and heard they were back in the hotel and settling in for a nap. After she hung up, she rejected a brief stab of jealousy that threatened to make her angry.

Now there was just the dinner to survive, and then the long drive home. And maybe some contemplation about how to tell if anyone else was going back in time. Maybe Ian could help her there. If Ian ever came back.

Where the hell was Ian anyway? She could feel his lips against hers, his heartbeat against her cheek. He was a crazy man, an apprentice shaman, not right for her at all. She couldn't stop herself from drifting off in thoughts of him whenever her brain had nothing else to chew on. There no real sense to what was happening to her, to them, to the world. She needed help to make sense of it. Where was he?

Was he safe?

CHAPTER 34

Ah Bahlam now wore only his own skin, and the afternoon sun licked it with heat. He wanted to go find Hun Kan, but it was his duty to stay with the other dancers. They had recovered from being overcome by their own totems, and were now just men, tired, sipping water, preparing to dance again, but as only men. Still, the mystery of the Dance of the Way sang inside Ah Bahlam, as if the sacred smoke and the jaguar both curled, nascent, inside his blood.

The women came through in their best finery and jewelry, stepping carefully in the spaces between the men. They gathered masks and pelts, belts and tails, everything except loincloths and sandals, and the staffs of the older dancers. They bent and touched and scooped and carried, but made no real sounds except the rustle of dresses and clatter of bone and antler, hoof and tooth. Ah Bahlam handed his heavy mask to his own mother. She brushed his hand with her cool fingertips before she moved on.

The high priest had retired to his temple to sleep before the evening rites. The crowd still existed, but its energy had shifted to the market, to drinks and abundant food. The spent dancers were of no immediate interest to them.

Ah K'in'ca sat across from Ah Bahlam, grinning, his eyes exhausted and elated at once, sweat drying in salty streaks down his face. "Good dance," he mouthed.

"Yes."

His father, beside him, looked over at the exchange, his eyes dark and clouded with worry. His father had been puma. Ah Bahlam had felt it, had walked beside him, the great son-cat beside the wise father-cat.

His father spoke directly. "I am worried for you. I remember when the dance took me as it took you, when the puma ran and I might as well have been a flea on its back." He fell silent and looked at Ah Bahlam, his brows knit together.

The amount of silence his father let fill the air between them reeked of import.

His father's continues, grave and serious. "Never did my Way challenge the Way of others who hold power. I would never have let it; that is not the road of our family." He leaned in closer to Ah Bahlam. "We rise as far as we can, gain our power, hold our power, and return our power to the people. We do not take it with force except from our enemies."

"I know this." Ah Bahlam shifted so that he looked his father full in the face, struggling not to flinch at the obsidian of his father's eyes. "It was not my choice. The jaguar that brought me home safely is not easy to control. He is a king in his prime."

"But you are not," his father snapped. "And you can be killed more easily than your Way. I am glad it helped you come home safe. But are you safe, now?"

"Are any of us? Times are changing."

His father looked away, past Ah Bahlam, then stretched, ignoring his son.

Ah Bahlam waited.

"You need to learn control."

Truth clung to his father's words, even though he didn't want to hear it. But he had done his best!

Before he could respond, his father pointed to people racing toward the gates. Their calls foretold who they rushed to greet.

Warriors.

His father, then he, then the others all rose to their feet. A wave of lords.

The warriors would go to the Wall of Skulls, a great stone platform adorned with carved and painted stone skulls modeled on the enemies of Chichén Itzá

The lords hurried to beat them there, their feet fueled by fear and possibilities. Had Chichén been attacked?

On the way, a tall man wearing the red-feathered uniform of the Warriors of K'uk'ulkan grabbed Ah Bahlam's arm and pulled him aside. "Your Way challenged the Way of our high priest."

Ah Bahlam waited for another rebuke.

"Some of us will try to see you live long enough to try harder." The warrior clapped him on the shoulder and disappeared into the crowd.

Ah Bahlam nearly tripped over his own feet.

He returned to his father's side by the time the lords reached the Wall of Skulls. The returning jungle warriors were visible as a few plumed headdresses buried in a crowd of celebrants. The crowd pushed them toward the Wall of Skulls.

Someone called out. "Stop!"

The leaders noticed the lords standing in front of them and turned, digging their heels in, slowing the momentum. They let the warriors pull free.

Five of them. Only five.

Ah Bahlam swallowed, reminded of the fight on the sacbe that only three had returned from.

The five walked with their heads up, blood streaming from surface wounds. One limped. Only three carried shields. Two had spears. No one had arrows. All five were damp with sweat.

None carried trophies to lay atop the Wall of Skulls.

The leader showed his teeth, part smile, part grimace.

When they reached the wall, the lords parted for them. The warriors turned and put their backs to the wall, facing the Lords, and behind them, the people of Chichén.

The crowd pressed in, heavy and sweaty and needy, nearly everyone who had been in the great plaza, celebrants and merchants, women clutching young children tightly to their breasts or herding knee-high offspring. Old men. Young women with faces desperate for news of brothers and husbands, worry painted across their squinting eyes. Warrior-age men like Ah Bahlam, who had other parts of their Ways to fulfill this day, this year, or this life, and had not been sent to battle. The sea of faces went back further than seemed possible: hopeful, worried, tense.

The oldest of the lords, their faces as impassive as the wall behind them, watched the warriors and the crowd, gauging the moment. Waiting.

Silence fell on the grounds of the great city.

"Tell us," Ah Beh demanded.

The leader stopped showing his teeth. "We did not lose." He paused. "We drove them away, and the celebration tomorrow will go on. But many enemies live to return. They ran, to fight again. Soon. They will return. Still, even now, our fastest runners hunt captives."

"Who is *they*?" a different lord asked.

The warrior looked at the lord who had asked, disgust and anger on his face. "Some were people I have never seen, but some have danced with us before."

The news rippled through the crowd, heading back toward the wall, moving from one mouth to another like the living thing it was.

Ah Bahlam remembered the boy who had given them water, and hoped he lived.

The crowd parted as the high priest came through it, striding quickly, purposefully. He glared at the Lords of Itzá, at the warriors, squinted at the Wall of Skulls. His eyes stopped at Ah Bahlam. They seemed to penetrate Ah Bahlam's very being, taking his measure.

Ah Bahlam trembled. The nascent being that was his Way rose in him, demanding voice and substance. He refused it, standing his ground until the high priest's gaze moved on.

With a mighty leap, an inhuman leap, the High Priest of K'uk'ulkan landed on top of the Wall of Skulls and paced its length once, then twice. He still wore his feathered armbands and leg bands, and his mask. He appeared ready to fly from the top of the wall. As he returned to the middle, he stopped and raised his arms. "You heard the news! We did not lose. We won. Our warriors were valiant and brave, and they are but part of our strength."

The crowd watched. Low whispers carried from near the back, but everyone who could see the high priest appeared mesmerized by his movement, his words, his presence.

"We are to celebrate as if there will be no tomorrow, demand of the gods that they visit us. That is *our* strength. It *will be* our strength. We will offer fit sacrifice and fit energy, we will offer our blood and the blood of our enemies. We will dance here atop our enemies' skulls years from now. We will dance here until time itself stops and the world turns to a new Way. Now, we will dance the rain back!"

The crowd began to stamp their feet. The lords stamped theirs. The high priest lowered his arms and raised them again, following and then leading the beat. He cried out; the crowd echoed him, drawn in the wake of his power like petals in the wind.

The sound of hundreds of feet stamping on stone surfaces rose, surely traveling all the way to the camps of their enemies.

CHAPTER 35

Alice approached a huge white canvas tent, with the flags of at least thirty countries flapping on poles outside. Layers of gauzy mosquito netting completed the circus-like effect. To reach the door, she had to walk between four black-clad men with rifles held close to their chests, and two big dark dogs that didn't so much as wag a tail at her. She could have pretended they were statues if their ears had stood still or they had no scent.

The gossamer nets parted for her and a hand took her invitation and ushered her into another world. Costumed waiters dressed like the Xcaret resort version of Mayans wandered about in body paint, feathers, and perfect tanned physiques. They looked thoroughly ridiculous carrying dainty trays with slender drinks or finger-food appetizers. Their female counterparts pulled the mix off a little better. While they were also perfectly built and ridiculously thin, they wore simple white dresses with flowers in their hair.

At least seventy people of various nationalities wandered about the crowd.

Alice had changed into a lacy sky-blue shirt and donned her best silver and turquoise jewelry, which meant she was only a little underdressed.

The tables were laid with white linen and each had a crystal vase with a different orchid in it. Bromeliads in full flower had been fastened to the tent poles. Alice found her hand-lettered name card on a table in the far corner.

As she was about to begin her second attempt at a casual slow circle through the crowd, she felt a light hand on her shoulder and turned to find Madam Roy, regal in a gold sari lined with a rainbow of colors. Her dark eyes sparkled warmly in her round, brown face. "Alice," she said. "I enjoyed your tour."

"Thank you, ma'am. It was my honor."

"Would you be willing to sit with me for a few moments?" the prime minister asked, walking over to a row of white chairs lining the side of the tent. "And, please, call me Aditi."

After they took their seats, Aditi turned serious eyes on her. "You know more than you told us today. I can feel it." She held up a slender hand decorated with silver rings. "Oh, not about politics. But about this place. You know something is happening. I've felt it, too. In India, many people are turning to the old ways. Rich old people have started wondering the streets as beggars. Many speak of the return of Buddha. The legislature is busy being modern, and doing a good job of it, and we are building and expanding our schools and industries. But there is a counter-movement. Is this also happening in the United States?"

Surely someone in Aditi's place would know. So was she testing Alice? "Some of our conservatives are becoming more rigid, but that isn't new. Mostly, people are scared by so much change. The weather seems to be turning on us and global economics is tougher than climate change. But America also has a strong core." She looked over and spotted the president next to Marie, pointing to him. "We have a good leader."

Aditi's voice was soft. "I am not questioning your loyalty. But the small stories often fall through the news like water through a sieve. Interesting things are hidden by the kinds of news that interest many people, like your daughter swimming with turtles."

Alice glanced at Marie, deep in conversation. Her protocol cram-session had said, don't offer unless asked. Aditi was asking. She took a deep breath and looked again at Aditi's brown, crinkly face with the warm eyes. Was she more likely to create a diplomatic incident by answering or not answering?

Aditi patted Alice's shoulder. "I'm asking as a woman, a mother. And as me."

All right. "I don't know why the turtles came to Nix," Alice said. "I'm a scientist, and not religious. I'm confused myself about some of the things that I see happening. That are happening to my family."

"Is your daughter confused?"

"I wish. Or at least scared."

Aditi blew out a short breath and put her hand over Alice's. "Healthy children are magical beings, and not easily frightened. The world is a strange place now. Do you think tomorrow will be stranger than today?"

Alice laughed, unable to ignore the surreal feeling of sitting beside the Indian Prime Minister and holding hands. "The question is what will the day after tomorrow be like? For a long time, I did not think it would be any different. But now I'm not so sure."

"I dreamed," Aditi said. "The night before last. You were in the dream, and you were here, but it was different than it looks today. When I woke up, I thought Chichén Itzá would look like my dream, but the place in my dream was much brighter. I am sure you are the woman who was in my dream."

"Was my daughter there, too?"

Aditi shook her head. "There was a man with a computer."

Peter? Alice held her tongue.

"And a young woman, but she had dark hair. I saw your daughter in the turtle picture and it wasn't her." She hesitated. "I just wanted to tell you about it. I don't know why. But I've learned to follow my instincts."

A bell rang, and the man in white who had been chief herd-dog on the tour stood at a podium. "Please take your seats," he called. Aditi squeezed Alice's hand before letting it go.

Alice said, "Thank you," and went to find her seat. Was Aditi's dark-haired woman Oriana or Hun Kan?

It turned out that no one at her table spoke English as a first language, and she and a French Canadian woman next to her managed to get through an awkward conversation in a mix of poor Spanish (Alice's was better), medium English, and poor French (Alice's was far worse).

The food was better than the sound system. The speeches and translations were hard to hear so far from the podium, and by the time dinner was over and the waiters picked up the empty banana sherbet bowls, she had smiled and nodded so many times that her cheeks hurt.

People began filing out. Alice hadn't managed more than a few long-distance smiles in Marie's direction, so she waited at her table until Marie came over and sat down in the same chair the French Canadian had been in. She had a glass of red wine in her hand. "Sorry for the lousy seating," she said. "Nice tour. Thanks."

Alice smiled and reached for her water glass.

"No wine?"

"Earlier. I have to drive home."

Marie raised her glass. "This is the first I've had. It's not bright to drink and save the world."

"Did you? Save the world?"

Marie shook her head and drank some more wine. "It's more like a never-ending process of small talk and big deal making. China is still refusing to talk about anything that matters. Mexico is too poor and there is too little governmental control. But the current administrations gets kudos for taking big bribes from us instead of a million small ones from their own dirty industries. I think. If I can trust my sources."

"And India?"

Marie glanced over at her. "I saw you talking to Aditi."

"She's had dreams. Dreams like ours. She said she saw me in one."

Marie nodded. "She is very earthy. Spiritual even. And she's convinced a lot of her country to use solar power. They're a nuclear power, and becoming a space power. They know it and use the strength that gives them—Aditi included. But in some ways they are still a beggar country. The double monsoon season almost killed them."

Alice knew. Hundreds of thousands dead. But that was out of her control, and her league. Marie's territory. "What do you think of her dreams?"

"I think she's honest. I'm glad more world leaders are women than at any other time. I have no idea what Emilio or Huo Jiang dream." She lowered her voice. "I hope they dream of something besides themselves and power."

The colorfully dressed waitstaff had been replaced by smaller, rounder busboys who moved quietly, only occasionally clanking dishes or forks as they filled blue plastic tubs.

"Will everyone who was here today be here tomorrow?"

Marie put down her empty glass and sighed. "Mostly. We have work sessions all day, so we won't get to the Ball Court until just before the game starts."

"I hope I see you again," Alice said, meaning it.

"Join me," Marie said. "I'll make sure there's room. I'd like to meet your daughter. That is, unless you have other plans?"

Ian. Damn him. "We'd love to. We have tickets for seats, and we'll be there early."

"Watch for me on my way in, and then I'll seat you with us. We have a great view."

She looked so earnest that Alice couldn't imagine turning her down. Maybe Ian would show up before the game. "Thanks." Her face flushed even though she'd been going easy on the wine. Hard to decide whether to be Marie's college friend or her citizen. Hard to be both. "I'm looking forward to tomorrow."

"Me, too," Marie said, "Me too." She stood up and offered Alice a hand. "Now go on. Get home to your daughter. If I don't sleep, I won't be awake to see your stars align."

Alice laughed. "Me either. May you have good dreams."

Marie stopped and looked at her, suddenly serious. "I hope so. I hope the whole damned world has good dreams."

On impulse, Alice leaned in and hugged Marie. Marie returned the hug, tight and quick, and plucked a vase with a bright purple orchid from the table. "Take this."

Alice smiled. "Thank you."

Marie was as mercurial as ever, and as strong as ever. Good thing.

CHAPTER 36

Drums sounded in the dark, coming toward Chichén from the jungle. Ah Bahlam tensed and sat up straighter, listening carefully. Not what he had feared. Not war drums. The drums of warriors coming in from the jungle, telling the people of Chichén that they returned with captives.

He stood, and his father and mother, who had been sitting with him, stood also. There would be news. They walked quickly, joining a steady stream of other aristocratic families heading across the great plaza they had all just left after a night of dancing, drinking balché, and praying.

The festivities had been fine: bright events to face down trouble and call the gods to their side. So what if an edginess hid just under the twirling women and the chattering men? Except it did matter. He hated the way people kept their children close and stayed in groups

The news could be good.

Ah Bahlam himself had danced to the memory of two young men who had been his classmates, had felt the double edge of despair and strength, had held his place, his Way, his role as a young Lord of Itzá. It had been hard. Perhaps this would be their reward.

Ah Bahlam's father carried a torch, and at least one torch drove the blackness away from each group. A convergence of lights in the dark, like heartbeats, all seeking good news.

They got near enough to the front of the crowd to see the drums and warriors and captives pour through the gate. Seven of the enemy had been caught, and all lived. A few of the warriors who returned with them had been counted among the missing, and cries of joy greeted them.

Torches passed, hand over hand, until each returning warrior held one. Beneath the flickering flames, seven stoic and sweaty captives were ringed by about twenty ecstatic and sweaty fighters of K'uk'ulkan.

A mother and her young daughter brought water to be passed through the returning warriors, and then another one gave water to the captives, honoring them, too, as was the Way of Chichén.

They would be honored until they died.

People pushed and crowded in to get a better look, and Ah Bahlam let some step between him and his parents.

He faded back, and then further back. In just a few moments, he had reached the crowd's edge. All attention would be here for some time while the warriors' stories traveled mouth to mouth through the crowd.

He had planned to wait until everyone slept to find Hun Kan, but this was even better, for the high priest himself would come here.

As soon as he stepped away from the plaza and neared the gate that would lead him to the quarters of the high priest, he slid into a slow, quiet jog, careful to avoid being seen by the few people that he passed, all still going the other way, toward the news.

The high priest lived inside a stone building. Along the outside, temporary wooden structures with thatched roofs stood a line. She would be kept here. The small huts served acolytes and students, but were never fully occupied.

He passed a painted white bone snake on the outside of the first building and peered inside the small window to find it empty of everything but a wooden table, a closed chest, and a sleeping mat. The peccary, the tapir, the ocelot, the puma, the jaguar, the macaw, the monkey, the quetzal—all empty except for various bits of simple furniture. The lower-level acolytes of the high priest did not share his opulent lifestyle.

He found Hun Kan inside a small room with Cauac's totem, a turtle, painted on the outside. He should have known to start there.

Her back was to both the door and the window. She lay on her side, her dark hair spilling across her face. Her feet were bound even though her arms were free. How dare he bind her feet! It made her test herself every moment since with her hands free, she could free herself. She had more honor than the high priest! But maybe that was what he tested—the extent to which her will bowed to his.

Ah Bahlam pushed hard on the door. It slammed open so easily he nearly stumbled. He rushed to her side. She flinched, not seeing him. "Go away!" Then she lifted her head and breathed out, "Ah Bahlam!" She sat up. "You should not be here. You have broken sacred law. You'll die if you get caught."

"I had to know you're all right. And you're not." Great streaks of blood stained her arm. Ni-ixie's bright blue gift remained on her wrist, but it had been scratched. The scratches that were shallow on the gift continued deep down her arm, still bleeding slowly. They were at least a few hours old.

She swallowed and looked up at him. Her eyes were rimmed in red from crying, but at the moment they were dry and clear. "There is nothing to be done. My family has asked after me, and been refused admittance. Only the high priest himself has talked to me."

He stroked her cheek. "I'm here."

"Please go," she said. "This is between me and the high priest, me and my fate. I won't be able to bear it if you're killed."

"But you may be," he hissed.

"You're not thinking," she insisted. "You're feeling. This is not the time to challenge the high priest."

An echo of exactly what he had told his jaguar in the Dance of the Way. He didn't tell her that.

Hun Kan continued. "Don't be weak. You must accept whatever happens to me." She looked away from him, but her voice didn't falter. "After all, I am here. I know the turtle is painted on the outside of my place of keeping. Gods and goddesses rise from the turtle's shell, but they must die first."

If she were a stranger, he would admire her words.

She had gone beyond him into some place of acceptance he refused to follow.

They couldn't just run away. If his father weren't so powerful, just the act of him being here could kill his family. "My father said the high priest is looking for sacrifices. He believes you could be chosen." He touched her face. "But there is good news, there are captives."

She lifted her bloody arm and put a finger across his lips. "Nothing certain has been said to me. I will live until tomorrow, at least. He says I will watch the game."

Ah Bahlam wanted Hun Kan free now! And yet there was no honorable path to that freedom. He would have to think, and plan, and pray, and hope.

Her great dark eyes, dry for herself, began to fill with bright water. "After the Dance of the Way, he came back and spoke to me. He wanted to know if you had ever spoken ill of him or of our traditions. I said of course not. But why did he ask?"

Ah Bahlam shook his head. "The jaguar is strong, and while it rode me in the dance it . . . hesitated when he challenged it."

Her eyes widened. "What does that mean? Hesitated?"

He recounted as much of the experience as he could, watching her lips grow tighter and her eyes rounder as he spoke.

She clutched his arm. "The Dance of the Way is beyond the men who dance it. I have heard him say so. What will he do?"

"I don't know." He hadn't told her about the red warrior who stopped him and suggested the priest's own elite might support a challenge. He needed to think about that, about what it meant for Chichén to be assaulted from inside and outside. He wanted her opinion, but fear for her held his tongue.

"Surely we have a few moments." He looked down at her wrist. Perhaps, if he could figure out how to remove the gift, the high priest would lose interest in Hun Kan. Her arm was so sliced and raw along one side that he paused before he touched it gently. "May I?"

She shook her head. "Don't take it even if you can. If I die, I wish to wear Ni-ixie's gift, to recall her smile. I want a friend among the gods."

"Pah," he spat, disappointed and a little angry. "If you don't act to save yourself, your friend among the gods will be Ixtab, goddess of suicide."

She flinched at his words, but reached her hand up and curled it around the back of his neck. "Perhaps Ni-ixie is one of her faces. We do not know." She pulled him down so that his face came close to hers, and then she lifted her head and kissed him.

She had not kissed him in all the days they raced home through the jungle. Touching her lips with his sent fire through him, a heat that melted his bones. The jaguar inside his belly uncurled. He cupped her head with his free hand and let himself fall into her scent, even the scent of her blood; it brought back a brief vision of their blood mingling with Cauac's in the altar bowl at Zama.

It would all be right. Whatever happened would be right. This moment, this kiss, was right. It was all so right that he wanted to scream, to hear his throaty growl bounce off of the boles of large trees in the depths of the sacred jungle.

She broke away first, whispering in his ear. "Footsteps. People come. You must go."

He fled.

His path didn't cross whoever made the footsteps, and he didn't think they saw him. He crouched low, running on all fours until he was back where he was free to walk. He headed for the gates, passing people drifting home. There must have been some cloud on his features, for very few people greeted him.

The jaguar was supposed to retreat from him after the Dance of the Way, to wait until it was called. It hadn't—it had stayed in his belly, a small thing, barely noticed, but watchful. He felt it inside him now, but at least it didn't ride him.

He passed through the stone markers of the same gate the captives had come in, empty now, and then moved along the outside of the wall, staying unseen. He followed human and animal paths, guided by moonlight, twisting his steps upon each other until he was nearly lost. Finally, he knew to stop at the edge of a short cliff. A great dark hole opened below him: the sacred cenote.

He sat with his legs folded under him and placed his knife in front of his knees on the earth.

Trees and bushes enveloped him, hard to name in the near-dark. Frog-song rose from below, and he heard the soft splashes of fish in the sacred water.

He let the jungle take away his thoughts. Eventually his heart slowed, he breathed with the leaves and the night birds and the sleeping daytime animals. He slithered against rough bark with the snakes and felt the trees in the way of bats.

But who, in this moment, should he pray to? K'inich Ahaw slept at night. Chaac turned his face. The jaguar god sat with him.

K'ul'ulkan. Did he dare?

He opened the question out to the jungle, the cenote, the power of this place.

The jaguar inside him stirred and he spoke to it. "It will be all right. This is a choice with honor."

The jaguar snarled at him, a low grumbling that resonated deep in his bones.

He chose the same arm he had cut in Zama. His knife drew a lightning stroke of pain across his skin and blood flowed wet down his arm.

K'uk'ulkan, accept my blood, my life, my center. Let Hun Kan live, a fit vessel for you. Let honor be found for all of us. Let the captives provide strong sacrifice for you, and let the ball stay in the air tomorrow as a sign of your pleasure. Let it pass through the hoop of the world.

He sat still as his blood flowed dark onto the dark earth. He breathed the jungle in and out, the palms and kapoks and ceibas and orchids and peccaries and wolves and birds, the stones and dirt and the scent of the sacred water below him. He became a jungle animal more than a man, the jaguar inside him and more than that, as if he were all the wild and sacred beings surrounding Chichén.

When he stood on weak legs and began to walk back, taking a more direct route, his head felt clear, although his heart still hurt. Maybe walking the right path always hurt the heart.

CHAPTER 37

Nixie sat up in bed, leaning against a yellow pillow propped up against the wall, her book open on her lap. The flying horses were interesting, and she would love to live in the world they lived in, where girls rode the great-hearted beasts to save their kingdom. If she had been reading this at home, she would have devoured it in a day. But here the black ink fuzzed into clouds on the page. She wasn't tired; she and Oriana had napped half the afternoon and then she'd swam in the pool while Oriana fussed with her costume for tomorrow—she was going to be a dancer at Chichén in the afternoon.

All in all, it had been an ordinary day. But now, with Oriana gone and her mom fast asleep (she had looked exhausted when she came home, and hugged Nixie and listened to her day and told her about seeing the president, but she had fallen asleep before Nixie, something she *never* did), Nixie was awake and nervous. Where was Ian? How was Hun Kan? She had learned nothing today.

She put the book down and picked up her feather, running it back and forth in her hand. Maybe she'd dream something tonight, but she needed to get to sleep first. She did like their new rooms. She and her mom both had big separate bedrooms so her mom didn't take up the living room every night.

She got up and walked out, staring at the television. She didn't really want to watch anything. She still held the feather in one hand. She set it down and went to the sliding glass door by the balcony, opening it a few inches. Ocean smells soaked into the room while soft waves whispered against the shore. There was no wind, and here, on the far end of the resort, she heard no voices beneath the balcony. Just the waves.

Nixie picked up the feather, and in her free hand she picked up Snake, wrapping the long green beast around her robe like a belt and clutching his head to her. She settled on the gold couch.

She closed her eyes and counted the breaks of the waves, an uneven metronome.

The waves flickered in and out, a soft, soothing sound in her ears that slowly saddened into sobs. The air cooled.

She opened her eyes.

Dream eyes.

She stood on a packed-dirt surface that felt cool under her feet. Stars filled the sky, and she recognized the ancient fullness that had arched over them all two nights ago by the sacbe.

Soft sobbing drew her attention. Like at Tulum. Hun Kan. It had to be Hun Kan. The sobs came from behind a wooden wall with a turtle painted on it. The image was almost as tall as Nixie, and crude.

There were other huts, a line close together. The bulky dark form of a stone temple blotted the stars just behind the huts.

There was a door in the wall with the turtle, at the far left. As she walked toward it, her feet made no sound. When she reached out for the door, it felt like putting her hand into a drift of sea-fog even though it looked like solid rough-hewn wood. It was closed. When she pushed on it, it didn't move.

She stared at it.

She pushed again. Nothing.

She ran at it, throwing her shoulder into it, and actually felt a stab of pain. The door barely registered her assault.

There had to be a way. This was a dream. She'd known she would dream tonight. But it wasn't like the dream from before, the time they could feel the thick roughness of the stones by the sacbe as solid things and when the jaguar's throaty roar had made her bones shake. Now, she felt like a ghost.

Her mom's hand had passed through the leather necklace the bead had been strung on.

She stepped through the door as if it weren't even there.

The room was empty except for Hun Kan lying alone on a dirt floor. She wore a red dress lined with yellow, bunched around her knees. A thick rope bound her feet. The skin under the rope was red and angry.

Nixie's eyes traveled up Hun Kan's body, stopping at her side. She not only breathed, she cried. Softly, like the waves through the resort window. Nixie bent down, whispering, "Hun Kan."

There was no answer, no change.

Hun Kan didn't open her eyes, but simply lay still, sobbing quietly. Every once in a while, a fresh teardrop ran down a track on her cheek and fell onto a quarter-sized patch of mud on the dirt floor. She must have been crying a long time.

What had happened?

Dream Nixie ran her hands over her friend, feeling her body, both of their bodies, but barely. Hun Kan stirred, and rolled over onto her back. One of her hands held the other wrist, the knuckles bloody. The wrist that held Nixie's watch.

Someone had tried to cut it from her! They'd cut Hun Kan cruelly, but only scratched the watch face. The band was made of woven Kevlar. Didn't they know nothing short of high-carbon stainless steel would cut it?

Well, of course not.

The face of the watch was visible. Nixie crouched beside her friend, staring at the watch for so long that her cheeks were soaked with tears.

Hun Kan didn't move.

When Nixie opened her eyes and found Snake's head soaked in her tears, it was midnight.

She had given Hun Kan the watch.

What had she done?

DECEMBER 21, 2012

CHAPTER 38

The big white bus they rode in smelled like plastic and old coffee. Nixie groaned as a security guard gave them lists of rules. You'd think that after her mom got to tour all those important people, they'd have been picked up by a black limo, or at least been able to drive their own car. By the time they got to Chichén Itzá, they were already two hours late.

At least they were here.

She had to find Hun Kan and show her how to take off the watch. She should have listened to Ian about not giving the old Mayans anything. She had to make this right.

The parking lot was closed to all traffic except buses and more buses. Nixie stood by her mom in a long, colorful line of people snaking toward the main gates of Chichén Itzá. She stared at the parts of the ruins she could see over people's heads. The bright primary colors she knew belonged to the real Chichén, the old one, streamed from this one on banners. It looked like a party.

Nixie fidgeted with the bead they had dug up from the past, which she'd stuck in her front pants pocket. The necklace draped over her white shirt, looped twice so it wouldn't catch on anything. Most important, the quetzal feather, wrapped carefully in cardboard, stuck in the back band of her pants. The top of it tickled her ear. Her mom had argued so much about the necklace Nixie hadn't said anything about the feather. Now, she stood a little sideways, hoping her mom wouldn't notice.

Her mom clutched Nixie's hand, but otherwise she seemed far away. She had woken tense and growly this morning, and every few minutes she glanced down at her phone, looking for messages.

For Ian. He hadn't come back, and her mom was worried. Not that she said so, but they were all doing it, Nixie and Oriana and Alice, talking about him from time to time and checking their phones obsessively.

Oriana had said he was supposed to be here, that he had a pass in as a security guy. Maybe Oriana had already found him.

Nixie rubbed the bead in her pocket for luck.

They shuffled forward a few more steps and then stopped again. A man in white shorts walked by with popsicles. Nixie's mom bought two juice sticks and handed one to Nixie, already dripping sugary-orange drops onto the dirty parking lot. Nixie's hand was sticky from clutching the empty stick by the time they got to the gates, and showed their tickets and ID. The gate guard seemed impressed by the paper her mom showed and talked to her in Spanish, pointing away from where he was sending most other people.

Inside, it was emptier than Nixie had expected after the long line. There *were* a lot of people, but there was still room to walk and space to sit.

Her mom led her to a small staff bathroom in the back of a building to wash the sticky juice from their fingers. She pulled a comb through Nixie's hair, fussing with it far more than usual. She cocked her head and used the comb to flip up the front side. "You might as well take that out, now."

Nixie slid the cardboard and the feather out from her back, relieved and a little apprehensive. "I might need it. Why else did he give it to me, if not for today?"

Her mom gave her a dark look. "You're to stay close to me. I don't want you going back."

Nixie stroked the feather softly, careful to brush it only down from the slightly crushed shaft to the delicate tip. "I might not be able to help it mom. I never choose to go back."

"What about Tulum?"

"I chose to hear who was crying."

"You chose on the sacbe."

There wasn't anything she could say to that so she turned and splashed water on her face.

Her mom gave an exaggerated I'm-not-happy-but-I-won't-get-you-in-trouble-now sigh. "I wish you hadn't brought it. You have to take care of it now."

"I will." She didn't want to talk about it—she just wanted to go back and find Hun Kan as fast as possible. "Let's go."

They neared the entrance to the Ball Court just as announcers began loudly exhorting, "Clear the center," in a rotation of Spanish, Mayan, and English.

They stood in another line of sweaty people and produced two more tickets to show they should be there. Her mom handed her one, smiling. "Don't lose this."

"I won't." At least her mom trusted her that far. They always did this at movies and plays, too.

Two sets of temporary bleachers had been erected along the sides of the Ball Court, away from the great stone wheels the players would eventually try to hip and elbow and head-bump the heavy balls through. It was crowded, all except for the tallest set of bleachers, closest to the middle, cordoned off with yellow and black VIP tape.

Security guards herded people to their seats until the main floor of the Ball Court was empty.

Drums sounded.

A man in a red costume stood at the top of the steps leading up to the Temple of the Jaguar. His headdress was as tall as he was, with bright macaw feathers that stuck out almost in a sunshine pattern. His face was masked like a bird and he wore a skirt with feathers and beads in it. His bare legs were long and brown. Below his knees, he wore leather circles that even more feathers dangled from. "He doesn't look real, mom."

"None of this looks real, anymore."

"No kidding."

The announcer was on an English round, and Nixie caught the words, "Last time a ball game was played here could have been five hundred years ago, or even seven hundred. And perhaps this is the last ball game that will be played here. You are . . . "

Nixie let the voice fuzz out, already knowing from Oriana that there would be dancers first. Oriana would be one of them, even though she was Italian and not Mayan. But she spoke a little Mayan and lived here, and had dark hair and eyes. That had been enough for a bit part.

Drums wafted in through the entrance. The drummers came in first, wearing white leather pants and vests and black boots. Women in simple white shirts and flaring white skirts followed them. Nixie looked for the red skirt Oriana had been working on, but everyone, even the men, wore white. The performers faced away from the drums, which picked up speed until the dancers flung themselves out, the women circling and the men doing acrobatics. It was too modern. She glanced up at her mom. "This isn't right. It's not even close."

Her mom whispered, "They're going backwards. Remember how in the Xcaret show they started with the old times and moved forward? This is starting with now and moving backward, and supposed to take us slowly to the ball game."

But Hun Kan needed her now. "Mom? In the old time, are they having ceremonies, too?"

"I suppose so. They had them every year here on the solstice. It's always the same date."

So if time was a stack of cards, there were hundreds of dances going on all at once, all on this day. Nothing was going to happen just sitting here. Clearly there'd been a ticket sold for every inch of hot silver seat on the bleachers. "Can I go walk around? I'm waiting for Oriana's dance and it's going to be *hours*."

"No."

She hated being eleven. Why couldn't she be sixteen or even twenty?

CHAPTER 39

The morning sun stung Ah Bahlam's eyes. Then his father's face blotted it out, his eyes angry and his jaw tight as a drumhead. "The High Priest of K'uk'ulkan sent a runner to me this morning. You will not play in the game. You will have no role in the game." He stared down, pain and anger both shaping his features. "You will watch it only."

Ah Bahlam blinked, silent for a long time as disappointment twisted to anger, souring his blood. "Will I dance the doors of the world open?"

"All the lords do," his father said. "Even the ones out of favor."

That stung.

Then he leaned down and grabbed Ah Bahlam's blood-streaked arm. He stared at the deep sacrificial cuts, still angry-red with dried blood. "Maybe the high priest is right." He jerked Ah Bahlam up, wrenching his sore arm and sending shooting pains all the way to his head. "You think you learned enough in less than a year with the shamans to mix your own sacrifices into the power of *this* ceremony? What will the high priest think when he sees this, especially after you challenged him in the dance?"

Ah Bahlam was getting tired of restraint. He pushed himself up, trembling with fatigue, anger, and fear. Tasting the fear allowed some of the anger to leak away, but he refused to back down into being a child at the mercy of his father's words. He made his own words come out slowly, demonstrating his control. "Father, I did what I needed to. Warriors are allowed to make personal sacrifices. It is done, and even if I wanted to, I can't undo it."

"I raised you to take my place."

Ah Bahlam sat quietly, waiting.

"Mayan lords must be brave. Courage without thought kills a lot of us. Perhaps you will dead before the year is over." Ah Bahlam's father turned his face away. "All I can hope now is that you have an honorable death."

He watched the back of his father's head, willing him to turn around and smile, to look proud of him even if he was worried. It had all started with Ni-ixie. He had not called her, had not chosen her. She had chosen him. He had to trust. "Father?"

"Yes?" His father did turn, and he looked as sad as Ah Bahlam felt.

No words would heal this rift. He drew a breath, surrendered. "It's time to go. We must eat and prepare to dance the world open before the game."

"Wash the blood from your arm before your mother sees it."

Ah Bahlam cut off a bitter laugh. He stood and headed toward a basin of water the kitchen slaves had just filled for the day.

At least the jaguar did not seem to live inside his skin this morning. He sensed that he could call it, but he wanted to be clearly and only himself for a while. He took a cup of water and walked away from the family compound to scrub his wounds. His arm stung, and he wished for Hun Kan's soft hands to clean his cut as she had the now-healing gash across his thigh. Even more, he longed for the simplicity of Zama, the ease of being a student. Chichén was so much more confusing and terrible than it had seemed when he was still a young man.

He had dreamed so hard of being a grown-up Lord of Itzá.

And all summer he had dreamed of playing in the game. This game.

He had to return to the basin twice to get enough water to wash all the blood off.

CHAPTER 40

Alice finally spotted Oriana swirling and dipping, third back in a line of four, her synchronization just a little off. The bright red skirts looked like carnations from a distance and roses when the women came closer. The men they danced with also wore red, with white shirts. The announcer was busy claiming that red stood for sacrifice, for blood, and that the dancers chose the color to symbolize death, and thus avoid it. The dance was the sacrifice.

Exactly the kind of nonsense Alice hated on tour buses. The sacrificial life and choices of ancient Mayans was neither simple nor completely understood, but they had clearly seen death as part of a life that continued after death. Kings had decapitated themselves at the height of their power. Mayans danced to please the gods and gain power, not to forestall death.

As Oriana came nearer, Alice leaned down close to her daughter. "She's having fun, isn't she?"

Nixie nodded, her eyes tracking Oriana, her hands stroking the feather, and her feet doing a staccato pound on the ground in front of them.

"Are you okay?" Alice asked. "You seem . . . so nervous." *Even more than me, and I'm nervous.* "Are you scared?"

Nixie kept her eyes on Oriana. She whispered, "I'm excited." She licked her lips. "And I want to see Ian."

Well, so did she.

"And Hun Kan," Nixie's eyes shone with determination.

Such focus. So much of her daughter's energy was centered on this other girl. "I can't help you there." Alice put a hand on Nixie's shoulder. "Do you want to meet my friend Marie?"

"When?"

Alice eyed the delegation she'd spotted coming in the gate, checking to make sure Marie was among them. "In about three minutes?"

Nixie turned around and blinked at her, then grinned. "Really?"

"She's asked us to sit with her."

"I . . . what if we just sit here?"

Why would Nixie say such a thing? And would she answer Alice if she asked? "She'll have better seats."

Nixie swallowed. "But I like these. We can see people come in and out the gate." She looked almost desperate. "Hun Kan," she whispered, just under her breath.

The first line of bodyguards already snaked behind their seats, moving toward the VIP bleachers. "Come on."

Alice breathed out a sigh of relief when Nixie actually stood. As they walked around to the back, Marie called a greeting to Alice and stopped to wait for them. The man in white was there again, and he stopped near Alice and Nixie, still unsmiling.

In just a moment, Marie reached them. She walked alone between two sets of bodyguards, and gestured Alice and Nix to her side. "Hello! You must be Nixie."

Nixie gazed at her evenly, as if taking her measure. No awe, no fear. Just curiosity. "I'm happy to meet you."

Marie smiled. "Will you tell me about the turtles?"

"Sure." Now Nix blushed. She didn't seem happy, though. They hadn't finished the conversation that Marie's arrival had interrupted.

The VIP bleachers filled in quickly. To Alice's surprise, they were actually seated just below Marie, close enough for conversation.

The dance started to wind down, and Oriana's group came close to the assembled VIP's. The drums rose to a strong beat and then fell, the dancers slowing, and slowing, matching the falling and softening drum until they stood completely still.

Applause erupted and dancers bowed. Oriana looked toward where they had been.

Nixie squeezed Alice's hand quickly. "She'll look for us by our old seats. I'll be right back." She handed Alice the long quetzal father, and without waiting for an answer, she was gone.

Alice shivered in spite of the sticky heat. She didn't want Nixie off alone, even though she should be able to see her from here.

Above her, Marie laughed softly. "Spunky."

Nix was eleven. She could find her way back. Alice stretched, trying to get rid of the worry riding her spine. "Marie? Did you have a good night?" *How were your dreams?*

"It was hard to get to sleep. I kept thinking about old times here and about how different everything is now."

I keep thinking about yesterday when we were on the temple of K'uk'ulkan. Or that's what Alice thought she meant. "I slept so well I don't even remember if I did dream. But maybe that's because it was so late when I got home."

"What did I miss here?" Marie asked.

"Nix's babysitter danced in that last dance—the one with the red dresses." She looked over and spotted Nix by the old seats, although Oriana wasn't with her. A new set of dancers, men dressed in costumes that made them look like birds and animals, trotted slowly onto the field. Good. The dance of the Wayob. Maybe this would be the last dance. It wasn't the right historical order, or even the right day for this particular dance. But it would be majestic. "There's a theory that in the old days the dances were supposed to open portals to the stars. Particularly to the Milky Way—to the dark rift I was telling you about yesterday."

"Maybe these dances will do the same," Marie mused.

Alice kept her eyes on Nix. "I think the old dancers had help. Mayan shamans used hallucinogens. And everyone was of one religious mind."

"Your friend who danced? What does she believe in?"

Alice frowned, surprised that the question was so hard to answer. "I don't know. She's been with us every day for a week, but I never asked her. She's a reef diver and she believes in conservation. She wants peace. But I don't know if she has a . . . a religion."

"Was she with you when you went hiking?"

Alice nodded, squinting, looking for Nix. She couldn't see her, but a small group of people milled about, letting someone down the bleachers. Surely Nix was just too small to see in a standing crowd.

"Can you find your babysitter, so I can talk to her?" Marie asked.

"Now?" Alice turned to look up at Marie, surprised. Clearly, Marie meant it. "Sure, I can try."

Marie held out her hand. "Want me to watch the feather for you?"

She handed it to Marie. "I'll be right back."

She stepped down into the crowd, looking for Oriana's slight, dark form, but even more, for Nixie's golden hair, which had disappeared in the moment she'd turned to hand the feather to Marie.

CHAPTER 41

A small crowd shifting unhappily to let a fat man down the bleachers gave Nix the perfect cover. If only her mom had let her go, so she didn't have to sneak away. But finding Hun Kan mattered more than anything.

She hurried past the guards, using a technique her mom had taught her a long time ago for foreign airports: Walk fast and look like you know exactly what you're doing. That got her out of the Ball Court, but then she stopped, unsure. Large crowds and guided groups milled noisily through the open spaces. The shadowy building she'd seen in her dream hadn't been very big, but it was stone. If it had survived, she'd recognize it. She needed a map. She started off for the entrance to find one.

Nixie was close enough to see the guards' faces when she stopped dead in her tracks. Ian. Coming toward her. He wore black pants and a white shirt, and carried a lightweight navy jacket with the bright yellow emblem for security on it. His dreadlocks were pulled back from his face and fell down his back in a neat ponytail. Peter walked on Ian's left. Ian leaned down, talking to an older man dressed in traditional Mayan clothes with a homemade pack slung around his middle and baby-blue tennis shoes on his feet. Don Thomas Arulo?

She raced toward them, cutting off three older women in her pell-mell rush, hardly noticing when one of them screeched at her in Spanish. Where had Ian been? What did he know?

She skidded to a stop when she got close, squinting. It wasn't Don Thomas Arulo. This man was older and more wrinkled, and his eyes were darker. Gray hair hung straight to his shoulders and a big home-made leather pouch was wrapped around his middle. Calm seemed to drip off of him, unless she looked directly at his eyes, which glittered with curiosity and looked a little . . . scared. As if he had great amounts of fear and quiet strength all at once, feelings Nixie had never seen together so clearly.

Ian's voice pulled her attention away. "Nixie! Am I ever glad to see you."

The old man's head whipped around faster than she would have thought possible. His dark eyes bored into hers, and then rolled up in his head as he bowed to her, so his eyes never left her even though he bent nearly in half. The fear still shone in his gaze, but also the same sort of wonder she'd seen in Hun Kan's eyes on the beach. When he stood back up, he said, "Ni-ixie?" in a voice so full of hope it plucked at her insides. He held out a hand to her, palm down.

She patted his hand. "Pleased to meet you."

"Cauac," he said, slowly, as if he wasn't sure she would understand. He reached out and touched the necklace from Hun Kan.

She glanced up at Ian.

He grinned at her. "Cauac," he repeated. "He's from Hun Kan and the bird-man's time. The bird man has a name—he's Ah Bahlam, which means 'jaguar.'"

Jaguar. She liked it. "How did you get here?" A car must have been hard on the old man. Besides, Ian's jeep was parked back at the resort. "Did you have Don Thomas Arulo's beetle?"

"Worse. We took a bus. Only way to get here. Line was two hours long."

She rolled her eyes. No wonder fear clung to Cauac. The modern world might be scary, but tourist buses were even worse.

Ian turned to Peter. "Can you take him and show him something close by?"

Peter nodded and led Cauac away.

"Where's your mom?" Ian asked.

She remembered the last time she saw him was when he and her mom kissed. Too bad she didn't have a copy of the picture with her. She watched his face closely as she said, "She's sitting with the President of the United States." She was rewarded for watching by seeing his eyes round and widen. "Well, and her friend, Marie. The science advisor."

He bit his lip for a second, looking over at Cauac and Peter, who had stopped by a tourist booth. "Are they watching the ball game?"

She nodded. "But it hasn't started yet. Just the dancing. Oriana already finished. She did great." She looked up into his eyes, trying to tell if he'd help her. "I have to find Hun Kan—I had a terrible dream. I dreamed she was locked up. They tied her up." She winced, and plowed into the next part, talking fast. "It's all my fault. I gave her my watch, remember? I dreamed her whole arm was bloody, but the watch was still on. Like they almost cut her arm off trying to get to it."

His lips drew together. "Why can't they just take it off? Did she see you put it on?"

She shook her head. "Well, maybe she did. But it's the kind with the clasp hidden in the band. The first time I got one, I had to work at it for a whole hour to figure it out. Even if she did see me put it on, she might not know how to take it off. I have to find her."

"Shhhh . . . I know." He knelt down so his eyes were at her level. "I know this is scary. And I know it matters. And I don't know why yet." He inclined his head toward Cauac and Peter. "I bet I can't get him into the Ball Court. Don't know if I want to. We'd have been inside an hour ago, even with the bus ride, but when he saw Chichén he just stopped and stared and then he cried and then he stared some more." Ian's eyes were sad. "He lived here once, when it was a real city. Makes me feel guilty for bringing him. But he has to be here. I don't know why, but I know he does."

"You can talk to him?"

Ian nodded. "Don Thomas was there to help me. At first I needed him, but once you learn it, Cauac's Mayan isn't so different from today. I can puzzle it out. The hard part is he doesn't have words for a lot of stuff we do, and he does have words for things I don't."

She nodded. "Is Don Thomas coming, too?"

"I think he's here. Have you seen him?"

"No. But we've mostly been in the Ball Court." She bit her lip. "I need to find Hun Kan. Are you coming?"

He stood back up. "Coming where?"

"I need a map."

He pulled one out of his back pocket. "I got it to show Cauac how we do maps. The Mayans had them, so I thought he'd like to see."

She took it from him and folded it out. "In my dream, there was a small pyramid. About four stories. Maybe a little bigger, but not like K'uk'ulkan. There were a lot of wooden huts around it and Hun Kan was in one of those. It had a turtle painted on it."

Ian's eyebrows rose. "Cauac's totem animal is a turtle."

She felt buoyant for a second, as if held up by hundreds of tiny turtles. Ian didn't even know she was turtle girl! He'd been gone so long. "I swam with turtles. A bunch of them. Back at the resort. They came to see me. Do you think that's why?"

Ian blinked at her, looking lost for words. "When?"

"The day before yesterday. The same day that we came back from getting the bead."

"Do you remember what time?"

"Sure. Late morning."

Ian gave her a big grin. "Maybe Cauac is a more powerful shaman than I thought."

She unfolded the map. "Why?"

"We went to Tulum. Straight from where we left you. Don Thomas wouldn't let us stop for food or coffee. He wouldn't tell me why. As soon as we got in, Don Thomas almost ran down to the beach, so fast we could barely keep up with him." Ian's voice had gone all storyteller, quick-paced and dramatic. "We raced down to the water, panting, and here was this old man climbing out of the water, naked. He just stood there, dripping wet, his feet getting stuck in the sand as the ends of the waves ran over him. When we walked up to him, he squinted at me, and you know what he asked?"

She shook her head.

"He asked if I was Ni-ixie." He drew out the pause in the middle of her name.

She giggled.

"He'd been out in the water calling for you. He told us he sent his turtle totem to fetch you. He'd heard about a fight and dead warriors, but he was sure Ah Bahlam and Hun Kan were okay. He seems to think they're special." He laughed. "They're so special they see you. Makes me special, too?"

She grinned again, but bent her head to the map, letting the idea that Cauac had sent the turtles sink in. Maybe if the turtles only spoke Mayan that explained why she hadn't quite gotten the message. She shook her head and stared at the map. "A small pyramid. It was stone, so it would still be there." She read the names by the squares that showed buildings. The smaller ones didn't have pictures. "Is it the High Priest's Tomb?"

Ian shook his head. "Too big. Maybe one of the buildings by the Las Monjas group?

She glanced down. "Maybe. But it says here that those were built later."

"Later than what?" Ian asked. "We never got an actual date. Although we can ask Cauac. He'd know it in the Mayan long count calendar. But I'd need a pencil or a computer to figure it out."

"Ask Peter."

Ian laughed.

There had to be a way to find the building. "Maybe there's a tourist book with pictures of everything over by Peter and Cauac."

"Good idea."

There was, and two or three places could have been right. She frowned and flipped back and forth between pages. "Can you tell Cauac what I saw, and ask him?"

Ian closed his eyes.

"Hurry," she whispered.

He nodded. "Wait here."

"Okay. Just hurry. Mom's going to be worried about me."

She shouldn't have said that. Ian's chin tightened and his eyes narrowed, but instead of a lecture he said, "Okay, I'll hurry."

Ian and Cauac talked. They did as much in gestures as words; maybe Ian didn't understand all that well after all. He called her over and had her talk about the dream, translating. Cauac's hands clenched and released, but he didn't show any other sign of worry. As he and Ian talked, and he gestured, ridged scars made red and white ropes of thin shadows down his forearms.

Ian asked her for a specific description of the hut, and how Hun Kan looked, and she described it and pantomimed Hun Kan's bound ankles. As soon as Ian finished translating, Cauac started walking.

Ian shrugged. "I guess we follow." He gestured to Peter, who fell in behind them. He still hadn't said anything more to her than a mumbled hello. She wasn't even sure he'd noticed her.

Part-way there, Ian leaned down and whispered, "It is in the Las Monjas."

He stopped in front of what could be the right building. It was the right height, but most of the edges had tumbled and worn to rounded ruin. "Is that it?"

She bit her lip. "It looked a lot sharper in my dreams."

He laughed. "Tulum was pretty sharp, too."

"The huts aren't there. But they weren't stone, so they wouldn't be. But how do we get back?"

Ian shook his head.

Nixie started walking around, imaging what it looked like in her dream. The paths, the huts, the glory of the brightly-colored building with its elaborate feathered serpent heads for decoration at every corner. It had been dirt then, where there was a neat green lawn now.

She tried to get all the dream-details, the whitish-brown dirt and the packed paths, the sharpness of the stone edges clear in her mind.

It didn't make any difference.

Nothing changed.

Cauac watched her silently. Peter sat down a distance away. Ian stood by Cauac and smiled at her from time to time, looking up up at the stars when he wasn't watching her.

Nixie bit her lip. Last night, dream-Nix had just walked through a wall. Could real-Nix just walk through time?

She paced. She closed her eyes. She tried calling, "Hun Kan," softly. The name fell in the modern world. She was here, felt here. There was no lightness in her.

She sat down on the grass and put her head in her hands.

CHAPTER 42

Drums and flutes and clapping kept a rhythm, rising and falling like the breath of the jungle. Everyone with a role in the game danced: the fire tenders who would keep the smoke of prayers rising from the walls, the players, the judges, the ball-retrievers who stood out of court, the high priest and the water boy. Even though he would only be a watcher, as a Lord of Itzá, Ah Bahlam had a role of his own. Not the one he'd wanted, but this wasn't the time to think about that. Swirling forms filled the Ball Court, costumed and not. Ah Bahlam wore his jaguar cloak, but not the awkward mask. Jaguar teeth rattled against his chest as he twirled and stamped.

Periodically, laughter rose.

The captives watched, solemn faced and serious. They had all been brought together at the top of the parapet of the game wall, surrounded by the warriors who captured them. No others stood beside them. Did that mean Hun Kan would not give her life?

Was he selfish to want life? He smiled and chanted, and the blood throbbed in his arm where he had sliced in ceremony the night before. His blood wanted to be free again, to flow like a river from his heart onto the Ball Court. It wanted to fill the underground rivers.

Blood like rain.

Blood heartbeat, loud in his ears. His feet stumbled as the dance dizzied him, but his beating heart and his jaguar did not let him fall.

Other dancers grinned giddily or grimaced as he caught flashes of their faces shining with afternoon sun, sweat dripping from their foreheads.

Dancing the portal open, so the players could game with the gods.

CHAPTER 43

Alice grew uneasy as walked through the crowds, searching the faces around her for Nix or Oriana. A man with the tail of a snake dragging in the packed earth behind him and a huge parrot-like head draped in red and green Macaw feathers passed close. His heavy footsteps and the sounds of shells rattling against his ankles drew her attention. What if Nixie wasn't here because she'd gone back? *Goneanywhen?*

She glanced at her phone. Nix was here, somewhere; her signal blinked right above Alice's.

She punched buttons quickly, demanding a close-in view. Dammit, if only she had the bandwidth to display a real-time aerial. Nix was close, but too far away to be in the Ball Court. Alice tried calling Nix's phone, but it went straight to voicemail.

She headed toward the gate, but she hadn't got five steps when she ran into Oriana coming toward her, dressed in jeans and a yellow T-shirt and an ear-to-ear grin.

"Did you see us? We hadn't done that well in any rehearsals, and we never got to practice here. It's like being in the Ball Court made us better."

"You looked great. Nix went to find you. But she's—I don't know. Out there somewhere." Alice pointed in the direction Nix's light indicated. "Did you see her?"

Oriana shook her head. "Want me to help look for her?"

Marie. She was supposed to get Oriana to Marie. At the least, she had to tell Marie she was going off to find Nix. "Look, come with me. Marie Healey wants to talk to you. Then I'll go look for Nixie."

Oriana gaped. "To me?"

"She wants to ask you about your dance. Maybe you can talk to her about the reefs. Come on, hurry. I need to go find Nix."

"I can help you."

"I can't just run off on the president's science advisor without telling her anything." She turned and started walking toward the VIP benches. Oriana came up beside her, whispering, "You really are worried, aren't you? You can see her beacon, right?"

Alice nodded.

"That's not so bad then," Oriana said.

"Maybe." Alice didn't like not being able to see Nix at all. "Have you heard from Ian?"

"No." Oriana sounded exasperated. "I told you he's a flake, sometimes. He's supposed to be here. He has security detail tonight. And I only have an hour's break. I just wanted to catch the start of the ball game."

The dance of the Wayob was still going on, but the dancers in the heaviest costumes already looked tired. "I don't think it will be long," Alice said.

They were almost at the VIP benches. Nix wasn't there.

She'd been right about the timing. The announcer's voice came over the air. "Please be seated. In ten minutes, the ball game will begin. Please be seated, the game is about to begin." The voice switched to Spanish.

Alice took the steps two at a time. Marie was deep in conversation with Aditi Roy, who now sat next to her. Some high end musical chairs. Marie put a finger up, forestalling Alice's planned interruption. *She had to go find Nix!*

Aditi smiled at her. "Alice! It's a pleasure to see you again. Who is your friend?"

Thank god for the prime minister's perceptiveness. Alice performed the introductions as quickly as she could, and then before anyone could start a conversation, she said, "I have to go find Nixie. She didn't come back, and her locator suggests she's not even in the Ball Court. I'll be right back."

Marie put a hand on Alice's forearm. "Let me send my folk. They'll find her. You don't want to miss the ball game."

"But . . . "

Marie shook her head. "I can send ten. After all, if anything bad is happening to her, armed soldiers with dogs will be able to stop it. We have her tracking ID and better bandwidth."

Of course they did. Marie didn't sound like "no" would be acceptable. Diplomatic teeth. Alice wanted to snarl back that armed soldiers with dogs wouldn't be able to stop Nix from going back in time. But neither would Alice.

The announcer had circled back around to English. "Please remain seated. Be prepared for a spectacle such as you've never seen before."

"Please?" Marie said. "My security people can go anywhere."

Alice bit back the reply she wanted to make and nodded. "But if they don't find her in twenty minutes I'm going, game or not."

Marie laughed. "They'll find her." She spoke a set of quick instructions into the air, ending with, "Use the turtle girl picture."

A reason to be glad of the damned picture. At least Nix's signal still burned bright blue. She wanted to look for Nix herself, but she finally turned toward Marie and said, "Thank you."

Marie nodded to acknowledge the thanks, but her jaw was tight and she seemed to have already dismissed the issue, her eyes far away as she listened to something someone said into her ear.

Marie used to make her mad when they were in school, too. Problem was, Marie was almost always right.

CHAPTER 44

Nix felt Ian sit down beside her. He smelled like sweat and dried saltwater and old adrenaline, and his voice was very, very soft. "Don Thomas always took us back. I don't know how to help you."

Nixie swallowed. "I have to find Hun Kan." She put her chin on her fists, wishing she could stare the ground back in time. Ian didn't think he could do it, so he couldn't do it. That was just how it worked. And Peter wouldn't be any help. As soon he got bored of watching her, he'd plunked down in the grass and opened up his computer. He stared at the screen, his brows knit so tight his narrow face looked squished. She could have poked him with a stick and he wouldn't notice.

Cauac had been watching her all along. He looked more like a raven than a turtle, full of curiosity. Nixie pointed at him and whispered, "Can he help? I've got to get back to mom, but I need to see Hun Kan."

Ian raised an eyebrow. "I'll ask." He pushed himself up and went over to Cauac, talking and gesturing, pointing at Nixie. Cauac went silent. He glanced over at Nixie then back at Ian. Ian bit his lip. "I don't know if he understands."

"Tell him I have to see her," she said. "Tell him she's in trouble."

Ian turned back to Cauac, looking far more serious than he should, almost as if he weren't Ian. Cauac remained stoic. When Ian finished explaining, he stood quietly for a long time before nodding.

Nix wanted to hug the old man, but she settled for sending him her best smile.

Cauac reached into the pack around his middle and pulled out a shell and two folded leaves. He set the shell on the ground, and sat in front of it, cross-legged. He rocked.

Ian sat down across from him and gestured to Nixie to scoot over so they almost made a square. Ian hissed, "Peter."

Peter didn't look up.

"Peter," Ian repeated, a little louder. "Join us."

Peter glanced over at him, looking like he was struggling to wake from a deep afternoon nap. He blinked and licked his lips, took a sip of water, and then blinked again. "But something's happening . . . there's data—" He seemed to be struggling with words. "You've got to see."

"Later."

Peter bit his lip, clearly torn.

Nixie needed him. Knew in her bones that she needed him. She leaned forward and put a hand on his knee. "Please. Something's happening here, too."

He stared at her then looked at Ian, his eyes almost pleading. "Leave me alone."

"Please!" Nixie repeated.

Peter sighed and closed his computer slowly, then slid it into his back pack. He still only seemed partially with them, like he was drifting into some other land in his head, his eyes not quite focused. There wasn't any sign of the man with the jokes in this Peter.

They made a square of people on the otherwise empty lawn, all close enough to touch, but no one actually touching.

Cauac reached into his pouch and pulled out a wadded up piece of paper. Ian raised his eyebrows as Cauac smoothed the paper out, revealing a dollar bill.

Nixie whispered, "It might be one of the ones I gave Jaguar-man."

Cauac laid the bill flat on the bottom of the shell, unfolded one of the leaves and poured a pinch of crackly-dry green herbs into his palm. He built a small mound on the bill in the center of the shell, then folded the pouch back up, carefully and deliberately.

He needed to hurry!

She looked around. At least it was empty here. The announcer's voice had returned, distant and droning, too garbled by old stone and distance for words to be clear, but it had to mean the ball game was starting. Big screens littered the plaza for people who didn't have tickets like she did. Maybe that explained why there was nobody immediately around them. They weren't near any of the projection screens.

The old Mayan sat completely still.

She'd been gone more than half an hour. Her mom must be frantic. Her mom had been working toward tonight for years. Nixie should be with her, helping her. She chewed on her lip.

Hun Kan might be dying. Her mom wasn't dying.

Cauac stared at the shell, brows knit almost like Peter's had been over his computer (the dual image almost made Nixie burst out laughing). If this worked, they'd be in the other time.

Nixie pulled her cell phone from her pocket, turned it on and quickly texted *I'm OK Mom*, and then, as an afterthought, added *Ian's here*. Maybe that would make her forget to be mad at Nix. She sent the message and turned the phone off again.

Cauac opened the second folded leaf and pulled out a lump of copal. He split the copal into a big and small lump, and lay the small one on top of the herbs, the dollar bill, and the shell. Even though it wasn't burning yet, its scent tickled her nose.

Next, he reached into a different pocket and took out two stones, his movements fast but measured and flowing, his gaze gone inward a little bit. He rubbed the stones together, and then struck one on the other.

Ian got it before she did. He pulled out a lighter and showed it to Cauac, flicking the flame on and off a few times. Cauac grinned, his eyes wide. He held his hand out, palm up. Ian frowned but dropped the lighter into Cauac's palm.

Cauac set the stones on his knee, lit the small pile, and held the lighter up, lighting it over and over. Ian stuck his hand out but Cauac slid the lighter into his pouch, along with the two stones.

If it had been her lighter, Nixie would have let him have it too. Then she remembered the watch and wanted Ian to take the lighter back.

Cauac pulled something dark and glittering from his pouch, and then held it and his other arm over the small fire. He whispered something in Mayan. Surely a prayer. His next movement was so quick his hand blurred.

A long thread of blood fell from his arm onto the edges of the bill, just a little way from the fire.

His prayer hadn't stopped, hadn't changed cadence or volume. The bleeding might have been as normal to him as breathing. She looked closer at the scars on his arms and understood.

She held her hand out.

Cauac stared at her, unblinking. She felt like she was failing a test.

He wasn't going to do it.

She didn't move. She sat there so long her arm began to tremble.

Finally, he smiled and dipped the edge of the knife into the fire. He took her finger and made a small cut, squeezing a tiny bit of her blood onto the flame.

The fire burned outward, touching the damp blood, releasing an iron scent.

Nixie closed her eyes, preparing to open them in the past.

CHAPTER 45

The gods of the directions had come to Cauac, even in this strange end-of-life dream. All around him, Chichén lay dead, shorn of most of her power. What were the gods telling him? Was this the result of turning his back on Chichén and choosing to live in Zama? Or was it a chance to rectify that, to use the strength of the turtle who changed worlds and birthed gods to help Chichén now?

The gods' only answer was to fill him, like they always filled him, and as he opened himself and let blood, the grass beneath the burning copal twisted to dirt. The scent of home filled his nostrils. He breathed it in, breathing out the fear that accompanied these days, letting the deep sadness of Chichén's death wash away from him in the smoke and smell of home. He breathed in again, filling himself and the gods with the sacred copal.

His vision no longer stuck to the grass or the dirt, but instead flitted both backward and forward before settling in the strange fog of the edges of Xibalba, the underworld, the otherworld, the place of the Hero Twins and the learning of the sky, the place the smokers of toad venom and the old dying dreamers went. He had not been here alone ever, and only twice before at all: his oldest teacher took him here to frighten him a long time past. He recognized it: the copal and too-sweet flowery smell of Xibalba had slept in his bones.

It took many beats of his heart to recall why he had ended up here.

He called the spirit of Hun Kan.

The fog had stubbornness.

He called again, louder, keening for her, demanding.

No change.

He fell deeper inside himself, remembering her scent (flowers and the sea) and the way her wide-set eyes often seemed contemplative, like the old turtles' eyes, even though Hun Kan herself was young. She didn't always obey—he remembered that, too. But she accepted what she must.

Fog parted.

She filled the place in between, her eyes wide, her mouth open as she recognized him riding the gods after her. He reached his bloody left arm toward her and with no hesitation, she took his hand, his blood smearing her smooth skin.

Now what?

He remained still, holding Hun Kan's hand. He could return them both to his time, but there was Ni-ixie. Her self had not followed him to the underworld.

He jerked, and Hun Kan followed.

As his self locked back into his body, Cauac blinked, opening his eyes to find Hun Kan lying on the grass between him and the others, her head toward Ian and her feet toward Peter. She wore the red dress of sacrifice and her legs were bound. Blood covered one arm where someone had tried to cut Ni-ixie's gift from her. His blood, fresher, stained her other arm. She was surely prepared to be blessed as a sacrifice, but the final commitment had not been made. Her skin was stained only with blood and limestone dust, and not with blue paint. Her eyes stared straight up at the sky, so far open that only the rise and fall of her chest said it was not a death stare.

The gods leaked away, their work completed, leaving him gasping at the memory of Xibalba.

Hun Kan's hands closed on the grass and she clenched them deeply, as if trying to hang onto the green shoots for life. She had noticed that Chaac smiled on this time and brought these people rain. In spite of how they looked and smelled and felt, they must be aligned with the gods.

Hun Kan blinked up at him. A soft moan escaped her parted lips. She looked at Peter and pushed herself up, bringing her legs together and smoothing her skirt. She spotted Ni-ixie. A wide smile broke across her face and she reached a hand out. Ni-ixie took her small, cool hand and smiled at her, then spoke to her in the words of the far-time ones.

Hun Kan released Ni-ixie's hand and turned to Cauac, her face bright and curious. "Did I die? What happened?"

"Tell me what you see," he asked her.

She looked around, slowly, her gaze traveling across the gray buildings, the green grass, the strange small white paths, across Peter and Ian and Ni-ixie, and then back to the horizon. Her eyes were drawn upward by one of the strange birds Ian had called "planes," and told him people flew in.

When she looked back at him her face had paled. She stumbled over her words. "It is Chichén and it is not. Is it Chichén in the underworld?" Her voice almost broke. "It frightens me."

He nodded, unwilling to show her it frightened him as well. "It is a place that I dreamed and now we are come to. Tell me what you see," he repeated.

She closed her eyes and opened them again. "Surely the gods did not kill Chichén just for my dream, my vision. If this is real, the years have worn on this place, like when we come across a village that has been abandoned to the jungle. But the jungle has not taken this. Did we protect it so well?"

"Wait," he said. "The two men are Peter," he nodded toward the tall thin one, "and Ian, behind you."

She twisted her head to look at Ian, who had his ear to their talk. He smiled at her and said, "Ba'ax ka wa'alik," the way an Aztec or Olmec traveler might. Emphasizing the wrong sounds.

She smiled at the greeting, and Cauac continued, feeling a need to hurry. "Ian told me the jungle did own this place, that jungle grew on the top of the temple of K'uk'ulkan, but that his people removed it all." He licked his lips, wanting to tell her more, to tell her of all the things he had seen here. What joy to have a familiar companion to help him cope with such strangeness.

Ni-ixie bent toward Hun Kan's bonds, but Hun Kan put a hand out, stopping her. Why didn't she see that Hun Kan's own hands were free, and she could free herself if she chose? Was she trying to help Hun Kan break her word to the high priest?

What did that mean?

"What was your Way?" he asked Hun Kan.

"People-of-unrest attacked us and Ah Bahlam's jaguar helped us get away. All others except Ah K'in'ca were lost."

He flinched, seeing the faces of the dead. They had all been so earnest in their studies and had been looking forward to bringing new skills home. Chichén needed them. He breathed in hard. Stay now. Mourn later.

Death at the hands of the enemy honored the enemy.

He gestured to her: continue.

She looked very pale. "We came upon the same warriors later, with many more tens of warriors, and watched Nimah sacrificed to bring the gods to them." She blinked, a tear glistening in the corner of her eye before she blinked again and took it back. "Ah Bahlam tried to turn that to us, to beseech the gods to make her sacrifice benefit Chichén." She drew her brows together, thinking very hard. "He did some good. His jaguar kept them from capturing us and we had the blessing to get away and go back . . . " Her voice trailed off and she looked around again. "Go back here. He saved us."

Good. Necessity had taught Ah Bahlam.

She told him about a meeting in the Temple of the Jaguar, and how she was taken from there by force and left by the High Priest's Temple. After, she twisted the brightness on her arm and looked at him with confusion filling her features. "Why did Nixie come to me? Why did she give me the gift that the priests want so badly and why do they want it?"

If only he knew as much as people believed he did. "Perhaps all we can do is trust." It was not his place to speak ill of the high priest. To do so could add to the bad luck Chichén already faced.

Ian cleared his throat, wanting attention. Once he saw he had it, he turned his focus to Hun Kan, speaking slowly and directly to her in his odd version of their language. "Nixie dreamed of you. She was frightened for you. She wanted to go to you to help you. How can she help you?"

Hun Kan looked solemn and still, and a bit unsure.

"Did you understand?" Cauac asked.

She nodded and glanced at Ni-ixie—or Nixie—he repeated it in his head. *Nixie* had scooted over by Peter and was staring at a soft paper with bright colors on it.

What language did both girls speak? Cauac glanced at her bound feet. "Will you walk with her?"

She blinked and stared at her hands. "It does not matter. I am not where the priest placed me now." Hun Kan removed her own bonds, tying the rope around her waist as if it were a belt. She rubbed at the red spots on her legs where the rope had been, and then stood, looking around her, wide-eyed. Her whole body shook.

Nixie stood, too. She took Hun Kan's wrist, the one with the watch on it. Cauac had become convinced she was a girl like Hun Kan, fearless, and very real.

After all, she bled.

Nixie's eyes burned with purpose, and she slid her finger under the band, leaving her thumb on the other side. She snapped her fingers, the way you did it to make noise, and the band slid silently open.

Hun Kan gasped and tried to hold the watch together.

Nixie put it back, then showed her again. She did it over and over until Hun Kan could do it with one hand. Hun Kan chose to leave it on in the end, and by then the exercise had calmed her.

They'd gotten about twenty steps from the others, still on the grass but close to the white path, when Hun Kan tugged on Nixie's hand. Nixie turned. Hun Kan held her free hand out: an invitation.

Nixie took it. The two girls stood looking at each other on the grass, sideways to the sun so neither of them had to squint at it.

Hun Kan's hips swayed. She picked up her right foot and, as she brought it down, she picked up her left. The pose held a moment, and then she stepped down a little to the side and started again. Nixie followed.

A dance.

Nixie looked into Hun Kan's eyes and smiled, and the girls' smiles bounced off each other and grew.

Hun Kan danced harder, the ends of the rope around her waist swaying back and forth. She was stronger and faster than Nixie.

Hun Kan led Nixie in the portal dance.

Cauac reached into his pouch and withdrew a small, short piece of heartwood, polished round with a stretched-leather cap tied to one end with sinew. He found a small rock and struck it experimentally. A little hollow, but not too bad. He started the steady heartbeat Hun Kan's dance demanded. She looked over at him, mouthed a "thank you," and turned back to the dance.

Aligning with the heart drum, Hun Kan began to turn the girls in the circle of creation, holding both of Nixie's hands and leaning back away from her, each dancer dependent on the other one, needing the other for balance.

They circled.

Hun Kan laughed when Nixie laughed, and yet her eyes remained serious, her steps fast but careful. Precise.

Sweat ran down Nixie's face.

Ian started to drum, too, rock on rock. He and Cauac shared a bright grin, and Ian drummed harder.

Peter sat hunched and staring at his moving pictures, not even noticing the dance in front of him, showing no sign he felt the shifts in energy as the girls danced the gods near.

Ian smiled like he was sleeping with a woman.

Cauac shifted the rock-drum to a different cadence and started to chant. Hun Kan heard him and picked up the pace. Both girls breathed hard. The late afternoon light turned their sweat gold. The gods were in them, of them, shining from their eyes.

They were beautiful.

The veil between now and then seemed to thin as they danced, as if they danced time open the way the Lords of Itzá did before the ball game. A dance of women balancing the dance of the men. Nothing showed this to his eyes, but it came in the scent of dry air in the breeze, the smell of corn soup cooking and a slight background noise that sounded like the laughter of slaves preparing for festival.

Finally, Hun Kan and Nixie collapsed, gasping, on the grass. He and Ian stopped on the same beat. Ian's hand was bright red from holding the rock, and looking into his eyes, it seemed the gods might have visited him during the girls' dance as well.

Cauac turned to compliment Hun Kan.

Nixie stared down at a bare patch of grass, one hand over her mouth.

CHAPTER 46

Ah Bahlam looked down on the Ball Court, waiting for the players to enter. He stood on top of the wide wall that the players would hit the ball against, near one of three small flame temples that sent prayers and messages out to the world on sacred smoke. Julu sat on his shoulder, ruffling his wings from time to time.

A sharp elbow stung his side. He turned to find a small page of the high priest's attached to the elbow. The boy could not be older than seven. His high child's voice cracked with excitement. "K'uk'ulkan requests you tell him the whereabouts of Hun Kan."

Hun Kan was not in the high priest's keeping? He struggled not to give away his happiness. He addressed the boy directly. "Tell K'uk'ulkan I have not seen her since she went with him. I offer myself to help him look."

The boy bit his lip and backed away, then climbed down the steps like a monkey.

Should he have followed him? But he had not been asked.

Ah Bahlam forced his attention back to the Ball Court. He had wanted to play, had daydreamed all the long summer of playing well, or ill.

He had dreamed these things since he was five summers old.

Disappointment burned inside, only slightly cooler than his desire for Hun Kan beside him. A part of his very being was glad to be Ah Bahlam and not a sacred ball player, a man rather than a god. A man might yet save Hun Kan.

He had been given no place of honor. Instead, he chose this place available to all of the minor Lords of Itzá; it was near enough to see the place they held captives. Here, he would be able to see Hun Kan if she were brought to join the others, be close enough to exchange glances if not words. The dishonorable feel of hoping her Way was to live and bear his children rode him like a slight ill wind. But he could not stop hoping it.

He would not betray Chichén to save her. He couldn't. Nor could he leave and let the night play out without him.

Ah K'in'ca was the only one of his friends chosen to play. The others were defending Chichén or dead, the men chosen to game with the gods below all older. The faces of those who died on the white road home danced inside him with the jaguar and his guilt and his dream for strength for Chichén.

The game needed to be good.

Ah Bahlam bit his lower lip as Ah K'in'ca walked into the court, cotton pads covering his elbows and knees, the great yoke settled against his hips. There were four others beside him, and five on the opposing team. They all entered from the same side of the Ball Court and stood in the center, with the Ball Court marker directly in front of them.

The High Priest of K'uk'ulkan, Ah Beh, and the High Priest of War stood in front of the players, solemn, dressed in full regalia.

Silence started with the players and the three high priests, flowed over the Ball Court and up the walls to the spectators, damping whispers and movement on the steps of the Temple of the Jaguars.

All of Chichén rested in the silence.

Sound began as a low hum, like butterfly wings or bees, then rose slowly, the sound separating out into the words that spoke of the birth of the sun, the passage of the sun into the well of the world, the game as symbol for the movement of the sun. The next words belonged to Ah Beh alone. "Let all who attend the festival be of one heart. Let all be of one blood. Let all be of one purpose. Let the very gods attend our game!"

The High Priest of War's turn was next: "Let all who defend Chichén be strong. May the Ways and the gods ride with them. May the enemy die! May the gods fight beside us."

The High Priest of K'uk'ulkan spoke last. "Let the blood of sacrifice bless this game, this day. Let the sun flow through the wheel of power and the proper side win. Let the gods game with us."

A rustling nearby told Ah Bahlam that one of the captives was being removed.

The chant of sacrifice started, the priests first, then the players and then the watchers, the sounds issuing from Ah Bahlam's mouth as well as the mouths of thousands of others, rising up to the sky as the high priest slowly ascended the steps of the Temple of the Jaguar to stop by a stone altar shaped like a man holding a bowl for blood: the Chac-Mool.

The sun's angle was so low it illuminated the high priest's mask and bounced from the shells and beads woven in his net skirt. Four of the warriors of K'uk'ulkan walked up the steps and stood behind the Chac-Mool. A naked man, painted blue, stood unbound in the midst of the four.

The man was not held or restrained in any way, although he stood as if he were, head bowed, hands folded in front of him.

The captive was about Ah Bahlam's age, maybe a year or two older. A person of unrest who might have fought beside the people of Chichén once, might have danced next to them in ceremony. Did he love a woman, or perhaps have a first child?

Ah Bahlam had never wondered such things about sacrifices before.

The high priest raised his hands, crying out, his voice full of fierce joy and demand, edged with the wild glory of his Way. The crowd's answer swelled from below him. New thoughts or not, Ah Bahlam's voice joined with all the other voices of Chichén, strong and sure.

It was in his blood.

The joined chant nearly drowned his doubt.

The bloody arms of the Chac-Mool cradled the blue-painted man.

The high priest held his hand out for the sacred obsidian knife.

The sacrifice spit in the priest's eye and screamed, "I die for freedom, for my people!"

That was wrong. The captive should not fight his Way, he should submit. Another sign of the long peace falling in on itself.

The high priest's hand clasped the rounded stone ball on the back of the obsidian knife and his hand rose and fell in a too-quick motion, ensuring the captive had no more breath to give cry with.

The heart glistened in the hand of the high priest, still pumping, blood falling to the body, the Chac-Mool, the floor, down the high priest's arm in a last splash of life.

Ah Bahlam fell silent. Did the balance of powers that kept Chichén strong feel so fragile to all of the other adults, or only to him? They had never seemed so before.

A red warrior walking by clapped Ah Bahlam on the shoulder, a congratulatory touch. It was the warrior who had accompanied him down the steps to the dance of the Way. He smiled and said, "Good dance."

"Thank you," Ah Bahlam replied, and nothing more. He did not want to feed the idea that he might attack the High Priest. Was he being set up? And if so, to succeed, or to fail?

He turned away from the sacrifice, glancing back toward the other captives.

A cry escaped his lips.

Hun Kan stood near them, a warrior of K'uk'ulkan beside her. Her eyes met his, glowing, happy, as if the sacrifice had somehow fed her even while it weakened him.

Her skin had been painted deep blue.

CHAPTER 47

Nixie stared at the empty patch of grass where Hun Kan had flopped down beside her moments before. They'd held hands and touched and been almost like one girl, like best friends. The world had shifted under their flying feet, dizzying her. She was dizzy still, and the place where Hun Kan should be, beside her, was empty.

Ian laid one of his long arms across Nixie's shoulder. "That was beautiful."

"But she's gone."

"I bet you still helped her," Ian said.

"It felt like dancing with sunshine and wind. Like something else danced with us."

Ian let her go, but stayed close. "What else?"

"Just . . . just something. Maybe the jungle." That wasn't quite right. Something bigger than her or Hun Kan or both of them, but there weren't any words for it. "Maybe Hun Kan can tell us what it was. She seemed to know." She wrapped her arms around her knees, drawing them up to her chin. "I miss her already."

Ian sat down on the grass with his knees drawn up near his chest, as if he were her mirror. "She thought this was a dream, but I think you gave her hope. Of some kind."

"She thinks she's going to die."

"Maybe she is." He was silent for a few minutes. "Nix, she's already dead in this time. It's just . . . just a choice."

"But I don't want her to die!"

"It's not *your* choice."

She flinched but stood up. "Let's go find Mom."

"A fabulous idea." He glanced at Cauac and Peter. "I can get in anywhere." He tugged on his security jacket. "But neither of these guys has a ticket."

She stuck her hand in her pocket, feeling the crisp edges of hers. "Mom is with the director, Marie. She can make anything happen. Maybe you can go in and explain, and I can wait out here with these guys."

He looked doubtful, but went and shook Peter on the shoulder. "Put that away, we need to go."

Peter blinked up at him. "We need to talk. Codes are falling out of the air."

"Codes?"

"Data. Codes. Ordered, like information. It's not from here, okay? You need to know this."

Ian shook his head. "Later. I need to get Nix back to her mom before we get in trouble for kidnapping."

Peter giggled, the sound odd from him, a little like he was breaking. "You need to see Alice. The whole world is changing and you need to see a girl."

Ian stared at Peter and then shook his head. "It's okay. Calm down. The girl is smart. Maybe she can help."

Peter brightened.

"Come on," Ian pressed him.

Nixie almost felt sorry for Peter as she listened to them. And he was still wearing the purple socks. Hopefully they'd at least been washed. He even acted like a perfect geek. She sat by Cauac, breathing in the last smells of copal and ash and his own smell which was only human with nothing of the modern world making it wild. Pleasant, like the jungle. Although she expected he wouldn't understand, she whispered, "Thank you."

He blew the ashes from his shell and packed it up, sliding shell and drumstick into their places in his pouch.

When he finished, she stood and offered him a hand up.

He took it, smiling at her thinly.

The four of them started toward the Ball Court, the sun now threading through the tops of the trees, making their shadows long and lacy.

As they rounded the corner and connected with a wide concrete path, two men dressed in black came up from behind them, walking close. They held rifles. The taller one said, "Stop."

They stopped.

Nixie looked up at them. Not Federales. Americans. She relaxed and put a hand on Cauac's arm, hoping to reassure him.

The same one asked, "Nixie Cameron?"

They were looking for her? She nodded, but Ian interrupted before she could say anything. "Why do you want to know?"

The soldier lifted a handheld up to Nixie's face, squinting a little, probably comparing a picture. He didn't answer Ian at all, but looked down at Nixie, his brows knit together. "Are you okay? Are these men hurting you?"

"I'm fine. They're my friends."

The soldier looked at the three men. "I'll need to see your identifications."

Uh oh. Cauac couldn't have one.

Peter produced his wallet immediately, and Ian started fumbling in his pocket, as if he was having trouble finding his ID.

She had to do something. She called her mom. "Mom. Are you there?"

"Nix? Are you okay?"

"Did you send soldiers after me?"

"Yes." A beat of silence. "Marie offered them to me. She said they'd find you faster."

"All right." Nixie cut her off. "I need you to help me. I was on my way. I was coming back to you."

"Good."

"I had to find Hun Kan. I'll explain later. I have to get Peter and another friend of ours in. Can you help?"

"Are you okay?" her Mom repeated. Then, "You had to . . . you did?"

"Yes. I was on my way back. You didn't have to send people after me!"

Silence for a moment. "That was before you texted me. I was worried."

Nixie bit back an angry reply. It was going to work out—if she could use them to get Peter in. "Please tell them to bring us all? It's me and Peter and Ian and another guy you don't know, but who knows Hun Kan."

There was a momentary silence. "Nix . . . I can't ask Marie to break the rules in someone else's country."

"I'll give Cauac my ticket. Ian can get in. He has a security jacket. But you want to talk to Peter." How could she convince her? Peter was such a geek. "Maybe Marie even wants to talk to Peter. He keeps trying to tell us about something happening on his computer. He's sure it's important."

"What is he saying?"

"Something about codes falling out of the sky. I wasn't paying much attention. I was dancing with Hun Kan, but he thinks it's really important. Mom, please?"

"Okay. I'll ask." She closed the connection.

Silence fell for a few long moments. Nixie stuck her hand in her pocket and palmed the ticket. Ian watched her and the men in black, looking caged. Peter opened his computer screen again, holding it awkwardly while standing, peering over it from time to time as the silence continued.

The security guard who'd demanded she come with him suddenly put a finger to his ear—listening.

Nixie held her hand out to Ian. "I'll leave with them. I'll have to."

He took her hand and she left her ticket behind in his palm. "Bring Cauac and follow."

The guard whistled softly. "Okay Nixie, and Peter, I'm Alan. Follow me."

Nixie took Peter's hand to make sure she didn't lose him.

CHAPTER 48

Ah Bahlam started toward Hun Kan, but forced his feet to stop. Never mind the warriors between him and the captives, never mind the shame it would bring on his family. She wasn't dead yet. Might not die. Her life depended on the high priest now, and maybe on the game. He swallowed.

It didn't depend on him. Not unless he did something smarter than just trying to take her from her destiny. She might not even go.

He couldn't help glancing at her from time to time, savoring the curve of her cheeks, the brave set of her shoulders and the fall of her dark hair. He kept hoping she'd return his glances, but she stared at the Chac-Mool, at the trail of fresh blood.

Did she long for death?

He felt for the jaguar, nothing now but a small wisp. His instinct at the cenote last night had been to call on K'uk'ulkan, the very same god she might die for. So he did it again, praying to Feathered Serpent. *Save her. Save us all. Make Chichén strong. Show me what to do.*

She fingered her wrist, the watch, as if it were a bead for prayer. A sad, quirked smile touched her lips.

Who did she pray to?

The high priest balanced on tiptoe, at the top of the steps leading to the Temple of the Jaguars, holding the heavy game ball above his head. "We call on the spirit of One Hunapu, whose sons' ball-playing skills banished the evil lords to Xibalba." He screamed, a high deep scream meant to invoke the spirit of Feathered Serpent. The ball flew through the air, aimed at the center of one of the team captains. The man thrust his hips to the side, sending the ball careening off the wall and out into space, where two men converged over it, one barely beating the other, both falling as the ball shot away from them in a high arc.

The game was on.

Sacred smoke rose from the small temple near Ah Bahlam, making his head light. People watched quietly, parents shushing children and young people whispering between themselves, trying not to be caught.

Hun Kan watched the game.

If only he knew what the high priest planned. What outcome would result in Hun Kan's life and what in death? Or would either promise death?

The ball flew back and forth the across the court. Players fell to their knees or slid on their sides, sending the ball careening with their hips, elbows, knees, or head. Sometimes their grunts and slight exclamations floated up to the parapet. Blood and sweat mixed with the dirt of the Ball Court.

Ah K'in'ca screeched his disappointment as one of his hits on the ball just missed the round circle below the captives.

If only he were down on the court beside his friend, racing to and from the ball, dancing the ball, playing the gods, every motion critical.

Below him, the players started to merge with the gods. They began to leap higher, to run faster.

The ball remained in play. His lip bled where he bit it each time it appeared the ball would hit the ground.

CHAPTER 49

Alice grimaced as the ball rolled out of the court yet again. As soon as it was returned by a course official in an incongruous black and white striped shirt, two players headed for it at once and managed to knock each other down. They grabbed each other's hands and pulled in order to right themselves. Theoretically, they'd practiced, but it looked like they'd practiced at rodeo clown school. The yokes about the player's waists were so heavy most of the men managed lumbering runs at best; only three out of ten seemed both comfortable and fast in the regalia. Two had already gone off to the sidelines with permanent injuries.

And yet all of the modern players were bigger than the old Mayans.

"Mom!"

Nixie raced up the stairs, trailing Peter behind her like a nerd balloon. Alice craned her neck. No Ian. She patted the bench beside her. "Nix! Thank God you're safe!"

Nix slid into a seat, Peter behind her. Nix held up her hands. "Shhhh . . . Hun Kan's in trouble and something weird is happening. It's freaking Peter out."

"What?" Alice asked.

"*I don't know,*" Nixie shook her head, her voice high and stressed. "But something's happening." She noticed Oriana. "You danced great!"

Oriana's face glowed.

Marie's hand snaked onto Nixie's shoulder from above. "Introduce me to your friend."

Nix shook Peter's shoulder to get him to look up. "Peter," she said, "Peter, this is the Director of the Office of Science and Technology Policy."

He blinked at Nixie.

"The Director of the Office of Science and Technology Policy. She works for the president."

Peter swallowed and glanced at his screen. He might have been willing to ignore a nuclear bomb.

"Marie Healey. She wants to know what you're seeing."

He stared at Marie with eyes as wide as flying saucers or plates, and Alice swore she could almost a see a thought balloon filled with exclamation points floating over his head. Finally the exclamation points seemed to leak out into the air and he held up a bony hand. "Okay, pleased to meet you." He flicked his eyes toward Alice. "Hi," and then looked back at Marie. "But *you* must know!"

"Know what?" Marie's eyes burned with curiosity inside a deadpan expression. She did know something. Alice wanted to giggle, except Peter looked so serious.

Nixie scooted closer to Peter. "What got you so excited right before we . . . *came back*?" she whispered, loud enough for Alice and Marie to hear. "What did you see in your computer?"

"Data." He licked his lips and looked at Alice, at Oriana, at Marie. "Data nobody understands. It's streaming down from the sky, like a sat-shot, except it's not from a satellite, it's from further away." He pointed at something she couldn't quite read on his screen. Maybe Marie and Nix could see it. "It's coming here, but also to Florida and Cuba, but not Europe or Asia or Chile or Canada, as if you drew a big circle and this was the middle of it. This very spot—the Yucatan anyway. Maybe even this Ball Court." He stopped and took a sip of water. "Okay, there's a flood of chatter on the nets, and everybody is trying to capture it." He set his screen down and looked more intently at the three women, as if sensing they weren't quite getting it. "There's so much data falling out of the sky—riding *our* wireless or being re-sent across it—I don't know, no one seems to know." His voice rose with tension. "It's like being inside the middle of a beam of light. It's filling our systems, shutting some down. I mean not everybody, okay, not all the computers, but the people getting the thread and trying to figure it out. The data is getting shuttled to universities and secure botnets in hope of finding anyplace with enough storage to hold it all."

Not enough storage in the world? She had terabytes just in her hotel room. Alice leaned across Nixie, speaking to Peter. "What does it *mean*?"

Peter shook his head and looked around and if someone could tell him the answer to her question. "I don't know," Peter said. "Okay. Nobody knows. The data isn't getting as far as any of the big SETI installations, I mean, there's a skeleton crew left at Arecibo, but they aren't getting anything except what people send them from here. The common thread is that it must be alien."

Alien?

Peter spoke directly to Nix. "Okay, there's cryptographers working on it—people that break codes."

Nix looked a little affronted, but then Alice knew she understood the word cryptographer. At least she didn't snap at Peter for talking down to her. "Are they succeeding?"

"I don't know."

Marie spoke. "They are. Sort of. Fragments of what seems like songs and poems. What are your friends saying?"

Peter got the exclamation point look again, and then dove back into his computer.

Alice glanced up, looking for Ian. No sign yet.

Peter mumbled, squinting at his screen and flicking his finger across it as he went, the colors shifting. "Same thing. Fragments. But there's layers. It's not English—but glyphs like Mayan or Egyptian glyphs—pictures that mean words or parts of words or many words. Only it's not Mayan or Egyptian, or any language we've decoded, although some linguists are suggesting a relationship. Kyle Mi—" He cut himself off, as if he didn't want to speak names. "Someone thinks they found the formula for the Mandelbrot set buried in what might be a poem."

Alice blinked at the impossible, the idea finally starting to sink in and seem real. Aliens? Strange messages?

"Like the Rosetta Stone?" Nix asked.

Alice grinned. Smart kid.

Peter squinted at his screen, swiped at it with his fingers. "It's a key of some kind."

Marie nodded. "Go on."

Nixie craned her neck, watching the crowd. Probably for Ian. She'd mentioned Hun Kan. How had she seen Hun Kan? It was tough to focus on any one thing.

Nixie stopped watching the crowd to look at Marie. "So does hearing from aliens mean we get world peace?"

Out of the mouth of babes! A cliché, but who cared?

"Alice!"

She stood, a thrill running through her. "Ian!"

He was walking up the path, an old man beside him in blue tennis shoes. But the shoes were a ruse. She knew it. He was an old Mayan. His forehead, his hair, the way he carried himself. Funny: she'd thought Don Thomas might be an old Mayan when he wasn't, but she *knew* the real thing when she saw it.

Ian and the old man turned up the steps between the rows of crowded bleachers. Alice bit her lip and looked around. "Marie," she spoke loudly enough to drag Marie's attention from Peter, pointing at Ian and the old man. "Marie—these two need a place to sit. By us."

Marie sighed, glancing from side to side at the full benches. She wet her lip with her teeth, and pulled her hair out of her face with one hand, a familiar gesture from college days.

She'd do it. Alice beckoned Ian up.

Ian returned her smile, just as broad, and Marie leaned down, a downright evil grin on her face. "This must be jungle-guy."

Alice blushed. Marie's watchers must have reported the kiss. "He has someone from . . . from what you and I saw yesterday morning with him."

Marie's eyes flickered with understanding.

Ian's eyes widened, but he didn't comment directly. He nodded at Marie. "Pleased to meet you."

"They can sit in the middle," Marie said. "On the steps." She glanced up toward the president, on the top steps. He was watching the Ball Court, but appeared to be listening to something else, almost as distracted as Peter. "Maybe that way it won't start a diplomatic incident."

"What took you so long?" Nix demanded.

Ian laughed and pointed at Cauac. "Remember when I said I didn't want him to see this game? He's horrified. I swear he wanted to run out there on the field and show the players what's what, even as old as he is." He helped make room for Cauac to sit down and then took a seat. Nix was between her and Ian. Alice really wanted to trade places so she could touch him, but how stupid and needy was that?

She smiled at him, and he smiled back, and it felt like a touch.

She was out of her mind. "Well, they are playing pretty badly." She focused on the old man: the creases around his eyes, the red, black and blue colors of his clothes, the patterns of the weave. Hopefully Nixie had a picture of him.

Marie looked down at the Mayan from one seat up. "Hello," she said. "My name is Marie Healey."

He shook his head.

"Tardes. Mi nombre esta Marie Healey," she said quickly.

Ian translated into Mayan, or something close to Mayan.

"Can you tell him who I am?" Marie asked.

Ian laughed. "I can try. All the Lords of the Chichén Itzá he knows are men."

Marie glanced up toward the top of the bleachers again. "There's no time to drag in anyone higher. Do your best. Get him up to speed." With that, she turned right back to Peter. "Yes, I'm getting reports on this. They say pretty much what yours do. It hasn't hit the major news sources yet, but there won't be any keeping it secret." She hesitated. "Will you work with my people?"

Peter licked his lips, staring at his computer. He didn't even look up. "Sure. But tonight I want to stay with my friends. There's things happening in real, too."

In real. It took a second for Alice to realize he meant in the physical world instead of a virtual one. But then he was the kind of guy who probably made his physical money virtually. Good for him. As weird as he was, Alice felt better with him around.

"I know about the real world." Marie gave Alice a meaningful glance before she turned back to Peter. "If you accept, you're officially hired now, and you can start tomorrow. Will that work?"

Peter nodded absently, his gaze already back on his screen.

Marie muttered into thin air, telling someone she'd just hired Peter.

Alice shook her head, amazed. She's never seen anyone so good at ignoring everyone around him. Even what little they'd said so far had been absorbed, and various people around them were also whispering into thin air, undoubtedly connected to their own minions or security goons. But then, no need to be secret if whatever it was fell from the sky like a river. She shivered. At least their faces showed more confusion than fear.

For now.

Surely it would come to fear, pass through fear, whatever it ended up as.

Below them, the game ball hit the ground again, and Cauac winced.

Oriana stood up. "I have to go," she said. "I promised to be in the food booths before the end of the game."

Nix grinned at her. "Find us afterward? Does Ian have your number?"

"Yes, and yes." Oriana scrambled over Alice and Nix, stepped carefully between Ian and Cauac, and then she was down the steps and gone.

Even if aliens were talking to the earth, people needed to eat. And all around them, except here in the VIP bleachers, most people seemed to just be watching the game or talking amongst themselves.

Alice whispered in Nix's ear. "Tell me about Hun Kan."

She sat still as she heard Nix's story. Only as she listened did it sink in that Cauac had come here, was here, sat on a metal bleacher, wincing at a bad modern rendition of something sacred to him, surrounded by the bones of his civilization.

It made her dizzy, made it seem like her own world was as stable as heck. Poor man. Strong man.

At the end of Nixie's story, Alice shivered. "It must have been hard when she—wasn't there anymore."

"Yeah." Nix went silent for a minute, then looked around, her gaze panicked. "Where's my feather?"

Marie must have ears on all sides of her head. She handed the quetzal feather to Nix without missing a beat and turned back to Peter's quiet babbling.

Nixie took the feather from her and sat, stroking it. She closed her eyes. "They're here," she said. "Hun Kan and the bird man. Ah Bahlam. They're here."

CHAPTER 50

Nixie sensed Hun Kan and Ah Bahlam, as if she could reach through time and touch them. In this place. She glanced around. It was a cinch they weren't on the bleachers. Those were from now. But they were close.

The bleachers backed up to a path behind them, and on the other side of the path, the wall of the Ball Court rose. Too steep to climb. But they were there. She'd read somewhere that people used to sit on the wide top and watch, that in the old days there were ladders on the back of the wall. She put a hand on her necklace, so she had one on the necklace and one on the feather, and closed her eyes. A whiff of the old world traveled down to her, carried on a stream of warmer air.

She had to trust herself.

There wasn't any ladder in this time, and if she chose to climb the wall she'd probably get arrested for assaulting an antiquity or something. She eyed the gap between the top of the bleachers and the top of the wall. She could jump it. Maybe. Falling might break her neck.

She needed help. "Mom?"

Her mom looked almost scared. "Yes?"

She looked around. "Mom, will you and Ian come get an ice cream with me? Or a water?" A thin excuse, but would her mom see it for what it was? She'd been careful in how she told her mom about Hun Kan and not mentioned time except to say that Hun Kan showed her the dance near some benches, so her mom would know it was this time. She stared at her mom, willing her to understand.

"Okay."

Nixie breathed out a long relieved sigh. "Come on Ian," her mom said, not asking.

He didn't question. "I have to bring Cauac."

Nix nodded. Good. She turned to Marie and gave her the most disarming smile she could come up with. "We're going to get Cauac some water. We'll be back."

Marie didn't look really happy, or even very fooled, but she nodded. "Hurry back." She put a hand on Peter's shoulder. "Will you stay?"

He glanced up, looking confused. Nixie felt like saying *he won't notice we're gone*, but Peter himself said, "Okay," and turned back to his computer screen.

In a few moments they were off the bleachers. Nixie led them behind the bleachers, and along the side of the wall, toward the gate. It wouldn't do to materialize in the middle of an ancient ball game. They had to figure out how to be in a crowd. She glanced down at her clothes. Between her and her mom and Ian, and Cauac's shoes, they were going to stick out.

Oh well. No choice.

She motioned them all close. "We have to go back to get them. I can feel them. I wouldn't be able to feel them if it didn't matter."

He mom looked really skeptical—Nix could practically see the word "no" leap to her lips.

"Mom—please. This is all happening for a reason."

People shouldered past them, and a few of the VIP guards watched them. "How?" Ian asked. "We can't exactly do the shell and bloodletting thing here."

He didn't really need to mention that part, did he?

Her mom narrowed her eyes.

Nixie did her best to sound confident. She'd needed Cauac to help her find Hun Kan. "I'll just have to do it. I did it on the sacbe."

Ian looked doubtful. "Maybe we can find Don Thomas."

That didn't deserve an answer. Unless Don Thomas found them, it would be like searching for a grain of sand on a beach. She closed her eyes, feeling for the past, feeling for Hun Kan.

Nothing.

She stroked her feather. It had come from the past. Another hand went to her necklace.

Someone put a hand on her hand where it held the quill. She didn't even have to look to know it was Cauac. His hand felt gentle, warm, and dry. His eyes were closed and he murmured something under his breath.

Did he even know what they were trying to do?

She closed her eyes again, struggling to shut out the modern noise of the announcer, the scent of hot dogs and popcorn and perfume. She tried to line up her breathing with Cauac's.

Someone bumped into her. "Excuse me."

A modern reply. She squeezed her eyes shut harder, and smelled the air, searching for the old world.

Sounds swirled around her. "Mom, I dropped my iPod . . . " a groan—probably at a bad move in the ballgame . . . the click of high heels . . . a monkey chattering . . . feet walking . . .

Bare feet.

She breathed in jungle and copal and heat and sweat.

Ian gasped. "Nix! Look!"

It would be nice if she at least felt a dizzy moment or something. But when she blinked, she wasn't all in one time. Like standing by the yellow hair-band, and for just a moment, seeing two times. People in colorful party clothes and modern sandals stared at the modern ball game, or talked between themselves, or spoke into phones, but just beyond, the Ball Court grass gave way to dirt. Standing in the dirt, Don Thomas beckoned to them.

She kept Cauac's hand in hers and raced toward the dirt, ignoring her mom's shriek of protest. She'd follow.

All four of them surrounded Don Thomas, the three men chattering in Mayan while Nixie craned her neck. Nothing now but the past. The ball game was on the far side of the court, and the watcher's attention almost all there. Still, if anyone looked, they'd be noticed.

She tugged on Ian's shirt. "I have to find Hun Kan."

He glanced down at her, nodded, and returned to speaking a stream of Mayan at Don Thomas. He'd better be doing what she needed him to. She bit her lip and looked around. People sat in tight groups on the parapet above the wall that had been behind the bleachers. Here there were no bleachers, of course. Not in this version of the world. Just the vast expanse of the Ball Court.

The ball players didn't slow down, or even seem to notice them. They moved like wild animals—like deer or wolves—darting and dipping, thrusting hips and elbows at the ball. The ball itself flew high and fast, and instead of two sides entirely at odds, Nix had the impression this was two teams moving together, almost as one. As if keeping the ball in the air mattered more than the competition itself, as if the game were part play, part ritual, part dance.

She shivered—it was beautiful and brutal. Not even close to the modern version. The modern players had been correctly decked out, but it was like watching five-year-olds dance *The Nutcracker*.

A group of women with gray hair and long white dresses turned their way. A young girl, maybe seven years old, saw them and stood with her mouth open, then took a step toward them. An old man with turquoise inlaid teeth grinned and watched them. Her mom took Nix's hand, whispering, "They see us."

"Don't look afraid." Nix said. "Even if you are afraid, don't look it. Keep your head up."

"I am afraid," her mom said from behind her, but there was a laugh in her voice. Maybe a kind of edgy one, but better than hysteria. Nixie smiled as her mom said, "Be careful."

Right. Most of the men carried knives or clubs, and a few had spears or bows and arrows. Even the women generally wore knives. Part of the ceremony? Were they always armed or were they at war? Her mom clutched Nixie's hand tighter and moaned lightly. "Stay brave," she told her mom. "Don't let them scare you."

The men behind her were still chattering. Nixie tugged at her mom, wishing she'd stayed back in the new time. Having her mom beside her, and so clearly scared, made Nix shiver.

She led her mom toward the wall. They were still behind the people watching the game, but the women who had seen them stepped away, hands on the knives in their belts and confusion on their faces.

She ignored them, watching only out of the corner of her eyes, and kept walking, slowly.

She and her mom got close enough to see individual stones in the wall. She stopped there and looked behind her. Ian, Cauac, and Don Thomas were finally following.

Drums kept a quiet heartbeat rhythm, so soft she hadn't picked it out at all at first. She wanted to move in time with the sound.

She turned her attention back up to the top of the wall. The bird-man—Ah Bahlam—stood on top of it, just above them. He stared down at her with a shocked look on his face. No, not at her. Well, at her, and at Cauac.

She waved at him.

He had a wide-eyed, confused look on his face.

She motioned Cauac closer, and whispered to Ian, "Tell Cauac to get us up on that wall."

He nodded, spoke, and then fell back so Cauac was in front, then Nixie and her mom, then Ian and Don Thomas.

Nixie liked that. It felt . . . safer somehow. Like Cauac was a good shield. Maybe he was. People kept their distance and one or two seemed to be calling to him, although the fast speech made it hard to tell for sure.

She kept looking around, drinking the bright lively colors, snapping pictures quietly from time to time. She framed the Temple of the Jaguars at the end of the Ball Court, zooming in.

Something dark and wet dripped from the Chac-Mool, black in the fading light.

She knew what it was.

Her stomach cramped and she almost retched.

Her mother glanced in the direction she had been looking, and leaned down, whispering in Nixie's ear. "Be brave."

Okay. She could do this. She could find her friend. Cauac's blood had helped her friend. As they neared the wall, more people surrounded them, close in but leaving room to pass. Nixie didn't look directly at anyone, afraid she'd get stopped. The air smelled of wool and animals and sweat, wood and jungle and the smoke from fires. She focused on Cauac's back, on keeping her mom's hand in hers.

Someone touched her hair. "It's okay, Mom," she whispered. "Let them touch you. Don't flinch."

"I know."

Cauac led them to a wooden ladder around the back of the wall, so wide it was more a scaffold then a ladder. Thick, smooth tree trunks had been tied together with sinew. She squinted down the long wall. The ladder followed the whole length. Like the huts from her dream, all of the wood would be long-rotted and turned to dust and soil before her own time. She took a picture.

Before they started the climb, Cauac glanced over his shoulder as if making sure everyone was with him, and his gaze stopped on Nixie's for just a second, full of warmth and . . . apprehension. It felt like he was hoping she could tell him what to do.

She shook her head, overwhelmed. Even on the sacbe it had been like watching a movie, and on the beach, it had been just her and Hun Kan. On the grass, tonight, it had been all people she knew.

This was an alien civilization.

Cauac gestured for her to go first, and she grasped the thick cross-beam just above her head and hopped up onto the lowest step. The sticks that made the steps were thinner than ladders, and set further apart. They gave a little under her weight. She felt like she was in a climbing-gym, with one long pull and big step after another.

Her mom came just after her, then Cauac and Ian and Don Thomas all in a line.

Even Ian looked scared.

CHAPTER 51

Ah Bahlam caught a flash of golden hair in the crowd below. He squinted, his heart racing. Ni-ixie! With Cauac. Ah Bahlam called Hun Kan's name, loudly, so she would be able to hear across the distance between them and over the noise of the crowd. She didn't turn, her gaze focused on the Chac-Mool.

He called again.

Hun Kan's jaw tightened. Angry. She glared at him.

He mouthed the word, "Ni-ixie" and touched his hand to his wrist.

Her eyes grew wide and she peered down the way he was pointing. When he was sure she had seen Ni-ixie, he turned and took the ten steps across the parapet as quickly as he could, stepping over seated watchers. He leaned. Coming up the ladders, he spotted Ni-ixie followed closely by a woman, taller than the girl, but with similar golden hair. Cauac came behind them, looking up grim-faced at Ah Bahlam. Behind him, a strange man with thick hair, and a man who looked a little like Cauac, but with short hair and clothes made by the gods.

He blinked and looked again. Cauac wore god-shoes.

He met his teacher's eyes and they shared both a worried glance and a small flash of happiness. He had never expected to see Cauac again.

Ah Bahlam extended a hand and Ni-ixie took it, scrambling up beside him.

Some of the others on the parapet turned to watch, the fear and mistrust in their eyes making him uneasy. As Ah Bahlam reached down to help the woman up, he spoke to Cauac, now just below him. "Why do you come here?"

"Nixie asked me to bring her to Hun Kan."

Ah Bahlam glanced to either side of him.

The wall was crowded. Almost half of the people now looked their way. Every few arms-lengths, warriors of K'uk'ulkan stood to keep peace, and further down the wall, more guarded the prisoners. The warriors already watched them. "We should go—"

"Wait!" Cauac pulled himself up so he crouched on the edge of the wall. "Look."

Nixie raced toward Hun Kan, head up, regal even though she was running. People made way for her. A golden girl heading toward the captives prepared for sacrifice. She passed through a crowd of old men and young boys, seemingly unaware that some watched her as if she were water in a drought.

One of the warriors of K'uk'ulkan even stepped aside, his eyes wide, his mouth open, clearly awed.

Hun Kan held out a blue hand as Nixie approached, Hun Kan's smile so broad her white teeth made a crescent moon. Nixie took her hand and leaned in, embracing her. When she let go, she turned so they both faced back toward Ah Bahlam and the others, who now stood side by side on top of the wall.

Nixie's hands were not stained blue where she had touched Hun Kan. The two of them, gold and dark, began to circle each other. They danced surefooted on the stone, controlled and measured, moving to a beat he couldn't hear.

They had not needed to speak to know what to do.

Young men and old gave them room, melting into each other to make clear space for the girls. More blue color leaked from Hun Kan's hand to Nixie's.

Two or three men began climbing down, looking like they were scared of both girls. One dragged a child with him, the child screaming.

Cowards.

The red warriors looked confused, but had started talking between themselves. They'd do something soon. What?

Ah Bahlam checked their escape route. The other two men had never climbed all the way up, but stood clinging to the ladders on the top of the wall, watching. The woman stood frozen beside him, smelling of fear. But she watched closely, and stood straight. Below them, on the ground, commotion and pointing, but still open space between people.

No one from below was climbing up.

Nixie and Hun Kan were close now, both of their eyes meeting his.

"Let's go," Ah Bahlam hissed at Cauac.

Cauac nodded, and motioned Ah Bahlam down. He wanted to protest, to be last so he could help Hun Kan off the wall, but the look in his teacher's eyes sent him scurrying, watching below.

The ladder felt strong and solid. He was not supposed to leave the wall, but Nixie was here and Hun Kan was beside him! Or just above him, anyway. He glanced up and saw the curve of her shoulder against the sky. The strength of hope and the jaguar poured into him, the moment heavy with destiny. He wanted to growl and scream with the joy of it.

As they descended, the grunts and shouts of the players floated over the wall. It felt right they were going away from the game, leaving it to succeed as it should without the disturbance of strangers.

They would be all right, they would get down the wall safely and the people would let them go. *K'uk'ulkan protect us. K'uk'ulkan protect us.* Hand over hand, down the ladder, the mantra of safety repeating each step. *K'uk'ulkan surround us. Tell me what to do!*

The woman climbed down beside him, her long legs taking the uneven steps easily. She had the same light skin as the girl, although hers had tiny red and brown spots on the tops of her arms and across her nose. Her form was more womanly: slender-waisted, but with rounded breasts and hips.

He spoke to Cauac, above him. "Are they gods?" Gods had mothers.

"I don't know." The tone of Cauac's voice said that he did not think so.

All the more important to get them away. They would be fragile. "Is that Nixie's mother?"

Cauac smiled. "I think so. But Ian is not her father."

"Who is Ian?"

Cauac wrapped an arm around a post for stability and pointed down at the man with the long strange hair. "The other is Don Thomas. They are from a year that falls after this year and the one after that and the one after that and many more."

Ah Bahlam put his right foot too far down and nearly slipped.

Hun Kan, who had heard the conversation, grinned down at him. She didn't have to tell him she had been right all along and Nixie was a girl and not a god.

A girl from another time. Scary. Like walking an edge.

His breath slammed against the inside of his chest, fluttering his heart. *K'uk'ulkan! I prayed to you last night. I pray to you again. Be beside me and beside Hun Kan, be on the side of the Itzá and of our gamers.*

His jaguar twitched inside him, nearly pulling him free of the ladder. It did not like him praying to the god it thought was weak. But this was K'uk'ulkan's festival and not the festival of the jaguar god. He looked up toward the top of the wall. Faces peered down, watching them.

What were his people thinking? He wanted to be down instead of halfway; to be away, to focus on Nixie and Cauac and Hun Kan and the new people.

K'uk'ulkan, the feathered serpent.

Below him, the High Priest of K'uk'ulkan stood in full regalia.

He had left the game.

Ah Bahlam's jaguar ears flicked back, listening. The game continued.

K'uk'ulkan's eyes were hard and bright, like banked coals. He hissed.

Ah Bahlam's jaguar took his teeth for its own and growled back, a deep rending sound that made him grip the wood under his fingers even harder.

Hesitation would not save him now. Nor prayer.

A breath and he was sideways above K'uk'ulkan, clinging to the wood with all fours, his haunches trembling with power. Then he went down hands-first, his forearms shaking with the effort.

Hun Kan gasped from above him and he heard no sounds to indicate the others moved at all. He could not stop for them. When he was still taller than man-height above the ground, he gathered himself and pushed off, away from the wall and toward the high priest.

The high priest stepped back, just out of range, his eyes wide, the man visible in them. Man and jaguar landed on two feet, staggering before standing straight.

The high priest hissed at him.

Ah Bahlam fell to all fours and twitched his tail. He crouched, but did not spring.

It was the Dance of the Way all over again, neither giving, neither moving. The moment seemed to freeze, for each breath to allow more challenge to build between him and the high priest.

Cauac stepped over to him and placed a hand on his shoulder. He spoke simply, quietly, as if there were no hurry in the world. "Control."

The word acted like water in the jaguar's face, making him shake his head and arch his back.

"No," Cauac said. "Control." He glanced at the high priest. "Before you forfeit your life."

Ah Bahlam stood. He breathed, and everyone around him watched him, still and silent. He balanced on his heels, calling earth up through his feet and sky down through the top of his head until he was bigger than the jaguar and could shrink the reluctant cat down into himself.

The high priest gave him a short imperious nod, his eyes focused on Nixie and Hun Kan, and on Nixie's mother. Nixie's mother's eyes had gone wide and her face paled to the color of paper bark. She grasped Nixie and pulled her to her side. It made Nixie look small and young.

Ian and Don Thomas stayed near them, hovering.

Hun Kan came close enough that Ah Bahlam smelled her sweat. She did not touch him, although her presence made him quiver ever so slightly. He saw something in her face that he had not seen in all the run, the sacrifice of Nimah, even in the hut last night.

Despair.

The high priest leaned in toward Cauac until his face was near the old man's face. But he would respect Cauac; all of Chichén respected Cauac. The priest glanced at the three women again. His words were low, but clipped and rushed. "What does this mean?"

Cauac pointed at Nixie. "I dreamed Nixie's people before I saw her. Ah Bahlam and Hun Kan saw her before I did, brought me tales of my dream walking in our time. I have seen the future."

"Is Chichén strong in the future?" the high priest demanded.

Cauac laughed, an edgy laugh that raised the hair on the back of Ah Bahlam's arms. "Chichén is remembered."

What did that mean?

Cauac looked at the high priest for a long time. When he did speak, he used his powerful teacher's voice. "Pray, and play ball, and manage the blood gifts of our moment." He spread his arms wide, encompassing the vibrant noise and life of Chichén in full festival. "I will see to the years that have not come yet."

Fear flashed in the high priest's eyes, but he stood firm, his muscles tight and his chin up. He looked regal, godlike, and except for the tiny flashes of fear, he looked exactly like he should.

A small white hand reached through the empty air toward the high priest. Nixie. She held out a gift, a yellow counterpart to the blue that circled Hun Kan's wrist. She spoke to Ian as she did so. Ian grimaced at her, glanced at the high priest, and shook his head. He looked like he was about to argue with Nixie, but he didn't.

The high priest looked at the gift, as if trying to decide if it was safe to hold. Cauac said, "It will keep the time of Chichén as if it were the very stars."

The high priest took the gift and wrapped it around his wrist. When he let go, it fell into the earth.

Nixie picked it up and spoke to Ian again. Ian said, "If Nixie puts it on you," he pointed to Hun Kan, "You may not be able to take it off."

The high priest apparently understood Ian's poor speech. He nodded.

Nixie fastened the yellow circle around his bony wrist. When she stepped back and looked at him in full regalia with the wide, yellow band around his wrist, she looked serious and awed.

Was Nixie trying to buy Hun Kan's life? Surely the high priest was too proud for that. He held his arm up and admired the pale yellow band. He spoke to Cauac. "The game needs me." His gaze stopped on Hun Kan. "You must come."

Hun Kan nodded. "Of course."

She didn't look at him. Before he could even think about it, Ah Bahlam stepped between her and the high priest.

Cauac glared at him, and Ah Bahlam couldn't look at him. He trembled, but kept his eyes on the high priest, breathing deeply, filling himself with the jaguar. He allowed his heart to become the heart of the jaguar, but kept his own head. "She is needed with us. She is part of the Way we must fulfill, like you must return to the game."

A condescending look filled the high priest's eyes. "I, too, have seen her Way and her blood. She must stay with me."

Golden hair tickled Ah Bahlam's shoulder. Nixie had come to stand beside him. Nixie's mother stood behind her, her hands resting lightly on Nixie's shoulders. They both looked determined and unafraid. The three of them made a wall between the High Priest and Hun Kan.

Hun Kan's hands were on his shoulder and Nixie's trying to separate them.

Ah Bahlam's jaguar roared, the sound pouring out of him, deep and feral. A sound no man could make.

The high priest's jaw shook, perhaps in anger, perhaps in fear. His gaze broke away from Ah Bahlam's. It was going to be enough. He would leave her.

Feathered Serpent turned away from them, back to the game.

CHAPTER 52

Alice glared at the receding back of the man in the netting and the feathered headdress. The High Priest of the Feathered Serpent. The man responsible for the spiritual life of Chichén Itzá, whether sacrifice or dance or prayer.

He had wanted her daughter. No, he had wanted to kill her daughter. Her hands and knees shook. She had never been so scared, ever. She swallowed, as weak now as she had been strong in front of the high priest.

She watched him until the only way to be sure of his location was to spot his headdress above the crowd. The top of his head came no higher than her chin and yet he seemed infinitely tall. His ancient, sad eyes had reminded her of pictures she'd seen of Geronimo and other Native American fighters. Serene and certain, and merciless.

If he had chosen to kill them, they would have died.

Nixie tugged at her hand. The high priest might be gone, but there were still men and boys watching them, some above, a few partway down the ladder, and some surrounding them. A few faces showed fear, the others were curious or fierce in the way of young men ready to prove themselves. The warriors were elsewhere.

Warriors or not, there were a lot of them, and more were drifting over. "We've got to go," Nixie said. "Now."

Alice wanted to be hundreds of years away from the high priest, but she might never see this again. She stared at the open wild innocence of the young boys' pale faces and wide dark eyes as they stood straight up near their grandfathers. Even though her blood still raced through shaking limbs, she tried to note the shape of weapons and the drape of clothes, the jewelry, the footwear. She took a deep breath of the clear ancient air. "Did you take pictures?"

"Some." Nix still clutched the feather close, like a talisman. The crowd around them felt bigger and closer. "We're out of time." Nix's voice shook, too. "Get ready."

Ah Bahlam raised one arm, and the quetzal appeared above his head, almost as if from nowhere, and dropped onto his shoulder. He reached up and touched the bird's beak and it made a soft chittering sound and rubbed its head against his finger.

Ian took Alice's free hand, his touch electric and tender. She stepped so they stood hip to hip, moving into him without thinking about it. Cauac held Ian's other hand, with Hun Kan between him and Ah Bahlam. Don Thomas

Arulo completed the circle, his large brown hand swallowing Nixie's small white one. He leaned down to Nixie and spoke a command. "You must help." He nodded at Alice and Ian. "Those two will need to be brought along."

Nix laughed. Alice blushed, until she heard Ian laugh, and laughed, too. The light shifted a tiny bit, from natural dusk to dusk with the odd whitened color of electric lighting that wasn't yet really needed.

English and Spanish, cell phones and the tap of heels on concrete.

Now. They were now. Alice felt relieved, but also regret.

Hun Kan and Ah Bahlam were with them. And Cauac. And everyone else who should be.

Tears sprang to her eyes, and she blinked them away, an unexpected reaction. Thank god she lived now.

Ian had his huge the-world-is-great grin on his face. He pulled her into him and gave her a hug, not even noticing that she didn't exactly return it, but felt stiff and shocked and relieved all at once, and as spacey as Peter. Ian winked at her, and then stepped over by Don Thomas.

She called Marie, who sounded as relieved as Alice felt. "Alice? Are you all right?"

She tried to keep her voice from shaking. "We went walkabout and brought back three more people. I don't think we'll all fit on the bleachers." Would Marie understand?

She did. "Maybe you'd best not come back in. I'll send the two who found Nixie this morning, tell them to do what you say. They can help you keep a safe distance from . . . anything."

Alice nodded, and whispered to Ian, filling him in. Before he answered, she added, into the phone, "Marie—can you send Peter out with the guards?" The Marie she knew a long time ago had always hated being excluded. "And . . . can you come?"

"I don't know. Hang on." Alice heard yearning in Marie's voice. The phone muted.

She watched Hun Kan stare at the crowds moving along the paths, more curious than afraid, one of her hands firmly in Ah Bahlam's. The painted blue caste of her skin made her look a bit like a statue. There was no denying her beauty, in a classic Mayan way. High cheekbones and wide eyes. A strong mouth. The way she looked at Ah Bahlam was the only soft thing about her.

Marie's voice pulled her attention back to the phone. "Can I bring the others?"

Wow. She'd done it now. She glanced over at the old Mayans.

"I mean, later. They won't all come, but after the game is over, I'll ask if anyone wants to have you show us the stars."

Alice laughed. "All right." She'd almost forgotten the great alignment. That would be like forgetting her name. She was Alice Cameron, right? Maybe now she understood Ian's bright smiles. After all, what else could you do in the face of a world so strange?

Maybe she was, after all, stark raving crazy. Or still dreaming. Whatever.

The four Mayans stood close together, and Alice dragged Nix near Ian, telling them about her conversation with Marie.

"So where should we go?" Nix asked, looking around. Every place was well-lit and full of people.

Alice smiled, real joy rising inside her. "Later, after the game, after people eat and the first few go home, they're going to turn off all the lights. It will be announced, so everyone can find a seat. We'll just go find a quiet spot now. There's probably plenty if you stay away from the buildings and the screens." And miss the game of the century, of the baktun. But the real game wasn't here anyway. She knew that now.

"I'm hungry," Nix proclaimed.

Alice burst out laughing. How incredibly, wonderfully normal.

Alice felt like a den mother as she settled them all on a large piece of grass near the back wall of the site, far from most of the people or festivities. There was no lighting close, and their shadows fell long and dark on dark grass. Alice verified that the guards, Alan and David, had flashlights.

Peter had come with them. Sort of. He had walked here with his screen in front of him, staring at it so intently Nix had to run interference so he wouldn't bump into a pole or anything. "What's going on?" Alice asked him.

Ian, who had come up beside her, asked, "Are aliens about to land?"

"Huh?" Peter shook his head absently. "No. Okay, I mean, maybe, but only the weirdest people think so. That doesn't have anything to do with the data. It must have originated tens of light years ago. We probably go through it at the end of every baktun, but we never had computers to get it before. So maybe no one got it."

"So that's not where the Mayans learned science?"

"How would I know?" Peter glanced up at her. "Maybe. Okay? We're just now even learning it exists."

Good. She'd been afraid he'd leap to conclusions. She didn't want to either—she was still a scientist. She glanced at the Mayans. She was. Really.

Ian said, "We know they didn't have computers, but what about just people? Could people get some of this? Like if they had taken mind-altering substances?"

"How would I know?" Peter repeated himself. He grinned. "Hell—you're the expert on that."

Ian cocked his head and raised an eyebrow.

Peter continued. "There's talk of building a probe to go sit in the data and read it. It's a total mystery how it's such a tight beam. It should be bigger than our solar system, but it's not even as big as little bitty Earth." He looked at Alice apologetically.

She laughed. "That's okay Peter. I like science mysteries more than supernatural mysteries."

Peter nodded at Ah Bahlam and Hun Kan, who sat close together, chattering quickly and quietly. "You seem to have a few of each."

"No kidding." She needed to do something normal, to ground, and think. "We'll need food." She supposed she and Ian were still in charge, like the night of the sacbe. And she wanted Ian where he wouldn't disappear. "I'll go to the stalls and get us food and water. I'll take Nix." She glanced at Ian. "Can you stay here and watch over everyone?"

"I'm not leaving Hun Kan," Nix snapped. Then she tempered her words with a pleading smile. "Please?"

Alice hesitated. She'd trapped herself. She didn't want to be anyplace different than Nixie, ever. "All right, I'll go." She took Ian's hand. "You'll keep her safe?"

Ian nodded. "But take Alan."

"I'm not the one you're trying to guard."

"Yes, you are."

She blushed.

CHAPTER 53

As soon as her mom left, Nixie raced over to Ian. "Come help me. I have to talk Hun Kan into staying here."

He pursed his lips and didn't budge.

She tugged on his arm. "Come *on*, Ian."

He still didn't budge.

Only after she stopped tugging on him did he kneel down a little and look her in the eyes. "I'll go with you to talk to Hun Kan, but I will not try to convince her to change her mind. I'll translate questions you have for her, but I won't translate orders or demands. Do you understand?"

She glared at him. It couldn't be right for Hun Kan to die! She knew that was what the priest planned. She'd known it since she dreamed her way into the little hut Hun Kan had been locked away in.

She couldn't let that happen. But she couldn't even talk to Hun Kan without Ian. She dropped her eyes. "All right. Questions it is."

Hun Kan and Ah Bahlam both smiled as Nixie and Ian came up and sat close to them. She knew what her first question was going to be, so she spoke it as soon as she sat down. "Do you like it here?"

Ian spoke in Mayan. Ah Bahlam answered him briefly, then Ian spoke again, looking directly at Hun Kan this time. Hun Kan met Nixie's eyes, then looked around at Chichén Itzá. From here, they could just see the top of the Temple of K'uk'ulkan washed in the gold of the sun's last direct rays for the evening. After she answered, Ian said, "She likes to see you. She thanks you for choosing her for a friend. She does not like this empty place. Much of the power has leaked from it."

Nixie swallowed. Okay. She could believe that. "Is she safe if she goes home?"

She watched Hun Kan as the Mayan words went two ways between the girl and Ian. "How can she not be safe in her home, in her path? She asks, is she safe here?"

Nixie swallowed. "She will not be sacrificed here."

Cauac came over and he and Hun Kan and Ah Bahlam spoke together in Mayan, leaving Nixie out of the conversation. She settled for watching the quetzal sit on Ah Bahlam's shoulder, hoping they'd finish soon so she could ask Hun Kan more questions.

When they started chattering with Hun Kan, Nixie coaxed Julu onto her shoulder, wincing as his feet dug into her. But she could take it. She's given blood for sacrifice.

Eventually Ian turned to Nixie.

"Will you answer a question from Hun Kan?"

Nixie nodded.

"How do you please the gods?"

She didn't. No one did, not really. Well, maybe some. But she wasn't sure she believed in any gods. "Tell her . . . tell her some people pray and go to church, but they do not kill each other for the sake of the gods."

Ian raised an eyebrow. "Are you asking me to lie?"

She pursed her lips. Wars. Terrorism. Demonstrations. "Well, we don't perform human sacrifices."

He still looked at her.

He knew what she meant! "We don't. Not like the Mayans. We don't cut the hearts from people!"

His jaw relaxed and he smiled at her. "Sorry, Nix. Maybe I'm oversensitive."

Ah Bahlam looked at Nixie as Ian spoke, and stopped him to ask questions.

Hun Kan watched the exchange between the two men silently before speaking her piece to Ian.

Hun Kan's answer, from Ian's lips was, "We all die." He had another question for Nixie. "Why did you come to me?"

Nixie and Hun Kan looked at each other. A tiny spark of distrust seemed to fester in Hun Kan's eyes, something Nixie had never seen there before. She scooted over closer and took Hun Kan's hand, rubbing it gently, trying to erase the distrust. Her hands turned bluer, Hun Kan's cleaner. If only she could talk to her friend directly! "Tell her I don't know. I just . . . heard her cry on the beach in Tulum all the way from my time and I knew I had to see who was crying. And it was her. And then I dreamed about her and I had to find her. Ask her if she'll stay here with me. She could go to school, learn English. I'm sure mom would let her stay. She could help mom with her studies."

Ian shook his head softly. "I'll ask, but don't expect to hear the answer you want."

As Ian talked, Hun Kan's hand tightened on Nix's hand. She looked at Nixie as she spoke the Mayan words to Ian. When he translated he said, "She is glad you came to her. She will follow her own path because she has to. Perhaps when you are as old as she is—seventeen summers—you will understand. In the meantime, she has a last question for you, but she doesn't want you to answer it. She wants to know what you can learn from her."

Being treated like a goddess had been easier than being treated like a kid sister. Nix swallowed, feeling hot tears behind her eyes. For Hun Kan, who might die? Or for herself, who might lose a friend? Her eyes slid away from

Hun Kan and down to the grass between them. "Tell her thank you and good luck. I will think about her question. I hope she stays here and I can see her again for many more days." She squeezed Hun Kan's hand, and then stood, managing to turn away from all of them before the first tears splashed down her cheeks.

Maybe she was just tired. Maybe too much was going on.

She went and sat by Peter, staring at the pictures on his computer screen until they finally sharpened as her eyes dried.

CHAPTER 54

Alice stared at the food in the cafeteria-style line. Sandwiches and cheese sticks wrapped tightly in plastic. Apples, which were surely grown in some other country. To make it worse, the place was picked over and expensive. What did Mayans eat nine hundred years ago? She didn't see any fish or peccary jerky or wild birds hanging.

A Mexican market in town would have better choices.

Alan stood beside her, stoic in the crowd, more watchful than a guard dog. She didn't feel as much protected as kept. At one point she tried to hand him a few bottles of water to carry and he stepped back, looking slightly regretful.

Probably needed to keep his hands free in case terrorists tried to attack her, the half-crazy scientist.

She finally settled for some too-brown bananas, a plastic container of ceviche, ten Mexican pastries, plus seven lukewarm hamburgers for the rest of them. As she rang out, she frowned at the idea that nothing—nothing—in the deli at the market at Chichén Itzá had anything she was sure anyone who lived here when the city was alive would even recognize as food.

What if she made them sick? What if whatever they did turned to a modern-day version of smallpox? God. Ian wasn't here to ask what he'd been feeding Cauac. At least she could still hear the announcer's voice faintly, even this far from the Ball Court. The game was still going, in spite of the way the light had fallen to half.

Maybe that was why Alan had played strong and silent the whole trip. "Sorry you had to miss the end of the ball game."

He shrugged, his face stoic. He was tall and dark, young enough to be one of her students. After they left the larger part of the crowd behind them, he finally took one of Alice's bags. "Who are those people? The old men? The blue woman and her boyfriend? The couple with the funny heads?"

That's right. The Secret Service hated secrets. "They're . . . indigenous. From Mayan colonies deep in the jungle, come in for the end of the calendar. I met them on a dig."

"We can't find any information about them."

"They probably don't have any ID."

"It's a law. They have to."

He sounded so earnest she had to laugh. "Tell *them* that. They probably won't understand you."

He lapsed into silence. They'd had to ID her and everyone she knew.

People like Oriana and even Nixie probably would never have gotten close to Marie if they hadn't come up as tangents in the interviews she'd had with the security goons.

"Look," she said, "They're safe enough. I'll vouch for them."

He didn't bother to answer her.

It would be full dark soon. Alice wandered through the small camp they'd become, picking up leftover scraps of the meal. After all her worry, the Mayans had refused food, and entertained themselves with a water bottle each.

Peter hunched over his computer, looking up from time to time. Oriana, who had just joined them, knelt beside Peter. Nixie sat beside them, watching Ah Bahlam and Hun Kan more than she watched the screen. The quetzal sat on Nixie's shoulder, its tail nearly touching the ground.

Why wasn't Nixie with Hun Kan? The look on her face didn't imply any desire for motherly intervention, so Alice let it go.

Cauac and Don Thomas watched the sky from prone positions, chattering so softly in Mayan she wouldn't have been able to tell what they were saying even if she understood the Mayan of everyday things. As she came near them, she noticed both men were smiling Ian-smiles, as if all was right with the world. They might have been two best friends who'd known each other all their lives.

Ah Bahlam and Hun Kan sat close together, Ah Bahlam's arm extended down behind Hun Kan's back. She leaned against him, the set of their bodies a touch awkward. They whispered together from time to time.

Alan and David paced circles around them all, border collies unhappy with the vulnerability of their flock.

Ian whispered at her. "Sit down."

He patted the ground beside him. She made another whole circuit, just as bad as Alan and David, and probably driving them crazy.

When she did sit down, Ian said "You remind me of a nervous cat. Back on the white road, when we stayed the night, you said you wanted to remember magic."

That wasn't exactly what she'd said, but it was close. "I'm not doubting it tonight." She glanced at Ah Bahlam and Hun Kan again. "But I'm no longer sure tomorrow will just be another day."

"Of course it will. It just might not be the day you expected."

How come everyone here, even Nixie, seemed to just accept that everything they knew had turned to dust and copal smoke? "Doesn't that scare you?"

He nodded toward the two shamans giggling together in the grass. "Live in the now. This moment, this night. It won't ever come again. And we have a piece of destiny here. You know that."

"Me? Or Nix? Or the Mayans?"

"Maybe everyone. Whatever it is, accept it."

She closed her eyes, feeling a bit dizzy. She couldn't deny that she was scared, deeply scared, scared in every nerve and cold with fear, but she was also excited. And awed. Like the day she first climbed the Temple of K'uk'ul'kan and sat on the bleached white step at the top of the narrow stairs, looking down on the huge Temple of the Warriors. This was that feeling.

"Relax," Ian said, his voice soothing. "Breathe with me."

She breathed in. He held his breath for a moment, and she held hers, a little off-time to him. Again. Again. And then they were breathing together and watching the stars and being silent. They leaned toward each other, palms on the ground, their thumbs touching. They probably looked as awkward as the young Mayans. She didn't care. It felt *good* to have him near, even though she didn't want to talk about it. Not yet. Maybe after whatever was going to happen did happen.

But maybe she'd never see him again after tonight.

Maybe it was okay not to know.

The announcer's voice began to sound from every PA system in the place. *"The game is over and has resulted in a draw. As the ancient Mayans would have said, the ball of the sun did not travel through the hoop of the sky this night."*

Ian laughed. "It didn't look to me like any of the players were good enough to get the ball through. They shouldn't have been so authentic. A lighter ball might have worked."

Alice smiled wryly. "Games didn't often play to a draw, but there was a paper by a grad student, Lisa something or other, last year. She suggested a draw outcome means the balance between Earth and Sky is off and large changes are needed in the spiritual life of the community."

"Ah. Appropriate for an age of climate disaster and terrorism." He glanced at his watch. "The schedule's screwed. There was supposed to be an hour between the game and dark for people to shop in."

She shrugged. "Mayan time. I bet they wanted a win for the news networks and played until it was too dark to see."

The announcer continued, *"Please take a seat. Please extinguish all lights, and become silent. You are about to witness the true end of the Mayan calendar as we know it."* The voice switched to Spanish.

The announcements had been pre-recorded, modulated to be calming, voices from before data fell from the sky or people traveled between times. They were all together now, everyone in one place and time, unless you counted the three old Mayans as out of place.

She wondered what they thought.

The announcer switched to a new message. *"This is the time the ancient texts of the Mayan people foretold. The beginning of a new world. A world of healing and magic. A world without war. These are the things the ancient Mayans promised for the start of this baktun. Some say they even prophesied the very chaos that has come before this day. Some say the Mayans predicted climate change and world wars."*

Claptrap. The Mayans were as muddy about this transformation as the Christians were about the Book of Revelations. The timing was universally clear in Mayan science, but the outcomes and signs had been portrayed differently at different sites.

Alice squeezed Ian's hand as the disembodied voice flipped to Spanish. She put her head on his shoulder and he turned a little and lifted her chin. In a soft, thick voice he said, "Kiss me."

"Why?" she asked.

"Because I'm a good kisser and this might be the end of the world."

He didn't mean the part about the end of the world, but he was right about the rest. She was still kissing him as the announcer said, *"The lights will go out in two minutes."*

She didn't stop until the artificial lights did go out, setting the sky ablaze with starlight.

CHAPTER 55

Ah Bahlam gasped as the cross of the world hung above him. The astronomers had spoken of the ending of the age and Cauac had told him and Hun Kan they were in that time. He had believed his teacher, but the blazing sky symbol shocked him anyway. The dark center was black as the void.

"We're here," Hun Kan's voice was the wind of beauty, thick with awe.

He smiled, shaking the strangeness of this fast talking place from his head. "What does it mean that we two are here?"

She held his hand. "It must be a gift, a reminder to us to do our duty at home, to follow our path and create harmony."

He bristled. Her blue skin reminded him of her idea of duty. "Maybe we are brought to this strange and dead Chichén to see the result of the path we follow now. My Way has been urging change. The jaguar challenged the high priest! Surely this is more of that message."

She turned to look at him, her eyes dark pools in the darkness, the reflected stars of the great cross scattered across them. She had never looked so like a goddess. "I prayed last night. After you left. I prayed to Ixtab."

The suicide goddess, the one goddess he didn't want her to think about, or follow. He held his tongue, though, and let her go on.

"I prayed to Chaac also, asking for his help. I prayed to K'uk'ulkan. I asked them all for help."

"And what did they tell you?"

"Acceptance." She glanced toward Nixie and the strange man with the light machine. "I came here earlier, pulled through Xibalba by Cauac, and danced with Nixie for Cauac and Ian. Like we danced on the wall, only more, and longer. A dance of power."

He shivered. "But Nixie is not a goddess."

"Neither are we." She fell silent, still looking up, her head tilted back so starlight bathed her face.

He wanted to touch her cheek, but the moment felt too charged with power to diminish with touch. "Maybe you and Nixie are both goddesses."

She shook her head. "We danced the portal open. It would have been the same time you danced the god-portal open to prepare the court. There was no time to tell you before." She looked almost guilty.

"It's all right. I'm glad you danced with Nixie." I'm glad you're safe.

"It took both of us to open the doorways."

He waited for her to go on.

"And then, when the dance was over, I found myself back in the turtle hut. Moments later an old woman and two of the serpent warriors came to me." She held up her blue arm. "The old woman painted me. They came so close after the dance, as if they just waited for me to return and walked in the door. Because of that, I know I danced the portal open for Ixtab."

"Can we know anything in this strange time?"

She looked away from him. "I don't want to lose you. Back in Zama, I dreamed many days of being your wife, of raising your sons and your daughters and running your hearth, your slaves."

She had never used words to tell him that. His mouth felt dry. "I want that, too."

"But I am blue, which means I walk dead. And you are thinking of challenging the high priest of K'uk'ulkan. After . . . " she fell silent a moment . . . "After watching Nimah die, I know that I can die as well. Paradise waits on the other side of sacrifice. Perhaps if you die in your challenge, we will meet together in paradise at the same time."

Her words stung "I don't want to die. If I challenge the high priest it will be in the name of the jaguar god and not in the name of Ixtab. Chichén needs life more than death. Maybe there has been enough death."

"It has always been so. We trade death for life every year."

"Why would the gods bring us here to see the time of change unless it is a message for *us* about change? Something to take back and make different." The idea was exciting and his voice rose with it, sped up. He held her hands in his, and looked her directly in the eye. "You and I, we can bring some small change to Chichén, re-align it with the gods, bring back a world Chaac wants to turn his rain onto."

She held up her hands. "I let the old woman paint me blue. That signifies my willing choice. I cannot break my word."

Then I will make sure you do not have to.

He looked around, suddenly filled with bitter sadness. This place reflected the death of his world. This was a faraway time, and he and Hun Kan would now both be dead, have been dead for so many years they would were no longer remembered. The changing of the world—the star pattern that hung above him in this very moment—meant turmoil. War, and unease, before and after. But legend said it needed duty, love and family. However it played out, he and Hun Kan would do their duty. As for the love? He leaned down and kissed her, softly and quickly, in case these strange people who watched them saw it. The taste of her blessed his tongue while he watched the stars.

CHAPTER 56

Four soldiers with dogs passed Alice and Ian, shadows and heavy breathing and boot steps in the dark of night. They stopped at compass points, surrounding them, touching the dogs to keep them quiet. Ian leaned in and whispered to her. "The dogs look like the stone lions in front of government buildings."

Other dark forms with guns fanned further out, and some of the families that had been picnicking near them moved.

Alice's phone rang. Marie, giving warning. After Alice hung up, she whispered to Ian. "They're about to be lions in front of government officials." She stood, pulling him up beside her, squeezing him and then letting him go. He walked back over by Cauac and Don Thomas, and she felt his every step away from her.

She looked in the direction the guards had come. Shadows emerged: Marie, Aditi, and Huo Jiang walking toward them, flanked by at least fifteen assorted guards and hangers-on.

Alice smiled in relief when Alan and David stopped everyone except the three leaders just far enough away to be out of hearing distance.

Marie came very close to Alice, bending down. "There are no private conversations tonight."

Alice pointed at Peter. "What's got data boy still so engrossed? What's happening out there?"

Marie shook her head. "Someone, somewhere, sent us a puzzle. I don't think it's going to get solved in one night. There are layers . . . maybe lifetimes worth of layers, all bathing us. It's starting to hit the world nets.

"From this day forward, the world is changed.

"My staff is crafting a press release I have to go approve." She looked up. "We can only stay long enough for you to explain the sky to us. But Aditi liked the idea, and well, Aditi put Huo Jiang in a position where he looked better for going than staying. We have fifteen minutes."

"Even you?" Alice asked.

Marie looked genuinely regretful. "Yes."

Well, she'd give them a good show. She pointed to the blazing visuals overhead, and spoke crisply. "The cross in the sky is the Milky Way—an arm of our galaxy—and the ecliptic plane, which is where all of the planets orbit the sun. That means it's how we see the constellations."

She stopped, drawing a long breath, feeling the stars before she pointed straight up. "There is the middle of our galaxy. At dawn this morning, the sun shone in the center of that cross. This is a rare alignment, and won't occur again in our lifetimes."

"Some people in India say it means the world will renew," Aditi said. "The old Brahmin class has new beggars that walk about proclaiming it."

Alice fell silent a moment, watching Ian chattering quietly with the Mayans. "If the Mayans could predict this hundreds of years ago, then we should be smart enough to find a way to salvage the Earth."

Aditi put a hand on her arm. "Yes."

Marie laughed softly. "Social change is harder to get than scientific knowledge."

Aditi nodded. "Some say the Mayans died because of climate change."

"Partly," Alice responded. "And if our civilization dies? Will we have died partly or all from climate change?"

"Partly," Aditi said. "The rest is from war and greed." Aditi grinned. "And if it lives, it will be from sheer stubbornness."

Ian cleared his throat. Marie glanced over at him. "Yes?"

He pointed to Cauac and Don Thomas at his feet, and to Hun Kan and Ah Bahlam. "These are Mayans." He glanced at Alice as if asking forgiveness. "I've been translating your star talk for them. They say you are mostly right."

She bit her lip, holding back a laugh. He saw it, and smiled at her. Then he bowed toward Marie, Aditi, and Huo Jiang. "Would you like to hear what they believe?"

"Of course," Aditi said.

Ian gestured to Don Thomas, who stood. He coughed and waited, gathering everyone's eyes to him before he started. "There is a tree between us and the stars, and it is our Way to tend that tree. Our shamans and priests can travel via the roots of the underworld or the branches of the tree to reach the stars. They exist all the time. The tree, the roots, the stars. There is no real distance between them, even though our souls pretend there is."

Alice licked her lips and shifted, uneasy. Marie watched closely, her eyes narrowed. Aditi simply smiled.

Don Thomas continued. "We do not travel in spaceships, or airplanes, or physically at all. We've always traveled to the grandfather stars with plant medicine."

She smiled, thinking of Ian.

"But now humans have space ships and are learning more. This is a new time. We'll be able to use spaceships and computers to travel to places we have only gone in our dream-bodies before." He paused, looking at the sky. "It will happen in this age which is coming. The tree flowers now, in the end of this baktun. Knowledge is coming to us." He glanced at Peter, who had looked up from his computer and was watching the speech closely. "Knowledge will be transparent to some of you, also."

Alice glanced around. His tone sounded way too New Age. But something about Don Thomas refused to be interrupted. Everyone watched the old man, even Huo Jiang.

"Now, we—which means you too—are able to climb the tree and pluck the knowledge of the stars. Sometimes the tree lets us up and down on different branches, and our Way crosses rivers of time.

"Now, our Way is crossing the many rivers that feed a single tree. Always, the equinox is like that, but this is an equinox like none ever recorded."

Don Thomas paused, and looked down at the ground and then up at the sky. He swept his gaze across all who watched him. "Use this gift for peace."

Ian grinned at Alice. He was an imp. An overplayed hand, except it barely seemed that way when Don Thomas spoke it.

The starlight on Marie and Aditi's faces shone a touch too softly for Alice to see their expressions. She nearly jumped when Huo Jiang spoke. "Show me." His voice was classic Chinese stereotype, inscrutable and calm. "Show me this travel. Take me."

Don Thomas and Ian exchanged a thoughtful look. Nixie stood by Hun Kan, taking the Mayan girl's hand.

A black shadow crossed the lawn, cat-shaped, dark enough to drink in the light around it.

Just as Alice recognized it, the jaguar roared.

The shadow and the cat were one, and the noise sang through the night.

Three Secret Service officers pulled guns and four dogs lunged toward the dark animal, but ended up converging on each other and empty air.

For a moment, everyone was still except the confused dogs, who circled and growled low in their throats.

"That may have been our invitation back," Ian said. He looked at Marie. "Are you ready?"

She nodded but glanced at Huo Jiang and Aditi. Her look held the question. *Go or stay?*

Aditi smiled serenely, and Huo Jiang gave a quick, brave nod that belied his startled eyes. After all, he had demanded this. The jaguar seemed to have given him belief in the impossible.

Marie looked like she had on the top of the Temple of K'uk'ulkan just yesterday morning, like nothing could be better than walking into a bloody and dangerous past. Only this time, Alice didn't try to stop her. Live in the now. Nixie was too far away from her, so she grabbed for Marie's hand.

Not smart. One of the Secret Service officers started heading her way, and then he was walking on hard-packed dirt, glancing around with wide eyes. He didn't stop heading unerringly toward Marie.

She turned to him. "Relax, Sofino. It's okay."

He looked like he wanted to grab Marie and run. Instead, he pulled a gun from behind his back.

"Put it away!" Marie demanded. "I don't want to see it again unless I say so."

Sofino sniffed at the air. "We're not in Kansas anymore."

Alice laughed at the cliché.

Marie wore her Executive face. "Only if one of the three of us is in immediate and real danger."

"Then don't do anything dangerous!" he snapped.

Alice tried to calm him. "We *are* in a different time. Do you believe me?"

He never stopped looking around. He hesitated. "Sure."

She couldn't tell if he meant it. "Okay," Alice said. "Stay watchful. I don't know who is around."

"When?" he asked.

"About nine hundred years ago. Give or take fifty years. I don't know exactly. Let me see who came through."

Alice had spoken loudly enough that the whole group gathered around her, curious. She squinted into the darkness until she picked out Huo Jiang, Aditi, Marie, all of the Mayans, and three Secret Service officers, including Alan but not David. Peter and Oriana. Two dogs.

CHAPTER 57

Nixie gasped. She hadn't wanted to go back, hadn't helped take them. She kept her grip on Hun Kan's hand and closed her eyes, trying to reach her own time.

The hot breath of one of the Secret Service dogs sniffed at her hand. A quivering voice called, "Max," and the dog smell left.

Secret Service people weren't supposed to get scared.

Hun Kan tugged on her hand, pulling her. She opened her eyes. Ah Bahlam stood nearby, gesturing them toward him.

Now she was scared of this time. It could kill Hun Kan. Maybe it could kill her, too.

Ah Bahlam and Cauac started off, Nixie and Hun Kan behind them. There was a brief argument between Marie and one of the guards; Alan took Marie's side, and the guards settled with one on each side and one in the rear. The dogs stayed to the side, watching the perimeter, leashed, sniffing like crazy. Nixie almost laughed. They knew they were in another world. Except it wasn't funny to be walking toward danger with all these important people. Surely they were headed for the high priest again, for the Ball Court.

For the Chac-Mool.

Why did they have to? All that the Chinese president, or whatever he was, had wanted was to see that they could travel. But all three leaders had actually pushed ahead of her and Hun Kan, and Ian and her mom. She'd have sworn they'd never done this before. They'd started out looking as lost as the Secret Service. But now they weren't showing fear any more, just curiosity and strength.

Maybe that was what it took to be them.

A young boy with long hair and a dark belt spotted them and turned, racing away. An old woman ran up to them, and stood in front of Ah Bahlam, speaking rapidly at him.

"She's scolding him," Ian whispered.

"What are we doing?" Nixie asked.

Ian shrugged. "I hope it's something good."

No kidding. Ah Bahlam spoke back to the woman, apparently mollifying her, and they kept going. There were paths. Not concrete like in home time, but stones that had been laid down and mortared like the sacbes, and painted a dark color. Probably red, but the pale starlight washed everything to shades of gray with faint hints of other color at best. This Chichén Itzá was full of wooden structures and animal pens and little buildings like the Mexican palapas; sticks with a thatched roof. It looked so much fuller than the gray Chichén of her time. What had Hun Kan said—the power had leaked out of the one they just came from? This was like . . . like Phoenix or some other big city. Well, maybe not that big, but almost. Alive and noisy.

Well, she wouldn't be scared. It wouldn't help. Couldn't help. Being scared was silly.

They had gathered an entourage. Mostly women and children, and a few old men, from what she could tell in the near-dark. Most of them wore white and looked a bit like ghosts, the whites of their eyes shining now and again in starlight as they looked up. That's what they'd seen last trip, too. Young people and old people. Ah Bahlam was the only warrior-aged man she saw.

From time to time the two Secret Service dogs growled low in their throats, and the people moved a little bit back. But not far. Their eyes glowed dark in shadowy faces, curious and strong and watchful.

Hun Kan and Nixie held hands, tight. Nixie reached back for her mom with her free hand. Alice came up, Ian on her far side, so the four of them stayed together in the middle of the whole group.

They seemed to walk a long time, but maybe it was the dark and the strange place, and the sickly-sweet copal scent that hung over everything and made her head spin.

They rounded a corner and were blinded by a row of torches. Nix shaded her eyes and blinked hard, peering through her fingers to see a large group blocking their way. Red-feathered warriors like the ones who had been around Hun Kan when she danced her off the wall. At least six of them.

The two dogs growled.

The warriors raised their torches, looking carefully and slowly at every one of their group, as if memorizing features and faces. One of them nodded at Ah Bahlam and smiled, but the others ignored all of the Mayans except for Cauac.

The numbers of the two groups were about even, but the warriors carried shields, clubs, knives, staffs, and in one case, arrows.

The warriors would have no way of recognizing a gun. So the dogs would be the only weapons they'd see.

The leader spoke to Cauac in rapid-fire Mayan.

Cauac turned and spoke to Don Thomas, who said, in English, "We are to let these men lead us to their high priest—that is the High Priest of K'uk'ulkan, or Feathered Serpent."

"And if we don't?" Alan spoke up.

Don Thomas smiled. "Then we will die."

Marie asked, "Can we leave when we want? Go back to our time?"

Don Thomas licked his lips. "The high priest may have powers that alter our own."

"Do you think we can?" she pressed.

"Yes. Let me ask another." He turned to Cauac and spoke softly and quickly to him. When he looked back at Marie he said, "Cauac believes he is as strong as the high priest."

Marie glanced at Aditi and Huo Jiang, who both nodded. "Tell them we are looking forward to the honor of speaking to the High Priest of K'uk'ulkan."

Nixie heard Ian whisper, "They didn't ask us. Well, then I guess we don't matter."

Her mom asked, "Why would we?"

"So this is what it was all for, this visit?" Ian asked.

"How can we know?" Her mom looked brave.

Was it? Was this why she had met Hun Kan and dreamed of her? It wasn't enough—this was a thing for the adults, a thing for the world, and there was something unresolved still. All of those turtles did not come to swim with her just to get these leaders together with those leaders. She didn't voice her certainty that there was more meaning in the events, something for her and Hun Kan.

Seven red-feathered warriors made a V in front of them, leading them down a cobbled path. At least five walked behind them. The Secret Service officer with the dogs flanked the group, looking confused and protective all at once, and feeling like weapons that could go off on accident.

The other Mayans who had been following them still trailed behind, but at a distance. The torchlight made it hard to see very far.

The Secret Service turned on flashlights and swung them back and forth, eliciting gasps from the children outside the circle of torches and ruining Nixie's night vision.

Nix expected Marie to stop them, but she just looked at the light playing across the ancient faces and licked her lips. The warriors eyes grew uneasy but they didn't react overtly.

They didn't go to the Ball Court. Instead, they went through the gates and down a proper sacbe like the one they had been on a few nights ago, and wound to a big, deep cenote. Even in all its wildness, even with the jungle looking entirely different than it did in this place in her own time, Nixie recognized the cliffs the torches illuminated.

The cliffs above the sacred cenote of sacrifice.

In both times, the pool was down inside a circle of earth topped by trees. But of course, there was no viewing platform with nice safe rails here. Smooth limestone rocks led to the top of the cliff, where the trees had been kept pruned on one side. Here, more Mayans waited for them.

The high priest stood in the middle of a group of warriors.

The warriors who led Nixie and her mom and everyone else turned them into a circle near the high priest, herding everyone inside except the Secret Service. The warriors gave hand-signals to Marie's guard to stand beside them in the outer circle. They obeyed only after a command from Marie, and kept looking behind them. Still, seeing them side by side made Nixie feel safer, more like the two sets of warriors weren't about to fight with each other.

The modern fighters looked deadlier, but there were a lot of Mayan warriors.

The high priest still wore the yellow band of Nixie's watch. It made her want to giggle a little, but the look on his face didn't.

CHAPTER 58

Ah Bahlam felt glad to stand under his own stars again.

He recalled Cauac's advice for confused moments—*concentrate on what you control*. Which was this moment, standing near the lip of the cenote with strangers and warriors and the forked choices of his possible futures. The jaguar curled inside him, at rest, a wild power insisting he could change Chichén's future. *Look around*, the jaguar demanded. *Be now. Know your surroundings. Know yourself.*

The high priest looked dizzy, sweat dripping from his chin, his movements less fluid than normal. His gaze kept flicking back as forth as he watched the god-dressed newcomers through narrowed eyes. A few times, he looked away from his contemplation of the strangers to glare warning at Ah Bahlam, as if he could sense Ah Bahlam's thoughts.

Ah Bahlam remained still and aware, ready. He extended his senses to feel and taste and hear the jungle all around them, but kept his focus most on the high priest and on Hun Kan.

From the chatter Ah Bahlam had managed to overhear on the walk to the cenote, the game had played—and played—until darkness forced a stop. A draw. Three players had withdrawn injured. One more captive had been sacrificed, and the high priest had not freed his heart on the first cut. The entire night had been a disaster of bad omens that the people of Chichén and her attackers could only see as a dangerous weakness.

This would be a good time to challenge the high priest's power.

Except he was alone, and he wasn't ready.

He reached for the jaguar, needing its counsel. It had gotten him safely back, after all. Kept him and Hun Kan safe. Driven them all back from the far away time to this place and this moment.

The jaguar was in him. But his Way stayed small enough that it was clear who thought. Who decided. Not the jaguar, but him. He felt its advice like a whisper. *Look around.*

The high priest's lips tightened and his jaw jumped where it met his neck, a steady heartbeat of anger.

The strangers in their turn watched the high priest. They looked calm and sure of themselves. A few of them, even a few of the women, felt like warriors. They would be able to move quickly under threat. The two who had physical manifestations of their Ways were the most dangerous, unless perhaps the beasts they held were worse. The eyes of the chained beasts and their handlers spoke of the predators inside them. If Ah Bahlam had not been to end of the world, he would have thought these were gods.

The high priest gestured for Don Thomas to come and stand beside him. "You will help us all speak," he said. "You will tell me the names of everyone."

Don Thomas spoke to the tallest woman in the group—the one who seemed to lead them all—in the god tongue. Why did he think of it like that when he knew they weren't gods? The future tongue. Don Thomas spoke the woman's words back in Mayan. "As long as you will also tell us who you are." His Mayan was good, smoother than Ian's, but he stumbled over sounds often enough to force Ah Bahlam to listen very carefully.

When he got to the three new people who had come just before they all crossed over—Marie, Aditi, and Huo Jiang—Don Thomas said, "These are equal to the lords of a larger Itzá."

The high priest did not look like he believed the words. But then, two of the high-ranking visitors were women and the other was too plain. Cauac saw the same thing because he broke in. "In the Itzá of the future, people do not hunt, they do not wear the skins of animals. Women lead beside men. Don Thomas speaks the truth. They are like you."

The high priest glared at Cauac, his jaw tight and his eyes narrowed in fury. He felt like a snake poised to strike.

Neither the men with the beasts nor the red warriors were introduced, but Ah Bahlam let his gaze wander across them. He recognized the man who had approached him on the way to the Wall of Skulls. Did he have their support? Or was he about to die?

The high priest said, "Welcome to the cenote of sacrifice. Let us feed the gods." He gestured to Hun Kan.

Don Thomas began repeating the words.

Hun Kan walked toward the lip of the cenote. Her face looked as it had when she watched the game. Lovely. Beautiful with purpose. She had once more become hungry to meet the gods.

Nixie took Hun Kan's hand and stood beside her.

The high priest smiled.

Don Thomas finished repeating the high priest's words.

Nixie's mother screeched and raced the few man-heights between her and Nixie and jerked Nixie back.

Nixie snarled at her mother, and tried to hang onto Hun Kan's hand, but Hun Kan freed her fingers from Nixie's. She offered Nixie a sad smile, then turned her back on the golden girl, staring out over the black mouth of the cenote. The water was two-man-heights below and hard to see, but it lapped softly at the rocks below and smelled of rotting leaves and fish.

Nixie's mother spoke into her ear and she stopped struggling. She stood in front of her mother, both of her mother's arms around her center, her eyes damp.

Bless her for wanting to save Hun Kan, but she was only a girl. When she fell in the cenote the day he met her, she was probably as scared as he was. Maybe more. The thought made him feel stronger. He had, in fact, learned much since then.

He called on his jaguar, breathed it into him, and moved between the high priest and Hun Kan, keeping his eyes on the avatar of K'uk'ulkan. Some of his own choices clarified.

I gave my blood to this pool last night. My sacrifice is done.

He felt stronger, as if K'uk'ulkan himself shielded him. His jaguar did not fight K'uk'ulkan. It fought the high priest.

They were and were not the same.

He opened his mouth and let the jaguar roar.

Cauac stared at him, took a step forward, his face full of rebuke, a demand for control.

That time was past.

Cauac must have seen it in his eyes. He stared at his student and then took a step back.

Ah Bahlam spoke to the high priest. "Sacrificing her gains you nothing. The gods you wanted are here." He gestured toward Nixie and her mother. "Chichén is damaged enough."

Hun Kan raked her fingers across his cheek from behind, repudiating his choice for her. "I go. It is my time."

Anger flared in him. "You choose."

She moaned. He desperately wanted a moment to tell her he loved her, but the high priest had called upon Feathered Serpent, and stood, full height, clearly still able to invoke the god.

Everyone near the high priest stepped back. With the others out of the way, Feathered Serpent and Jaguar faced each other, clothed in strength alone, holding no weapons.

A small scuffle among the red warriors drew Ah Bahlam's attention for a moment. One of them glared death at him, but three others surrounded that one. The red warrior he had spoken to flashed him a smile and a good luck gesture.

He gave a small nod, acknowledging that he might live.

K'uk'ulkan leaped at him, an extended foot catching him in the hip and almost felling him, driving the breath from his chest in a startled exclamation.

His focus narrowed. He backed up a few steps, getting some room.

He watched closely as the high priest stood sweating in front of him, poised.

Ah Bahlam circled, slowly, testing.

The high priest moved with him, circling inside Ah Bahlam's larger circle, fluid and ready to strike at any weakness.

Ah Bahlam rushed him, head down, his movements strong, full of grace and cat.

He passed the high priest, who had glided three steps away. A slight quirky smile broke his lips.

Ah Bahlam dropped his head and rolled, staying in a crouch. He leapt upon the high priest.

Who was again not there.

He stopped, waiting and watching. A slight wind blew. Julu flew a circle overhead. A cat did not fight straight out. It hovered and pounced; it surprised.

Not possible now; surprise was gone. He had to be man and cat together.

He rushed toward the priest and turned sideways at the last moment. It turned out the priest had again moved, in the other direction. Ah Bahlam laughed and then growled low in his throat. He kept his eyes on the priest, his cat's vision sharper, clearer. The individual hairs on the man's head could be separated with this vision.

Feathered Serpent looked back, its eyes dark above the priest's mask.

Ah Bahlam circled, holding its gaze. Was it a balance game of who could mix the right amount of man with god?

His opponent had years of experience. The raw will in its gaze was a physical force, like a wind in his face, pushing against his chest. He leaned into it, growling.

The high priest hissed and leaned forward.

Ah Bahlam stepped back.

Nixie screamed, "Hun Kan!"

The splash of a body hitting water, crystal clear to the jaguar's ears. Drops falling back into the water and the splash of a hand.

Ah Bahlam took the split second the sound stole from the high priest's gaze and leapt. He raked the man's neck with his hands as he passed, knocking him off balance.

Ah Bahlam landed easily, driven by the splash, the need to know if Hun Kan lived.

The only way to see was to kill the high priest.

As soon as his feet touched the ground, he bent his knees into a crouch and exploded out, sheer force bringing the high priest to the ground.

A figure streaked by in the torchlight: Nixie rushing to the edge of the cenote, her golden hair a fire in the flickering torchlight.

Her mother screamed.

Hands closed around his throat, pushing him away. He leapt up, forcing the high priest to first rise with him to keep his hold on Ah Bahlam's neck and then to let go. Ah Bahlam fell again, getting his own powerful paws around the head of the man below him. He pushed his face near the high priest's mask, snarling.

He took a deep breath and twisted his hands.

The high priest's neck cracked and his eyes flew open wide before his head fell back—broken.

A shriek of pain sounded behind him, followed by more of triumph. The red warriors. Mostly pleased.

His heightened hearing picked up a small clear sound in the water that gave him hope: Hun Kan moving.

In death, the spirit of K'uk'ulkan had fled, and the high priest's body looked shriveled and small, hardly like a worthy opponent. Ah Bahlam stood looking down on his enemy's face, recalling that he had once looked up to the man.

The tall fighter who had supported him brought out a black obsidian blade and set it on Ah Bahlam's outstretched palm. "We honor you."

He closed his fist around the hilt, felt its heft, and glanced at Cauac. His teacher's eyes were wide and full of surprise. And pleasure. Cauac nodded.

Ah Bahlam closed his eyes. *Jaguar, help me! I have never taken a heart. I never want to take another one. But I must take this one!* He lifted his arm above his head, hesitating at the top, gathering strength. He plunged the blade into the still-warm chest in front of him and extracted the high priest's heart, the thrust and movement clearly guided by his Way. His arm and hand knew how hard to fall, how to twist, how to shatter bone. His fingers released the blade once it had cut the heart free. He clasped his hands, bloody and slick with life, around the warm heart.

The jaguar shrank back inside him, falling away into infinity, into a small tiny place deep inside. It felt satisfied.

Perhaps this was a moment to be a man.

He held the heart up to the blazing night sky. He spoke aloud for the first time since the fight began. "K'uk'ulkan! Honor your high priest's sacrifice and bring us water and plenty. Honor our sacrifices of the past few years and give our warriors the strength to make peace."

He wanted to race to the edge of the water, but there was something more to say. He made himself stay, blood dripping down his wrists, staring at the sky until the gods gave him the answer. "Give the strangers what they need. The leaders and Ni-ixie. Bless their time. Bless us all and let me walk my Way to the glory and health of all the Itzá in all of our lands."

Finally, enough words. As he raced to the edge of the pool, he heard Don Thomas beginning to translate for the strangers.

Ah Bahlam flung the heart into the pool, aiming far from where he felt Hun Kan.

Warriors began to approach him.

Later. He could accept them later. He nodded at them as he backed to the edge of the cenote. "Thank you. I will speak with you in a moment."

The tall one nodded, and stopped.

Ah Bahlam caught his weight on a branch and leaned over the edge of cenote. Hun Kan splashed in the water, clearly alive. It was too dark to see her face, but the whites of her eyes and her teeth shone in the starlight. Thank all the gods. *Thank you K'uk'ulkan!*

He dove for the center of the pool, head first, not caring that the living should not leap into this cenote. Hun Kan was there, alive.

Warm water greeted his pointed fingers and then they struck cold and he felt almost reborn, digging down an extra stroke, honoring the water he swam through and the way it had accepted the high priest's blood, and left the woman in the center of his heart alive.

He came up next to Hun Kan.

Her face was the most beautiful thing he'd ever seen. Everything was clear and bright, defined; as if he still saw through the jaguar's eyes even though he was entirely himself in this moment.

He held his hand out.

She stayed where she was, treading water. "You killed the high priest," she said. "Because of me?"

"No. Because we need a new leader and we were saved for that. Both of us." He knew that now, that he would take the high priest's place with her at his side. They had seen the future together, and they understood death. Perhaps Hun Kan understood it even more than he did. "Your leap into the water gave me the moment I needed."

She blinked at him, absorbing his words.

He wiped the last of the blue paint from her cheeks and forehead before he guided her to the edge of the cenote near where he had spilled his blood and prayed the night before. He reached for a root with his free hand, helping her balance on his shoulders and start climbing up.

As they navigated the cliff, he reveled in the curve of Hun Kan's waist, the way her wet clothing clung to her hips. She looked like a goddess of fertility. "Will you have my children?" he asked.

She was a little above him. She looked over her shoulder and smiled down at him, the look in her eyes all the answer he needed.

There was no more time to talk because they were near the top and Alice and Nixie reached their hands down toward them. At first he thought Nixie would take Hun Kan's hand, but at the last moment she grinned and said something to her mom, then reached for him.

He understood.

When they met he had pulled her from a cenote.

CHAPTER 59

Cauac smiled as Nixie pulled Ah Bahlam, dripping and somewhat undignified, from the cenote. The boy had done well.

A great weight had lifted from his own shoulders. After all, would Ah Bahlam have been here to change the order if Cauac himself had not been in Zama to teach him?

Or was that an old man's fancy?

He shrugged and checked on the people-of-the-future who had chosen to witness. The leaders talked among themselves. Their guards had managed to separate them from both the warriors and the lip of the cenote. Cauac had been so focused on Ah Bahlam and the high priest during the fight that he had missed their reactions.

The red warriors still stood by the body of the high priest. The situation in Chichén must have been even worse than they had thought in Zama for most of the high priest's own elite bodyguards to shriek joy at his death.

But now they stood looking confused. Ah Bahlam had thrown the heart into the water, but this cenote had not seen human sacrifice since the dedication of the Ball Court a generation ago.

As he walked over to the small knot of seven or eight warriors, he recognized two as past students of his. "K'inti! P'oh! Good to see you!"

"Good to see you, too!" K'inti smiled at him. "You taught Ah Bahlam."

It wasn't a question, but he nodded anyway. "He was always on the path of the warrior priest." He knelt down, staring at the yellow band on the high priest's arm. What had Nixie shown Hun Kan? He twisted. Nothing. It took three tries, but he finally placed the watch in the pouch around his waist. It told time, and he wanted to learn how it did that.

"Will he lead us well?" P'oh asked. "Will Chaac smile upon us?"

After seeing Chichén dead and gray, Cauac knew it didn't really matter. Enough time changed all things. If the Mayans were to live on, it wasn't going to be as themselves, not exactly. He glanced at Don Thomas, who stood chattering with Ian and watching the foreign leaders. Perhaps the Mayans had lived on in a way. A Way. He looked up at the sky. "See, the stars are already a little obscured. Perhaps rain clouds will come in to honor the passing of the High Priest of K'uk'ulkan."

One of the other warriors grunted. "Or the rise of the new one."

"Either way, Chaac may be paying homage to Feathered Serpent and Jaguar. You will know what happens tomorrow. For now, perhaps it would be best to burn this body so the animals do not eat it and the water does not foul with it."

K'inti asked, "Will you stay with us?"

Cauac looked over at Ah Bahlam, who was headed toward them, his head high and Hun Kan on one arm. He looked up at the sky, which was indeed clouding over a bit.

The doorway between the two times was still open, like a wind in his face. "You do not need me."

CHAPTER 60

Alice watched as Ah Bahlam and Hun Kan left her and Nixie, two small people with dripping wet hair and well-made but scratched and scarred bodies. They walked close together, hips almost but not quite touching, heads high. They each had a lightness in their step.

Power had just changed hands in Chichén Itzá.

Twenty minutes ago, Ah Bahlam had ripped the heart from an old man's chest. Five minutes ago, he and Hun Kan had laughed like two teenagers in love as they climbed up over the lip of the cliff.

She shook her head and reached for her daughter's hand. "I wonder if we'll see them again after tonight?"

"I don't think so." Nixie's smile looked sad.

Alice didn't have any idea how to make her feel better. "We'd best go see if everyone else is all right."

Marie, Aditi, Huo Jiang, Peter, Oriana, the Secret Service, and the dogs stood in a knot a few steps back from the edge of the cenote. An unusual silence gave away the depth to which the violent passing of power had affected them.

Three stoic red warriors watched them quietly, their eyes flicking to the dogs more often than the people.

Every pair of eyes looked at Alice and Nixie as they walked up.

What was she supposed to say? At least they were all safe. "It's . . . it's not a dream." She paused. "It's magic, except . . . " she glanced at Marie, "except there's messages coming down in our time that are following the rules of science. Maybe we are, too."

Aditi smiled. "Let it be, Alice. Maybe science and magic are one and the same."

Marie laughed. "I guess I asked to come here. It . . . I . . . "

She'd never heard Marie run out of words. Aditi picked up the silence. "How often can any of us see history? It's very beautiful here. Raw. Like we can never be. Smell the air."

A short silence fell, and everyone looked around, as if suddenly reprieved and allowed to do so. Stars blazed overhead and somewhere far off, a monkey screeched. The air smelled of flowers and leaves and limestone. Bats made tiny dark arrows through the sky. Alice savored the moment, wishing she knew how it had come to her. Magic in her bones. She sucked it into her like air, so she expanded and for just a heartbeat, a breath, she felt like she was the entire jungle and the ancient night sky.

Marie broke the silence by leaning over to Nixie. "I know why the turtles came to you. You're the only one who tried to go to your friend's side."

Nixie's sounded amazingly poised as she said, "Well, I wasn't being guarded by the Secret Service. And I knew they wanted to kill her. You didn't."

Alice blinked back a tear. When had her daughter grown so much?

Huo Jiang had been silent. He shifted on his feet, quietly drawing attention to himself. When he had it, he looked at Alice, Aditi, and Nixie. "I am sorry I doubted you." He looked straight ahead, toward the cenote. "But you could come here, and I could not have. You have the respect of these people from the past. I could not have done that. And you were no more afraid than I."

Alice looked to Marie to answer, but Aditi spoke next. "If we are so lucky that an equal miracle takes us back, I will not question the Brahmin's insistence in belief in the supernatural anymore."

A fleeting smile crossed Huo Jiang's face before his mask of inscrutability returned.

Alice recognized herself in Aditi's words. How differently might she study the stars now?

Peter was still staring at his computer screen. Marie asked, "Is the same kind of data landing in this time, too?"

"No." He looked up at Marie, his eyes pleading. "But I'm running some decoding algorithms. Can we go back before I run out of battery, too?"

Alice wanted to burst out laughing. Such a modern and unspiritual request. So Peter. She looked around. Cauac had joined Ian and Don Thomas, and otherwise they were all close by.

Marie spoke. "We need to make history in our own time. We've got to meet the press." She didn't look indifferent. She looked like she wanted to stay here more than anything.

"Ian," Alice called. "Can you ask Don Thomas to take us back?"

He came over and took her in his arms, pulling her in close. He kissed her so hard it nearly bruised her face, and she didn't want to let him go. Ever. Her hand curled around the back of his neck and kept him close to her.

When he pushed her gently away, he said, "Nix can take you. I'll be along."

"But you will?" she asked.

He smiled. "There's still tomorrow to see, right?"

She initiated the kiss this time, smiling as he turned back toward Don Thomas.

Nixie said, "Wait. Ian? Can you tell Hun Kan something for me?"

He nodded.

"Tell her what I learned from her is to be brave and do what I know I have to do, even if it scares me. Tell her I also learned about friendship."

After Ian was done speaking in Mayan, Hun Kan separated from Ah Bahlam and gave Nixie a long look, her eyes wet and shining. She stepped forward and kissed Nixie on the cheek, a regal kiss, but equal to equal. The Mayan girl was not much older than Nix, and now she would help shape a whole culture. There was much glory left before the Mayan culture would die.

Alice struggled not to cry.

"Everyone hold hands," Nixie said, and everyone did except Ian, Don Thomas, and Cauac, who stepped back. Alice had the strange sense she was in the middle of a nursery rhyme or a kids television show, or that maybe the whole group of them holding hands should just break out and sing *Kum-bay-ah, My Lord, Kum-bay-ah*, but they simply ended up with the great tree and the cross of the ecliptic burning above them like a beacon and a welcome.

The cenote was still there, of course.

One of the dogs bayed and was shushed. They began to sniff at the air and the ground.

The guards flashed their lights across the group, counting.

Huo Jiang looked greatly relieved to be back in the time with the wrongly-restored sacbe and the historical sign in front of the cenote. He reached into his pocket and took something out, and then quite loudly said, "For peace and clean air . . . and this time I mean it with the greatest of sincerity." His arm drew back and swung forward, a dark silhouette against a dark gray background. Something small flew from his hand. A short sharp splash announced its contact with the water of the cenote of sacrifice.

A feeling of the sacred settled over Alice.

Then the dogs barked and two of the three Secret Service men started chattering at the empty air. Peter already had his laptop out and happily exclaimed as his screen lit so brightly it threw blue and orange bars on their faces.

Marie stepped over by Alice. "Thank you."

She shook her head. "I didn't do anything."

"Would you and Nixie come to DC? I don't know how to work it yet, but I'm sure we need an archeoastronomer on the project to decode all of this data falling from the sky."

"Will I see you?" Alice asked.

Marie looked away. "Sometimes. Not too much. But you'd make a difference, and there are good schools there for Nixie."

She took in a long breath, and it seemed like the sweetness of the Mayan past came into her for a last time. Even though she wasn't Nixie or Don Thomas, she knew the door would close tonight, and they'd be done. "Can I be based here?" she asked.

Marie bit her lip, then smiled. "You'll have to come to DC sometimes. Maybe as much as once a month."

She'd be crazy not to take it. "Of course. Will the phone number I have work for you tomorrow?"

Marie nodded. "I'll make sure that number gets extended another day." She leaned in and hugged Alice. "I will take you with me to DC in a few days."

Alice nodded.

"Enjoy a few days on the beach."

Alice glanced at Nix. "I will. Good to see you." She felt awkward.

Marie folded her in a warm hug, and then whispered in her ear. "Ian's quite cute."

Alice blushed.

Marie leaned in and hugged Nixie, too. "Take care of your mom, and remember to carry the turtles with you. I think you've only just started on the destiny they hinted at."

Nixie nodded. "Me, too."

Marie fidgeted, anxious now. "I'll leave you Alan."

Like she wanted a keeper for these last two days on the beach. "No need."

"Sure?"

Alice nodded. "Go meet the press."

Marie gestured to Peter, who gave Alice a long, apologetic look but followed Marie, who would have access to power and information far faster and deeper than Alice would. Oriana trailed along behind him, as if Peter needed her for balance. The dogs and keepers made up the last of the entourage, Marie querying Peter as they went.

The quiet behind them felt like heaven. They were alone.

Alice sat down on the stone, pulling Nix down beside her. "We'll wait here. Ian will be along soon."

"Okay," Nix mumbled and scooted close to Alice, putting her head on her shoulder.

Alice stared up at the sky, entranced. Nixie slept, the starlight shining on her face. As always, she looked years younger and more vulnerable in her sleep. But not, perhaps, as young as she'd looked a week ago.

A hint of raw magic seemed to have settled permanently over her.

DECEMBER 22, 2012

CHAPTER 61

A knock on the door woke Nixie. It was clearly morning, maybe past; the brightness of the day intruded even through closed curtains. She shoved aside the covers and padded through the living room to peer through the keyhole like Oriana had taught her those two days when every journalist and blogger in the Yucatan had been chasing her.

It was Oriana, looking ready for the beach. She had on a light shift over her blue one-piece swimsuit, and yellow swim goggles and fins stuck haphazardly out of a white canvas bag she carried. Nixie flung the door open. "Oriana!"

"Good morning, World Turtle Girl."

"Good morning." She glanced at the bag full of swim stuff. "World Turtle Girl?"

"Hmmm . . . Marie talked about you last night. Said you and people like you might save the world just by being innocent."

Nixie laughed. "Did you come to take me snorkeling?"

"Yeah." Oriana grinned. "I thought we should go one more time. Is your mom up?"

Nixie shook her head. "We can leave her a note. But I'm hungry."

Oriana patted the canvas bag. "I packed us a lunch."

The door to Alice's room swung open. "I'm here," she mumbled, pushing sleep-mussed hair back from her face. "We'll go with you."

"We?"

The door opened wider to show Ian's grin.

He'd spent the night? In her mom's room? Nixie wasn't such a baby she didn't know what that meant. Her cheeks grew hot. "Good morning, Mr. Ian."

He laughed and said, "Good morning, Turtle Girl." He glanced at Oriana. "So how is the morning after the end of the world doing so far?"

"Pretty normal. But I'm hungry for the salty sea, so come on."

He narrowed his eyes, and stuck his tongue out at her. "If it's normal, we have time for coffee."

Nixie grinned evilly. "So use a to-go cup."

They piled into Ian's jeep, driving through the warm wind of the first day of winter proper in the Yucatan.

Nixie and Oriana left Ian and Alice up on the beach under palms, holding hands and finishing their coffee, while they sat on the wet sand near the high tide mark, watching the water.

"Looking for turtles?" Oriana asked.

Nixie shook her head. "They'll come when I need them." She ran her fingers through the sand.

Oriana watched her. "You know that's not sand."

Huh? Nixie scooped up a handful and splayed her fingers out so the sun caught on hundreds of tiny shells. Shells so small it would probably take a million to fill a coffee cup, mostly tiny versions of the ones you could hear the sea in. "Wow."

"You should see them through a magnifying glass or microscope sometime."

"Things are never what they seem, are they?"

Oriana let out a long, soft sigh. "Not often. Will you miss her?"

"Of course." It felt like a punch. She really wouldn't see Hun Kan again. They'd said it last night, when Ian and Cauac and Don Thomas came through to this time, but she'd been half-asleep even walking out of Chichén and getting in line for the bus with the tourists. She didn't remember the ride. Only now the idea that it was over, that she'd never go back, sank in. "I hope I remember everything about her."

"You've got your pictures," Oriana said. "Maybe you can take a handful of those little shells. They're so small they look like fairy shells, so maybe they'll remind you of magic."

"They'll remind me of you, too. What are you going to do?"

"Maybe I'll go work at the clinic again. And keep diving. I can't imagine leaving the coast here. Peter asked me to come to DC, but I told him no."

"Did he ever go to sleep last night?"

"No. The data stopped flowing around dawn, but the whole world is working on understanding it. There appear to be stories and poemsscience facts and pictures, but no one has figured out how it all goes together. Peter thinks it'll take years."

"He'll like that."

Oriana stared out toward the horizon line where the blue sky and the blue of the sea fuzzed into each other. She stood up. "Are you ready?"

Nix grinned. "You bet."

They walked out into the ocean, stopping to put on their fins and mask when the water was just below their waists.

ACKNOWLEDGEMENTS

I wrote this book because I have been to Palenque once and I have been to the Riviera Maya twice. I've sat at the top of the Temple of K'uk'ulkan at Chichén Itzá and climbed crumbling half-restored steps at Coba to look out over jungle canopy far below me. I have been swimming at the beach in Xcaret and Akumal. I love the land and the people there, and the mystery of their past seemed worth exploring.

Many thanks to the Mayanists of our time: the people who study the historical Mayan culture. I read widely in preparation for writing this book, starting with Diego de Landa's *Yucatan before and after the conquest"* which was written in 1566, and through many far more modern works by Linda Schele, David Friedel, Joy Parker, Anthony F. Aveni and John Major Jenkins (a full bibliography can be found at www.mayandecember.com). I read work by academics and spiritualists, and by optimists and doomsayers. Nothing that I read had the same thing to say about either the Mayan culture or its relationship to our own modern world. Perhaps that's as it should be; the ancient Mayans probably could not have imagined the modern world any more than we can truly see and understand their world.

But it was sure fun to try!

Note that this is a work of fiction: while well researched, there are bits of the world I portray here that are simply made up. That's what fiction writers get to do.

Thanks to my immediate family Toni and Katie Cramer, and to my mom and dad for reading and commenting, as well as to a host of other first readers like John Pitts, Darragh Metzger, Cat Rambo, Louise Marley, and others. Every writer needs good feedback to make a book better.

Thanks to Sean Wallace at Prime Books for believing in this book. Thanks to Paula Guran for the many fine comments and corrections that helped make this better. And as always, thanks to my agent, Eleanor Wood.

ABOUT THE AUTHOR

Brenda Cooper has published fiction in *Analog, Oceans of the Mind, Nature,* and in multiple anthologies. She is the author of the Endeavor award winner for 2008: *The Silver Ship and the Sea,* and of the sequels, *Reading the Wind* and *Wings of Creation.* By day, she is the City of Kirkland's CIO, and at night and in early morning hours, she's a futurist and writer.